WORLDSHAKER

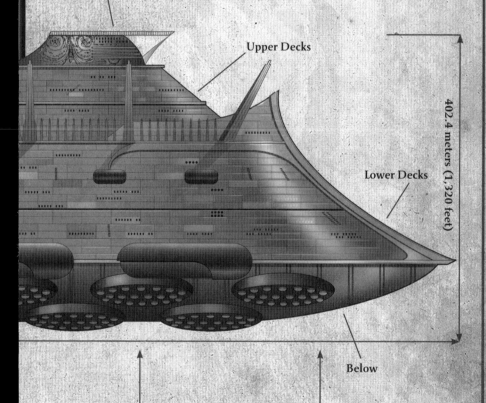

Bridge

Upper Decks

Lower Decks

402.4 meters (1,320 feet)

Below

UPPER DECKS POPULATION: 10,040 approx.
FILTHIES: 2,130 approx.

WORLDSHAKER

Richard Harland

SIMON & SCHUSTER BFYR

New York London Toronto Sydney

SIMON & SCHUSTER BFYR

An imprint of Simon & Schuster Children's Publishing Division
1230 Avenue of the Americas, New York, New York 10020

First published in Australia in 2009 by Allen & Unwin
First U.S. edition 2010

For information about special discounts for bulk purchases, please contact Simon & Schuster
Special Sales at 1-866-506-1949 or business@simonandschuster.com.
The Simon & Schuster Speakers Bureau can bring authors to your live event.
For more information or to book an event, contact the
Simon & Schuster Speakers Bureau at 1-866-248-3049 or visit
our website at www.simonspeakers.com.
Book design by Laurent Linn
Endpaper illustrations by Patrick Reilly
The text for this book is set in Augustal.
Manufactured in the United States of America
2 4 6 8 10 9 7 5 3 1
Library of Congress Cataloging-in-Publication Data
Harland, Richard.
Worldshaker / Richard Harland. — 1st U.S. ed.
p. cm.
Summary: Sixteen-year-old Col Porpentine is being groomed as the next Commander
of Worldshaker, a juggernaut where elite families live on the upper decks while
the Filthies toil below, but when he meets Riff, a Filthy girl on the run,
he discovers how ignorant he is of his home and its residents.
ISBN 978-1-4169-9552-4 (hardcover)
[1. Fantasy. 2. Social classes—Fiction.] I. Title.
PZ7.H22652Wor 2010
[Fic]—dc22
2009016924
ISBN 978-1-4169-9554-8 (eBook)

FIRST
EDITION

For Erica, Sarah, Angela, Selwa, and Selina

ACKNOWLEDGMENTS

For historical research: Henri Jeanjean,
of the University of Wollongong, for information on
Albert Mathieu-Favier's under-the-Channel tunnel project.

For much-valued feedback: the ROR writers' group
(Margo Lanagan, Marianne de Pierres, Rowena Cory Daniells,
Maxine McArthur, Trent Jamieson, and Tansy Rayner Roberts).

For helpful critiques on individual chapters:
Cat Sparks, Rob Hood, Ann Charlton/Whitehead, and Chris McTrustry.

As always, I'm hugely indebted to my wonderful agent, Selwa Anthony,
and also to Selena Hanet-Hutchins, for creative suggestions.

Last but not least, my gratitude to David and Navah at Simon & Schuster.
Thank you for believing in this book!

1

A sound brought Col out of a deep sleep. Something was happening out in the corridor. Urgent footsteps, orders and questions, the clangs of many doors opening and closing. Cabin by cabin the disturbance came closer.

His own cabin remained in darkness—until suddenly the door was flung open. Two menacing shapes stood silhouetted against the dim blue light of the corridor.

"Room light on!" came the order.

The figures sprang forward into the room, flourishing their weapons. Col switched on his bedside lamp.

In the warm yellow-pink glow the figures diminished to a pair of ordinary warrant officers. The pounding of Col's heart eased. Warrant officers were responsible for security, and their heavy wooden batons were for his protection. But what were they doing in this part of the ship?

"Ah, Master Porpentine, isn't it?" The senior officer fingered his gray walrus mustache. "Sorry to disturb you, sir. We have to search your room."

"What for?"

Ignoring the question the officer went on. "How long have you been awake, sir? Have you seen or heard anything unusual in the last few minutes?"

Col raised himself higher on his pillow. "Doors clanging. And you clumping along the corridor."

"She must have run on," the junior officer whispered to the senior. "We're wasting our time on this deck."

"Who's 'she'?" Col demanded.

"A Filthy," the junior blurted—then clapped his hand over his mouth. "I mean . . ."

"Hold your tongue, Jull!" The senior officer swung his baton and gave Jull a cracking blow on the wrist. Col was shocked.

The senior officer turned to him again. "You didn't hear what he said, did you, sir?"

"Yes, I did. What's a Filthy doing on the Upper Decks?"

"You wouldn't want to know. My colleague got carried away."

"I'll forget about it if you answer my question."

"She . . ." The senior officer's cheeks were red, and he was visibly sweating. "Well, she escaped. That's all I can say."

He prodded Jull with his baton and pushed him toward the doorway. "So, if you'll just forget about it, thank you, sir . . ."

Out in the corridor he began an angry whispered conversation with his junior. Col caught the words "grandson of Sir Mormus Porpentine," then the door closed behind them, and they moved off down the corridor. More clanging doors, more questioning.

He still couldn't believe it. A female Filthy running around on the Upper Decks? Inconceivable!

He looked round at his own safe, civilized bedroom. Green carpet, brown velvet curtains, cream wallpaper . . . On the walls were framed pictures of the most dignified creatures: the wise owl, noble lion, and brave bear. A metal plate above the door was stamped with the name WORLDSHAKER and the date 1845, which was when *Worldshaker* had been constructed, one hundred and fifty years ago. The washstand, bookcase, and full-length mirror bore similar stamped plates. Only the massive wardrobe cupboard lacked a plate: It was an antique of carved oak from earlier times in the Old Country.

All proper, all normal—like the distant thrum of *Worldshaker's* turbines, driving the great juggernaut forward. Time to go back to sleep.

He reached out to switch off the lamp—when a sudden thought set his heart pounding again. The sound that had woken him up *wasn't* the clang of a door! Now that he thought back, there *had* been something else. Something much closer.

Don't panic, he told himself. There was no one else in his room. Where could they hide? Unless in the cupboard . . . or under his bed . . .

He twisted over, lifted the fringed edge of the bedspread, and looked under his bed.

Two eyes looked back at him.

The female Filthy!

For ten long seconds he couldn't move. So close, separated only by the thickness of his mattress! He was lying almost on top of her!

The eyes studied him, sizing him up.

Then she moved first. Quick as a whip she slid out and knelt at the side of his bed. Nostrils wide and flaring, hollow cheeks below sharp cheekbones. Her hair was a knotted tangle, black in some places and blond in others. Huge, burning eyes dominated her face.

He wriggled away and fell off the other side of the bed.

Fighting free of sheets and blankets he stumbled to his feet.

She opened her mouth and spoke. "Don't let 'em take me."

It wasn't a grunt, but actual proper words! Pronounced in a rough and uncouth accent, but definitely words!

Col goggled. "You can speak?"

"Course I can speak. Why wouldn't I?"

"I thought . . . I didn't know Filthies could speak. Menials can't."

"Yeah, I heard about Menials."

"We train Filthies and make them into Menials. Then they can understand human language."

"Untrain 'em, more like. They could understand *and* speak, before."

Col had no answer. His head was spinning; he couldn't adjust.

She jumped up suddenly. She was all muscle and sinew, lithe and slight, quite unlike a Menial. Col had a general impression of darkness and dirtiness. She wore rags around her hips and torso, leaving her limbs shockingly naked. Her skin was streaked with smudges of soot and grease.

"See, they brought *me* up from Below to make me into a Menial." She faced him across the bed. "Fished me up on their hook and tried to march me to the Changing Room. But I give 'em the slip."

Col shook his head. "What do you mean, Changing Room?"

"Where they change us. They torture our bodies and do horrible things to us."

"Nonsense, there's no such place. How would you know, anyway?"

Col was quite sure that Upper Decks people would never do "horrible things." Mere Filthy ignorance! He had studied ethics with his tutor, so he knew torture was against proper moral principles.

He put on the kind of dignity he'd seen his elders assume. "You're lucky to have the chance to become a Menial. You're too young to know what's good for you."

"I'm not young. I'm fourteen."

"Well, I'm sixteen."

"You oughta know about the Changing Room, then."

It was hopeless trying to reason with a Filthy. *And I shouldn't even be trying,* he told himself.

He turned to the door and raised his voice. "Officers!"

She was across the room in a flash. He had always pictured Filthies as slow and brutish, but not this one. She opened the door a fraction, peeked out, then closed it again in a hurry.

"They're still there," she muttered.

He took a deep breath for a louder shout.

She flew back across the room and stood before him, hands clasped in appeal. "Please!" The bravado had fallen away, leaving only abject terror. "Don't let 'em take me!"

Footsteps came tramping along the corridor.

"I'm scared," she whispered, and stared at the door.

In that moment he remembered his own feeling of a few minutes ago. Seeing the two menacing figures in the doorway, flourishing their batons, ready to hit and beat . . .

She made a dart for the antique cupboard. While Col stood openmouthed, she jumped inside and pulled the door shut behind her.

The footsteps came up level with his room—then went past. If it was the warrant officers, they hadn't heard his call.

He didn't think of calling out again. He was still strangely churned up inside, as though her fear of the officers had transferred itself to him.

He went over and spoke through the cupboard door. "They've gone past."

"Thank you," said a muffled voice. "Thank you."

He didn't want her thanks; all he wanted was time to think. He turned the key in the cupboard door.

"I'm locking you in," he told her.

"Hey! No! You don't need to do that."

Col didn't reply. He was sure she couldn't escape: The wood of the cupboard was solid, and the lock was strong. She was his prisoner. But what was he going to do with her?

She rattled the door. "C'mon, let me out. You won't never see me again."

He removed the key from the lock and retreated to his bed. She was still trying to talk through the door, so he climbed in between the sheets and pulled the pillow over his ear. The key stayed safe in his clenched fist.

He felt hot, then cold, then hot again. It was like a bad dream. Had he actually been having a conversation with a Filthy? A Filthy who could not only speak but answer back? Instead of making her aware of her ignorance, he'd ended up feeling *he* didn't know as much as he should. Like a child!

He stared at the antique cupboard. It no longer looked the same, was no longer his old familiar cupboard, but a menacing, alien presence in the room. The girl had long since stopped shaking the door, but she was still inside, pressed up against his clothes. Her Filthy smell would be seeping into his suits and shirts! He would never be able to wear any of them again.

It was all unthinkable and unreal. And his own actions were the most unreal of all. Where had he gone wrong? He went back over it step by step. Why hadn't he called the officers before ever starting to talk to her? Or, when he did call, why hadn't he gone right out into the corridor? Or why hadn't he called again after she'd hidden in the cupboard? That was the most inexplicable moment of all. His behavior when the footsteps went past seemed to belong to someone else, not Colbert Porpentine. Crazy, crazy, crazy! If only he could take that moment back!

How had it happened? Was it the look in her eyes? So large and . . . not attractive—a Filthy couldn't be attractive—but it was as though her feeling of terror had jumped right out at him. He shouldn't be able to sympathize with a Filthy, and yet . . .

Creaking sounds came from the cupboard. He lifted the pillow from his ear to listen. The girl must be adjusting her position, perhaps settling down to sleep. He lay with the bedclothes pulled up to his chin.

The sounds continued for a while, then stopped. Now he seemed to hear breathing, faint and steady, in and out. His hearing had become almost preternaturally sharp.

An unpleasant thought came into his mind: If he was listening to her, perhaps she was listening to *him*. Each listening to the other's sounds! He took smaller and smaller breaths until the sheets stopped rustling over his chest.

How much did he truly know about Filthies? They weren't the sort of thing he discussed with his tutor, Professor Twillip. He must have picked up hints and worked out for himself that they couldn't speak. Only he'd worked it out wrong.

In polite society people only ever hinted at the existence of Filthies. His impressions came not from what anyone said so much as the look on their faces when they avoided the topic.

His main impression was that the Filthies were both dangerous and necessary. They were dangerous because they were always *breeding* and *multiplying*, which meant they might some day outnumber the civilized people on the Upper Decks. He had no idea why they were necessary.

What did it mean anyway, "breeding and multiplying"? Such dreadful, fascinating words, which stirred strange feelings in him. Going round and round in his mind, they brought up related words like "obscene," "brutish," "bestial." Fearful images from old nightmares floated before him: heavy lumbering shapes, hairy unclothed bodies, hideous cannibal faces with leering mouths. Doing things, hidden things, filthinesses—he couldn't even imagine the things they might do.

This girl didn't match up with his nightmares, though. He'd always pictured Filthies as a savage, uncivilized version of Menials. But she was the complete opposite, swift and athletic, flickering like a flame. . . .

He knew he ought to decide what to do with her. But somehow the right moment for making decisions had passed. Although a million thoughts chased around in his head, his mind refused to work on solutions. It was all too difficult.

He calmed himself by concentrating on words that always filled him with good and proper feelings: "duty," "empire," "Queen Victoria." For what seemed like hours the good words competed against the dreadful words, slowly driving them out. Waves of drowsiness washed over him.

When he finally fell asleep, he was thinking of his favorite words of all: "Her Imperial Majesty."

But his dreams didn't follow on from the good and proper feelings. In one dream his cupboard developed a thick coat of hair and flapped its door at him in a suggestive manner. In another he discovered a person wearing one of his shirts beside him in bed. Other dreams were filled with wise owls that frowned at him, noble lions that shook their heads at him, brave bears that turned their backs on him. . . . On and on, for the rest of the night.

When a *rap-rap-rap* on his door woke him up, it seemed as though he'd hardly been asleep.

3

He opened his eyes and saw that the ceiling light had come on, with its white daylike radiance. There was a second, louder *rap-rap-rap*. Then the cabin door flew open, and his sister, Gillabeth, marched in.

"Why are you still in bed?" she demanded. "Didn't you hear the morning bell? Why is your bedside lamp on? You know you're not allowed to sleep with it on."

She was only two years older than Col but always acted as if she were ten years his senior. Her black hair was cut very straight and plain, and she wore a sensible brown frock with a white bib and white cuffs. Her only ornamentation was the name GILLABETH embroidered on the bib. Everything about Gillabeth was straight and plain and sensible.

She and Col divided the family traits between them. While Col was growing up tall like his grandfather, with the same broad forehead, black eyebrows, and gray eyes, it was Gillabeth who had inherited the square Porpentine jaw. She stood now with jaw outthrust and hands on hips.

"It's a special day," she told him. "Grandfather has an announcement to make at breakfast. You'll need to wear your best sailor suit."

Col was about to get up when he felt the key in his hand. Last night's events came flooding back into his mind. The

Filthy girl in the cupboard! He prayed she'd have enough sense to keep quiet.

"Can you guess what it is?" asked Gillabeth. "It's about you."

"What is?"

"Grandfather's announcement."

"Oh. Why me?"

"You're such an innocent, Colbert Porpentine. You and your Professor Twillip. You have no idea what goes on."

"Is it good or bad?"

"Good, of course. Only good things happen to you. The world falls into your lap, and you never know why."

Col paid no attention to the sharpness of tone. It was just Gillabeth's normal way of speaking to him.

"I'll get your sailor suit ready," she said, and marched across to his cupboard.

"No!"

"Why not?" Gillabeth directed a smug look of conscious virtue upon him. "I'm your sister. I'm here to help."

At least the cupboard was locked and he had the key. Col plunged his hand deeper under the bedclothes.

But when Gillabeth pulled on the handle, the door swung wide open.

This was the end of everything! A Filthy discovered in his cupboard!

"Now, where is it?" She reached in and rummaged about. "Why don't you keep your clothes in proper order?" She lifted out Col's best sailor suit on its hanger. "Here you are."

Col didn't understand; he only felt a vast relief.

"Now hurry up." She laid out the suit across the bed, over

his feet. "The family is waiting." In her mouth the word "family" always seemed like an imperial command.

"Gillabeth, what do you know about Filthies? You know so much more than Professor Twillip and me. Are they like Menials?"

She shook her head. "We don't think about them."

"But can they speak?"

"Maybe."

"Are they slow and heavy like Menials?"

Gillabeth averted her eyes. "Why would you ask that?"

He had the impression that she knew some things about Filthies he didn't. But it was impossible to probe her without giving himself away.

"Doesn't matter." He tried to sound casual. "I'll get dressed now."

He waited until she was out of the room. Then he threw off the bedclothes and rushed over to investigate the cupboard.

There was no one there. Gillabeth hadn't missed seeing the Filthy girl, because she'd already gone. He swished his clothes back and forth to be sure.

Then he noticed something stuck into the lock on the inside. His Young Patriots button! Unbelievable! The girl must have found the button on his jacket lapel, then used the pin to pick the lock. He was amazed that a Filthy could be so cunning.

Well, good riddance to her. His spirits lifted. The problem had been solved; she'd escaped by herself. What happened to her next wasn't his concern.

He washed using the hand basin, dressed, and combed his hair. He grinned at his reflection in the mirror. What was this announcement Grandfather was going to make?

Breakfast took place in the Northumberland Room, three corridors away from Col's cabin in the middle of Forty-second Deck. It was a room for the exclusive use of the Porpentine family, and the five branches of the family were already seated at separate tables when Col arrived. White tablecloths, fresh napkins, silver cutlery, gleaming cups and plates—after last night it was all so right and normal. The linen was decorated with pretty pink motifs, while the cups and plates had borders of primrose yellow. Even the legs of the tables were decently clothed in white ruffs and flounces.

Col took his seat next to his mother and father, Quinnea and Orris. Facing him across the table were Gillabeth and his baby brother, Antrobus. His grandfather and grandmother sat at the head of the table: the twin pillars of his world, Sir Mormus and Lady Ebnolia Porpentine.

Six Menials wheeled a trolley around from table to table, unloading teapots, kippers, and racks of toast under the supervision of two stewards. The stewards were far inferior in rank to the elite Porpentines, but they were still Upper Decks people. Menials, on the other hand, didn't count as people at all. You looked over them or through them, but never really *at* them.

Col studied these six out of the corner of his eye. They wore the gray pajama-like uniforms of all Menials—in fact everything about them was gray. Compared to the young Filthy girl they seemed incredibly old and lumbering.

"Grace." Sir Mormus rapped on the table and produced an instant hush. "In the name of Her Imperial Majesty Queen Victoria the Second, may we be truly grateful for the good things here before us. Amen."

Evidently, he intended to make his announcement at the end of breakfast. As the meal began amid a tinkle of cutlery and murmur of polite conversation, Col turned his attention to his grandfather. There was something magnificently solid and immovable about Sir Mormus's massive shoulders and large head. His very presence was as much a statement of authority as were his braided jacket and high starched collar, or the keys of office on the gold chain round his neck.

Col couldn't imagine what it would be like to be so powerful and self-assured. Sir Mormus always gave orders in a tone of absolute command. Col didn't know exactly what a supreme commander did, but he knew that his grandfather was the most important person on *Worldshaker* after the queen and her consort. He was glad to be a Porpentine and share some of the reflected glory.

"Eat up, Colbert," said Quinnea. "Not too fast, though."

Col focused on the kipper and toast on his plate. Kippers for breakfast was a tradition from the Old Country, though the kippers they ate came from everywhere else in the world, never the Old Country.

His mother was more interested in Col's eating than her own, and she had pushed aside her plate after a few mouthfuls. Other people were watching him too—he sensed half smiles and glances directed his way. Did they already guess something about the forthcoming announcement? Adults usually took no notice of the younger generation at all.

Ten minutes later Sir Mormus concluded breakfast by wiping his mouth on an enormous handkerchief. When he rose to his feet, every conversation died away.

He nodded toward the five tables in turn. "Morpice Porpentines. Rumpley Porpentines. Leath Porpentines. Oblett Porpentines. Sir Mormus Porpentines." Each branch was named after its most senior member. Naturally the Sir Mormus Porpentines were the most important. "I have an announcement that concerns you all." He crooked a finger at Col. "Stand up, young man, stand up."

Col stood. He held himself very upright, though his heart was hammering.

"My grandson Colbert." Sir Mormus spoke with slow deliberation, as though every word had been weighed and found worthy. "Eldest male child of Orris and Quinnea Porpentine. What have you achieved so far in your life, Colbert?"

Col thought and came up with an answer. "Education, sir."

"Go on."

"Lessons with Professor Twillip, sir. My tutor."

"That's all?"

Quinnea uttered a little pleading sound. "He tutored my sister's daughter, Sir Mormus. . . . Highly recommended . . ."

Sir Mormus hardly seemed to hear her. "What do you know about the real world, my boy? Not much, I suppose?"

"No, sir. Not much."

"You've had a sheltered upbringing, my boy. From now on you will attend school. I have come to a decision about you."

Sir Mormus swung to face the other four tables. "Look at

him, all of you. See how tall he stands? Straight back, fine chest, firm mouth. Particularly good eyebrows. Very black. What do you think?"

The Porpentines at the other four tables looked attentive.

"I'll tell you what to think. This boy is the future of our family. He will go to school and learn control and authority. I nominate him as my successor. I shall prepare him to become the next supreme commander."

Col's gasp was lost among all the other gasps. Successor! Supreme commander! The idea was so staggering he couldn't take it in. He wanted to look round at his mother and father. But something told him to maintain his posture, keep his eyes straight ahead.

"What do you have to say, my boy?"

"I shall do my best, sir."

"Only your best? You have some doubts about yourself?"

"No, sir. I shall become the next supreme commander after you."

Col had no notion where the words were coming from, but he knew exactly what to say. It was as though Sir Mormus's influence had spread across to him. Although the announcement was completely unexpected, it was also right, very right. He felt that some part of him had known all along.

"Good, good." Sir Mormus approved. "You will have competitors, of course. But if you possess the true fiber of a Porpentine, my support will see you through. We have had a Porpentine as supreme commander for all but twelve of the last one hundred and fifty years. The tradition is in your hands, my boy."

The entire Porpentine family broke into applause. Even Baby Brother Antrobus brought his hands together like a little mechanical toy, imitating the adults. Gillabeth clapped, but with an expression on her face as though she were having teeth pulled.

Col continued to look serious, though inside he was grinning fit to burst. *I can do this,* he thought. *I can really do it.*

When the applause died down, Sir Mormus lowered his voice to a meditative rumble. "I once stood as you stand, Colbert Porpentine. When I was your age, my father made the same announcement about me. I was overwhelmed. I feared I wasn't ready. I trembled at the prospect."

"No, no." Murmurs of protest came from around the room.

"Yes, I trembled. Even I. Yet I rose to fulfill the role bestowed upon me. When summoned, I found the necessary strength of character. Willpower is what it takes, my boy."

And I'm not even trembling, Col exulted inwardly. Aloud he said, "I have willpower, sir. I shall do as you did. I shall serve my family and my queen."

Another round of applause confirmed that he had said exactly the right thing once more. Col had never in his life been the center of attention—but yes, he could get used to it!

"Sir, I have a request." Sir Mormus's stare was like a battering ram, but Col refused to flinch. "I don't know much about the real world, sir, as you said. I've never gone beyond the upper levels of the Upper Decks. If I'm to be prepared for supreme command, I'd like to see the whole of our juggernaut, sir. From top to bottom, sir."

There was a fraught silence. Had he pushed too far? Although he hadn't actually said "Below," that was what the word "bottom" implied.

Sir Mormus let out a snort like a trumpet blast. "Very good, my boy." It was a snort of approval. "A suitable request. I shall take you from top to bottom myself. The top first. Is that all?"

"That's all, sir."

Sir Mormus turned to the room again. "I shall be on the bridge at nine o'clock. Someone can escort him there. This breakfast is at an end."

The head steward hurried up with the chit for Sir Mormus to sign. Then Lady Ebnolia rose and attached herself to her husband's arm. With slow and stately steps they made their exit from the Northumberland Room.

5

Col remained the center of attention for the next half hour.
The male heads of the four other branches shook his hand
and wished him well. The women fussed over him and seemed
surprised that he'd grown so tall without their noticing.

"You must come to one of our whist evenings, young man."

"Perhaps you'd like to attend our book club?"

"Will you take him to the Fefferleys' high tea, Quinnea?"

Col's mother nodded silently and dabbed at her cheeks
with a tiny handkerchief.

"Oh, he really must get out into society more. I hear the
Dollimonts are having a soirée."

"And don't forget the Imperial Gala Reception coming up."

"You've been hiding him away, Orris, I do declare."

Col's father responded with one of his slow, sad smiles.
"No, no. We've been waiting and hoping for this moment to
arrive."

Eventually, the crowd thinned out, until only the members
of Col's own family branch remained. Then Orris spoke up in
his funereal voice.

"I'll escort you to the bridge now, Colbert. As your father I
think that's appropriate."

So they set out. As always, Orris's presence had a depress-
ing effect. Col loved his father like a dutiful son, of course,

but he had always been aware that there was something not quite right about him. Something more than the droop of his shoulders or the sag of his jowls. An air of perpetual gloom clung to him like a shroud.

They ascended a staircase to Forty-third Deck and walked past the Wiltshire Room and the Imperial Staterooms. Then more staircases, up to Forty-eighth Deck. Here they left behind the residential regions and arrived at the administrative regions of the juggernaut.

They passed offices with glass doors, offices with maps on the walls and metal filing cabinets. The carpets were plain, unpatterned green or brown and the paintwork a dull cream color.

"This is the highest I've ever been," said Col. "Forty-eighth Deck."

"Ah, well. The bridge is six decks higher."

"Can you see outside from the bridge?"

"Yes. It'll be a new experience for you."

Col thought back. "I've seen outside before. On Garden Deck, when we went on our holidays."

"It's not the same, Colbert. Garden Deck is walled in at the sides."

"I saw the sky, though. Real day and night. Real sunshine."

"That's nothing compared to what you'll see from the bridge." Orris pulled thoughtfully at his chin. "Let me show you."

He turned suddenly down a side passage and arrived at an oil painting of their own juggernaut hanging on the wall. Col had seen similar paintings before; in fact his only idea of how *Worldshaker* might look from the outside came from such pictures. But the settings were always dramatically obscure, with clouds or swirling haze, dazzling sun or jags of lightning.

This one was clearer than most: *Worldshaker* by moonlight. Tier by tier it rose, like a mountain blotting out the stars.

"So big," Col breathed.

"Two and a half miles long, three quarters of a mile wide. Still the largest human construction on the face of the earth. Here's the bridge, up here."

Orris pointed to a spot of brightness at the top of the black silhouette. The bridge faced forward from the brim of a towering cliff of superstructure.

"Twenty-six years ago," he went on, musing to himself, "I looked out there once." He cleared his throat. "And this is Garden Deck, down here."

He moved his finger to indicate an area below the cliff, toward the front of the juggernaut.

"What about Below?" asked Col. "Where's that?"

Orris sketched a rough line across the silhouette. "The bottom quarter of the hull. I . . . well . . ." He broke off.

Col studied the painting, but there was no visible division on the black side of the juggernaut. Then he noticed something else.

"What's that?" He pointed to a shape in the background. "Another juggernaut?"

"*Lebensraum.* The Prussian . . . juggernaut. We're over . . . overtaking it."

Orris seemed to be having difficulties with his words. Col turned and saw that his father was blinking back tears. Suddenly it all fell into place.

"You looked out from the bridge twenty-six years ago?"

Orris nodded. "I was fourteen years old."

"Grandfather showed you from top to bottom of the juggernaut, didn't he? Just like me?"

Another nod. "I was to be his successor. Until I failed."

Of course—it was obvious. Col was amazed he hadn't realized before. Sir Mormus's son should have been first choice to follow in his footsteps, not his grandson.

"How did you fail?" he demanded. Then, realizing he might sound less than respectful, he added, "Can you tell me, sir?"

This time Orris shook his head. "That would be inappropriate, Colbert. Come. You wouldn't want to be late for your grandfather."

Col was used to the way the word "inappropriate" closed off all further discussion. They walked on up through Forty-ninth, Fiftieth, and Fifty-first decks. On Fifty-second Deck Orris came suddenly to a halt.

"Yes, I *will* tell you." He turned to Col. "You ought to be prepared."

Still, he didn't speak immediately. When he did, he lowered his voice to a whisper. "A softness of the heart betrayed me, Colbert. It was my weakness that no one had ever suspected. I'd never suspected it myself. But when I looked down Below and saw them . . ."

"You mean the Filthies, sir?"

"Yes, yes. We can speak frankly about them now that you're moving beyond childhood. You'll have to face up to many hard facts of life we don't mention before women and children. You'll see sights you never imagined."

"You went down *among* them?" Col was horrified at the thought.

"Not among them, no. There are viewing bays for looking out Below. Sir Mormus will take you to one, eventually. Not close. But you can still hear them. . . . Sometimes you can see them. . . ."

For a moment Orris couldn't go on. His Adam's apple went up and down as if he were trying to swallow something painful.

"My reason told me that the Filthies aren't like us. They're not sensitive to pain and suffering in the same way. But I felt something for them. I couldn't help it. I couldn't bear to stay. I broke and ran, and I said mad, hysterical things. . . . Oh, the shame, Colbert! The shame of it!"

Col felt ashamed for him too. Before, he'd been curious, but now he only wished his father would keep his secrets to himself.

"I'm sorry," Col said. "I'm sorry to be taking your place."

"No, *don't* be sorry!" Orris spoke with sudden forcefulness. "I don't want you to be sorry. I want you to glory in your success. Be proud of your strength of character. Be thankful you don't have my kind of weakness. You mustn't make the mistakes I made."

With his father's lugubrious, froglike eyes upon him Col could only think to say what he'd said in the Northumberland Room. "I shall serve my family and my queen, sir."

Orris appeared satisfied. "Yes, there's no morbid taint in you. You'll prove it was only an aberration. Whatever happened to me, the Porpentine bloodline runs true in my son."

In silence they continued up to Fifty-third Deck. Col made a promise to himself: He would honor his father as a dutiful son, but he would be as unlike him as possible. He understood now what wasn't quite right about Orris Porpentine: the aura of failure he carried like a smell. Col vowed he would never, ever have that aura.

The last flight of steps led up to a steel-paneled door. Guarding the door was an ensign armed with a long-barreled rifle. Col goggled. He had seen pictures of guns, but he'd never seen one in real life.

"Master Colbert Porpentine," said Orris, standing back. "To see Sir Mormus Porpentine."

The ensign snapped to attention, turned a handle, and flung open the door.

"The bridge is through there, Colbert." Orris lowered his voice. "You'll do what is right, I know you will."

"Aren't you coming too?"

"No, not me. But you go in."

Col could hardly bear the sight of his father's sad, hopeful smile. He went in to meet his grandfather.

6

The bridge was a hubbub of organized activity, with thirty or more officers pulling on levers, rotating wheels, speaking into voice pipes. Control units stood in rows: square cabinets of dark, polished wood with glass dials and gleaming brasswork. Bells rang; buzzers buzzed; orders were shouted.

Looking in from the doorway, Col saw that the floor rose level by level to a curving strip of clear glass windows at the front. Sir Mormus Porpentine sat enthroned in a carved wooden chair on the topmost level. Blue sky and white clouds were visible through the glass, so much bluer and whiter than in any picture.

A senior officer caught sight of Col and spoke in the supreme commander's ear.

"Maintain course for Palk Strait," Sir Mormus boomed.

He rose from his chair and came down to where Col waited. "Well, Grandson. What do you think of the bridge?"

"Amazing, sir. So many controls."

Sir Mormus nodded. "Every officer knows his role. If anyone did the wrong thing at the wrong time, the consequences would be disastrous." He pointed to a particular bank of dials monitored by three officers. "For example, without those officers, our axles would overheat through lack of lubrication, and our turbines would go into meltdown." He pointed to another five officers hovering over a row of levers. "And if those officers didn't balance the steam pressure in our boilers, the boilers would explode and destroy us all. A finely tuned system, my boy."

"Do *you* know what every control does, sir?"

"Enough, enough. I control the controls." He touched the keys on the gold chain around his neck, and a complacent smile passed across his features. "These aren't just ceremonial, you know."

Then he turned and snapped his fingers at the nearest officer. "My grandson needs your jacket, Mawser."

Mawser took off his jacket, embellished with the gold braid of a master lieutenant. Col was big enough to fill out the arms and shoulders, though not the breadth of the chest.

"Today we're going to look out from on top," Sir Mormus announced.

Col followed him to a staircase that went up steeply at the side of the bridge. The metal steps shuddered under Sir Mormus's weight.

They went up through the ceiling and into a small round chamber like a turret. Then Sir Mormus unbolted a door and strode out.

It was incredible. Following his grandfather, Col walked out into a world of fresh air and sunshine. Openness on every side! He had never known anything so glorious. The cold wind fanned his hair and made his cheeks tingle. He opened his mouth and let the freshness fill his lungs.

They had come out onto a platform above the bridge. All around were masts and wires, which sighed and sang in the wind. Col watched half a dozen small puffs of cloud—so close it seemed he could reach out and touch them. He could have stayed there forever, just feeling the sun and air on his face. It was like sailing in the sky.

But already his grandfather was striding forward to a waist-high barrier of solid steel that ran round the front of the platform. Col hurried to join him. He too leaned forward and looked out.

His vision swam with the vast scale of it all. There were the gray metal decks of *Worldshaker* far, far below—but even more, the landscape spreading out all around, unfolding into the distance! A panorama of forests, hills, and seas!

"What do you think, my boy?"

What did Col think? He didn't know how to put it into words. It was as though the maps in his atlas had come to life. With his eyes he traced a winding boundary between the blue of the sea and the colors of the land.

"Where are we, sir?" He pointed. "What's that?"

"That? The east coast of southern India. We've traveled over the Nilgiri Hills and the Amaravati River. See those light green and brown patches?"

Col followed his grandfather's gaze. "Yes, sir."

"Cultivated plains. Primitive agriculture. See those paler yellow patches?"

"Yes, sir."

"Native towns and cities. Little centers of tin-pot kingdoms. We'll reach the coast in another three hours and cross Palk Strait to Ceylon."

Ceylon was a dim shape of low-lying land, barely visible on the horizon.

"The water is so shallow we can cross it on our rollers, without changing to propellers," Sir Mormus continued. "As a future supreme commander you'll need to understand these things."

Col was puzzled. "We don't seem to be moving at all."

Sir Mormus rumbled with amusement. "We're thirteen hundred feet above the ground, my boy. On the ground we're traveling faster than a galloping horse. Keep your eyes on that dark line there."

"What is it, sir?"

"The Vaigai River. We'll be rolling over it in a couple of minutes."

The dark line ran across just a little way above the juggernaut's blunt prow. Col stared and saw how the interval between them grew less and less. For one moment he glimpsed the glitter of the river itself; in the next moment the prow had blotted it from view.

"Sir, what do our rollers look like?"

"Three hundred and forty of them, each weighing eight hundred tons."

Col tried to picture the rollers rolling over the Vaigai River, but his imagination failed him.

"We have them cleaned whenever we stop at a coaling station," Sir Mormus went on. "Do you know what a coaling station is, my boy?"

"No, sir."

"It's a base where we take on coal and raw materials. We have to restock every eighteen months. Next due in three months' time."

Col remembered the red dots on different continents in his atlas. "Is that like Gibraltar and Hong Kong, sir?"

"Yes, and Singapore and the Cape and Botany Bay.

Outposts of the Old Country. Forts and depots." Sir Mormus's hands clamped down on Col's shoulders and turned him around. "Now take a look the other way."

The view to the stern was largely hidden by a huge black funnel at the back of the platform—and an endless row of similar funnels behind it. They were all pumping out smoke, leaving a long, dirty trail in the sky.

"Look at our cranes," said Sir Mormus. He meant the steel arms that stuck out at various angles from the sides of the juggernaut. "That's what we use for loading coal."

Even from this restricted angle Col could see dozens and dozens of cranes. Mighty scoops like jaws swung out on cables through the air. They were swiveling and lowering even as he watched.

"What are they doing now, sir?"

"Trading, my boy. Our juggernaut lives by trade. We exchange manufactured goods for raw materials. Trade and profit: the imperial principle. A supreme commander plans the route where the trading will be best. Do you want to do that, Colbert?"

"Yes, sir."

Still gripping Col's shoulders, Sir Mormus rotated him through a complete circle. The busy cranes . . . the tremendous superstructure . . . the landscape spread out like a map . . .

"All yours, Colbert. You will rule this juggernaut and everyone in it. Ten thousand people."

"Including the Filthies, sir?"

"Ten thousand people and two thousand Filthies."

Another rotation. The wind roared in Col's ears and made his eyes go blurry.

"This iron colossus, Colbert, this mechanical mountain, this predominator. You will be it and it will be you. Do you want that?"

"Sir, I do."

And he did, he did. He felt dizzy and drunk with the greatness of it all. He wasn't thinking of his duty to the Porpentine family or Queen Victoria. This was what he was born for; this was his inheritance! *Yes! Yes! Yes!*

Sir Mormus released his shoulders. "You'll do, my boy. You'll do."

Col leaned back slightly, planted his feet, and drank in the tremendous panorama all around. *Iron colossus. Mechanical mountain. Predominator.* His heart filled with pride.

But his grandfather was no longer beside him. Col turned and saw that Sir Mormus had returned to the turret. Reluctantly, he followed.

"Do we go down to the bottom now, sir?"

"Are you ready to see Below, my boy? Ready for the engines and the Filthies?"

"Sir, I believe I am." Col felt ready for anything.

Sir Mormus uttered a grunt of approval. "Good. But not today." He ushered Col into the turret and closed the door. "I shall take you to a viewing bay tomorrow morning."

7

Col didn't go for lessons with his tutor that morning. When he returned to Forty-second Deck, his mother summoned him to be measured for a school uniform. She had even decided to take him to the tailor herself. They set out accompanied by Quinnea's favorite Menial, Missy Jip, who carried her mistress's bags, spare clothing, and fold-up stool.

Col's mother was a wispy, ethereal woman with flyaway hair the color of dead leaves. Her skin was so pale that the veins showed through, and even her teeth had a glassy appearance. Col loved her, of course, but she had always been a vague, ghostly presence in his life.

The tailor was Mr. Prounce on Thirty-third Deck. Thirty-third Deck and the two decks under it made up the manufacturing area of the juggernaut, where every kind of light industry was carried out, from clock making to boot making, stonemasonry to joinery. The corridors had bare lightbulbs, and the workshops smelled of paint, glue, leather, and a hundred other powerful odors.

Quinnea held her nose pinched shut and walked with exaggerated caution, as though stepping on eggshells.

Mr. Prounce occupied one of the grandest workshops. He had a dozen Menials working for him, bowed over clacking machines on long, narrow tables.

So this is how clothes are made, Col thought, and was surprised to realize that he'd never pondered the question before.

"Two complete school uniforms." Mr. Prounce stroked the thin line of his pencil mustache. "Of course, of course, my lady."

His hands were infinitely respectful as he held the measuring tape across Col's shoulders, around his waist, and down his leg. Quinnea averted her eyes.

"Before Monday," she told him.

"I shall deliver them personally by Saturday evening." Mr. Prounce bowed as he presented the chit for her to sign.

"What a vulgar man!" she remarked afterward. "Such low standards one meets among the artisan class!"

She insisted on escorting Col back to his cabin. She behaved like a mother about to lose her beloved son forever.

"I must take another look at your dear little room," she said. "How many more times will I get to see it now?"

While Missy Jip waited in the corridor, Quinnea entered and looked round. She was out of breath from the walk and the stairs.

"No chair? I shall have to sit on the side of the bed. I'm feeling so faint."

She perched herself on the edge of his bed and patted her hair.

"Oh, Colbert, Colbert," she murmured. "To think of you wearing a school uniform. It seems no time at all since I was dressing you in baby clothes."

So far as Col could remember, he had always been dressed by Missy Jip or some other Menial. But perhaps when he was very, very small . . .

"I'm afraid for you going out into the world," she went on. "Growing up, becoming a man . . . It's all too much."

"I hope you'll be proud of me, Mother."

"Oh, I will. Terribly proud. But a mother's heart . . . a mother's care . . . a mother's panic attacks . . ."

"And I have to finish school first."

"But *school*, Colbert! Do you know how many other pupils there are? Hundreds! *Hundreds!* Boys and girls!"

"What school, Mother?"

"Dr. Blessamy's Academy, of course. The only school for children from superior families. But none as superior as ours. Who will look after you?"

"I can look after myself."

"Oh, they can be so rough, Colbert. So boisterous! Playing games in the recess! Running around! Shouting out! I've seen them!"

She was working herself up into a fit of nerves. Her hands shook, and she patted her hair so hard that one of her combs fell out. The left side of her hairdo immediately collapsed into loose, straggling strands.

"I had to be taken out of school, you know. I couldn't bear the chalk. And all the desks . . . the pencils . . ."

Col bent down to retrieve the fallen comb. He was about to say he didn't mind chalk and desks and pencils—but gasped instead.

Quinnea jumped and gasped ten times louder. "Oh! Ooh! What is it?"

Col straightened up with the comb in his hand. "Nothing. Nothing at all."

"Is it my feet? Is it my ankles?"

"No, mother. You're fine. Your ankles are fine."

He tried to appear calm and forced himself to look away.

But in the corner of his eye he could still see the Filthy girl's face peering out from under his bed. Horror gripped him. It was a nightmare come to life.

He held out the comb to his mother, who took it but didn't know what to do with it. She adjusted her dress over her knees and brought her ankles closer together.

"Oh, my poor head! I shouldn't let myself feel so much. Strong feelings aren't good for me. I'm all over the place. Look at me!"

Col was desperate. "Do you want your smelling salts?"

"No. Yes. No. Yes. No." Quinnea couldn't decide. Her hands were still fluttering, her knees still quivering.

Under the bed the Filthy girl looked out around the side of Quinnea's legs. She was grinning at him!

"You must be tired," Col told his mother. "You should go back to your rooms for a long lie-down."

The girl pulled a face and mimicked a yawn. Col's blood boiled. The mockery!

As if from a distance he heard his mother sigh and say, "Oh, Colbert!" over and over again. She didn't seem opposed to the idea of a long lie-down.

"Come on, then." He helped her to her feet. If she glanced down now . . . He kept up a constant stream of chatter as he steered her, tottering, toward the door.

"Here we go. Very good. Here's the corridor. Are you all right to go with Missy Jip?"

He didn't wait for an answer. With a hasty good-bye he swung back into his room and closed the door.

The Filthy girl was still under the bed. He dropped down on all fours to confront her.

"What . . . you . . . how dare you!" The words came out in a splutter.

"And hi to you, *Col-bert*. Just passin' by, so I thought I'd drop in. Ain't ya pleased to see me, *Col-bert*?"

She pronounced the name as his mother had done, in a quavering, drawn-out tone. He couldn't believe her impudence.

"How dare you make fun of my mother!"

"Oh, ah. The son defends his mother, is it?"

"I love and respect my mother."

"Didn't look very loving to me. Strange sort of family you have, Col-bert."

"What would you know about families? We're Porpentines. The most important family in this whole juggernaut."

"Is that right? So your name is Col-bert Porping-tine?"

"Porpentine. My grandfather is supreme commander, and I'm going to be supreme commander after him."

"Well, ain't you the fortunate one."

The sarcastic grin never left her face as she slid out from under the bed and stood up to face him. He noticed something different about her appearance . . . and then he noticed the book in her hand.

"Hey! Where did you get that?" It was *his* book, a book about mountains and volcanoes. "You've been stealing from my bookcase!"

"Just lookin' at it. Keep yer hair on."

"Looking? Why would a Filthy look at a book? You can't read."

"Only 'cause I never got a chance to learn. If I'd learned, I bet I could read ten times better'n you."

Col snorted. "If you've dirtied it . . ."

Then he realized what was different about her appearance. She was no longer dirty! Her skin was glowing, and even her hair seemed softer and silkier. . . .

"Yeah, I had a wash," she said, and pointed to his washstand. "Don't mind, do ya?"

She was sneering at him. He stared at the marks on the white enamel basin, the smears on his towel. He was amazed to think that a Filthy would actually *want* to wash.

"Get out!" he snapped. "Go back down where you belong!"

"I will when I find a way."

"Go back the same way you came up."

"Don't be stupid. They fished me up on their hook. It don't work the other way. I gotta find a ladder or steps or somethin'."

"Get looking, then."

"What do you think I been doin'?" She frowned. "Searchin' all over your lower levels is what. Kitchens and laundries and storerooms."

Col had never been to any of those places. "You'll get caught. You're lucky you've lasted so long."

"Lucky? Don't make me laugh. Who's goin' to catch me? You Upper Decks people are too slow. I see your officers long before they see me. I'm speedy."

She performed a kind of boastful dance, arms flickering. She *was* speedy, Col had to admit, almost faster than the eye could see. But flashy, mere slickness and show. A proper person would have more dignity.

"You're all a waste of space," she jeered. "Just standin' around lookin' pompous."

"We do the planning." Col quoted his tutor: "'The role of the head is to make plans for the body.' We're the head and you're the body."

"That's just your excuse for hoggin' all the good stuff." Her gesture took in the furnishings of Col's cabin. "Books an' beds an' pillows an' carpets . . . You don't deserve any of it! It oughta be taken off of you!"

Col was horrified. "Right. That does it. I'm calling the officers."

"Call away." Her eyes narrowed. "But I'll tell 'em what you did before."

"What?"

"You hid me in your cupboard. So's they wouldn't find me."

This was a trap Col hadn't foreseen. "They won't listen to you."

"Wanna bet? They'll think we got partnered."

Col was nonplussed. She gave him a malicious smile.

"I'll be goin' now," she said. "Maybe I'll drop in again soon."

She moved to the door. Just in time Col saw that she still had his book—deliberately hiding it behind her back!

"No!" His frustration boiled up in a burst of rage. He sprang after her and grabbed the book with both hands.

Still she refused to let go. He wrenched at it, wrestled her for it. Arm to arm, hip to hip. In the heat of the moment he forgot about being disgusted by the touch of a Filthy.

She was wiry, and twisty as a snake, but he had the better grip on the book. He pulled it away and held it safe against his chest. She turned away with a shrug.

"Okay, Col-bert. Now I'll drop in again for sure." She opened the door a crack and peered out into the corridor. Then she glanced back round at him. "By the way, you never asked, but the name's Riff."

Next moment she was gone.

8

Col stood in front of the mirror and examined his reflection. He was still panting from the struggle, and his cheeks were on fire. He went across to the washstand, dampened his wash-cloth, and pressed it against his cheeks. It took several minutes before his face went back to normal.

Then he removed his shirt and washed his arms and chest . . . anywhere he might have touched her, even through the shirt. He used a great deal of soap and the scrubbing brush. He cleaned the basin too, removing even the faintest Filthy smear.

It was so unfair. Why him? Why now? Just when everything else was going so right in his life, why did this one thing have to go so wrong?

If only she would go back down Below . . . But the more he thought about it, the more he doubted it was possible. A way to go down would also be a way for Filthies to climb up. Surely the builders of *Worldshaker* would have made sure that couldn't happen?

At least he didn't see her again that afternoon. He had dancing practice with Mrs. Landry, followed by foils practice with Mr. Bantling, followed by supervised jigsaw-puzzling with Mrs. Canabriss. Then it was time for dinner in the Northumberland Room.

Dinner was roast beef, potatoes, and something like cabbage, served with pools of imperial brown gravy. But

Col couldn't concentrate on his food. He kept remembering those words: *I'll drop in again soon*. It was like a curse hanging over him.

"You're not eating," Gillabeth observed sharply from the other side of the table. "What's wrong with you?"

Col took a new grip on his cutlery and dug in.

Antrobus was watching him too. Col's baby brother had reached the age of three without uttering a single childish word or even babbling, yet his eyes fixed upon things with a look of deep concentration. All through dinner they were fixed upon Col.

Col found it unnerving. Feeling guilty in himself, he imagined accusations everywhere. And still he couldn't stop thinking about Riff. It was maddening that even her name had stuck in his mind. Until today he would never have guessed that Filthies had names.

So many things he didn't know and couldn't ask his family. But perhaps he could ask Professor Twillip. When dinner ended, he decided to pay a visit to the Norfolk Library.

The library was a soothing, civilized domain on Forty-fourth Deck. Shelf upon shelf of leather-bound books rose up out of the gloom on all sides. When Col entered, he saw Professor Twillip working at a table under the sole electric light.

"Hello?" He swung round at the sound of Col's approach and looked out over the top of his glasses. "Why, Colbert. Name the most important Greek philosopher before Plato."

"Er . . . Socrates?"

"Correct. Spell 'philology.'"

Tutorials with Professor Twillip always started with quick-fire questions. He was a chubby man with a face so pink it shone like a beacon. Though he was middle-aged, his skin was boyishly unlined; as if to compensate, his fleecy hair had turned absolutely white. He was always brimming over with scholarly enthusiasms—of which philology was the most recent.

Col shook his head. He wasn't here for a tutorial.

"Oh, yes, of course, of course." Professor Twillip readjusted his glasses. "I was falling into old habits. No more tutorials. You'll be moving on to school, and then even higher prospects, so I hear. Well done, Colbert."

He smiled the smile of a man who never said anything he didn't truly mean.

"What will you do when you don't have anyone to tutor?" Col asked.

"Oh, I'll get used to it, I expect." Professor Twillip encompassed the library with a sweeping gesture. "So many books still to read. I haven't finished with the Greek philosophers yet. Then there are the Rationalists and Empiricists of the seventeenth and eighteenth centuries. Then the Imperial era and the modern Paternalists."

Col saw his opportunity. "Who was it who said, 'The role of the head is to make plans for the body?'"

"That was Fenwick, one of the leading Paternalists. In *The Hierarchy of Man*, 1872."

"Because the body doesn't have the intelligence to plan for itself?"

"That's right. While the head is the seat of reason, logic, and language."

"Language?" Col frowned. "So Filthies and Menials can't speak?"

If Professor Twillip was surprised by the outright mention of Filthies, he soon recovered.

"Well, Menials can understand but not speak. As for the Filthies . . . do you know, I've never really considered it."

"What happens in training?"

"Training?"

"When Filthies are turned into Menials."

"Oh, dear. You know me, Colbert, always the scholar. I'm afraid I'm rather ignorant about such practical matters." Professor Twillip scanned the shelves. "I wonder where I could look it up. It's not the sort of thing that books are written about."

"It *ought* to be," said Col.

"Why are you so curious?" Professor Twillip pushed his glasses back on his forehead and looked out from underneath. "Ah, I think I can guess. You're going to be concerned with such matters very soon, aren't you? Then, perhaps, you'll be the one telling *me*."

Their relationship had changed, Col realized. He'd always looked up to Professor Twillip, but now there was a sense in which his tutor looked up to him.

"I'll miss our tutorials," he said suddenly.

"So shall I, Colbert, so shall I. You've been an excellent, hardworking student. But I think it's right for you to move on. Deep down you're more of a doer than a thinker."

"I wish I could be as good a man as you, Professor Twillip."

"Ah, Colbert, it's much easier to be good in theory. You'll make a difference to the world one day. I have great faith in you."

He steepled his fingers and smiled. He was looking

straight into Col's eyes, yet he didn't guess a thing. *If you only knew what I've been doing,* Col wanted to say.

But instead he said, "Truth is the most important of all virtues. That's what you taught me."

"Yes, Colbert, and I'm sure you'll live up to it. Telling the truth is the only reason we stand at the top of the natural hierarchy. Lower creatures don't have our instinct for honesty and integrity, as Fenwick said. Or was it Carrington?"

Col had the strange notion that his eyes had become a screen and he could think whatever he liked behind them. He'd hardly had secrets in his life, so he was amazed to discover how easily they could be kept hidden.

Professor Twillip was scanning the shelves again; in another minute he would be searching for the volumes of Fenwick and Carrington. The subject of Filthies had been left behind. It was time to leave.

"I've been fortunate to have had you as my tutor, Professor Twillip," Col said.

The Professor beamed with pleasure. "Well, thank you, thank you. That's very kind of you."

Col considered shaking his hand but decided it would be inappropriate. He headed for the library door.

He felt as though new spaces were opening up inside him, deep private places that had never existed before. He didn't much like the feeling. Who would ever have guessed that inside and outside could be so different?

9

That night Col barricaded his room by pulling his bookcase across in front of the door. No way would he let that Filthy girl—that Riff—come creeping in. When he woke to the morning bell, eight hours later, he was refreshed from a full night's sleep, and Riff no longer seemed so important. What mattered was the magnificence of his future career.

Sir Mormus was absent from the breakfast table, but he'd left a message for Col with Grandmother Ebnolia.

"He said he'll meet you on First Deck," she repeated. She was small and dainty, with the tiniest of waists and the sweetest of smiles. "Chief Petty Officer Drummel will escort you down there after breakfast."

After breakfast Col found Chief Petty Officer Drummel waiting for him in the corridor outside the Northumberland Room. They started down the same staircases he had descended yesterday on his way to the tailor's, then angled off on a different route. They continued past the manufacturing decks to lower levels he had never seen before.

Twenty-first and Twentieth decks were the dormitory decks, where Menial drudges slept between shifts. On Nineteenth Deck Col saw the kitchens, where cooks supervised the preparation of food in enormous ovens. On Tenth Deck they passed by laundries smelling of detergent and pressed linen.

He remembered what Riff had said about kitchens and

laundries. So she must have visited these levels too . . . but no. He shook his head. He didn't want to think about her.

On Sixth Deck they walked past dark rooms filled with earth to a depth of several feet. Glancing in through openings like unglassed windows, Col could see upright slabs of stone rising in pale rows. The earth itself gave off a musty, moldering smell.

"What's in those rooms?" he asked.

"People buried," Drummel answered shortly. "We call them the Graveyard Rooms."

Col couldn't help wondering where the earth came from. Had it been scooped up along the way by the cranes he'd seen? Or loaded in place when *Worldshaker* was constructed, a century and a half ago? The thought of rooms filled with age-old earth and long-dead bodies made the hairs stand up on the back of his neck.

Fourth Deck was a repair area, with stacks of timber, metal sheeting, cork, burlap, coils of rope, and spools of wire. Below that was a deck given over to live animals in coops or pens. Col was able to recognize chickens, goats, and sheep from illustrations in his *Boy's Book of Animals*. Crammed side by side, dull-eyed and sad, they lacked even the spirit to lift their heads.

The two lowest decks were used for food storage. Col smelled grain, tea, dried fruit, pickles, and smoked meats. Drummel led the way to a clearing among the boxes and bags, then stopped.

"We wait here," he said.

Col tapped his foot on the metal floor. "The engines must be right underneath us?"

"No, this is only First Deck. Bottom Deck is under this. *Then* Below."

Five minutes later Sir Mormus arrived. He rode down on an elevator platform that emerged through the ceiling on four vertical rails. There was a chuffing and hissing, a rattle of chains and a clank of machinery. The platform came to a stop with a great *foosh!* of escaping steam.

Stepping out through the steam, Sir Mormus dismissed Drummel and beckoned for Col to follow. They marched between barrels and crates to another clearing. In the middle was a deep trough with steps going down.

They descended to a massive steel door with red lettering that announced:

· DOOR 17 ·
AUTHORIZED PERSONNEL ONLY

"Look away," Sir Mormus ordered.

There were three small wheels set into the door, with numbers round the rims. Col looked away as his grandfather rested a hand on the uppermost wheel. Three times he heard the *click-click-click* of wheels rotating and tumblers falling into place. When he looked again, the door was open.

Sir Mormus ushered him through. Col gaped at the strange world of Bottom Deck: rows of iron piers braced with crisscross struts, towering black mounds, pools of blue-white light alternating with areas of shadow. From floor to ceiling it was at least three times the height of a normal deck.

Sir Mormus closed and locked the door by turning more

wheels on the inside, then led the way forward. As they detoured around puddles of water and slicks of grease, Col felt a warmth rise up through the soles of his shoes.

"That's the coal that feeds the engines, my boy." Sir Mormus pointed to the black mounds.

"Yes, sir. How does it get down Below, sir?"

"Drops through chutes." Sir Mormus indicated a group of officers winding crank handles. "Those men are about to release a quantity of coal from one of the bunkers. We have other chutes for feeding the Filthies. See over there?"

Col didn't see a chute, but he saw a circular manhole cover. Piles of bags and sacks were stacked nearby.

"What do we feed them, sir?"

"Whatever we don't want ourselves."

Coal dust scrunched under their feet. They passed an array of hoses and pipes and arrived at a special fenced-off zone around a canvas tent. Warning orange lights flashed on top of the fence poles.

"Yes, go into the tent," said Sir Mormus.

Inside the tent was a flat hatch raised on a coaming a few inches above the floor. The words on the hatch were in the same red lettering as before:

VIEWING BAY 17

"Open it up," Sir Mormus ordered.

Col crouched, turned the handle, and heaved. The hatch came open with a great blast of heat. The noise from Below was like a million pounding hammers.

Sir Mormus lowered himself through the hatch and onto a ladder. Col saw a pulsing red glow and billows of smoke. . . .

Then the smoke got into his eyes and he was blinded by tears. He climbed down after his grandfather.

It was like one of his old childhood nightmares, when floors gave way beneath him and he went tumbling down to the depths below. So many times he had woken in terror, clutching the sheets in desperate hands as nameless horrors rushed up to overwhelm him. But he couldn't show weakness now. He clenched his jaw and kept going.

The smoke had a foul smell like rotten eggs. He fought down an urge to cough and concentrated on the rungs of the ladder.

When the ladder came to an end, he found himself standing not on solid floor but on thin wire mesh. The mesh shuddered to the rhythm of the engines as if shaken by giant hands. Col reeled and nearly lost his balance. He planted his feet wide apart and felt the vibrations drumming up through his bones.

Rubbing the tears from his eyes, he saw that the viewing bay was a kind of cage. About fifteen feet square, it hung suspended from the bottom of Bottom Deck. He stared down through the mesh and glimpsed huge dark shapes and glints of fire, like lava from a volcano. Insubstantial strands of wire were all that kept him from falling into the vast pit of Below.

He looked away in a hurry. At the other end of the cage Sir Mormus was talking to the officer on duty. They were little more than silhouettes in the smoky murk, but Col caught fragments of Sir Mormus's booming speech.

"Stop sweating, man. . . . Fasten yourself up. . . . Remember who you are. . . ."

It seemed he was angry that the officer had loosened his collar in the heat. The officer mopped his brow and fumbled at his top button.

Col went across to the side of the cage, hooked his fingers through the mesh, and looked out.

He could have been looking out over a boiling black ocean. There were no walls or bulkheads, only endless cavernous space. The echoes of sound suggested dimensions as wide and as long as the juggernaut itself. Tremendous metal wheels and beams rose and fell through rifts in the smoke, looming and vanishing. Sometimes the nearest beams came scything toward the cage, until Col thought his last moment had come—but always they swung away again. More threatening were the sprays of hot oil that flew through the air and spattered the roof.

He gritted his teeth and hung on. Reason told him that officers stood on duty here for hours at a time. He had to block out instinctual reactions.

He was just starting to relax when something new started up. Far below, in some deep gulf, a screech of metal rose above the general pounding din. Then showers of sparks, shower after shower, casting an eerie yellow glow through the smoke. The screech grew louder, a jagged seesawing sound.

Sir Mormus turned to the duty officer. "Give them some steam . . . aisles five and six . . ."

The officer reached for a row of levers that angled down from the roof. He pulled on one, then another. A roaring, jetting sound added itself to all the other noises in the pit.

Down Below, a cloud of white vapor appeared and spread. Surging and turbulent, it filled the depths where the sparks had been. Col couldn't guess what was happening, only that it involved steam.

After two minutes the officer returned the levers to their original position. The cloud continued to expand, but now with a lazier, drifting motion. The roaring, jetting sound had gone, and so had the screech of metal.

But what was that other sound? Straining his ears, Col heard a multitude of voices. It must be the Filthies! Were they howling abuse or crying out in pain?

For a moment he thought he glimpsed a mass of bodies at the bottom of the pit. Gleaming skin and waving arms . . .

The image of Riff flashed into his mind. It could have been her down there, writhing in agony, swearing and cursing. He let go of the mesh and backed away.

Sir Mormus turned and saw. "Hold firm, Colbert! Be a man!"

"It's the Filthies, sir!"

"Of course it's the Filthies. They shovel the coal and feed the engines."

"But the steam . . ."

"Gingers them up when they start slacking off."

He was staring at Col with heavy, frowning brows. Col knew exactly what he was thinking. *So the son is like the father after all.*

Col stiffened. He *would not* be like his father! Never that smell of failure! Never!

He drove the image of Riff out of his mind. *The Filthies are not like us,* he told himself, *not sensitive to pain and suffering. Not like us, not like us.*

He repeated it over and over, and as he repeated it, he stepped back to the mesh. Once more he took up his position and looked out.

The massed bodies must have existed only in his imagination. And even the cries . . . The Filthies were cursing because they hadn't been allowed to slack off. *That's all, nothing more,* he told himself.

After thirty seconds he knew he was going to make it. Besides, the white cloud blanketed out more and more of the view, and the cries of the Filthies grew more and more muffled.

Sir Mormus kept him there for another ten minutes. Col concentrated on working out the pattern of the beams as they rose and fell. He studied the cage itself: the bolted door in the side of the mesh, the metal poles and other equipment clipped to the roof overhead. There were dozens of ways to occupy his mind without falling into unwanted thoughts.

Finally Sir Mormus was satisfied. His hand descended on Col's shoulder. "Very good, my boy. A true Porpentine."

They went back up the ladder to Bottom Deck. Col felt shaken and numb, but triumphant.

Anyway, he thought, it couldn't be so bad Below, since Riff said she wanted to return. If it was as bad as it looked, she wouldn't be searching for a way back down. . . .

Walking through Bottom Deck, he suddenly realized that there *was* a way back down. The food chute! If it was big enough for a sack of food, it was big enough for Riff.

He looked at it as they went past and saw how the manhole cover was fastened by four large bolts. Yes! A one-way drop from the Upper Decks to Below, which could be opened only from above!

He needed only one more piece of information. When they came to the steel door and Sir Mormus told him to look away, Col secretly continued to watch.

His grandfather turned the top wheel to number 4, the middle wheel to number 9, and the bottom wheel to number 2.

Col recited the number and fixed it in his mind: 4-9-2. 4-9-2. 4-9-2. He was hardly aware of going up in the steam elevator when Sir Mormus took him back to Forty-second Deck. Now he knew how to get the Filthy girl out of his life!

10

The usual routine of Col's days was left behind as preparations for school took over. After lunch he accompanied Grandmother Ebnolia on a visit to Dr. Blessamy's Academy. Grandmother walked with a faint grinding of stays and corsets, past the nursery rooms and down to Thirty-seventh Deck.

Ebnolia was renowned for her past beauty and the kindness of her disposition. Her skin was still as soft as suede, and a cloud of strawberry perfume hung in the air around her. For Col the scent of strawberries was inextricably associated with the idea of kindness.

"A proper school with proper teachers." She chatted as they walked along. "This is the start of a new life for you, my dear."

More than you know, Col thought. When he reflected back on his existence so far, it was as though he'd hardly been there. He was like a sleepwalker who'd just woken up.

"But I still expect to be your favorite grandma!" Ebnolia bobbed and showed her tiny pearl-white teeth in a smile. "Will you always love your favorite grandma?"

"Always," said Col without thinking. Didn't everyone love their grandmother?

There was a convergence of corridors and a square of open space in front of the academy. The entrance itself was an antique arch from the Old Country, decorated with carved stone owls. It bore the motto LOYALTY, INTEGRITY, SELF-DISCIPLINE.

They passed under the arch and into an immense school-yard. The yard might have felt like the openness of outside—if Col hadn't experienced real openness on the platform above the bridge. It rose up through four levels of deck to white day-lighting high above. On each level there were doors and windows and a wrought-iron gallery running round. Ramps sloped up from gallery to gallery, and a footbridge crossed all the way from side to side on the third level.

They made a circuit of the bottom level until they came to a door labeled DR. BLESSAMY. DO NOT KNOCK. Ebnolia knocked.

"Who is it?" came a sleepy voice from within. "Can't you read—"

"Lady Porpentine," said Ebnolia sweetly. "How would you like to open this door for me?"

Creaks and scrapes, sounds of furniture being rearranged. Then the door opened.

"Dear Lady Porpentine. Welcome to my humble . . . er, humble . . . ah, yes. My room and study."

The face that looked out was crusty with age. Although Dr. Blessamy's skull was bald, hair sprouted luxuriantly from his nostrils and ears. There were dry, flaky deposits in his eyebrows and round his ears.

Ebnolia sailed into the room and perched on the edge of an armchair, while Col stayed standing. Dr. Blessamy moved round to sit facing them across his desk. He found a mortarboard and clapped it on his head.

"Paperwork, paperwork," he said, wafting his hands over some pens and papers on the desk.

"This is my grandson Colbert," said Ebnolia. "He's enrolled to start school on Monday."

"Ah, Monday, Monday. And this is Friday." Dr. Blessamy turned to Col. "Will you work hard for me, young man? Will you make me a happy old headmaster?"

"His presence will be an honor to your school," said Ebnolia on Col's behalf. "What class will you put him in?"

"Well, he's, ah, how old? Seventeen? Sixteen? Er . . . nineteen? Twelve?"

"Age isn't important. He's a Porpentine. What class are the Squellingham twins in?"

"That would be 4A."

"Good. He can go into that one."

A troubled look passed over Dr. Blessamy's face. "It's, er, Mr. Gibber's class."

"What's wrong with Mr. Gibber?"

"Oh nothing, nothing." Dr. Blessamy sighed, causing the hairs in his nostrils to flutter. "All the teachers at this academy have the very highest standards of . . . er . . . standards. Mr. Bartrim Gibber is . . . yes, one of them."

"That's settled, then. Now tell me about the subjects on your curriculum."

Col hardly listened as they talked about geography, geometry, chemistry, algebra, English language, and more. He would have plenty of time to concentrate on school subjects when he had gotten rid of Riff. He thought his own thoughts and waited for the interview to end.

Finally, the discussion came round to the equipment that Col would need for his lessons, and Dr. Blessamy rose stiffly upright. "I can do better than tell you, your ladyship. I'll take you to Mr. Gibber and he can . . . himself."

He led them out into the yard, up the nearest ramp, and

onto the first-floor gallery. Halting at a particular door, he opened it just wide enough to call inside.

"Er, Mr. Gibber, if you please."

Peering over Dr. Blessamy's shoulder, Col glimpsed a dimly lit room and rows of pale schoolboy faces. Then Mr. Bartrim Gibber bounded out, slamming the door behind him.

He had red, rubbery lips and slicked-back gingery hair that made his head look as round as a ball. He stood before them on short bowed legs, rocking back and forth, pulling all kinds of facial expressions. Col was reminded of the monkey illustrations in his *Boy's Book of Animals.*

"Mr. Gibber, you are to be honored with a new pupil," said Dr. Blessamy. "Lady Porpentine's grandson, no less."

"No less, no less." Mr. Gibber performed a little bow. "Honored indeed. Oh, yes. Excuse me."

He broke off and disappeared back into the classroom. They could hear him barking at his students, "Quiet! No talking! I said, *no talking!*"

By the time he stepped back out, there was even more noise inside.

"Lady Porpentine wishes to know about equipment for lessons," said Dr. Blessamy. "Such as a ruler and . . . things similar to a ruler."

Grins followed grimaces across Mr. Gibber's face. It was impossible to tell what they expressed: triumph or servility, gratitude or vanity. His eyes kept darting from Ebnolia to Col and back again.

"A ruler, yes, certainly. A protractor. Two pens. Two pencils. A rubber eraser. Definitely a rubber eraser. And three exercise books. An imperial dictionary. Did I say a protractor?"

He seemed hardly able to hold himself in. With another "excuse me," he bounced back into his classroom.

More barking. "Be silent! Sit still! What did I tell you just now? Well? Well? I'll make you wish you hadn't said that, Chervish!"

He looked strangely pleased with himself when he reemerged, though the noise had risen to an uproar.

"And a satchel," he concluded. "A leather school satchel."

"Thank you, Mr. Gibber." Dr. Blessamy turned to Col and his grandmother. "I'm sure this young man will make us all very proud to have been . . . extremely . . . all of us . . ."

The *clang-clang-clang* of a bell interrupted him. Mr. Gibber flapped his gown and dived back into his classroom without even an "excuse me."

"Close your desks!" they heard him yelling. "Put your books away! No, open your desks, put your books away, *then* close them! Your desk, Trant! When I say *go*—"

There was a stampede of thundering feet. Dr. Blessamy, Ebnolia, and Col stood back as a mob of schoolboys streamed out through the door. They all wore green jackets with red piping and badges labeled DR. BLESSAMY'S ACADEMY. They scarcely noticed the visitors as they charged for the nearest ramp.

Other students poured out onto other galleries: boys on the first and bottom floors, girls on the second and third floors. The whole horde rushed down into the yard.

"Ah, dear boys, dear boys," murmured Dr. Blessamy. "And girls. So very young and boyish. Or girlish . . ."

11

Col was eager to act on his plan for getting rid of Riff, but he needed her to pay him another visit, as she'd threatened. For two whole days she stayed away. When she finally turned up, it was in the middle of the night.

Thud-d!

He woke to the sound of a book falling flat on the floor—the book he'd propped against his door as a warning alarm. Riff stood half in and half out of the doorway, hissing a muffled curse.

Col sat up in bed in his nightgown. "Come in."

She came all the way in, closing the door behind her. Her eyes were enormous and unblinking.

"So." He felt very much in charge of the situation. "You still haven't found a way back down Below."

"No."

"I have."

"You?"

"The only possible way."

"How?"

"Down a food chute."

"Where?"

"You'll find out. Do you want me to take you there or not?"

"Yeah, I told you."

"Turn your back, then. I have to get dressed."

"What's to see?" she mocked, with a return to her old impudence.

Still, she did turn her back. He stood on the other side of the bed and pulled on breeches, a jacket, socks, and shoes. He didn't want to remove his nightgown in front of her, so he tucked it in like a shirt. Folds of flannel bulged uncomfortably under his breeches.

She said nothing all the time he was dressing. He found out why when he finished and looked round. She had taken a book from his bookcase and was thumbing through the pages.

"Put that back," he ordered.

She glanced up with an odd expression, part aggressive and part appealing. "I was goin' to ask to borrow it."

"Borrow? How do you return it when you're down Below?"

"A gift then. A good-bye gift."

"No."

She scowled, closed the book, and put it back in the bookcase. It was the book on mountains and volcanoes that she'd been looking at before.

Col nodded. "Now I'll lead you to the food chute. You'll have to follow out of sight. Can you do that?"

She snorted scornfully. "I've been keepin' out of sight for days, remember?"

"Just be careful."

"*You* be careful. I like takin' risks. More fun."

"You're nothing to do with me if you get caught," he growled.

"Are you scared, Col-bert?" She snapped her fingers. "Scare easy, don't ya?"

Ignoring her taunts, he opened the door and went out into

the corridor. He didn't look back over his shoulder but began retracing the route he'd taken with Chief Petty Officer Drummel.

He *was* scared, his heart thumping in his chest. Everything he was doing was wrong and forbidden. He prayed for it to be over as soon as possible.

All the lights were dimmed for the night, and the corridors and stairs were generally deserted. Whenever he heard footsteps in the distance, he stopped and waited for them to pass. He couldn't see Riff even when he did look round, but from time to time he heard the sound of a low, two-tone whistle. He took it as a signal she was still following.

He wondered what excuse he could give if an officer questioned him. Perhaps he could say he'd dropped something valuable on the way down yesterday, and now he was looking for it. Yes, that would do. Interesting. He'd never realized how easy it was to invent a lie.

There was a little more activity on the lower levels, where groups of Menials were engaged in nighttime tasks under the command of supervisors. Fortunately, the supervisors were too busy to spare him a second glance.

Down and down he went, through the kitchens and laundries. On Sixth Deck he arrived at the Graveyard Rooms. Still keeping to Drummel's route, he walked along the corridor past the unglassed, windowlike openings.

Riff materialized suddenly at his elbow. "I don't like this place. What is it?"

He was about to order her away when he saw she was trembling. She was scared herself now.

"The Graveyard Rooms. People are buried under the tombstones."

She refused to look where he pointed. "There's ghosts in there."

"Ghosts!" Col laughed. He had almost forgotten she was only an ignorant Filthy. "Nobody believes in ghosts."

"I do. Let me walk beside you just this bit, hey?"

She asked so humbly he couldn't refuse. "Okay."

He peered in through the openings as they went by. Pale stone slabs glimmered in the darkness, catching faint light from the corridor. Riff shivered and kept close.

They were approaching the staircase down to the next floor when Col froze. Someone was coming up from below, someone wearing a white officer's cap and jacket with epaulettes.

They turned and ran back along the corridor. But there were no corners or intersections. In another moment the officer would reach the top of the steps and see Riff—and Col with her!

Col made the decision for both of them. He turned to the first opening and dived over the sill. Riff had no choice but to dive after him. They landed side by side on soft, bare earth.

The officer might still see them, though. Col crawled further into the room, away from the light. Riff stifled a moan and followed.

The officer's footsteps came striding along the corridor, louder and louder. Col took cover behind one of the stone slabs, Riff behind another.

"Ugh-ugh!" At the worst possible moment she let out a shuddering gasp.

The officer grunted and his footsteps came to a halt.

Riff wasn't even thinking about him. "A ghost-thing! It touched me!"

She jumped to her feet and ran.

"Who's there?" the officer called out.

His silhouette appeared in the opening. Col couldn't see any ghost-things, but he saw the silhouette raise a leg and begin climbing in over the sill. He jumped up and ran after Riff, lurching and stumbling over thick, lumpy earth. At the back of this room was another opening into a farther room.

"Who's there?" bellowed the officer again.

He was still coming after them.

The next room was almost lightless, with an overpowering smell of mold and decay. Riff was running and flapping her hands as though she were being chased by some unimaginable horror. She disappeared though an opening into yet another room.

Col banged his shin on a stone slab but kept going.

The third room was pitch-black, and at first he couldn't see a thing. The stale air stuck in his throat like dry felt.

"Where are you?" he whispered.

"Here," came a tiny, terrified voice.

She had come to a halt in the middle of the room. He approached carefully, feeling for tombstones in his way.

"Ah!" she cried when he bumped into her.

She reached out and clutched his hand. They stood motionless for a moment.

The officer had stopped bellowing and seemed to have given up. Perhaps he didn't like the dark either.

"I have to get out of here," Riff muttered. "Can't you feel them?"

"No."

"Touching and groping. They're all around."

"We can't go back." Col surveyed the blackness.

"Wait." Riff let go of his hand. "Is that an opening?"

They made their way toward it and discovered another room, a fraction less dark than the one they were in.

Col guessed they must be approaching a different corridor on the other side. They passed through two more rooms, and each time, the light grew a little stronger, the air a little less stale.

When they came to a room with a whole row of window-like openings, Riff couldn't hold back any longer. She took off running and jumped straight over the nearest sill, not caring if there was anyone outside.

By good luck there wasn't. When Col climbed out into the corridor, she was all alone and slumped against a wall. She kept brushing herself with both hands, as though removing invisible cobwebs.

Col chewed his lip. "I have to get back to the route I know. I can't find the food chute otherwise."

Riff shook her head violently. "I'm not going through *there* again."

He had it on the tip of his tongue to use her own phrase against her: *Scare easy, don't you?* But he didn't.

"Okay. We'll find some other stairs down, then work back across on a lower deck."

She flashed him a grateful look. "Now?"

"Yes."

She jumped to her feet, and they headed along the corridor, side by side.

12

They found a flight of stairs and descended to Fifth Deck. There were no walls between rooms here, only ceiling-high racks of metal shelves. It made Col think of a hugely expanded version of the Norfolk Library. He threaded between the racks, cutting back in the direction of his previous route.

The shelves were filled with painted plaster statuettes of the imperial family. There were representations of Queen Victoria seated, Queen Victoria standing, Queen Victoria and Prince Albert seated, and Queen Victoria seated and Prince Albert standing.

Riff took one down to examine. "What are these for?"

"No idea."

"Must be millions of 'em."

After a while they emerged from the racks into a corridor Col recognized.

"Yes!" he exulted. "Back on track!"

They met no one else as they descended to First Deck. Col found the place with the steam elevator, then the place where the steps went down to Door Seventeen.

"I never explored round here," Riff muttered.

"You couldn't have got through, anyway," Col told her. "It's a special lock. Authorized personnel only. Look away."

He waited for her to turn her head before he began spinning

the wheels. Top wheel to 4, middle wheel to 9, bottom wheel to 2. The steel door unlocked with a sudden clack. *Done it!*

Now came another nerve-racking moment. He pushed the door open, just a crack, and peered through. Nobody close by . . . Their luck still held.

He swung the door wider and entered, with Riff at his heels. She hurried on to hide behind the nearest iron pier while he closed and locked the door on the inside.

He rejoined her a moment later. "That way." He pointed. "Keep to the shadows."

Creeping and darting, they moved forward from pier to pier and coal mound to coal mound. They could see officers in pools of light, but all at a distance and occupied with their tasks.

Col halted behind a final mound of coal. "There it is," he whispered.

Surrounded by a semicircle of sacks and bags, the manhole cover was in relative darkness.

"That's where the food comes from?" Riff eyed it thoughtfully.

"Yes. We open it up, then you jump in and slide down. Easy." Col hoped she wasn't having second thoughts, yet he couldn't help asking, "You really *want* to go back Below?"

"Yeah. Why?"

"All the smoke and heat and noise."

"You've seen it, huh?"

"From one of our viewing bays. But it can't be as bad as it looks."

"It's worse. Smoke and heat and noise is nothin'. It's dangerous like you wouldn't believe. If you ain't quick down there, you're dead. But I'd sooner die Below than live half a life like yer Menials up here." There was a perverse kind of pride in her voice. "Anyway, down there I'm a leader."

"Leader? Filthies don't need leaders."

"They do, and I'm one of 'em. I'm on our Revolutionary Council."

The word "revolution" gave Col a jolt. "No!"

"Yeah. We're makin' plans. Didn't I tell ya? We don't aim to stay down there forever."

"You're just boasting."

"If you like." She broke into a grin. "Ready, then?"

She didn't wait for his answer but skipped out to the manhole. Col shook his head and focused on the immediate goal. She was already unfastening one of the bolts.

He hurried to join her, crouching down opposite. He slid back another bolt; she slid back the third. No time to check what the officers were doing.

He slid back the final bolt. Then, together, they took hold of the cover and lifted it up on its hinges. It was heavy, but manageable.

Under the cover was the chute itself: a wide circular pipe that dropped down at a steep angle. Its inner surfaces were shiny and silvery, faintly reflecting a red glow from Below.

Riff released her side of the cover, but not to jump into the chute. Instead, she moved round to Col.

"So it's good-bye," she said. "I owe you for this."

Col was left supporting the full weight of the cover. "I'll never see you again."

"Who knows? You may need my help sometime."

Col held his tongue. *Just go,* he thought.

"You're okay, Col-bert Porping-tine," she said, and reached up suddenly with her thin, muscular arms. She drew down his head and kissed him on the mouth.

It was so unthinkable that he stopped thinking. He couldn't free his hands to push her away. Helplessly, he felt her lips on his. It was as though the whole world narrowed to that one shocking contact: warm, moist, soft . . .

Then it was over. She grinned at him.

"Doesn't mean we're partnered or anythin'," she said.

She stepped forward into the chute, tucked her arms in at the sides, and went down with a *whoosh!*

Everything happened so fast it ran together in his head. His mouth still felt the touch of her mouth even as his eyes saw her hair fly up and vanish down the chute. Gone!

He stood staring stupidly.

But not for long. An officer might come by at any moment. He lowered the cover and slid the bolts back into place. His actions seemed remote, as though someone else were performing them.

Then he hurried away into the shadows and stopped to think about it all. A Filthy kiss! He ran his tongue over his lips. Did it taste of anything? Dirt? Sweat? Grease? He knew it had to taste disgusting.

It was completely different from kisses that mothers gave their babies on the Upper Decks, or from the pecks on the cheek that women exchanged with other family members. That was only the same as men shaking hands. No one on the Upper Decks ever kissed like Riff. What did it mean? Why would she do a thing like that?

He rubbed the back of his hand over his mouth. No, he

needed water to wash it off. But where? It would take ages to get back to his room on Forty-second Deck. Perhaps there was a tap on one of the lower decks?

He set off at once toward the steel door. He had to remove the taste before it left a lasting imprint.

13

Returning to his own proper life was like coming out of a strange, dark tunnel. Col vowed he would never do anything wrong or forbidden again. Now he could look forward to starting school on Monday.

In the meanwhile his weekend was filled with a new round of social activities. On Saturday morning he went along to be introduced to the ladies of his mother's embroidery club, who met in a room belonging to the Postlefrith family on Fortieth Deck. There were twelve ladies, each accompanied by one or more Menial servants. It was the Menials who did the actual embroidering, while their mistresses compared patterns, exchanged tips, and gave instructions.

Col was introduced to Mrs. Postlefrith, Mrs. Bassimor, and a great many other women whose names he couldn't remember. Quinnea smiled, sighed, fanned herself, and bathed in a general glow of successful motherhood.

Col was embarrassed to be the object of so much admiration. But embarrassment gave way to boredom as the morning wore on. The conversation of the embroidery club soon turned into reports and rumors of who said what to whom. Col would have preferred to discuss Plato and Aristotle and ethics with Professor Twillip. He had to make a deliberate effort to stop from drifting off into thoughts of Riff.

The afternoon was more interesting, because his school

equipment started to arrive. Middle-class tradespeople from the manufacturing decks brought each ordered item to Lady Ebnolia Porpentine. Col stowed everything in his new satchel, and inked his initials under the leather flap. Later his two school uniforms were also delivered: green jackets with red piping and badges labeled DR. BLESSAMY'S ACADEMY.

The social event after dinner was a whist evening in the Wiltshire Room. It was a tournament among families: Porpentines versus Turbots versus Frakes. Col accompanied Grandmother Ebnolia, along with Orris, Gillabeth, and the adults of the Leath Porpentine branch.

A Menial called Wicky Popo came with them too. With his large, sad eyes and drooping expression he was Ebnolia's new favorite, and she wanted to show him off to her acquaintances.

Col was still the main attraction, though. Everyone wanted to meet Sir Mormus's nominated successor. When the adults sat down and the games began, various ladies kept asking him for advice on how to play their cards. Since Col was a complete beginner at whist, he had the impression no one took the tournament very seriously.

While Col was summoned this way and that, his father as usual faded into the background. Gillabeth wasn't a player but stood at Ebnolia's elbow, ready for any errand that might be needed. Mostly she was sent to check on Wicky Popo, who stood propped against the wall by the door. It seemed that the hot air of the room made him unwell.

After an hour or so the requests for Col's advice fell away. Instead one lady took it upon herself to teach him the rules and strategies of the game. The Honorable Hommelia Turbot was a large, florid woman in a billowing, flowery dress. In a whisper she explained about following suit, calling trumps, taking or yielding the lead. Col listened and learned, but he wasn't much interested.

When Hommelia caught him covering up a yawn, she seemed more delighted than offended.

"Ah, this is all too trivial for you." She patted his arm with her cards. "You want to be thinking about serious male things."

"It's not that."

"Oh, you men! I know, I know. You want to be thinking about trade and routes and navigation. Big decisions about *Worldshaker*. My husband is just the same." She turned and raised her voice to Ebnolia at the next table. "I'm sure we've made him do his penance, Lady Porpentine. Can we let him go now, do you think?"

Ebnolia pursed her lips. "*Dear* Hommelia." She switched her attention to Col. "Yes, go if you want, Colbert. Your sister will escort you back."

Col didn't like the frown that swept across his sister's face. "It's all right," he said. "I can find my own way."

"No, no. Gillabeth has been a spectator long enough, haven't you?" Ebnolia clearly didn't expect an answer, and Gillabeth didn't give one. "Off you go, both of you."

So Col made his farewells. Hommelia asked if he was going to attend the Imperial Gala Reception tomorrow night, but Col didn't know.

"Oh, I hope so," she gushed. "You must! You must!"

Col walked with Gillabeth back to Forty-second Deck.

"Sorry," he said. "Did you want to stay?"

"I'm doing what Grandmother asked me to do," she replied tartly.

She was simmering inside, Col suspected, but he didn't know how to make peace with her. He had never been able to talk to Gillabeth as brother to sister. She preferred to take on the manner of an adult with him.

"You realize why they're all fawning over you?" she said suddenly.

"Who?"

"The women. The mothers."

"Why?"

"They're angling to land you for their daughters."

Col didn't understand. Gillabeth gave him one of her *what-I-have-to-put-up-with* looks.

"You're a future supreme commander. They hope to get you married into their families."

"But . . . I'm not old enough to marry anyone."

"When you turn twenty-one. They're planning long-term."

Col considered. He didn't like the idea of being angled for—and indirectly, by the mothers not the daughters.

"What's this Imperial Gala Reception?" he asked after a while.

Another one of Gillabeth's looks. "Tomorrow night in the Grand Assembly Hall."

"Will I be going?"

"Yes, by special invitation. Grandfather will present you formally to Queen Victoria."

"Are you going?"

"I'm not invited."

"Oh. So it's only if you're being formally presented?"

"Not me. I've *never* been formally presented." Suddenly Gillabeth boiled over. "Listen. You may have become a future supreme commander, but you're the same for me as you always were. Don't expect *me* to start fawning over you!"

"I never expected—"

"Here's your corridor. There's your cabin." She pointed to his door ahead. "Don't get lost now," she added savagely.

Then she swung on her heel and marched off to her own cabin in the next corridor.

He stood staring after her. Whatever he did, he always ended up on the wrong side of Gillabeth. She was an absolute mystery to him.

14

Over Sunday breakfast Sir Mormus made the official announcement that he would present his grandson to Queen Victoria and her consort tonight at the Imperial Gala Reception. The heads of the other four family branches and their wives were also invited.

"Best clothes and best behavior, my boy," he told Col.

Col had often seen Queen Victoria at a distance, but never close up. Her full title was Her Imperial Majesty Victoria II, and she had reigned for ten years. As official head of the Imperial Church, she was the embodiment of all things good and great and glorious. She had taken as consort a nobleman from the juggernaut *Denmark*, who after marriage had become His Imperial Highness Prince Albert.

Col's clothes for the occasion were very solemn and dignified: a long jacket, waistcoat, and dress shirt. His mother and grandmother fussed over him for hours, while Gillabeth looked on with folded arms. Finally, the moment arrived.

For the entry into the Grand Assembly Hall, Col walked alongside his grandparents and in front of the other invited Porpentines. Then Ebnolia, too, dropped back, and Col found himself advancing over the carpet in step with Sir Mormus.

The hall was a large oval space rising to a height of forty feet under the domed ceiling. He gazed in awe at white columns, velvet drapes, and a chandelier that glittered with a thousand candles. There were marble statues on fluted plinths and dark-leaved aspidistras in terra-cotta urns. Col had never seen the hall fully lit up and decorated before.

There were at least a hundred people present. Menials displaying the Imperial V & A insignia moved among the throng with bowed heads, holding out teacups and tidbits on silver trays. The crowd parted like a bow wave before Sir Mormus's jutting brow and chest.

Smiles and greetings were directed toward the Porpentines from every side. Sir Mormus inclined his head in silent acknowledgment, and Col did the same. The guests were all members of the juggernaut's thirty elite families.

Sir Mormus commented on the most important representatives in a low, rumbling voice intended for Col alone to hear.

"Lord Fefferley to your left. Prestige and title, a stickler for his rights . . .

"Rear Admiral Haugh on your right. Haughs were important in the nineteenth century, but they've come down a few notches since . . .

"Chief Helmsman Turbot over there. Influential on the Executive. Family of navigation specialists . . ."

Col recognized the Honorable Hommelia Turbot, nodding to him alongside her husband. But Sir Mormus's commentary on important people paid no account to any of the females.

There was one family head to whom Sir Mormus drew special attention. "Squellingham ahead. Sir Wisley Squellingham."

Sir Wisley had deep-set eyes and a sharply ridged nose. Sir

Mormus replied to his greeting with a "How d'ye do" and a deeper inclination of the head.

They moved on past, and Sir Mormus tapped the keys that dangled on his chest. "Ha! These are what he wants," he rumbled. "My greatest rival. Hungry for power and cunning as a rat. The Squellinghams have always hoped to displace the Porpentines. Watch out for them, my boy."

A path had now opened up all the way to Queen Victoria and her consort in the center of the hall. They sat on a raised dais, gripping the armrests of their thrones. Queen Victoria's throne was larger and higher than Prince Albert's, and so was her crown: a massive construction of steel and gold.

"Chest out," Sir Mormus told Col. "The Porpentines are known for their chests. Always maintain a firm and forceful chest."

Col took a deep breath and thrust out his chest.

Queen Victoria's features were exactly like her portraits: noble and majestic as a thoroughbred racehorse. The only difference was the furrow in her brow, which looked less like sternness and more like a headache coming on.

Sir Mormus bowed first to the queen and then to her consort. Col followed suit.

"Well, well, well," said Queen Victoria.

Sir Mormus cleared his throat. "May I present my grandson Colbert Porpentine."

"Your grandson." She studied them both. "So you must be his grandfather."

"He has the qualities of a true Porpentine, Your Majesty. When I pass on, Colbert will make a worthy supreme commander."

"Oh, dear. You're passing on?"

"In the future, Your Majesty. Not for many years yet."

Prince Albert nodded approval. "Glad to hear it, Porpentine. Glad to hear it." His voice was a rusty bass, with just a hint of his original Danish accent.

"He starts school tomorrow," Sir Mormus continued.

"Ah, school. Education. Learning." Queen Victoria seemed to have difficulty focusing under the weight of her crown. "Ask the boy a question, Albert."

"What sort of question, my dear?"

"Ah . . . something times something."

"Seven," said Prince Albert. "Seven times . . . er . . . seven."

"Forty-nine," said Col immediately.

"Excellent effort," said Queen Victoria.

"Commendable, commendable," Prince Albert agreed.

"Also correct, Your Majesties," said Sir Mormus.

"Even better." Queen Victoria turned to her consort. "Ask another question, my dear."

"Umm . . ." Prince Albert chewed on his mustache for half a minute. "I don't seem to have any more."

"Sir Mormus, then." Queen Victoria turned to her supreme commander.

"Very well." Sir Mormus had been ready for the request. "A question for my nominated successor. At this moment we're halfway across the island of Ceylon. Should we travel up the east coast of India and risk meeting the French juggernaut? Or should we go straight across the sea to Burma?"

Col caught the hint of a wink as his grandfather named the second option. He faced the imperial couple and said, "We should go by sea to Burma, Your Majesties."

"A decisive answer." Queen Victoria bestowed a smile.

"I like a decisive answer," said Prince Albert.

"Is it correct, Sir Mormus?"

"I believe so, Your Majesty. It is the view I shall be putting to the Executive tomorrow morning."

"Then I'm sure it will be carried unanimously."

The presentation was over. Prince Albert gave Col a final nod. "We shall expect great things from you, young man."

Queen Victoria whispered loudly behind her hand. "And look at his chest, my dear."

Col followed Sir Mormus's lead as he bowed and turned away. He could hear Prince Albert muttering his agreement. "Very fine chest. Very fine."

Sir Mormus marched up to the nearest Menial with a tray, helped himself to two meat-paste triangles, and put them both in his mouth at once. He took another two and handed them to Col.

"Sir?"

"Yes, my boy?" Sir Mormus sprayed crumbs as he spoke.

"The queen doesn't decide anything, does she?"

Sir Mormus looked around. "She's a figurehead," he said in a lowered voice. "While I'm her supreme commander, she decides what *I* decide."

"So when we say we serve Queen Victoria the Second . . ."

"Say it as much as you like. Just remember who's really in control." Sir Mormus gestured to the keys of office on his chest. "And now I have matters to arrange with my supporters on the Executive. You're in demand over there, my boy."

Col followed his gaze and saw Grandmother Ebnolia signaling from the middle of a group of ladies.

"Go and meet your admirers," said Sir Mormus. "You'll get used to it, my boy."

He strode off, with a curt command of "Come" to the Menial with the tray. His personal supply of tidbits accompanied him across the hall.

Col chewed on a meat-paste triangle. Another revelation! When he became supreme commander, he would be telling even the queen what to do. He felt as though he'd been let into the secrets of a male world of power. Everything was different from the way he'd thought—but he liked it!

Still, Grandmother Ebnolia was signaling to him. He went across to meet his admirers. Yes, he was starting to get used to his new role.

15

Col's mother escorted him to within thirty paces of Dr. Blessamy's Academy. But she couldn't face the square of open space in front of the entrance arch. The noise of students in the schoolyard was clearly audible.

"Oh dear . . . oh dear . . ."

She took the handkerchief that Missy Jip produced, and dabbed at her forehead.

"It's all right," said Col. "I'll go by myself now."

"You must speak to the headmaster, Colbert. Tell him to make the noisy children be quiet."

Other students were marching in under the arch. Col took his satchel from Missy Jip and fell into step with one boy who had just emerged from the same corridor.

"Hello, there."

"Hello." The boy kept walking. He had straw-colored hair and long, gangling limbs.

"I'm Colbert. Col for short. Who are you?"

"You looked into our classroom on Friday. You're a Porpentine."

"Yes. Who are you?"

"Trant."

"Trant what?"

"Septimus Trant. We use surnames in the boys' classes."

They passed in under the arch. The yard was already full of

students, some running, some standing in groups. The boys' groups were all on the left-hand side, the girls' on the right. A single master on playground duty sat and rocked on a swing suspended from the footbridge.

"So where do we go?" Col asked Septimus.

Septimus appeared uncomfortable. "Er . . . it's hard to explain."

"Where are your friends?"

Septimus pointed to a far corner of the yard.

"Let's go, then."

With a silent shrug Septimus led the way to his group of friends. Their jackets were old and worn compared to Col's and their satchels positively shabby. They seemed awkward and tongue-tied in the presence of a Porpentine and reluctant to give their names.

They opened up a little more when Col asked about Mr. Gibber.

"Watch out for his tweaker," said one.

"And his Number Two," said another.

A third shook his head. "He'd never use his Number Two on a Porpentine. He wouldn't dare."

"Don't go near his pet, though," warned Septimus. "Murgatrude's the apple of his—"

"Out of the way, grindboys!" A big, burly student shouldered forward into the circle. He spoke to Col as though the others weren't there. "You don't want to talk to *these*."

He made as if to take Col by the elbow, then thought better of it.

Col stayed where he was. "Who are you?"

"Lumbridge. And you're Porpentine." Lumbridge lowered

his voice. "You belong with us. This is the toilets' end of the yard."

Col might have resisted. But when he looked round, Septimus and his friends were already turning away, abandoning all claim to him. He accompanied Lumbridge to the opposite end near the entrance arch.

"Who's this 'us' I belong with?"

"The best families. I'll introduce you."

A group of three students awaited their approach. A chalk circle drawn on the asphalt separated their space from the rest of the yard. Other students veered away, even in the wildest running games.

"Here he is," said Lumbridge. "Porpentine, meet—"

"Fefferley." The first member of the group introduced himself. He was round as a butterball, almost bursting out of his school uniform.

"I'm Flarrow." The second member twisted his pimply features into an ingratiating smile.

The third student had his hair in a pompadour and wore a silk waistcoat under his jacket. "I'm Haugh," he drawled.

Col recognized two of the names as belonging to families Sir Mormus had pointed out at the reception.

"The Squellinghams will be along in a minute," said Lumbridge.

"Are you all in Mr. Gibber's class?" asked Col.

"Yes," answered Flarrow. "You should stay away from the grindboys, Porpentine. They're the lowest of the low."

"Why 'grindboys'?"

"Their fathers are supervisor class and tradespeople. They're only allowed in the academy because they're supposed to be brainy. So they grind it out. Work, work, work."

"I was planning to work too," said Col.

"Not like them!" Fefferley's smooth, smarmy face creased with laughter. "We put their heads down the toilets."

"We'll look after you," said Lumbridge. "You're all right with us."

It was obvious no one would ever try to put Lumbridge's head down a toilet. His shoulders were massive, and he had a neck like a bull's.

Flarrow indicated a group of boys who were tossing a ball back and forth. "There's another lot. We call them the blockies. When they leave school, they'll go to work as officers on the bridge or Bottom Deck. Very upright, very moral, very dumb."

"And very boring." Haugh affected a yawn.

"Like blocks of wood. They take their orders from us." Flarrow swung to point to another part of the yard. "See those two groups? The climbers and the crawlers. Their fathers are mostly professional class, doctors or engineers or second-rank administrators. The climbers want to count with the best families. They'd do anything to have us accept them."

Even as he spoke, some of the climbers noticed the attention and waved back optimistically.

"Go take a running jump, Bodworthy," muttered Flarrow.

"You were friendly with him once," said Lumbridge. "The Squellinghams only let you up last year."

Flarrow flushed and suddenly ran out of words. There was a moment's silence until Fefferley took over.

"The crawlers are climbers without the expectations," he told Col. "They admire us, but they never hope to rise to our level. In their own pathetic way they copy us."

"Here come the twins," said Haugh.

"The Squellinghams," Fefferley explained for Col's benefit.

Though similar in appearance the Squellinghams weren't identical twins. Like Sir Wisley they had a sharpness around the nose and deep-set eyes, but Hythe had the sharper nose and Pugh the more deeply set eyes. Otherwise they looked like ordinary students, with ordinary clothes and ordinary haircuts.

Remembering his grandfather's warning, Col wondered about their attitude toward him. If Sir Wisley was Sir Mormus's greatest rival, then the twins would have to be *his* greatest rivals.

"Porpentine, meet Hythe Squellingham." Fefferley gestured. "Meet Pugh Squellingham."

Lumbridge moved to stand behind the twins, as if on guard for them.

"Pleased to meet you," Hythe said, and extended a hand. Col shook hands with each in turn.

Then Pugh turned to Hythe. "I think we should do a round with our new member."

"Yes." Hythe looked even sharper around the nose. "Let everyone see that Porpentine's with us."

So Lumbridge and Flarrow went ahead to clear a circuit around the yard. Lumbridge pushed aside anyone who was slow to move, while Flarrow called out in a loud voice: "Grandson of Sir Mormus Porpentine! Coming through, coming through!"

It was a kind of procession, with Col at the head. The Squellinghams followed half a pace behind, while Fefferley and Haugh brought up the rear. The games and running stopped as everyone turned to stare. Passing the boys' groups, Col caught mixed looks of envy and deference. Passing the girls' groups, he was the object of outright adoration. Some ventured a smile, then bashfully dropped their eyes. He could hear the whispers.

"Isn't he tall?"

"Did he look at you?"

"I think he smiled at me."

"No, that was me."

By the time they returned to the chalk circle, Col was in a daze of embarrassment and exhilaration.

"I didn't know being a Porpentine was so important," he confessed.

"And being nominated as Sir Mormus's successor," said Pugh.

Col looked into Pugh's eyes and saw no hint of resentment. In fact the faces of both Squellinghams were completely expressionless.

16

The *clang-clang-clang* of the school bell summoned the students to class. Mr. Gibber stood by the door as 4A filed in. He flexed his fingers and cracked his knuckles. A mad grin broke out on his face when Col passed in front of him.

The Squellinghams led Col to a desk at the far right of the room. The desks were made of wood with iron frames and bench seats. Previous generations of students had scored initials and doodles into every desk lid.

"You have to sit in front of us," said Hythe.

"Hang on!" For once, Haugh's languid manner deserted him. "That's my desk!"

"You can move," said Pugh.

"Next row across," said Hythe.

"But . . . but . . . the Gibber won't like it."

"Yes, he will."

"If we want him to."

Lumbridge emptied out the desk and dumped everything into Haugh's arms. Haugh gazed off into the distance in silent protest. A student in the next row was pushed out to make room for him.

The student was no happier about it than Haugh, and no more successful in his protests. The Squellinghams directed him to a spare desk on the other side of the room, while Lumbridge flung his books and equipment after him.

Col unloaded the contents of his satchel into his desk. He sat behind Fefferley and in front of Hythe and Pugh, while Lumbridge, Flarrow, and now Haugh sat in the row on the left. Slinging his satchel over the back of his seat, he studied his new surroundings.

The room had a dingy look under the yellow lightbulbs overhead. Three walls supported tottering piles of books and papers as high as the ceiling. The teacher's desk was on the fourth side, along with a blackboard, a cupboard, and a rack of canes.

Mr. Gibber strode across to the blackboard, collected two sticks of chalk, and tucked them behind his ears.

"Silence! *Silence!*" He faced the class and flapped his gown like a demented bat. "I can hardly hear myself shout. That's better."

Grinning and grimacing, he stepped forward and performed a small bow in Col's direction. "Now, 4A, we are most humbly delighted to have a new student added to our class. Welcome to Master Porpentine."

He didn't look at all humble, though he was certainly delighted. He swung round and singled out a student in the front row on the opposite side of the class.

"Master Porpentine will learn to address me as Mr. Gibber, won't he, Snellshott? Not Gibber. Not the Gibber. Because gibbering suggests a kind of animal, doesn't it, Snellshott?"

"Don't know, sir."

"A kind of animal that gibbers. What could it be?" He uttered a monkeylike *hoot-hoot* and let his arms dangle. "Tell him, class. Anyone?"

There was no reply. Mr. Gibber swept his eyes from side

to side as though he'd caught a hint of a whisper.

"Did I hear the word 'monkey'? Did any boy think the word 'monkey'? Because any boy who tries to make a monkey out of me will soon feel the weight of my Number Eight."

He bounded across to his rack of canes and stroked one particular cane lovingly, meaningfully. Then back to the front of the class.

"Now, 4A, what subject shall we start with today?" He rolled his eyes toward Col, then away again. Col had the sense that he was a special audience.

"Chemistry, sir," one student volunteered.

"Chem-is-ter-ee!" mocked Mr. Gibber. "And why chem-is-ter-ee, Clatterick?"

"It's on the timetable, sir."

"On the timetable! Ha! Ha! Ha! Who teaches you, Clatterick? The timetable or Mr. Gibber? *I* decide what to teach. Your humble Mr. Gibber. And I decide—geometry!" He beat on his chest with one fist. "Take out your rulers, pencils, protractors, and geometry books."

Another student spoke up. "But, sir, we don't have geometry books!"

"Swiddlington, Swiddlington." Mr. Gibber sighed deeply. "Why are you such an irredeemable imbecile? Take out an exercise book and write 'geometry' on the cover."

"How do you spell it, sir?" asked another student.

Mr. Gibber strutted across to the blackboard, took a stick of chalk from behind his ear, and wrote G-E-O-M-E-T-R-Y. He made the chalk squeak as loudly as possible. There was a mirror clipped to the blackboard so that he could keep watch on the class while his back was turned.

Col wrote *GEOMETRY* on the front of an exercise book. Looking across, he noticed that Flarrow's book was already covered with previous subject headings: *MULTIPLICATION, RELIGION, GEOGRAPHY, LANGUAGE, HISTORY.*

"Now." Mr. Gibber drew a line on the board. "What's this?"

The class remained silent. Mr. Gibber pulled an extraordinary series of facetious faces. "Is it a star? Is it an Eskimo? Is it a bunch of roses?"

"It's a line, sir."

"No!" Mr. Gibber stamped his foot. "Do you want our new student to think you're a brainless dunce, Wunstable? Do you want him to think he's come to a class of driveling idiots? This, Wunstable, is no ordinary line. It's a *straight* line."

"It's not completely straight, sir. It's got a bit of a wobble—"

"*Silence!*" Mr. Gibber sprang across the room and stood quivering over the student who'd spoken. "It's what *I* call a straight line. It's what your teacher, Mr. Gibber, calls a straight line. Do you think you know more than your teacher? No? Anyone else? Not an Eskimo or a star or a bunch of roses! A straight line! And"—he sprang back to the board —"here comes another!"

He drew a second line to join up with the first. "Now what have we got, 4A? If anyone says two straight lines, they'll feel the sting of my Number Thirteen."

The class held its breath. Mr. Gibber sniggered. "Well, you ignoramuses? Well, you dolts? You numskulls? You pinheads? Well, you blithering nincompoops?" He was obviously enjoying himself.

Col put up a hand. Geometry had been one of his favorite subjects with Professor Twillip. "An angle, sir."

"Ah, yes, an angle." Mr. Gibber seemed disappointed. "But can anybody tell me what sort of angle?"

"An acute angle, sir," said Col.

"Very good, very good." Mr. Gibber turned to shout at the rest of the class. "Ignoramuses! Morons! Retards! An acute angle!"

He jabbed at it with his stick of chalk, which broke in pieces and scattered across the floor. Mr. Gibber ground it to dust with his heel.

"Consider the acute angle," he resumed. "Clean, keen, sharp, and wholesome. An acute angle is a *good* angle. Now, who can tell me what's a *bad* angle?"

He rolled his eyes toward Col. But Professor Twillip's geometry lessons had never included good versus bad angles.

Mr. Gibber took the other stick of chalk from behind his other ear and drew two more lines, meeting at about 130 degrees.

"This," he said, "is a *bad* angle. Observe how wide open, how lax and undisciplined. Sloppy, slack, degenerate. We call this an obtuse angle. Shameful and disgraceful. Don't let me ever catch any of you drawing obtuse angles, 4A."

He picked up the eraser and rubbed his obtuse angle from the board.

"Now. Who can tell me the best angle of all? Nobody? The best and finest angle is the right angle."

He drew an angle of ninety degrees on the board and stepped back to admire it. "There! Observe the right angle, boys. Straightforward and upright. Observe and benefit from its example." He swung around to the class. "Hold up your protractors."

With much scuffling, the boys held up their protractors. Mr. Gibber seized the nearest and flourished it in the air.

"This is your aid to right angles, 4A. At your age you haven't had time to develop firmness and strength of character. Still full of nasty little tricks. Eh, Prewitt? That's why we have protractors for you. Draw one line at zero degrees and one line at ninety degrees. Then you can produce a perfect right angle every time. Even you, Trant."

He handed back the protractor he had taken. "I want fifty perfect right angles from every boy. All clearly labeled with the words 'right angle.' Start work."

Silence fell as the class opened their exercise books and applied their protractors.

"I shall be coming round to inspect," warned Mr. Gibber. "If any boy is producing immoral angles, he'll feel the full force of my Number Four."

Mr. Gibber limited his inspection to grindboys, climbers, and crawlers. Sometimes he launched into torrents of abuse, while students protested, "But, sir, you jogged my elbow!"

They spent a whole period drawing and labeling right angles.

17

The rest of the day continued in the same way. In chemistry they learned the difference between the purity of elements and the dirtiness of compounds; in music they recited the words of imperial hymns; in algebra they learned to prefer honest numbers over sly, secretive x's and y's. All of Mr. Gibber's lessons were very moral, and very different from anything Professor Twillip had taught.

It was in a religion test that Mr. Gibber first used his tweaker: a long rod with a clothespin on the end and a string to work the pin. While students wrote answers to the test, Mr. Gibber prowled up and down between the desks. When he grew tired of prowling, he snapped the clothespin onto the pen of a student three desks away.

"Writing too fast, Nebblethwaite!" he barked. "How much do you think I want to mark?"

He lifted the pen high in the air, pulled the string, and deposited the offending object on top of Nebblethwaite's head.

"Keep concentrating!" he cried. "No cheating!"

There was a short recess in the middle of the morning and a longer break for lunch. Two Menials served school food from a trestle table in the yard: pies, sausage rolls, and sandwiches. The sausage rolls looked good to Col, but Flarrow soon put him right.

"We don't eat that muck. We eat from the Squellinghams' special hamper."

The hamper had been delivered just inside the entrance arch. The twins handed out plates, and the members of the group tucked into pâté, pastries, fruitcake, and other delicacies. Lumbridge carried a slice of cake across to the master on playground duty.

After lunch Mr. Gibber decided to teach history. His history was as strange as all his other lessons. When one of the students asked, "What's history, sir?" Mr. Gibber answered, "It's whatever I say it is, Weffington. Take out your history exercise books."

Col was used to the procedure by now. He crossed out *ALGEBRA* and wrote *HISTORY* on the cover of the same exercise book.

"In history I teach you about the past. Who can tell me something that happened in the past? And I don't mean the day before yesterday, Hegglenock. Anyone? Anyone?"

Col put up a hand. "The ancient Greeks and Romans, sir. Athens and Sparta, Rome and Carthage."

"Yes, them, of course, of course. But they're not historical enough. Something *really* historical?" He cracked his knuckles one by one: *crack-crack-crack!* "I'll tell you something really, really historical. History begins with a very important man called Noah. Write it down in your books. N-O-A-H. Noah was the man who built the first juggernaut."

"Was he from the Old Country, sir?" asked the student called Prewitt.

"Why not? He was a very wise man and the ancestor of our present Queen Victoria the Second. He heard there was going to be a flood, so . . . do you know what a flood is?"

Several hands shot up, but Mr. Gibber snorted scornfully.

"No, you don't, because this was a bigger flood than *you* know about. A worldwide flood. When Noah heard it was coming, he built a juggernaut and called it the *Ark*."

He drew a shape on the blackboard that could have been anything.

"Noah's Ark. He built it in wood because he didn't have iron. Then he invited two of every class and species on board."

"Did it have steam engines, sir?"

"It had . . . its own kind of engines. Don't distract me, Wunstable; I'm telling you about who he invited on board to be saved. There were two officers and two supervisors and two engineers and so on for every type of human being. Then there were two chickens and two goats and two geese and two pigs and two Filthies and—stop *sniggering!*"

The word "Filthies" had produced a wave of muffled titters around the class.

"Why two of each, sir?"

"Were they a male and a female, sir?"

Mr. Gibber glared, permitted himself a brief snigger of his own, then glared again.

"Quiet, 4A. There were two of each because that's the way it was and you don't need to know any more. This isn't smut, this is history. When they were all on board and the flood came, then every class and species had to learn to *cooperate*. Yes, I know it's a long word for your brain, Melstruther. It means doing things together. So the supervisors supervised and the engineers engineered, the chickens laid their eggs and the pigs gave their bacon. They all played their parts and lived in harmony. Which is why we all play our parts and live in harmony today, don't we, Trant? I serve as your teacher and you serve as my pupils. Sit up and serve properly, Nebblethwaite!"

Pugh nudged Flarrow, who nudged a boy in the next row, who asked, "Sir, did the Filthies learn to play their parts and live in harmony, sir?"

"Ah, ah." Mr. Gibber licked his rubbery lips and shuddered. "No, the Filthies didn't want to cooperate. They went off to live in the dark at the bottom of the Ark. They *multiplied.*"

Col didn't know what to think. Professor Twillip's lessons had never covered history before the Greeks and Romans— nor after them, either.

He raised a hand to ask a question. "What about the other species, sir?"

"What about them?"

"Didn't they multiply too?"

"No, no, no! Not in a Filthy way!" Mr. Gibber could hardly control himself. "Not in the dark! Not in a dirty, lewd, indecent way! Ugh!"

"Ugh!" went the class. "Ugh! Ugh! Ugh!"

A memory rushed into Col's mind, so vivid he could taste and feel it. The Filthy girl's kiss! Soft, warm lips pressed against his own!

Disgusting!

A glowing sensation came to his cheeks. He lowered his head and prayed no one would notice. He twisted his mouth into a different shape, nothing like the shape of a kiss.

The lesson continued. For a long time Mr. Gibber's voice was just background noise to Col. The memory of the kiss was followed by a memory of her parting words: *You're okay, Colbert Porping-tine!* He could recall the exact look on her face as she said it.

He couldn't *stop* recalling it.

Why did this have to happen now? She was out of his life; he was sure he'd forgotten her. *Out, out, out!*

After a while Mr. Gibber lost interest in history. He set the class to drawing pictures of Noah's Ark, leaving off the bottom part where the Filthies were. The class tittered and started work.

Mr. Gibber yawned and sat behind his desk. From time to time he reached down to his wastepaper basket and appeared to be patting something inside.

"That's Murgatrude," Hythe leaned forward to whisper from behind. "The Gibber's pet."

Murgatrude made a deep *rumm-rumm* sound, somewhere between the purr of a cat and the growl of a dog.

The afternoon wore on. Fefferley and Haugh took pillows out of their desks, laid down their heads, and fell fast asleep. Some students amused themselves by flicking little inked balls of blotting paper at one another; some tried to repel the attacks by building defensive walls of books on their desks.

Still, Col couldn't get the memory of Riff completely out of his mind.

18

Col came home after school to afternoon tea in the Somerset Room—Grandmother Ebnolia's private parlor, with satin-upholstered chairs and little lace-covered tables. Ebnolia and Quinnea pounced on him immediately.

"How was your first day?" asked Ebnolia.

"Did it give you a headache?" added Quinnea.

Col didn't know what to say. The truth was that school hadn't lived up to his expectations at all, and Mr. Gibber's lessons had been a complete disappointment. But perhaps it wasn't a good idea to say so when Sir Mormus was also in the room, along with Orris, Gillabeth, and Baby Brother Antrobus.

"A hug for your favorite grandmother," said Ebnolia.

Hugs with Ebnolia involved more contact with her perfume than her person. The overpowering strawberry sweetness made Col's senses swim.

"Now, tell us what you learned," she said.

"Umm. Strange things about acute angles and obtuse angles. Compounds and elements. Noah's Ark. Is it true that Noah's Ark was the first juggernaut?"

"Oh, I wouldn't know, my dear." Ebnolia showed tiny white teeth in a smile. "The females in our family have never bothered with education."

"The females in other families do," said Gillabeth from across the room.

"Yes, dear, but they're not Porpentines."

Gillabeth dropped her head in submission. She turned her attention back to Antrobus and decided that his collar and cuffs needed straightening. Antrobus received her savage ministrations as he received everything else, in wide-eyed silence.

"If your teacher says it, it must be right," said Quinnea.

From his chair beside the cake stand Sir Mormus cleared his throat as if blasting out a blocked pipe. "Harrr-arrr-uuph!"

Ebnolia looked across and bobbed her head. "I think your grandfather wants to talk to you, dear," she told Col.

Sir Mormus had a lemon tart in one hand and a cup of tea in the other. Col went across and stood before his chair.

"Shall I tell you about my first day at school, sir?"

"I heard, my boy. Angles, compounds, Noah's Ark. Stuff and nonsense. You're not going to school to learn about things like that."

"I'm not?"

"Of course not. You're there to learn about power."

"I don't understand, sir."

Sir Mormus lowered his voice to a resonant whisper. "We don't say this in front of women and children. No need for them to know the world isn't all sugar and spice. It's about obeying or being obeyed. Power isn't a gift, my boy—it has to be earned. You earn it by subduing other people. Starting in school."

"Other students, you mean?" Col was so surprised he forgot to say "sir."

"Yes, other students. Don't expect to do it all at once. Practice on the lower boys first, then work up to the elite. The Squellingham twins are in your class, aren't they?"

"Yes, sir."

"Good. So you have the opportunity to dominate them from an early age. Break their spirit, make them recognize your power. If you build up their habit of subservience now, it'll last a lifetime. Grind them down and rub their noses in it."

"But they like me and I like—"

"Liking has nothing to do with it. They must be afraid of you. You want to be supreme commander, don't you?"

"Yes, sir."

"Then learn supremacy."

Sir Mormus swallowed his tart and drained his tea in one huge sip. His digestive processes made a deep-down gurgling sound.

"Now go back and talk to the others," he said.

Col returned to Ebnolia and Quinnea in a somber state of mind. He no longer felt so good about fitting into his new role.

19

Grinding people down didn't come naturally to Col. He tucked Sir Mormus's precepts away in a corner of his mind and gradually forgot about them.

In any case he was already in a position of supremacy. Crawlers and climbers in all classes at the academy admired him from a distance and tried to copy his behavior. Then, in the second half of the week, little presents started to turn up in his desk: packets of fudge, bars of nougat, boxes of chocolates. There was always a small card attached: *From ST*, or *Admiringly, MB*, or *Thinking of you, JW*.

"Girls," said Hythe. "Those are their initials."

Col shared the sweets around, while the group tried to work out who owned the initials. More than half the presents came from *ST*.

"I know," said Pugh. "That's Sephaltina Turbot in 4B."

"It could be Shevaleen Thorlish," Flarrow suggested.

"No, her father's only a doctor," said Hythe. "She wouldn't have the nerve."

"Sephaltina's father is chief helmsman," added Fefferley.

They pointed Sephaltina out in the recess. She had a heart-shaped face, rosebud lips, and yellow ribbons in her hair. Her cheeks were her most striking feature, blushing constantly on and off. They blushed a great deal more when she saw Col looking at her.

The twins weren't jealous of his popularity so far as Col could see. Nor did they resent it when he outscored them to come first in the religion test. Then in a chemistry test he came second to Pugh but ahead of Hythe, and in an algebra test he came second to Hythe but ahead of Pugh. He was amazed to be getting such high marks after only a few days at school.

Fefferley, Haugh, and Flarrow usually did well in tests too. Only Lumbridge scored poorly, often beaten by the blockies and some of the climbers. But Lumbridge had a special position in the group because of the way he stood guard over the twins. They looked after him as he looked after them. It was Flarrow who came lowest in the group's pecking order.

Col saw how it worked when the Squellinghams decided to show him Mr. Gibber's pet. The whole group sneaked back into the classroom during the Thursday lunch break, and Lumbridge lifted the wastepaper basket up onto Mr. Gibber's desk.

"That's him," said Hythe. "That's Murgatrude."

All Col could make out was a curled-up lump of hair or fur at the bottom of the basket. "What is he? A cat?"

Hythe turned to Flarrow. "Lift him out."

Flarrow took a backward step. "He'll go berserk."

"Do it," said Pugh.

"I'll get scratched."

"So?"

Flarrow looked round the circle of faces and surrendered to his fate. He buttoned his jacket up to the neck for protection, then reached into the basket with both hands.

Murgatrude exploded into action like a coiled spring. He

raked at Flarrow, flew through the air, and crashed into the blackboard, then zoomed around like a hurricane, banging into desk frames and skimming along walls. Col glimpsed a half-bald body, a nose like a pug dog, and whiskers like a cat.

The animal made a complete circuit of the room, then jumped up onto the desk and back into the basket.

Everyone laughed except for Flarrow, who was bleeding from scratches on his hands and chin.

"Now do you know what it is?" Pugh asked Col. "A cat or a dog?"

Col shook his head.

"Nobody does," said Hythe. "Nobody has ever worked it out."

"Lift him out again," Lumbridge ordered Flarrow.

There was a warning growl from Murgatrude in his wastepaper basket.

"No, don't," said Col. "Stop."

It was an outright command, of which Sir Mormus might have approved. Lumbridge shrugged and desisted—but only after exchanging glances with the Squellinghams. Even Flarrow looked in their direction first.

20

"Right." Mr. Gibber cracked his knuckles. "The next subject will be . . . will be . . ." He waited for attention. "Will be geography. What's geography, Clatterick?"

"Don't know, sir."

"Because you're a dimwit and a doodlebrain. But *I* know. Your humble teacher, Mr. Bartrim Gibber, knows."

It was Friday afternoon, and Fefferley and Haugh had already brought out their pillows. Mr. Gibber unrolled two maps and pinned them up on the blackboard: a map of the world and a map of the Old Country.

Mr. Gibber's geography was as moral as all his other lessons. He divided the world into good coastlines and bad coastlines. Good coastlines like Florida and Cape York were firm and proud and pushed forward into the ocean. Bad coastlines like the Gulf of Mexico and the Great Australian Bight bent weakly inward. In general the coastline of Europe was the best of all coastlines, and the coastline of the Old Country was absolutely perfect.

"See Wales pushing forward." He used one of his canes to point on the map. "And Cornwall here. Kent. East Anglia. All outstanding coastlines. Coastlines with character."

Col put up a hand. Mr. Gibber licked his rubbery lips and took up a pose of listening.

"Silence, everyone! A question from the grandson of Sir Mormus Porpentine. What would you like to know?"

"I don't see how you can have one without the other, sir. The bits that stick out need bits going in between them. Like the Bristol Channel between Wales and Cornwall. Or the Thames Estuary between Kent and East Anglia."

"Oh, he knows all about the Bristol Channel and the Thames Estuary." Mr. Gibber went into an ecstasy of grinning and grimacing. "'Going in,' he says. Disgusting! Where are they? There!"

Mr. Gibber drew back his cane and gave the map a mighty whack. "That's what I think of the Thames Estuary!" Another whack. "And that's what I think of the Bristol Channel!"

The map of the Old Country fell off the blackboard.

Flarrow put up a hand. "What about the Great Australian Bight, sir!"

Whack! Mr. Gibber vented his spleen on the Great Australian Bight.

Another student chimed in. "The Gulf of Mexico, sir!"

Whack!

The map of the world joined the map of the Old Country on the floor. Mr. Gibber whirled around and started whacking desks at the front of the class.

"This is what I do to a bad coastline! And anyone in favor of a bad coastline! Are you in favor of a bad coastline, Trant?"

He brought his cane down so hard on Septimus Trant's desk that Septimus let out a yell.

"Oh, you are, are you?" Whack! "Perhaps you're in favor of the Thames Estuary? Even though Porpentine has shown us how bad it is?"

"No, sir, I—"

Whack! Whack! Whack! Mr. Gibber jumped up and down, thrashing Septimus's desk from all angles. Septimus shrank back as the blows just missed him.

"Tell me, Trant! You think I'm a moron, don't you? You think I'm a monkey brain!"

"No, sir."

"Yes, yes, I am! You don't respect me, do you? I'm a clown and an idiot! Say it!"

Mr. Gibber had gone red in the face and seemed about to burst a blood vessel. Septimus kept shaking his head, unable to make himself heard.

"And what about my nose?" Mr. Gibber pointed to his nose. "It makes you want to laugh, doesn't it? Like a squashed tomato! You think it's the most stupid nose that ever existed! Yes, you do! I can see you do!"

He whacked so hard that his cane broke in two. One half went zinging across the room, until Lumbridge stood up in his seat and caught it. The class cheered.

Mr. Gibber quieted down, staring at the stump in his hand. "That was my Number Eleven. Now see what you've done."

He sat behind his desk and ordered the class to write out lines. "Fifty times. 'The Thames Estuary is a very bad coastline.'"

The class groaned.

"Yes, yes. Get started."

While Mr. Gibber sulked, the class pretended to write lines in their exercise books. Fefferley tilted his book to show Col what he was really producing: a picture of Mr. Gibber leading an army of firm outstanding coastlines against an army of weak and inward coastlines. The coastlines snapped at one another with balloon cries of *"YARAGH!" "HAI!" "TAKE THAT!"* and *"KERSPLUNK!"*

Col was sorry he'd gotten Septimus into trouble. He understood the hierarchy well enough by now. Mr. Gibber put on an exaggerated servility toward the elite group, ignored the blockies, and showered his sarcasm on the crawlers and climbers. When he really wanted to bluster and perform, it was always a grindboy he picked on.

21

Col's weekend was filled with social activities. On Saturday he accompanied Ebnolia on three family calls and attended a committee meeting of the Imperial Charitable Society and an evening of amateur theatricals put on by the Bassimors. His life moved at a different pace now that his diffident, dreamy mother no longer organized his days. There was never a spare moment with his grandmother in charge.

For Sunday she had arranged a picnic at a play park on Thirty-sixth Deck. She took the younger family members— Col, Gillabeth, and Antrobus—and four Menials, including her new favorite, Wicky Popo.

The play park was half an hour's walk away at the back of *Worldshaker*. It was an enclosed court surrounded by high metal walls but open at the top. Col could see smoke drifting across overhead, though he couldn't see the funnels from which it came. He had a much better grasp on the geography of the juggernaut now.

A dozen families were already present. Respectable ladies under white parasols supervised children playing in the sandbox, or on seesaws, slides, and merry-go-rounds.

Several ladies whose family status was not too far below the Porpentines' came across to pay their respects to Ebnolia. Others from lesser, professional families merely smiled from a distance and warned their children to play in a well-bred manner.

Gillabeth took Antrobus over to the slides. She tucked his knickerbockers into his socks and helped him to the top of the lowest slide.

"No flapping, no waving," she ordered. "You know how Grandmother likes to see you slide."

Antrobus came sliding down, arms fixed at his sides like a wooden doll. There was no way of telling whether he enjoyed or hated the experience.

"Now again," said Gillabeth.

Meanwhile the Menials had begun setting up the picnic things. Wicky Popo struggled helplessly with a fold-up chair. He had looked frail the last time Col had seen him, but now he looked downright sickly.

"Poor Wicky Popo." Ebnolia had finished with civilities and bobbed up beside Col. "Not well at all."

Grandmother was known for her soft heart and compassion toward Menials, Col remembered. They watched as Wicky Popo studied the chairs that other Menials had unfolded, yet still couldn't work out the trick of it.

"Look at the poor darling!" Grandmother hugged herself in delight. "So puzzled he looks! Did you ever see anything so sweet?"

One of the other Menials took the chair from Wicky Popo and unfolded it. Grandmother was disappointed.

"What a shame he couldn't do it himself. How sorry he looks! Wrinkling up his nose. I just love his dear little nose! And those big, sad eyes!"

The other Menial took a pile of plates from a hamper and showed Wicky Popo how to lay them out on the table.

"Oh, he's trying so hard." Grandmother was all sympathy.

"He wants to do it properly. If only he could speak and tell everyone how hard he's trying."

Col frowned. "But they never do, do they?"

"What's that, dear?"

"Speak."

"No, of course not. They're Menials, so they don't need to. They have very simple lives, with none of our worries."

"Are you sure? You said Wicky Popo looks sad."

"Sad *eyes*, dear. Not sadness as we'd feel it. He's still contented because he doesn't desire anything more."

Col remembered Riff's view on the contentment of Menials. *Half a life*, she'd called it.

"What if a Filthy didn't want to be made into a Menial?" he asked.

The word "Filthy" made Grandmother Ebnolia raise her eyebrows. "Tch, tch, Colbert. Such silly ideas you have. Of course they want to be made into Menials."

"I heard of one who didn't."

"What?"

"Ten days ago. Two officers came checking my cabin for a Filthy who'd escaped in the middle of the night."

"They told you that?" Grandmother clicked her tongue against her tiny white teeth. "Ah, yes, I remember now. A very ignorant Filthy girl."

"The officers said she didn't want to be made into a Menial." Col bent the facts a little.

"That's because Filthies get frightened, Colbert. They're not rational beings, you know." Grandmother smiled brightly. "Anyway, that particular girl was found soon after. Now she's a perfectly happy Menial, working in the kitchens."

By sheer force of habit Col almost believed her. Throughout his entire life anything that Grandmother told him was as good as if he'd seen it with his own eyes. But this time he knew better!

"Where did they find her?"

Grandmother reflected a moment. "Ah, yes, she was hiding under the stairs by the Warwickshire Lounge."

She was making it up! Yet she said it with such conviction, nodding her head like a little bird. Looking into her eyes, Col felt dizzy from the abyss yawning in front of him. How many other times had she been making things up?

There was a crash of breaking china, and Wicky Popo stood looking down at a plate he'd dropped. Grandmother clapped her hands together.

"Oh dear! Oh dear! Now see what he's done! Isn't he hopeless! I'll have to give him a tiny treat to make him feel better. Something to eat, perhaps." She tut-tutted sweetly to herself. "I know I shouldn't, but he's so adorable."

Col wasn't listening. He was thinking back on all the things that he'd always known that seemed to have come from his own experience. But what if they were only things he'd been told? The more he thought back, the more his childhood disappeared into a strange obscurity. Perhaps his whole world was created out of things he'd been told. . . .

"I'm going to have a go on the swings," he said, and hurried off to the other side of the play park.

22

Col's second week at school was much like the first. On Monday Mr. Gibber taught them the admirable qualities of proper nouns but could hardly contain his contempt for indefinite articles. On Tuesday he went into an apoplectic fit over an algebra equation that refused to work out. On Wednesday he picked on the grindboy called Swiddlington and hurled abuse at him like a monkey hurling coconuts.

Col had always had doubts about Mr. Gibber's lessons. Now he suspected that his teacher was making things up, just as much as Grandmother Ebnolia had been. He stopped paying attention in class and let his mind wander.

There were other things he didn't believe at school, such as the mythology of the toilets at the far end of the yard. They were smelly, lightless cubicles, and the students went there as little as possible.

"They go all the way down Below," Fefferley said, giggling.

"So whatever you do—," Flarrow began.

"—drops onto the heads of the Filthies," Hythe finished.

"Then they try to come and get you," said Haugh.

"Wriggle up through the hole," said Lumbridge.

Col shook his head. "It's too narrow."

But nobody was listening.

"You wouldn't want to be on the seat when a Filthy makes a grab for you," said Pugh.

They were half laughing and half shuddering. Col was amazed they could believe such nonsense. Did they think that Filthies were like snakes? But he didn't argue. He couldn't afford to let on that he knew what a Filthy really looked like.

In the Tuesday lunch break the group played a joke on the crawler called Weffington, who had gone into one of the toilets. Creeping up outside, they made sounds of grunting, gobbling, and heavy breathing, supposedly like a Filthy climbing up the pipe. When Weffington tried to escape, Lumbridge held on to the outside door handle and stopped him from opening the door.

Col felt a bit sorry for him when they finally let him out. After five minutes he was obviously in a state of terror. For the rest of the group his white face only made the joke better.

When Col had started school, he'd felt like a beginner compared to other students; now he felt older and more mature. The silliness over the toilets was just one part of the general naïveté. They could be naughty in a schoolboy way, but they had no idea of real wrongdoing . . . like hiding and helping a Filthy.

He thought more and more about Riff. When his mind wandered in class, it was to her that it wandered. He remembered her changed appearance after she'd washed in his washbasin . . . her skin glowing, her blond-and-black hair almost silky . . . and the fast, flickering dance she'd done. Then there was the time she'd tried to hold on to his book and the boast she'd made: *I bet I could read ten times better'n you.*

Such an incredible few days . . . He felt guilty about his thoughts, but it was a sweet, melancholy sort of guilt that he didn't want to relinquish. It spread all through him and made a strange tightness in his throat and chest.

He'd actually touched her when he'd wrestled the book from her hands!

He looked round the classroom and wondered what the students would say if they could see into his mind. Here he was sitting in the middle of them, and they could never begin to guess. Even that thought was oddly pleasing, oddly seductive.

Although he had cut off from Mr. Gibber's lessons, his marks hardly suffered. He came first in a physics test, second in a spelling test, and third in a grammar test. But he was starting to have doubts about Mr. Gibber's marking.

The thing that most puzzled him was that the grindboys always wrote the longest answers yet always received the lowest marks. Septimus Trant, who wrote more than anyone, was usually bottom of the class. Col watched him in a history test on Wednesday afternoon as he filled up page after page. Was he writing complete drivel, or what?

The paths of grindboys and the elite never crossed, and Col hadn't talked to Septimus since his first day at the academy. Today, though, he decided to quiz him after school.

23

"**W**ait up!"

Col had followed Septimus for a couple of corridors on his way home. Septimus stopped and turned. He seemed nervous, his Adam's apple bobbing in his throat.

"You shouldn't be seen with me," he said. "It'll make trouble for you."

"Why?"

"Because I'm a grindboy and you're a Porpentine."

"I don't care."

"You should. The Squellinghams will drag you down if they get the chance."

"I don't believe you."

"Everyone knows it."

Col shook his head. This wasn't what he wanted to talk about.

"I watched you write eight pages in the history test," he said. "Why do you keep getting bottom marks?"

Septimus shrugged and remained silent.

"Is it because you don't answer the question?"

"Of course I answer the question." An angry, defensive look came over Septimus's face. "I get bottom marks because the Gibber never reads what I write."

"What?"

His pale eyes stared full into Col's. "You don't get it, do

you? The Gibber decides the marks with the Squellingham twins. They have meetings after school. They're probably deciding the history marks right now. Sometimes they write in answers to fit the marks."

"But I beat Hythe in spelling. I beat both of them in physics."

"Only because they wanted you to. They've probably decided to make you best in some subjects and second best in others."

"What about wanting to drag me down, like you said?"

"They won't do it *that* way. The system works for people like you."

"You ought to complain."

Septimus snorted. "Who to?"

When he turned and walked on, Col still kept him company. Septimus seemed to be teetering on the edge of a confession.

Finally, he burst out with it. "I can prove Mr. Gibber doesn't read my answers. Because if he did, I'd be expelled."

"Why?"

"Because my answers contradict everything he says."

"You don't agree with his lessons?"

"No. Do you?"

Col grinned. "No. Moral right angles. Immoral coastlines. Pure elements and dirty compounds."

Septimus grinned too. "Proper proper nouns. Noah's Ark as the first juggernaut. I contradicted that in my answer this afternoon."

"You don't believe it?"

"It's rubbish. I've read books about the Crusades and the

Spanish Armada and Oliver Cromwell. There were no juggernauts then."

Col knew nothing about the Crusades or the Spanish Armada or Oliver Cromwell, but he knew all about one historical period. "Not in the time of the Greeks or Romans, either. Unless they were invented and then forgotten."

"Impossible. Like Noah being our queen's ancestor."

"What about the Filthies?"

Septimus didn't snigger over the word. "They weren't around either. They didn't exist in the seventeenth century."

"So where did they come from?"

"Don't know. I can't find any books on later history in the school library."

"Maybe they arrived at the same time as the juggernauts," Col suggested.

"Don't know," Septimus repeated. "I don't even know what Filthies look like."

It was on the tip of Col's tongue to say he *did* know what they looked like. The urge to share his secret was overwhelming; he'd been holding it in so long. But no, too risky . . .

They walked on again in silence.

Then Col had an idea. "We could ask my old tutor to find out."

"Why would he do that?"

"Because he loves research and finding out the truth. He'd do it out of interest. And he has the whole Norfolk Library to look things up in."

"The Norfolk Library?" Septimus's eyes went wide. "That's huge, isn't it?"

"Thousands and thousands of books." Col knitted his

brow. "I know. We'll tell him we've got a school history project. For Mr. Gibber."

Septimus laughed. "The early history of juggernauts and Filthies," he proposed.

"Yes. Good. Let's see if he's in the Norfolk Library now."

Col led the way to the Forty-fourth Deck. Septimus had turned into a different person, almost quivering with excitement.

He was even more excited when they entered the library. The sight of so many books made him gasp out loud. He veered at once toward the shelves, as if itching to touch the leather-bound spines.

Col reminded him of their purpose. "Professor Twillip. Over there."

As usual Professor Twillip was working at a table in the main reading room. His white hair gleamed under the single electric light. He looked up with surprise, then pleasure, as the two boys approached.

"Well, well, Colbert. Revisiting old haunts, eh? And who's this with you?"

Col introduced Septimus. Professor Twillip clearly had no notion of the Trant family's lower rank on the social scale.

"We were hoping you could help us with a history project," said Col.

"History, eh?" Professor Twillip rubbed his hands together. "Not my specialty. But tell me, tell me."

"The early history of juggernauts and Filthies," said Col.

"Where they came from," added Septimus.

"Hmm. There were no juggernauts or Filthies at the time of the Roman Empire. So I suppose . . ." Professor Twillip drummed on the table with his fingertips, then broke out in a smile. "I suppose I shall have to look it up." He surveyed the shelves in the gloom. "I wonder where to start."

Septimus gazed around too. "Isn't there a list?"

"No. These books are all very old. They've never been catalogued. Nor even arranged by subject matter."

"That's crazy!"

For the first time Professor Twillip peered over the top of his glasses and took a close look at Septimus. "Yes, it does seem a little foolish," he agreed mildly. "I usually know where to find the books I want. But history after the Greeks and Romans . . ."

"And after Oliver Cromwell," said Septimus. "Eighteenth or nineteenth century."

"So recent?" Professor Twillip rose to his feet. "Well, we can start by looking for any book with eighteenth or nineteenth century in the title."

"If we find one book, it might lead us to others," said Septimus.

"Exactly, exactly."

They were like trackers on a trail. Professor Twillip headed over to a particular row of shelves and started examining book after book. Septimus took another row and did the same.

"Look for bibliographies at the back," Professor Twillip advised.

"What about indexes?"

"Yes. If they list 'juggernaut' or 'Filthies.'"

Professor Twillip was in his element—and so was Septimus, Col realized. He watched them for a few minutes, not sharing their scholarly instincts. He had to get back for high tea, followed by a game of charades that Ebnolia had arranged with the Postlefrith family.

"This will take ages, won't it?" he asked.

"Ages and ages," Professor Twillip agreed happily.

"I'll leave the two of you to it, shall I?"

Septimus looked up in sudden alarm. "But I can't stay if you go."

"Why not?" asked Professor Twillip.

"I don't have permission to be in the Norfolk Library on my own."

"No problem," said the Professor. "I can give you permission."

"What if it takes longer than just today?"

"Oh, it will, it will. If you want all the facts, it'll take days. But so long as I'm here, I can give you permission."

"That's settled, then," said Col.

Septimus was grinning as though all his Christmases had come at once.

24

The next day at school Col was a little wary of the Squellingham twins. He couldn't believe they were looking for a chance to drag him down . . . and yet Septimus had sounded so sure about it. He watched for signs but saw nothing.

The day passed by in its usual way until the last lesson of the afternoon. Then there was a knock on the door, and Dr. Blessamy walked in.

"Stand up, 4A!" roared Mr. Gibber. He made a low bow to the headmaster, then roared again, "Sit down, 4A!"

"Dear boys." Dr. Blessamy stood in front of the class, while Mr. Gibber capered about behind his back. "Tomorrow is Friday and . . . another day as well. Our Founder's Day. A day in memory of the very first Dr. Blessamy. My great-great-grandfather . . . or possibly great-great-great-grandfather." He seemed to lose track of his thoughts for a moment, then redis-covered them. "The Dr. Blessamy who founded this academy in 1851. Without our Founder, we wouldn't have this school today." He gestured expansively. "I wouldn't be standing here speaking to you, and you wouldn't be listening. I wouldn't be your headmaster, and you wouldn't be my pupils. And instead, here we all are. Standing. Speaking. Listening. Pupils."

He surveyed the class with a benevolent air. Mr. Gibber, who had been emphasizing every gesture with gestures of his own, surveyed the class with a belligerent air.

"For tomorrow, dear boys, your thoughtful old head-master has arranged a very special . . . er . . . something. Excursion. Yes, an excursion to the tomb of our Founder in the Graveyard Rooms. We shall meditate and pay our respects to the first Dr. Blessamy. Then free time for every-one to go and pay their respects before the tombs of their own forefathers. It will be a day of respects and meditation and . . . er . . . more respects . . ."

As Dr. Blessamy ran out of words, Mr. Gibber stepped forward to bawl, "What do we say, 4A? We say, 'Thank you, Headmaster!'"

The class bawled, "Thank you, Headmaster!" in perfect imitation of Mr. Gibber.

Dr. Blessamy winced, blinked, smiled vaguely, and withdrew.

Col was busy with his own thoughts. The Graveyard Rooms . . . where he'd gone with Riff, fleeing from the officer and the invisible ghosts. He remembered the soft, crumbling earth, the musty, moldering smell. And one memory leaped into his mind most vividly of all—the way she'd clutched at his hand in her terror. He could almost feel the touch of her fingers.

He kept thinking about the Graveyard Rooms for the rest of the lesson, then on the walk back from school, then all through afternoon tea in the Somerset Room. A plan was starting to form in his head.

It was so wild that at first it was more like a daydream. Yet the more he mulled over it, the more he fell in love with it. It tied in with another memory of Riff, when she had tried to "borrow" his book on mountains and volcanoes.

After high tea there was a piano recital by Gillabeth in the Lancashire Room. Ebnolia had invited guests from many families, and the chairs had been set up in rows. Gillabeth's severe brown frock was softened by flowery bows for the occasion, but nothing could soften her massive Porpentine chin. She played correctly and competently, as she did everything correctly and competently. The audience applauded a succession of pieces by a famous Old Country composer. Still, Gillabeth gave the impression that she would sooner strangle the keys than play them.

Col had to remind himself to applaud. The elements of his plan were falling into place. He was relying on the fact that Dr. Blessamy had promised free time for students to visit the tombs of their forefathers. If he could slip away then, if he could find Door Seventeen, if he could retrace his steps to the food chute on Bottom Deck . . .

Gillabeth continued to batter the piano into submission. Several ladies began to whisper among themselves, their voices covered by the crashing chords.

Yes, a present from him to Riff . . . Of course, she could hardly learn how to read by herself. Although he no longer thought of her as dumb, nobody could be *that* smart. But she could look at the pictures and see the words. She would recognize the book and know who had dropped it down the chute. . . .

A thunderous crescendo concluded the recital. Gillabeth glared at the piano while the audience clapped. Quinnea Porpentine had to be helped from the room, hair hanging in loose strands, face drained of color.

"It's the emotion of the music," Orris explained. "Too much feeling."

Col took the opportunity to go with her. He supported her on one side while Orris supported her on the other.

"It was the high notes," she breathed faintly. "Too many high notes."

Missy Jip was waiting inside the door of Quinnea and Orris's private reception room. While his mother tottered off for a long lie-down, Col told Missy Jip to find him some scissors, some safety pins, a ball of string, and a sheet of brown paper. It was all part of the plan. Orris didn't think to ask why his son needed such things—and Missy Jip couldn't.

Back in his own room he took the book on mountains and volcanoes from his bookcase. He wrapped it in brown paper and used a pencil to address it. Since the Filthies couldn't read the name Riff, he drew a picture of her with blond-and-black hair. He couldn't help grinning at the likeness.

Then he tied the package round with string. He loved the idea of her pulling off the wrapping and discovering the book inside. . . .

Still, he hadn't finished. This was what the safety pins were for. With string and pins he made a kind of sling inside his school jacket and tucked the book into it. When he studied the effect in his mirror, the bulge was scarcely noticeable.

All prepared for tomorrow! If he'd been asked why he was doing it, he wouldn't have been able to answer. But he *had* to go through with it now.

25

The Graveyard Rooms were not as Col remembered them. For one thing the lights had been turned on, so that students looking in from the corridors could see names and dates engraved on every tomb. For another thing Dr. Blessamy had brought them to a much grander section of the rooms, where tombs were sculpted with scrolls and angels and the ground was covered with green stone chips. Even the moldering smell was less noticeable.

The tomb of the first Dr. Blessamy was especially sumptuous: a black marble monument in the shape of *Worldshaker* itself, with a line of funnels along the top. The students took turns looking in through the windowlike openings, while the present Dr. Blessamy delivered a rambling fifteen-minute talk.

The air grew more and more stifling. Col was the only student who kept his jacket buttoned. He was sweating with the heat, but he had to keep the package out of view.

He had come down with the Squellingham group, marching behind Mr. Gibber at the head of 4A. Now, though, he took advantage of the circulating crowd to drift away and lose himself among the younger students of 1A and 1B. He hoped his absence wouldn't be too obvious.

At the end of his talk Dr. Blessamy called for a minute's silence. Then it was time for the students to go and pay their respects before the tombs of their own forefathers.

"Your teachers have maps," Dr. Blessamy announced. "If you haven't been to pay your respects before, they can give you directions. Think solemn and serious thoughts, boys and girls. Reassemble here in an hour's time."

There was more milling around in all directions. Col strode off along the corridor as if he already knew exactly where to find the tombs of the Porpentines.

In fact he had only a rough idea of where he was in relation to where he needed to arrive. He suspected that the route he'd followed with Drummel and then Riff had been further back in the juggernaut.

He walked on and on without finding anywhere familiar. When he came to empty rooms where the earth was unturned, without tombs or headstones, he realized he had come too far. He gritted his teeth and retraced his steps. This was going to be harder than he'd thought.

Now he encountered gaggles of wandering, chattering students. They seemed to be making a social occasion of it, visiting one another's family tombs. Col still strode along as if he knew exactly where he was going—until he ran into the Squellingham group.

"We lost you," said Fefferley.

"Where have you been?" asked Flarrow.

Col avoided a straight answer. "I'm heading for the Porpentine rooms."

"Oh?" Hythe seemed to be studying him. "Where are they?"

Col waved an arm in a vague gesture. "That way."

"Not back there?" Pugh pointed in the direction from which Col had just come.

"No, that way."

"Well, okay. So . . ."

Col guessed what was coming next. They expected him to rejoin the group and visit one another's family tombs together.

"Bye, then," he said, and walked on, leaving them standing.

He felt their eyes burning into the back of his neck, but he didn't look round. Had Hythe been studying the faint bulge of the package under his jacket?

He turned off into the next corridor to the side. Ahead was a flight of stairs going down to the level below. Yes, safer to try and pick up his old route on Fifth Deck, where there were no students to run into.

On Fifth Deck his luck changed. He walked through racks of plaster statuettes and came out into a corridor he recognized. At last!

He went on at a fast jog. Dr. Blessamy had allowed an hour of free time, but Col had already wasted fifteen or twenty minutes.

His heart was pounding, yet he felt reckless and lightheaded. He remembered Riff's words: *I like taking risks.* Now he understood what she meant!

Down he went through Fourth Deck, with its piles of timber, wire, and rope.

Down through Third Deck, with its penned animals.

Down through the two food storage decks . . . on to the steps that descended to Door Seventeen.

For the first time in a fortnight he seemed to have come fully alive. After all the mind-numbing hours in Mr. Gibber's classroom he felt the same thrill of adrenaline he'd experienced with Riff. This was what he'd been missing!

The numbers for the lock flashed up before his mind: 4-9-2. He spun the wheels and slipped inside.

He slowed down then, moving almost as soundlessly as Riff. He took the same way as before, flitting behind iron piers and mounds of coal, hiding in the exact same shadows. It was as though some fate had hold of him.

In the last shadow of the last black mound, he stopped to unbutton his jacket. He unpinned the sling and brought out the brown-paper package.

All going to plan . . . except one thing. Suddenly he remembered the wheels on the inside of Door Seventeen. Had he locked them?

He considered going back to check. But no, it would take only a minute to open the manhole and deliver his package. Then he'd be back at the door anyway.

Again he looked round at the nearest pools of light and made sure no officer could see him. He was alert to every tiny sound. A creak of coal settling in the bunkers over there . . . and that must be a faint hiss of escaping steam . . .

He darted out to the food chute. Putting his package down beside the manhole, he began working the bolts free. One . . . two . . . three . . . four . . . He swung the cover up and over, and lowered it to the floor.

A thunder of deep-down hammering rose from Below, a red glow reflected on the chute's shiny surfaces.

He tried not to think about the last time he had stood here, when Riff had reached up with her arms and . . . *You're okay, Col-bert Porping-tine.*

It was an unconscious reflex to wipe the back of his hand across his mouth. Then he picked up the package and dropped it down the chute.

"From me to you," he said.

There was another hiss, sharper and louder. Was that really the sound of escaping steam? He stared into the shadows all around.

The next sound wasn't a hiss but an unmistakable whisper.

He was frozen with indecision. Someone had seen him, someone hiding behind the sacks and bags of food for the Filthies. Should he close the manhole or leave it open and run?

"We're on to you, Porpentine."

"You've been found out."

He recognized the second voice. "Lumbridge? Is that you?"

Lumbridge stepped out, followed by Flarrow, Haugh, Fefferley, and the Squellingham twins. Their faces were ugly, threatening, triumphant.

"You followed me?" Col couldn't believe it.

"Got it in one," said Pugh. "We guessed you were up to no good."

Col tried to go on the attack. "You're not authorized personnel. You're not allowed down here."

Hythe sneered. "And you are?"

"Yes." Even as he said it, Col knew it sounded unconvincing. He was too poor a liar to bluff.

"Tell it to the officers," said Hythe.

"We're going to call them," said Pugh.

"And we'll tell them what *we* saw," said Haugh. "You dropping stuff to the Filthies."

"What was in that package?" asked Flarrow.

"You must be some kind of Filthy-lover," said Lumbridge.

All at once, they began chanting. "Filthy-lover! Filthy-lover! Filthy-lover! Filthy-lover!"

From another part of the deck an adult voice shouted, "Who's there?"

"Come and see!" Pugh shouted back.

The others joined in. "Over here! Over here!"

Col was desperate. "I'll get you into more trouble than me. I'll say *you* opened the food chute. I followed you down to see what *you* were doing."

"They'll never believe you," said Hythe.

"Six against one," said Pugh.

"But I'm a Porpentine," said Col.

Hythe and Pugh exchanged glances.

"You're the one standing over the food chute," Hythe pointed out.

Col went to move away, but Lumbridge moved to block him. "Stay where you are, Filthy-lover."

A tramp of many boots approaching! It wasn't a single officer but a whole group of them!

Col made a bid to dodge past Lumbridge's outspread arms. Lumbridge seized hold of his school jacket and swung him back toward the food chute.

"Don't let him escape," urged Pugh.

Col tried to wriggle out of his jacket. Lumbridge switched his grip to Col's hair. Agony tearing at his scalp, Col drove his fist into the bully's face.

Blood spurted from Lumbridge's nose. His smirk vanished, replaced by an expression of sheer disbelief. His eyes crossed as he tried to look at his nose.

The leading officer strode into view around the sacks and bags.

"Stop that!" He clapped his hands.

But Lumbridge lunged for Col again. Taken by surprise, Col took a backward step. His foot hung over empty space—the open manhole!

He tried to grip onto Lumbridge, who staggered. For one second he stared into Lumbridge's small, piggy eyes and nostrils trickling blood. He never knew what went on in that second behind those eyes. Was it deliberate or accidental?

Both of Col's feet now hung over empty space. Lumbridge raised his arms, broke Col's grip, and dropped him down into the hole.

26

Down, down, down. His very worst childhood nightmare had come true. Utter helplessness, nothing to clutch on to. Scrabbling at the smooth metal of the chute, he only added a corkscrew twist to his fall.

By the time he hit bottom, he was traveling at tremendous speed. All he knew was that something caught him under the feet and bounced him back up. For a moment he was spinning, over and over. Then he landed once more, this time on his back.

He lay winded. There was a rotten-egg smell and a dull pounding of machinery. He tried to open his eyes, then discovered they were already open. The world was a blur of hellish red and black.

"Somethin' else come down!" roared a voice nearby.

"Food!" cried another.

The red and black separated out into a band of red sky between towering cliffs. The cliffs were actually walls of iron; the red sky was a glow reflected on smoke.

Then faces appeared, hideous faces with glinting eyes. One was disfigured by crinkled scar tissue; another lacked teeth; a third was clotted with yellow grease. As they loomed over him, Col had an impression of bare, sweating shoulders and chests. Surely they were hairy and dark as beasts!

Panic took over; his deepest fears resurfaced. They had called him "food"! Filthy cannibals!

He struggled to rise up off his back. But he was in some kind of net and couldn't get a purchase. His left foot sank through between the cords, leaving him snagged and trapped.

"What we got here?" growled Scarface.

"Must be a one of 'em," said Greasy.

"Urr, fell down from above," agreed Toothless.

Col could hardly hear for the noise of machinery, but he could read the words on their lips. Toothless was holding Col's book on mountains and volcanoes under his arm. He had already torn off the paper and string.

A wiry hand caught hold of Col's chin and twisted the angle of his head. "Let's have a look at 'im," said Scarface.

With a frantic tug Col managed to pull his foot free. He felt the side of a hand in front of his mouth and bit down with all the strength of his jaws. Teeth into flesh, teeth meeting on bone.

"Aaaaaghh!"

As Scarface snatched his hand away, Col rolled sideways on the net. Over and over—he didn't try to stand but kept rolling until he fell off.

"Get 'im down!"

The three Filthies were on the opposite side of the net. Scarface stood wringing his hand, and the other two had to run round him. It was just enough time for Col. He scrambled to his feet and fled.

Massive blocks of black metal ringed him in, but he found one narrow gap like a ravine. He darted along it, came to a T-junction, then swung right into another ravine.

"Get 'im down! Get 'im down! Get 'im down!"

He heard the yells of his pursuers, felt the vibration of

their footsteps through the floor. Vague impressions flashed past, of pipes, bolt heads, iron plates. But he had eyes only for the gaps between the black metal blocks. If he ran into a dead end, he was finished.

Catapulting round corners, he kept banging into bits of machinery: some oily, some grimy, some burning hot. He ducked under projections that seemed to leap out at him, jumped over ground-level ducts and sills.

All at once the floor came to an end, and there was nothing ahead, only a smoke-filled void. He skidded to a halt on the very edge. Peering through the smoke, he could just make out the monstrous shape of a cylindrical steel tank, so big that he could see neither its top nor bottom.

His pursuers were almost upon him when he spotted a ladder attached to the outside of the edge, going down. He flung himself onto it. Missing more rungs than he touched, he half slid and half fell for twenty feet. A succession of floors rushed past in front of him, narrow passages between the dark bulk of the machinery.

Choosing a floor at random, he swung off the ladder and ran back in the reverse direction. He had to run in a crouch because the ceiling was so low. The light dimmed, no longer a glow of red but a sickly yellow from occasional bulbs along the passage.

On either side were niches like wire cages, stacked one on top of the other. Four levels of them, each barely a couple of handsbreadths high—yet Filthies lived in them. Col glimpsed bodies curled up under rags, their backs turned to the passage. Sometimes they lay huddled in groups or pairs, pressed tightly up against one another. Col didn't like to think about what they might be doing. Dirty, disgusting Filthies!

He took a turn to the right, then a turn to the left. Shouts rang out behind: "Where'd he go?" "Which way?" Scarface, Greasy, and Toothless were still on his trail. Glancing back over his shoulder, he saw bodies roll over and heads pop out of niches. With squinting eyes the Filthies stared after him.

"Wassa noise?"

"Who's shoutin'?"

They were rousing up ahead of him too. It was hopeless. The news was traveling faster than he could run.

He came to an intersection and turned left again. Here rags hung across the roof of the passage: Filthy clothes spread out to dry. Forced to duck even lower, he noticed a row of empty niches on the bottom level. He flung himself into one before his pursuers came round the corner, rolling as far as possible away from the light.

Lumpy objects jabbed into the small of his back. He dug them out and discovered three tiny figurines carved from pieces of coal.

The niche had other forms of decoration too. Lengths of string had been knotted onto the wire in a pattern round the sides, and tufts of hair had been fastened onto the wire overhead. Human hair? Col shuddered at the thought. What else could it be down here?

Someone had even tried to make the niche more comfortable with a soft bag like a pillow. It seemed to be filled with soot or very fine ash. When Col pulled it toward himself, he found a metal spike hidden underneath. A weapon, sharpened to a murderous point.

He gripped it in his fist. At the same moment the pounding feet of Scarface, Greasy, and Toothless swept by outside.

He counted them past. They had fallen for his trick; they were chasing a phantom. Still gripping his spike, he rolled out of the niche and turned to run the other way.

But he was too soon. A whole horde of Filthies had joined the pursuit—and now they were rushing toward him along the passage.

He had no choice but to turn again and run on in the same direction. Scarface, Greasy, and Toothless were no more than twenty paces ahead—they only had to look back and see him, and then he'd be trapped between the two groups. But there was a farther intersection ahead too.

He made it to the intersection just as Greasy spotted him and yelled, "There he is!" He swung left along another passage. Arms reached out from niches as he raced past, and hands clutched to hold him. He slashed in great arcs with his spike and the hands dropped away.

They were all after him now. He heard the chant swelling louder and louder: "Get 'im down! Get 'im down! Get 'im down!"

He took another turn, and suddenly there were no more niches, only massive blank plates of metal. He darted forward, and the floor whirled under his feet. A moving turntable! Hurled sideways, he slammed into a wall of metal. The spike fell from his hand, and he dropped into the gap between wall and turntable.

With a bone-jarring *clang!* he crashed down onto another floor. Huge rotating spindles and humming drive belts hemmed him in on all sides. The belts moved so fast he could see them only as a blur, even inches in front of his face. One touch and he would be sucked in and ground to a pulp.

Still, he had to keep moving. He staggered to his feet and edged his way forward, bending and swaying to avoid the belts. Their hum was hypnotic; their wind fanned his cheeks. Finally, he climbed over a rim and found himself in a kind of trough.

The Filthies hadn't followed him through the spindles, but they were approaching from other directions. All around he saw them, clambering down ladders, swarming along walkways. The ladders and walkways hung as if suspended in the smoky air.

Which way now? Before he had time to think, there was a thunderous sound, and an avalanche came surging down the trough toward him. Hot slag—red embers and gray cinders! He sprang across the trough and somersaulted over the rim on the other side. The avalanche passed by behind him.

Now he was in an area of flues and chimneys. They rose out of the floor, tapering upward, and radiated waves of heat that almost knocked him off his feet. The sound from inside was like rushing, roaring fires.

He broke into a stumbling run. He had to escape. His clothes were starting to smolder, he could hardly draw breath, and his eyeballs were stinging from the heat.

By the time he got through, the threads of his jacket were alight with tiny flames. He beat out the flames, blinked the tears from his eyes, and stared at a track of shiny rollers ahead, sloping down between black walls. Where did it lead? He could see nothing but darkness.

He took a flying leap and dived full-length onto the rollers. He would choose his own death sooner than be captured by Filthies.

Down the slope he went, as the rollers turned under him. Darker and darker . . . until the slope came to an end and the rollers pitched him forward.

He had a sense of dropping through some kind of hole.

It was pure instinct to reach out with his arms, pure luck to catch on to a chain he couldn't even see. The instant deceleration nearly wrenched his arm from its socket.

He hung in midair, swinging from side to side, hearing the creak of the chain. An acrid stench came to his nostrils, a strange fizzing sound to his ears. Looking down, he made out a faint phosphorescence that floated on a thick, porridge-like sea.

He must have arrived at the very bottom of *Worldshaker*.

"Get 'im down! Get 'im down! Get 'im down!" The cries of the Filthies were coming closer.

Raising his eyes, he saw a grille of bars overhead. The hole through which he had dropped was a large square opening in the center of the grille. Several chains spanned the darkness, including the one to which he clung.

"He ain't down yet!" snarled a voice. "I see 'im!"

Filthies walked out across the grille. Viewed from beneath they were vague, misshapen shadows, all feet and legs. They squatted to peer down between the bars or through the central opening.

"I'm not your enemy!" Col shouted.

The only answer was a barrage of jeers and abuse. A missile went whizzing past in front of his nose.

"Aim for 'is hands!" someone bellowed. "Get 'im down! Into the bilge!"

They were trying to knock him off his chain. So that was

what they meant by "Get 'im down." They wanted him to die in the porridge.

Another missile skimmed his chest, another struck him on the shoulder. When one bounced off the chain, he saw they were hurling chunks of cold cinder.

Down below he could hear ominous fizzing sounds as the chunks landed in the porridge. The stuff was in a state of yeasty ferment.

One chunk hit him on the wrist, and he nearly lost his grip. He was trying to jink and dodge, but it was only a matter of time.

Then a new voice spoke out overhead, lighter yet somehow authoritative. "Stop that!"

The bombardment of missiles ceased at once.

"Pull up the chain," the voice commanded. "Bring him up here."

27

The chain rattled, and Col seesawed through the air. They were hauling him up toward the opening. He didn't understand—he was thankful for the reprieve—but what would they do with him?

Many hands reached down as he approached. They grabbed him by his jacket, hoisted him up, and deposited him on the bars. His feet slipped through, and he ended up half kneeling, half sitting.

Filthies clustered around. He recognized Scarface, Greasy, and Toothless, all grinning with vicious satisfaction.

"Stand back!"

Again the authoritative voice. It was a female voice, Col realized. As the crowd stepped back, he saw that the person giving the orders was a girl with blond-and-black hair, sharp cheekbones, and large eyes.

Riff!

He gasped in disbelief. Riff merely nodded at him. She must have already recognized him on the chain.

He remembered what she'd said about being a leader down Below. Now she was his one and only lifeline.

"Riff, please!" he appealed. "You said you owed me once. You promised help if I ever had to ask."

She frowned and bit her lip. A ripple of muttering ran through the crowd.

Riff turned to face them. "Yeah, it's true. You all heard the story. This is the boy that hid me in his cupboard."

The muttering changed tone. Less hostile? Col looked around and noticed how young most of the Filthies were.

But Scarface didn't change. He held out his hand, displaying Col's teeth marks etched in blood. "See what he did to me? I say he dies now."

Riff nodded at the teeth marks. "I made a promise to help him, though."

"Help him how?" asked one of the other Filthies.

"Dunno. Save him for the Revolutionary Council to decide."

"No!" Scarface was livid. "He's a one of 'em! He has to pay!" He turned to the crowd. "For everything they've done to us, right? For all the blasts of steam!" He pointed to the puckered tissue that disfigured half his face. "Like this, right?"

The Filthies appeared undecided.

"Only one place for his kind!" Scarface pointed to the porridge. "Into the bilge!"

He advanced on Col, but Riff stepped forward and blocked him.

"Okay," she said. "If that's the way you want it. I'm ready."

What now? Col wondered.

The Filthies spread out to form a ring, linking arms. Scarface and Riff backed off to a distance of twenty paces, flexed their arms, and bent at the knees. They were going to fight over him.

Col's hopes crashed. It was a totally one-sided contest. Scarface was older and bigger and stronger. His only disadvantage was his injured hand, and even that didn't seem to bother him. Riff wouldn't stand a chance.

For a minute or two the combatants circled each other. They were both sure-footed on the bars, as though they sensed the gaps without needing to look. They kept clear of the opening in the center of the grille and Col beside it.

When Scarface launched forward with a roar, Riff remained poised until the very last moment, then ducked under his reaching arms and sprang to the side. She flung herself against the ring of Filthies, rebounded, somersaulted lightly on both hands, and flew through the air feetfirst. Her scything kick caught Scarface just above the kidneys.

Col winced at the savagery of the blow. Scarface coughed and doubled up but quickly recovered. He swiveled to face Riff as she went onto the attack.

She danced forward, feinting left and right. Scarface balled his fist and swung. A tremendous punch—if it had landed. But Riff caught his fist and deflected the punch over her shoulder, then hooked a foot round his ankles and overbalanced him with his own momentum. He ended up punching downward, driving his fist between the bars. For a moment his arm was trapped up to the armpit.

The Filthies cheered, and Riff responded with a bow. Very deliberately, she turned her back on Scarface and sauntered across to Col.

"It's all in the timing, see?" She squatted to talk to him. "Timing and technique. I use his own strength to defeat him."

What was she doing? The fight wasn't over. Scarface had freed his arm and was getting back on his feet.

Col opened his mouth to shout a warning—in the same instant that Scarface charged forward like a raging bull. He was aiming to knock Riff through the opening in the grille.

"Watch—!"

No need for the warning. Riff had been waiting for this very move. She pushed Col aside and burst into action.

Everything happened in a split-second blur. As Col sprawled sideways, Riff kicked off in a great leap across the opening. Scarface tried to skid to a halt—too late. He slid off the edge of the grille, twisted as he fell, and managed to catch on to the very last bar. He hung dangling over the void.

Riff ran back around the opening, knelt, and grabbed him by the wrists. She gave him a moment to contemplate the bubbling porridge below.

"Who wins?" she asked.

"You do."

"Who decides what happens to the boy?"

"You do."

She hauled him back up onto the bars, where he lay sullen and defeated. The Filthies unlinked arms. As the crowd began to disperse, Riff picked out half a dozen of them by name.

"Swale. Tobbs. Jarvie. Channa. Gart and Sess. Go find the other members of the Revolutionary Council. Tell them I'm calling a meeting now."

Col saw Greasy and Toothless slinking away, without waiting for Scarface. Toothless had something tucked under his arm—the book on mountains and volcanoes.

"Hey!" Col jumped to his feet. "That's not yours!"

Riff followed his pointing finger. "What?"

"It's *yours*," Col told her.

"How do you mean?"

"It's that book you wanted to borrow. I dropped it down the food chute for you."

"Yeah? Why would you do that?"

"As a present. I wrapped it up and drew a picture of you on the front." Col turned to Toothless. "Tell her."

Toothless gave a reluctant grunt of agreement.

"Bring it here." Riff snapped her fingers.

Toothless came forward and handed her the book. She opened it up and turned the pages. Col sensed a growing delight behind her severe expression.

"I thought you deserved it," he said. "Because you wanted to learn to read. You said you never had the chance."

"No, I never had the chance." She closed the book with a snap. "Okay, I'll argue your case with the Council." Suddenly, she was beaming from ear to ear. "Let's go."

28

Col followed Riff up ladders and along walkways. When they came to a narrow defile between gleaming, oiled machinery, she turned with a warning. "Move as I move."

The defile was a death trap, where huge pistons shot out and slammed across from side to side. Or it would have been a death trap, but for Riff's guidance. She took Col by the hand and pulled him forward in sudden jumps and halts.

"Now," she said. "Wait. Now. Wait. Now."

Riff's movements were as unpredictable as the pistons, but he learned to react to the pressure of her hand. Half a dozen times he barely escaped being crushed to a pulp.

"You gotta have fast reactions down here," she explained, when they were through. "That's why I beat Sculler so easy. He's gettin' too old. Reactions slow down after you turn twenty. Ain't no one here lives much past thirty."

Col remembered how young most of the Filthies were. It no longer seemed so strange that Riff was a leader at the age of fourteen.

He would have asked more, but Riff hushed him with her instructions for the next part of the journey. "Thick smoke now. We climb four ladders. When you get to the top of each ladder, run left on the platform, lean out, take a deep breath. Make it last while you climb. Got that?"

He nodded. Riff breathed in and clapped her hand over

mouth and nose. Col did the same. The smoke rose in billowing plumes of brown and gray, with flurries of red sparks.

For the next five minutes he concentrated on survival. The smoke blinded him and the sparks pricked his skin. Four times his lungs were ready to burst; four times he ran left and leaned out, gasping for air. He had to will himself to turn and plunge back in.

Not once did Riff glance over her shoulder to check on his progress. It was up to him to follow. There were no second chances in this world, he realized.

After the smoke and ladders they walked up a sloping ramp in the shadow of an immense cylindrical tank, like the one Col had seen before. The curving sides of this tank were covered by a kind of scaffolding, on which balanced a multitude of Filthies.

"What are they doing?" Col asked.

"Cookin' food. Heatin' water."

"How?"

"Against the sides of the boiler."

"It's a boiler?"

"Yeah. Hot enough to burn yer skin off."

There was a cry of "Look out!" as a metal pan came clattering down. It bounced from one level of scaffolding to another, passed Col and Riff, and disappeared into the depths below.

"Who did that?" hollered Riff.

A guilty face peered down from a level above. "Sorry. It was empty."

"Lucky for you."

Col shook his head. "What a madhouse!"

Riff transferred her anger to him. "Think so, do ya?"

"I mean, everyone living on top of each other. It's chaos."

"Phh! You don't see what's in front of yer eyes. Look again, Col-bert Porping-tine."

Col looked and saw the Filthies passing heated pans along from hand to hand. To change position they had to climb over one another on the scaffolding. Impossibly precarious! A hundred times it seemed that someone would burn themselves on the boiler or lose their footing or drop another pan—but nobody did. At the last minute there was always another Filthy to lend support, to catch an arm or grip a shoulder. The whole operation continued at amazing speed.

"Do you see now?" Riff demanded.

Col shook his head. It must be only by luck that there were no accidents. It surely couldn't be all calculated and intentional.

"We gotta cooperate *because* of livin' on top of each other," said Riff. "We gotta be better organized than your lot, else we'd never survive."

Col didn't want to see it, but in the end he did. There was a pattern to the chaos, a pattern so complicated it was almost beyond comprehension. The actions of every Filthy fitted in with the actions of everyone else. It was like a dance where the dancers were all perfectly practiced in their steps.

Once he'd seen it, he saw it everywhere. They moved on up through a series of floors where people were washing clothes, and he saw how some did the sorting, some the scrubbing, some the rinsing, some the hanging up to dry. Bundles of clothes flew back and forth through the air almost faster than the eye could see. The clothes were mere rags, but the system was incredibly slick and smooth.

He felt dizzy just from watching them. He could no more imagine being able to wash clothes like the Filthies than he could imagine being able to fight like Riff. Their abilities seemed superhuman.

After the laundry floors, Riff led him through a maze of zigzag pipes. She pointed to small nozzles that stuck out here and there.

"Don't get caught in front of these," she warned.

Avoiding the nozzles, they stepped high or crouched low or sometimes crawled flat on their bellies.

"What was that about?" he asked when they emerged.

"Steam. That's where your lot shoots steam at us."

Col remembered Sir Mormus's explanation for the steam. "To ginger you up."

"Don't be stupid!" Riff snapped. "They make us work by controllin' the food. All the steam does is slow us down. They do it 'cause they enjoy hurtin' us."

Col had no answer. "So why don't you stay away from the nozzles?"

"Ain't you worked it out yet? There's nowhere down here that's not dangerous." Riff's eyes flashed. "You know your problem?"

"What?"

"You only look at one thing at a time. If you want to survive, keep yer mind wide and yer senses open. Don't concentrate—be ready in all directions."

For the rest of the journey Col tried to keep his mind wide and his senses open. Perhaps he improved a little.

Climbing higher, they came to boxlike frames of girders and struts. Every surface was slippery with gobbets of yellow grease. Col looked ahead and saw where they had to cross from frame to frame—and the only bridge was a single girder.

"I can't do it," he groaned.

"You can. Take a run-up. Watch me."

Riff accelerated toward the girder, held her arms out to the sides, bent at the knees, and skated across. The grease under her feet created an ideal sliding surface. On the other side she caught hold of a strut and brought herself to a stop.

"The faster the better," she encouraged Col. "Don't look down."

He had no choice. He ran full speed, extended his arms, bent at the knees, and skated. Only momentum kept him upright. He tilted to the right, corrected to the left, overcorrected to the right. Too far! The gulf gaped below him.

Just in time he caught hold of the strut.

No word of approval from Riff. She turned immediately on her heel and set off again.

Overhead, huge beams rocked back and forth to a mighty rhythm. They must be close to the underside of Bottom Deck, Col guessed, though nothing was clearly visible in the murk.

"Not far to our meeting place now," Riff told him. "The rest of the Council should be there by now."

"Already?" One small corner of Col's mind remained capable of calculation. "How could they get there before us?"

"Oh, they'll have taken the shortcuts."

"What did we take?"

"The long way round. Shortcuts'd be too hard for ya."

So this was the *easy* route? Col's mind boggled at the thought.

29

The meeting place was an outsize hammock slung like a spider's web in the space between two enormous flywheels. Rotating at high speed, the flywheels threw off a wind all around, but the space between was as still as the eye of a storm. Col had grown used to shouting to be heard above the constant noise of Below. Only in the meeting place was it possible to talk in a normal voice.

At Riff's prompting he leaped forward into the hammock and rolled to the bottom. The members of the Council were ranged along one side, leaning back comfortably, feet braced against the ropes. They stared down at him with inquisitorial eyes.

"Stay where you are," snapped a tattooed girl with close-cropped hair as he struggled to rise.

There were six of them including Riff. They were all similar in build, thin and wiry and muscular. Most seemed to be in their late teens or early twenties, except for one woman in a red headband, who could have been thirty.

A boy with a bandaged leg ordered Col to explain what he was doing Below. It seemed that the Revolutionary Council already knew the story of his previous encounters with Riff. He told them about dropping the book down the food chute, the fight with Lumbridge, then falling down the chute himself. They listened in silence, only snorting with amazement at some of the details. Riff passed the book around for the Council members to examine.

Then they shot questions at him, which he answered as best he could. The questions came from them all equally, and Col had the impression that no one outranked anyone else.

"So you think Riff owes you a favor," said Red Headband at last. "What favor do you want?"

"To go back up on the Upper Decks."

"Yeah, and how do you expect us to do that?" asked a boy with a high, domed forehead and cold, assessing eyes.

Riff spoke up. "There is a way, Shiv."

"For him but not for us?"

"For us when they want new Menials." Riff shrugged. "You know how they use a hook to haul us up. So they could do the same with him. All we gotta do is put him where they can see him."

"Right." The boy with the bandaged leg nodded. "Somewhere high, near one of their cages."

"Okay, we could," said a young man with a stubbled chin. "I still don't see why we should."

Riff exchanged glances with him. "I made a promise, Padder."

Red Headband cocked an eyebrow. "Nothing personal in this, is there?" She looked from Riff to Col and back again. "You and him?"

"Course not," Riff bit back at once.

The young man called Padder scowled. "I heard you already fought Sculler for him. You done him enough of a favor."

"I fought Sculler 'cause he refused my orders," said Riff. "That was for me."

Red Headband grinned. "Mind, he's not bad-lookin'. Except them stupid clothes. I daresay, if ya took off his clothes . . ."

"Shut yer face, Fossie!" Riff was furious.

Padder growled threateningly. "Yeah, shut up. Looks has nothin' to do with it. He's a one of 'em."

Again he exchanged glances with Riff. *There's something between them,* Col thought, and his heart did an odd sort of flip-flop. Were they somehow partnered? Yet Riff was only fourteen. On the Upper Decks no one could think of getting engaged until eighteen, or married until twenty-one.

"Lettin' him live is enough of a favor," Padder said. "Let him find out what it's like to live down Below."

Col grimaced. "I wouldn't last long. You might as well kill me straight off."

The girl with the tattooed arms and close-cropped hair spoke up. "That's true. He wouldn't last a day down here."

There was a moment of silence. Then the boy with the bandaged leg made a suggestion. "We oughta trade him. If they want him up there, they gotta give us somethin' in return."

"Like what, Zeb?" asked the tattooed girl.

"Dunno. More food. Less steam."

"Phuh!" The cold-eyed boy called Shiv made a spitting sound. "They'll go back on their word, soon as they get what they want. They'll punish us with more steam, less food."

"We could make the talks last a long time," said Zeb, no longer so confident.

"Yeah, and they'll make the punishment last a hundred times longer," said Shiv. "We can't trust 'em."

Col spoke up. "You can trust *me*."

Fossie looked at him curiously "What can you do?"

"I'll be supreme commander one day. Then I'll make it an order: no steam ever again."

They all burst out laughing.

"You don't believe me?" Col appealed to Riff, who was laughing along with the rest. "I told you, remember? I'm next in line after my grandfather."

But Riff wouldn't back him up. "When? Ten, twenty years?"

"Maybe. When my grandfather retires."

"And we'll all be dead by then," said Padder.

Col was about to say, *Don't be ridiculous,* until he remembered that no one Below lived much past the age of thirty.

"Anyway, we have bigger plans," said the tattooed girl.

"Hush, Dunga." The others frowned and shook their heads at her.

Then they began whispering among themselves, in voices too low for Col to hear. *Deciding what to do with me,* he thought, and his throat tightened.

Finally, there was a general nodding of heads.

"Okay, it's agreed." Riff addressed Col. "We'll help you get back to the Upper Decks, on one condition."

"What?"

"You have to help one of us get up there too."

This was unexpected. "How?"

"You go to a food chute afterwards and let down a rope."

Col fumbled for excuses. "I don't know where there's a rope that long."

"You'll find one," said Riff.

"What would this person do?"

"Explore the Upper Decks," said the boy called Shiv.

"Be a spy, you mean?"

"That's our business."

Col didn't trust them. What had they been whispering about before? What were their bigger plans?

"Only one person?" he asked.

"Yeah."

He pointed to Riff. "Her, then."

"Exactly what we were thinkin'." Riff grinned. "Me."

Her willingness increased his suspicions. "But two weeks ago . . . all you wanted was to get back Below."

"'Cause I thought I was stuck up there. It's different now."

"Will you do it?" Shiv demanded. "Yes or no?"

Col nodded. "Yes."

Riff leaned forward, eyes boring into his. "Give us your word. Give *me* your word."

"I give you my word."

"Okay." She extended a hand and helped him to his feet. He stood swaying as the hammock rocked back and forth.

"Let's hope you don't regret this, Riff," said Dunga.

"He'll do it," she answered. "You'll see."

30

The plan was simple: to put Col on display where he could be spotted from above. The officers on watch would do the rest. The six Council members led Col to the nearest viewing bay.

Higher and higher they climbed, through a zone of foul-smelling gas. Huge dark shapes moved in the fumes: cogged wheels, interlocking shafts, and sliding rods. Above them Col could see the roof of Below, which was also the underneath of Bottom Deck.

They went up the side of a greasy black chimney, dodged a cascade of boiling water, and climbed a ladder to a platform at the top. The platform was the only thing that stayed static in a world of moving parts.

"It's up there." Riff pointed and spoke into Col's ear above the noise. "Where they lower the hook."

"Can't see it."

"Nah, not yet. You go up on that."

As she spoke, a great metal beam rose in front of them. It swept past the platform with a mighty *swoosh*, spraying drop-lets of oil in its wake.

"That?"

"Yeah, you won't fall off. Pretend you're escapin' from us."

"We'll shout like we're chasin' you," added Fossie in Col's other ear.

In the next moment the beam plunged down with a further *swoosh*.

"Lock your hands together." Riff demonstrated. "Like this."

Col interlaced the fingers of both hands.

"Now arms above your head."

No sooner had he raised his arms than the Filthies took hold of him and swung him off the ground.

"Hey!" he protested.

The beam was coming up again. They rocked him back, then flung him forward as if tossing a log.

Swoosh!

He sailed helplessly though the air—then crashed against the ascending beam. As his locked hands looped over a projecting spur of metal, he was jerked so suddenly upward that his stomach was left behind.

Up, up, up, passing dark shapes in the fumes. He almost blacked out from the acceleration. The beam soared to the top of its arc, then reversed direction and dropped back down. For a second time Col's stomach stayed behind.

He caught a blurred impression of the Council members watching from the platform. He went past them on the way down, then again on the way back up.

He twisted his head as he approached the top of the arc once more. Yes, there was the wire cage suspended beneath Bottom Deck. Inside, an officer stared down through the mesh of the floor.

Had he spotted Col? The beam reversed direction before Col could call out for help.

"Remember yer promise!" cried Riff as he went past.

Down again, then up again. Now the officer had disappeared. Was that good or bad?

Col was starting to feel nauseous. He had no way to return to the platform: If he wasn't hooked up from above, he would be stuck on the beam forever. Or at least until he let go and fell to his death . . .

Then he noticed that the Filthies were shaking their fists, howling abuse at him. He was so dizzy it took him a few seconds to understand that they were putting on a show.

Raising his eyes, he saw that half a dozen officers had now appeared inside the viewing bay. They held out a long rod through the open door of the cage. And something was being lowered toward him on a cable, some shining, curved device: the hook!

He never grasped exactly how it worked. It must have been more like Mr. Gibber's tweaker than a simple form of hook. He only heard a snap like a trap springing shut. At the top of his arc he was suddenly gripped round the waist in a ring of metal.

Then the beam went down, the hook took his weight, and his interlaced hands were left holding nothing but air.

The officers hauled him up a few feet at a time. He heard the rattle of a ratchet and a voice calling: "Pull! And—pull! And—pull!"

He'd survived. That was all he could think as he rotated on the end of the cable, head down, feet up. The Council members had finished their pretense of pursuing him and were no longer visible.

Louder and louder came the sounds of the ratchet and the officer's voice. Then strong hands clamped round his arms and legs. He was pulled up over the edge and onto the wire mesh floor of the viewing bay.

With another metallic snap the hook opened to release him.

He rolled over, eyes filling with tears of relief. The officers stood round in a respectful half circle. He wanted to blurt out words of heartfelt gratitude. But he owed it to Sir Mormus to maintain an attitude of appropriate dignity.

"Thank you," he said. "I shall recommend your prompt action to my grandfather. Who spotted me first?"

They made no reply. What was wrong with them? Col blinked and took another look.

The expression in their eyes wasn't respect, but revulsion.

31

Of course, he was dirty. His clothes were stained with oil and grease, his hands were black with smoke and grime, and his face no doubt the same. Perhaps he smelled of all those things as well. But what made the officers recoil was something more than dirt.

"Did you see me get away from the Filthies?" he asked. "I was too smart for them. Did you see them chasing me?"

No one said anything to the contrary. They must have seen the Filthies howling and shaking their fists. Yet the expression in their eyes remained unchanged.

Col realized then. It wasn't the way he'd returned, but the very thought of where he'd been: down Below, down among the Filthies.

He rose to his feet, and they retreated a pace farther away. It was as though he carried some contagious disease.

"You fell down the food chute," said one officer.

"Ah. Yes." What had been happening in the time he'd been Below? "You know about that?"

"Yes. Sir." The "sir" sounded like an afterthought. "The supreme commander has been conducting interviews with all concerned."

"He'll be on his way now," said a second officer. "I sent a messenger to tell him you'd been sighted."

"He never expected to see you again," added a third.

"We'll take you to meet him now," said the officer who'd spoken first.

In silence they escorted him up from the viewing bay. This was a different viewing bay from the one Col knew, but the ladder and hatch were similar, and the canvas tent, and the cordon fence with flashing orange lights. Even the coal mounds and iron piers looked much the same.

They had walked only a short distance when the leading officer called a halt. "Here they come now," he said.

Advancing along Bottom Deck was a party of a dozen officers, led by the towering figure of Sir Mormus Porpentine. Col ran a hand through his hair and smoothed down his clothes. The only effect was to leave new marks on his shirt and jacket.

Sir Mormus's face was set and grim, and his brow was like thunder. Ignoring Col, he addressed himself to the officers from the viewing bay. "Well?"

"We hooked him up off a beam, sir."

"He appeared to be escaping, sir. From a pack of Filthies, sir."

Sir Mormus drew himself up to even greater height. "Good. Then return to your duties. All of you." He flicked a hand toward Col. "You come with me."

Col could feel the officers' stares of disapproval burning into his back as he went off with his grandfather. Sir Mormus didn't spare him a glance, but stomped straight across puddles, coal grit, and patches of oil.

Col attempted an explanation. "It was Lumbridge who pushed me down the food chute, sir."

Sir Mormus snorted. "What were you doing on Bottom Deck, boy?"

"I, er, followed them down, sir. The Squellingham twins and their group. I suspected they were up to no good."

"No, they followed you."

"That's what *they* say, sir. But—"

"Don't trifle with me, boy. You were the one who'd been taken to Bottom Deck before. Only you could have known the numbers to unlock the door."

Col fell silent as his explanation collapsed in a heap.

They left Bottom Deck by a door labeled DOOR 21. Sir Mormus led the way to a steam elevator nearby.

"Listen, boy," he said, as the platform started up. "We're going to the Executive Chamber. There's an imperial inquiry already underway. When you appear, Sir Wisley will turn it into a trial. You'll be on trial, I'll be on trial, and the Porpentine family will be on trial. So *I'll* do the explaining. You back up everything I say. Understand?"

"Yes, sir. But what if—"

"Not another word."

At Fifty-first Deck the elevator puffed and wheezed to a halt. They passed through a screen of wooden swing doors and green velvet curtains. Col had never been to the Executive Chamber before, but he knew it was where the most important decisions for the future of *Worldshaker* were made.

He understood the situation he was in now. Sir Mormus would defend him because the reputation of the Porpentines depended on it. But from his grandfather's point of view it would have been better and simpler if Col had stayed lost down Below.

They walked a hundred yards along a corridor and came

to a door with panels of polished oak. Sir Mormus flung it open and marched in.

The Executive Chamber swam before Col's gaze. Somber portraits . . . busts in niches . . . plush green carpet . . . a semicircle of tables. Queen Victoria and Prince Albert were seated on their imperial thrones, flanked by members of the Executive. Dr. Blessamy stood in the center of the semicircle and appeared to have been giving evidence.

Col took a deep breath as every eye in the room turned on him.

32

"**E**xtraordinary," muttered Prince Albert. "Extraordinary. *Most* extraordinary."

Col was painfully aware of the stains on his school uniform, the grime on his face and hands.

Queen Victoria frowned under her massive crown. She swiveled her head a few degrees toward Dr. Blessamy. "Thank you, headmaster. You can step down now."

Col recognized several members of the Executive: Chief Helmsman Turbot, Rear Admiral Haugh, Lord Fefferley, and Sir Wisley Squellingham. Sir Wisley sat at the end of the semicircle with a stack of papers on the table before him. He smiled to see Col, showing the gold fillings in his teeth. It was not a pleasant smile.

"Please tell us, Sir Mormus." Queen Victoria swiveled her head back in the opposite direction. "How did your grandson get up from Below?"

She seemed to know about Col's reappearance, but not the details of the rescue. Col realized that Sir Mormus must have been at the inquiry when the summons to the viewing bay arrived.

Now Sir Mormus propelled Col forward to the spot vacated by Dr. Blessamy and positioned himself behind. His account of Col's rescue made it sound like a heroic escape: His grandson had deliberately climbed to the highest point below the viewing bay, fighting off all Filthy attempts to drag him down.

Col only half listened. He was distracted when he noticed other people at the back of the chamber. There in a row of chairs sat Hythe, Pugh, Lumbridge, Fefferley, Haugh, and Flarrow. Dr. Blessamy stood next to them, and five officers next to him.

Sir Mormus concluded with a flourish. "All observed by many witnesses, Your Majesty. I can bring them up to testify, if you wish."

"No, no, no," Sir Wisley jumped in. "Not necessary. Not relevant. Let's keep our eyes on the main issue." His own eyes darted rapidly in every direction. "Let's hear the officers confirm what the boys have told us."

Queen Victoria winced under the weight of her crown. "Very well. But first, let Master Colbert hear what the boys have said against him." She extended a hand toward her consort. "If you would care to summarize, my dear."

"Humph." Prince Albert pulled on alternate ends of his mustache. "School excursion. Master Colbert and six school friends. He opened a locked door to Bottom Deck. Secret numbers."

Sir Wisley was eager to elaborate. "They followed him down because they were suspicious. They knew they were doing wrong, but their actions were not nearly so wrong as his." He inclined his head respectfully. "Excuse the interruption, Your Highness."

"Yes, yes, I was going to say all of that," Prince Albert huffed. "Follow down. Suspicious. Wrong. Just so, just so. Then Master Colbert opened a thing called a food chute. Threw something down. Then the officers came."

"Because the boys called them," Sir Wisley broke in again. "Pardon me, Your Highness. Then, when the officers ran up, Porpentine jumped down the food chute."

"That's not true!" Col protested. "I never—"

A heavy hand clamped down over his shoulder. "Wait, boy."

Sir Mormus exuded confidence and authority. Col couldn't imagine how he could be so confident.

"If we could hear from the officers themselves, Your Imperial Majesty?" Sir Wisley suggested.

Queen Victoria agreed. "Stand forward, please, officers."

The five officers advanced from the back of the chamber. Sir Mormus held his place with Col, so the officers formed a line in front of them.

"We were on duty in Area Seventeen," said one of the five. "We heard cries of 'Over here! Over here!'"

"Many cries?" Sir Wisley interrupted.

"Yes, sir."

"So. My sons and their friends. And what did you see when you ran up?"

The officer had taken on the role of spokesman for the rest. "Two boys were fighting beside the food chute, sir."

"Which two?"

The officer turned to point. "Master Colbert. And Master Lumbridge. The others were watching."

Sir Wisley drummed with his fingers on the table. "Would you say that Master Lumbridge was trying to stop Master Colbert from jumping down the food chute?"

"I couldn't say, sir. They were wrestling back and forth."

Sir Mormus spoke up suddenly. "Podwin, isn't it? Petty Officer Podwin?"

Podwin swung around to face his supreme commander. "Yes, sir."

Sir Mormus's tone was almost fatherly. "Well, Podwin. You couldn't say that Master Lumbridge was trying to hold my grandson back?"

"No, sir."

Sir Mormus stepped closer, towering over the petty officer. "Could it be that Master Lumbridge was trying to force my grandson forward? Deliberately trying to push him down the food chute?"

There was a gasp from all round the chamber. Podwin gulped and goggled like a stranded fish.

"Speak up, man," rumbled Sir Mormus. "I can't hear you."

"This is outrageous," Sir Wisley objected. "Lumbridge wouldn't do that."

"Unless he'd been told to." Sir Mormus addressed himself to Queen Victoria and Prince Albert. "By some boy who had an interest in getting rid of a future supreme commander. Some boy who would have a clear path to the position once my grandson was gone. Or should I say, some two boys?"

"No!" squawked Hythe and Pugh in the same breath.

Sir Mormus turned to Col. "Did you try to jump down that chute, Colbert?"

"No, sir."

"Did Master Lumbridge try to push you down? Look your queen in the eyes and tell the truth. Did Master Lumbridge try to push you down?"

Col had a momentary image of Professor Twillip saying, "Truth is the most important of all virtues, Colbert." But this was no time for ethics . . . and anyway, he'd never been sure exactly what Lumbridge had intended.

He repressed a twinge of conscience, looked Queen Victoria straight in the eyes, and said, "Yes, he did, sir."

There was a long silence. Had he convinced them? New, radiating furrows appeared on Queen Victoria's brow, until she seemed to be in pain. The members of the Executive were stunned, some nodding and some shaking their heads. Sir Wisley ran a finger round the inside of his high wing collar.

It was Prince Albert who finally broke the silence. "This is a very serious accusation, Porpentine. We've never heard an accusation like this before. Have we, my dear?"

"Never," said Queen Victoria. "Dreadful, dreadful."

Col sensed that the tide might be turning in his favor. But Sir Wisley wasn't finished yet.

"His word against theirs," he said. "It comes down to a question of character. Who'd be most likely to tell the truth? I think we're forgetting one small fact here."

He rose to his feet behind the table. Everyone's attention was upon him. His sharp nose stabbed like a beak in Col's direction.

"What was the thing he threw down the food chute? What was it he dropped to his friends the Filthies?"

A ripple of shock ran around the room. "His friends the Filthies" was a deliberate provocation.

Col looked at his grandfather. Surely he had to claim they were all lying? But Sir Mormus's expression provided no clue.

"Well, Colbert," said Queen Victoria. "What was this thing?"

Col was about to say, *It never existed,* when Sir Mormus boomed out, "I gave it to him."

The shock of a moment ago was nothing compared to the shock now.

"I don't understand," said Queen Victoria faintly.

"It's very simple, Your Majesty. He was on a mission for me. I gave it to him and told him the numbers to unlock the door."

"What? Why?" Sir Wisley snarled as he saw his prey slipping away.

Sir Mormus spoke to the queen alone. "I can't explain in front of these people, Your Majesty." His gesture took in the five officers, the six boys, and Dr. Blessamy. "Only the Executive."

"Hmm." Queen Victoria pursed her lips. "Sensitive information. Executive only. Very well. Everyone else leave the room."

Dr. Blessamy left first, followed by the Squellingham group, then the officers. Nobody had asked Col to leave, so he stayed.

Sir Mormus cleared his throat and spoke very slowly, very deliberately. "I gave my grandson a sealed container filled with a special drug. It would have shattered at the bottom of the food chute and vaporized in a cloud. The Filthies would have breathed it in."

"But the purpose, man!" huffed Prince Albert. "What was it for?"

"To keep them awake, Your Highness. The drug was a powerful stimulant. Keep them awake to work longer hours."

"Longer hours?" murmured Rear Admiral Haugh.

"An unofficial experiment," Sir Mormus continued. "As the Executive is aware, the Prussian and Austrian juggernauts have recently been traveling as fast as *Worldshaker*. Since our engines are still the biggest and the best, I believe they must be working their Filthies harder. Ours are sleeping too much and slowing us down. We have to find a way of getting more work out of them."

Sir Wisley sneered. "With a drug?"

"Yes." Sir Mormus was solid as a rock.

Col couldn't imagine that anyone accepted Sir Mormus's story. It was too obviously ridiculous. But only Sir Wisley was willing to call his bluff.

"So. Your grandson would have fallen into this cloud, this vaporized drug?"

Col knew it was up to him. "I did," he said. "It made me cough."

Sir Wisley turned on Col with a glint of gold fillings. "And speeded you up, I suppose?"

"Yes." Col had a flash of inspiration. "I was so fast the Filthies couldn't catch me. That was how I climbed up through the machinery."

"I don't believe it."

"Do you doubt his word? Do you doubt my word?" Sir Mormus lowered his brow like a bull about to charge.

"Yes."

"Are you challenging me?" Sir Mormus's voice rose to a blustering roar. "Do you challenge your supreme commander?"

"I don't believe it."

"How dare you!"

The chamber was in an uproar. The head of the Porpentines and the head of the Squellinghams confronted each other face-to-face. Neither could stare the other down.

Like Riff and Scarface, thought Col. *Only this quarrel won't be settled by fighting.*

In fact it was settled by Queen Victoria. She rose from her throne with her hands over her ears—or perhaps she was just trying to ease the weight of her crown. "I have a headache," she said.

Prince Albert jumped up too, and studied her with concern. "Your forehead is all in lines, my dear."

"I don't know who to believe," she moaned. "It's impossible."

Prince Albert turned to the room at large. "We'll all have headaches soon," he said. "I declare this inquiry over."

"But what's the decision?" Sir Wisley demanded.

"Nothing." Prince Albert's upraised palm forbade further discussion. "Status quo."

Sir Wisley's gaze flickered to the keys of office on Sir Mormus's chest. "Not for me, Porpentine," he hissed. "I'm only just beginning."

33

Thirty minutes later the extended family of Porpentines gathered in the Northumberland Room. They sat at tables laid out for dinner, but no one was thinking of food. When Sir Mormus entered with Col, he immediately dismissed the Menials and their supervisor, then closed all the doors.

The Porpentines had the look of people anticipating bad news. Col guessed that rumors about him were already in circulation. He'd had time to wash off the dirt and change his clothes, yet the men still scowled at him, while the ladies wrinkled their noses as though there were a smell in the air.

Sir Mormus stood with legs firmly planted and hands folded over his belly, back to his full pomp and dignity. He recounted the story of what had happened according to his explanations before the inquiry. All other questions were left unanswered.

"Now you know as much as you need to know," he boomed. "Have faith in what I have told you. For the good of our family. For the survival of our family."

The Porpentines gasped at the word "survival."

Oblett Porpentine raised a hand to speak. "But you said the inquiry was over. They accepted your explanation."

Sir Mormus snorted. "The *official* inquiry is over. My explanation wasn't *rejected*. But people will talk. The Executive will plot. Sir Wisley will see to that."

"What can he prove, though?" asked Rumpley Porpentine.

"He can create doubts and make people think too much." Sir Mormus was visibly controlling himself now. "He won't challenge me about my grandson, but he'll try to swing the Executive against me on small decisions, until they get used to not following my lead. He needs seven votes to bring on a no-confidence motion against me. Bassimor, Frake, and Postlefrith will vote with him, and he'll work to win over Fefferley, Haugh, and Turbot."

The Porpentines looked blank and bemused. It appeared that no one understood the consequences of a no-confidence motion.

"But doesn't it depend on the queen?" asked Leath Porpentine.

"And she always does what you tell her," added Morpice Porpentine.

Sir Mormus was breathing heavily through his nostrils. "She's in the habit of doing what I tell her, but she's also in the habit of following tradition."

Still they hadn't understood. Sir Mormus's composure cracked completely.

"Fools!" he roared. "If I lose the confidence of the Executive, Queen Victoria will replace me. Sir Wisley will become the new supreme commander."

Horrified cries of "No!" and "Impossible!" echoed round the room.

"Yes," said Sir Mormus. "Sir Wisley instead of me."

Col couldn't believe it either. His grandfather as supreme commander was part of the natural order of things. He felt the weight of the family's angry stares upon him.

"If he wasn't the nominated successor . . . ," someone muttered.

"Dragging us down," said someone else.

"What if . . . ," another voice began.

It was Morpice Porpentine who pointed at Col and came out with what they were all thinking. "Can't we disown him?"

There were nods of agreement on all sides.

"We don't want to associate with someone who's been Below," said an uncle from the Leath Porpentine branch.

Only Orris and Quinnea objected. Orris groaned and shook his head, while Quinnea let out a long, quavering wail.

"You could nominate your other grandson as successor," Morpice suggested.

All eyes turned to the solemn little figure of Antrobus, seated beside Gillabeth. Gillabeth patted him on the back to make him sit up even straighter.

"No." Sir Mormus raised a hand to quell further discussion. "To disown my eldest grandson now would be seen as an admission of guilt. My reputation would be ruined along with his. The die is cast. We stand our ground."

Grandmother Ebnolia nodded her birdlike head. "And you'll counteract Sir Wisley on the Executive?"

"I will."

Morpice Porpentine still wasn't convinced. "But what do we say when people . . . you know . . ."

"You outface them." Sir Mormus thrust out his chin. "You ignore them. Or you speak up for him. Praise him, be proud of him, and express complete confidence in him. Let no one suspect a moment of doubt."

There was a long silence as the Porpentines digested Sir

Mormus's strategy. Col looked down at his feet and wished that the floor would open and swallow him up.

Then Ebnolia spoke again. "So he goes back to school tomorrow, as though nothing ever happened?"

"Precisely."

A hand rose with another question. Col was surprised to see that it belonged to Gillabeth. Normally, his sister was far too proper to put herself forward in a gathering of adults.

The hand remained aloft until Sir Mormus deigned to notice it. "Well?"

"Sir, would it be a good idea to have someone at school to keep a watch on him? Report on any trouble brewing?"

"Who?"

"I'd do it, sir. If you enrolled me at Dr. Blessamy's Academy."

Ebnolia tut-tutted disapprovingly and Quinnea let out a little snuffle of dismay. But the general mood of the room was in favor.

"Only for the sake of the family, sir," Gillabeth added.

After due consideration, Sir Mormus agreed with the general mood. "So be it. We shall make the arrangements."

Gillabeth lowered her eyes with an air of duty performed and virtue vindicated.

Then Sir Mormus strode to the doors and flung them open. "Serve dinner!" he called out.

Col went and took his seat at his grandfather's table. On all sides people were discussing the situation in animated voices. But no one wanted to discuss it with Col. He almost wished they'd turn on him with their blame and accusations. But no one wanted to have anything to do with him.

34

Col's weekend was a social agony. On Saturday he went with his mother and grandmother to a knitting bee, where Menial servants knitted for charity while their mistresses chatted over tea and scones. Quinnea was no more eager to attend than Col, but Grandmother Ebnolia insisted. Sitting in a circle with the other ladies, Ebnolia kept steering the conversation onto Col's successes at school. Never before had he been required to do so much talking, going through every result of every test in which he'd top-scored. Ebnolia was effusive in her praise and confident he would soon be first in every subject. Knowing how Mr. Gibber decided the marks made it even more of a mockery in Col's ears.

Later there was an evening of parlor games with the Rumpley Porpentines. Adults and children from all branches of the family were present, along with selected guests from other families. I Spy was the main game played, in a room where every possible object had been "spied" a hundred times before. The adult Porpentines smiled at Col and made a point of applauding his correct guesses.

It was a polite façade, and they kept it up perfectly. Yet Col was always aware of their secret shame and underlying hostility. He looked across at his father and began to understand the inward torture he'd endured for so many years. Every pleasant word was like the twist of a knife.

On Sunday there was a subtle change. The stories about Col must have spread, and the Porpentines were no longer the only ones who knew the secret. Still no one spoke out openly, yet there was a wariness in the way the other families looked at him. He sensed it in a morning social visit to the Trumpingtons and an afternoon social visit to the Jessicles. But the worst was a supper party at the Paramoughs'.

It was a party to celebrate the decoration of the Paramoughs' new lounge room. Everyone admired the huge wall mirrors, gilded cornices, and frescoed ceiling. Menials with trays kept the guests supplied with food and drink.

As the throng circulated, Col stayed close to Ebnolia or Sir Mormus or both. He was conscious of being watched, his every action noted and examined. It was as though he were still coated in grease and grime. The moment he turned, the watchers looked the other way.

When people came up to talk, Ebnolia included him in the conversation. They talked of recent news, of children and families, social and public events. But there was always a silence around Friday's events, the day when he'd fallen Below. He was sure they were all deliberately steering clear of it.

He tried to follow his grandparents' lead and outface the look in people's eyes. He would blot that Friday out of existence. But he made a serious blunder toward the end of the supper party.

It happened when a piece of the cupcake he was eating broke off and dropped to the floor. Quick as a flash he bent down and retrieved it. It was an instantaneous reaction—like the reactions of the Filthies in their deadly, dangerous environment. But it was not proper here.

He realized what he'd done wrong even as he straightened up with the cake in his hand. There was an "Ah!" of indrawn breath from around the room, and a pause in the flow of conversation.

Of course it wasn't for a Porpentine to clean up after himself! Of course he should have waited for a Menial to do it! Of course, of course, of course!

Ebnolia deflected attention by snapping at the nearest Menial. "You, come here. At once. Stay alert." She made it appear that the Menial had been slow to respond. "My grandson will have something to say to you."

Col took his cue and addressed the Menial in a loud, stern voice. "Be quicker next time. You shouldn't need to be called. Put out your hand." The Menial put out a hand, and Col deposited the cake into his open palm. "Now go. Out of my sight."

Even as he spoke, he seemed to hear himself like another person. His tyrannical tone sounded unreal and unconvincing.

"As I was saying . . . ," Sir Mormus resumed.

The moment had passed. But Col had no heart for making small talk anymore.

So this is how it will be, he reflected. His future seemed to stretch out ahead in an infinity of wretchedness. He would be always acting a role, while everyone pretended to carry on as normal. He would know what people were really thinking . . . and they would know he knew . . . yet nobody would ever speak of it aloud. He was locked in this strange twilight state forever.

By the end of the supper party he just wanted to scream. Instead he hurried to his room and flung himself on his bed.

It was a relief to turn his mind to that other world of

Below, where fast reactions were the difference between life and death. He remembered his journey with Riff and her amazing acrobatic skills.

But that memory led to other, less pleasant memories. He recalled the meeting of the Revolutionary Council, where he'd promised to lower a rope for her to climb up. The tattooed girl called Dunga had said, *Let's hope you don't regret this,* and Riff had answered, *He'll do it.* But he still hadn't done it. . . .

What would she think of him now? He couldn't tell her what had happened on his return, how everything had become so much more difficult.

And there was another memory from the Council meeting. In his mind's eye he saw the glances Riff and Padder had exchanged when Fossie had said Col wasn't bad-looking. There was a connection between them, no doubt about it.

He groaned. He knew he ought to keep his promise. Professor Twillip had always taught that a man's word was his bond, with countless examples from the ancient Greeks and Romans. But surely the ancient Greeks and Romans had never had to deal with a problem like this.

He *couldn't* just walk down to the food chute and lower a rope. Perhaps later, when the situation had settled down . . .

35

On Monday Col dawdled to school with a sinking sensation in the pit of his stomach. He took so long on the way that the bell was ringing by the time he approached the entrance arch. But it wasn't an ordinary start to the school day. Instead of streaming up the ramps to their classrooms, the pupils were forming up in class groups in the yard. Teachers barked orders and tried to tidy their classes into compact squares.

Col went across to stand with 4A. The Squellingham group didn't notice him until Fefferley let out a sudden squawk. Then they stared at him in silent amazement.

They never expected to see me back at school, Col thought grimly.

"Quiet! Quiet!" shouted Mr. Dandrum, the deputy principal. "Dr. Blessamy will address you now."

Dr. Blessamy must have mounted a set of portable steps, because he stood head and shoulders above the throng in the yard.

"Dear, dear boys and girls," he began. "Those of you who *are* dear. This is a sad day for your old headmaster. I have to tell you about an incident which . . . an incident that . . . in short, *that* kind of incident. A dropping-down. I'm sure I don't have to say any more."

He pulled out a large white handkerchief and mopped his forehead. "After all my years of devotion to our academy.

Every one of you, a sacred trust. And now . . . in the autumn of my . . . autumnal years . . ."

He broke off, blew his nose into his handkerchief, then dabbed around his eyes with it.

"It is not for me to pass judgment. But someone has gone where they should not have gone. Someone has seen what they should not have seen. Dear boys and girls, be on your guard against lowering influences. Avoid them like . . . er . . . things to be avoided."

His eyes roamed over the assembly, yet always managed to miss looking at Col.

"We must maintain our reputation. We must live pure lives and think pure thoughts. Your teachers will be your role models, and I will be *their* role model. Never forget our school motto: Loyalty, Integrity, and . . . the other one."

Col wondered whether the students had already heard the story. Did they know which pupil they were being warned against?

When classes began, half an hour late, Mr. Gibber launched into a campaign against lowering influences.

"We shall follow our headmaster's example, or my name's not Bartrim Gibber. That's *Mr.* Gibber to you, 4A." He stood at the front of the class with his hands behind his back. "Are we all ready to think pure thoughts? I shall be your role model. Like this." He put on an expression like a half-dazed sheep. "Start thinking, everyone. That goes for you too, Nebblethwaite."

There was silence around the classroom as the pupils tried out a variety of facial expressions.

"Good, good." Mr. Gibber cracked his knuckles. "Only pure thoughts. None of the other kind. If I suspected any of *those . . ."* He went to his cane rack, selected three canes, and laid them out side by side on his desk. "That should take care of all possibilities. My Number Three, Number Seven, and Number Thirteen. Now. Is anyone in this classroom thinking those other thoughts?"

There was a general shaking of heads. Mr. Gibber homed in on a boy in the front row.

"What about you, Snellshott? A bit uncertain, are you?"

"No, sir."

"Melstruther?"

"No, sir."

"What are *you* thinking, Hegglenock?"

"The same thoughts as you, sir."

"The same as me, the same as me." Mr. Gibber seemed highly delighted. "Is anyone not thinking the same as me?"

He picked up one of his canes and swished it through the air. Faster and faster until it was no more than a blur.

"Because I'd have to drive out those other thoughts, wouldn't I? Nasty little ideas! Dirty pictures in the mind! Not in my classroom! No, sir!"

He began dancing back and forth, shooting sharp glances in every direction.

"Do you know what I'd do to those thoughts, Prewitt? Do you know what I'd do, Clatterick? I'd beat them into oblivion! Ob-liv-ee-un!"

He darted suddenly into the aisle between the desks of the Squellingham group and stopped right next to Col. He wasn't looking at Col, yet Col had become the center of everyone's attention.

"Disgusting, shameful thoughts. Filthiness, filthiness,

such filthy filthiness." Mr. Gibber raised his left hand and glared at it. "If this was the hand of a boy having impure thoughts, do you know what I'd do? I'd teach him a lesson he wouldn't forget! No mercy! I wouldn't think twice!"

He placed his hand flat on Col's desk and swung at it with his cane.

"Take that! Ow!"

He jumped back and waggled his fingers as if to cool them. He had worked up to a state of manic excitement.

"No!" he yelled. "Take your punishment! You don't get off as easily as that!"

He put his hand on someone else's desk and dealt himself another stroke of the cane.

"Yeee-ow!"

The pupils were cheering and egging him on. He repeated the performance a third time.

"Filthiness! Filthiness! Want some more, do you? Drive it out! Out, out—*aaaaaagh!*"

This time he had really hurt himself. He dropped the cane and retreated to the front of the room, blowing on his injured fingers.

"That'll do," he told the class. "Now you know what you can expect if you think impure thoughts. Take out your chemistry books."

Normal lessons resumed for the rest of the day. Mr. Gibber kept his left hand in his breeches pocket and came back after morning recess with a bandage wrapped around it. He continued to prowl about and throw out unexpected questions. "Are you thinking what I think you're thinking, Wunstable?" "What's that in your mind, Swiddlington?"

Col sensed it was all directed at him, though Mr. Gibber didn't dare make open attacks on a Porpentine. Clearly, the teachers knew the identity of the "someone" Dr. Blessamy had been talking about. It was only a matter of time before the whole school knew.

Col kept away from the Squellingham group all day. When the twins opened their hamper for lunch, Col opted for school food: a sausage roll and a fish-paste sandwich. In the afternoon they whispered and passed notes to one another.

Col suspected they were plotting against him, but it seemed somehow muffled and distant. He had the impression that a pane of glass had risen around him, cutting him off from the rest of the classroom. He let his mind float away into memories of Riff.

The strange thing was, he couldn't quite remember what she looked like—or he could remember too well. There were too many pictures in his mind to pin her down in any one version. Riff angry, Riff mocking, Riff amused, Riff boastful . . . There were so many different Riffs, so unpredictable!

When he counted back over his encounters with her, he was amazed to realize he'd met her only four times. It seemed more like four hundred. . . .

Tuesday began in the same way as Monday. Perhaps the Squellingham group's whispering was more malevolent; probably more of the other students now looked at Col askance. He found himself standing alone at morning recess and again at lunch. Then he saw his sister in the schoolyard.

When had she arrived? This must be her first day at school. She looked neat and tidy in her new school uniform, as only Gillabeth could look neat and tidy.

She too was standing on her own. He waved and went across, but she only glared at him.

"No," she hissed. "I'm here to report on what other students are saying about you. I won't hear anything if we're seen together."

"But . . ."

"I have a job to do for the family. I can't afford to be friendly with you."

You wouldn't know what friendly means, Col thought. "Okay," he said aloud. "Let me know what you find out."

Gillabeth bridled as though what he'd suggested was the height of immorality. "Of course not. I report to Grandfather and the family. *They* can repeat it to you if they want."

She turned away and marched off. Col stared at her

retreating back. Something told him that her reports would show him in a very bad light indeed.

But if Gillabeth didn't want to be friendly, someone else did. Before the end of the lunch break a cluster of 4B girls approached him, giggling and nudging one another. Presumably, they hadn't heard any rumors about him yet. One of them was Sephaltina Turbot.

"Go on, Sephaltina," the others prompted.

"Tell him."

"You're a Turbot. A Turbot can talk with a Porpentine."

Sephaltina was half reluctant and half willing as they pushed her forward. She looked at Col, dropped her eyes, and blushed furiously.

The others spoke up for her.

"Do you know who ST is?"

"Did you like the chocs and sweets?"

"She thinks you're—"

"Back off!" roared an ugly, threatening voice.

It was Lumbridge, striding across from the Squellingham group. He shook his fist at the girls, who quailed but stood their ground.

"You don't talk to him, understand?" Lumbridge towered over them. "Move away. Or else."

"Hey, pick on someone your own size," said Col.

Lumbridge whirled to face him, rage burning in his small piggy eyes. He was obviously itching for revenge over the bloody nose that Col had given him. He barged the girls aside and raised both fists—

"Wait," said another voice. "Not on your own. Not now."

The Squellingham twins had followed Lumbridge across

the yard. Pugh laid a restraining hand on the bully's shoulder.

"When the time's right," said Hythe. "He knows what's coming to him."

It was all over as quickly as it had started. The girls dispersed and the twins escorted Lumbridge back to the lunch hamper.

But Lumbridge hadn't forgotten. Back in the classroom after lunch he glowered at Col and clenched his fist under his desk. Col shrugged and looked away.

How long before the twins decided that the time was right? Col could put up a fight against Lumbridge alone, but not against the whole Squellingham group.

He let the mental pane of glass rise up around him and drifted off into thoughts of Riff again. This time, though, it was her fighting skills he remembered. The way she'd beaten Scarface . . . How easily she could beat Lumbridge and the rest!

He imagined Lumbridge taking a swing at her as Scarface had done . . . and she'd wait until the last second, then deflect the blow and trip him up. Using his own size and weight to send him sprawling on the ground. No problem!

And when the rest of the group came against her, she'd pick them off one by one. Somersaulting away from Haugh . . . chopping Fefferley down from behind . . . kicking Hythe where it hurt . . . punching Pugh in the throat and Flarrow in the stomach . . .

The daydream expanded to include a role for himself as well. Perhaps Lumbridge would attack him first, and he and Riff would work as a team to bring the bully down. Or he could drop back and stop the others from interfering . . .

tackling Haugh to the ground . . . spinning Hythe around . . . twisting Pugh's arm up behind his back . . .

In the end his daydream included Mr. Gibber and half the class. He and Riff could outfight them all. "Watch my back!" "I'll deal with this one!" Of course it was impossible; if he ever had a Filthy fighting alongside him, everyone on the Upper Decks would be his enemy. Yet it was so enjoyable, he couldn't stop fantasizing.

Then a thought came to him that wasn't fantasy. Riff couldn't fight alongside him, but she might help in another way. She could teach him her fighting skills. If he could learn how she did it . . .

The idea took his breath away. Of course, he would need to bring her up from Below, as he had promised to do four days ago. Suddenly it didn't seem so difficult to keep his promise.

He began to calculate. Where could he get a rope to lower down through the food chute? He remembered seeing coils of rope among the repair stores on Fourth Deck. If need be, he could knot several ropes together. Then creep on down to Bottom Deck . . .

By the end of the school day he was ready to put his plan into action. Professor Twillip had once called him a doer not a thinker—well, he was ready to do something now. No more excuses. He would do it tonight.

It was well after midnight when he made his way down to Door Seventeen. His main worry was whether he would be able to open the lock. Would they have changed the combination numbers for the wheels? Could they change them?

His worry proved needless. When he spun the wheels to 4 and 9 and 2, the lock sprang open with the familiar clack. He slipped through and this time remembered to relock the door from the inside.

He moved silently and secretly through Bottom Deck, dressed in a black sweater and dark breeches. Over his shoulder he carried a rope made up of three ropes knotted together—surely long enough to reach all the way to the bottom of the food chute.

He got a shock when he neared the chute. Voices and flashlights! He ducked low and slunk forward in the shadows.

Half a dozen officers were busy around the open manhole cover. In orderly procession they lugged sacks of food across and dropped them down the chute. Feeding time in the middle of the night? But all hours of day or night were probably the same Below.

"Here it comes!" one officer called down the hole. "Garbage for the pigs!"

"Enjoy your nice muck!"

"Dirty animals!"

"Don't eat it all at once!"

The last witticism brought on guffaws of laughter. The Filthies were too far below to hear, but the abuse made Col's blood boil. *You make them live like animals, then blame them for it,* he thought.

"Okay, lock it down," said the officer in charge.

They slammed down the manhole cover and slid home the bolts. Then they dusted their hands and moved off at a smart marching pace.

Col guessed they were moving on to repeat the operation at the next chute. He waited until the sound of their footsteps faded and all was quiet. Then he crept out, pulled back the bolts, and heaved up the cover. Unslinging his rope, he started paying it out down the hole.

There would certainly be Filthies underneath the chute so soon after a delivery of food. He pictured Scarface, Greasy, and Toothless standing around the net, lifting the sacks off one by one. He could only hope they'd been told of his deal with the Revolutionary Council and wouldn't try to climb up themselves.

The rope flew through his fingers. First length . . . first knot . . . second length . . . second knot . . . At last he felt a slight lessening of weight, as though the lower end had touched down. Confirmation came a moment later with a sudden sharp tug. Someone was testing the rope. Once. Twice. Three times.

He signaled back with three tugs of his own. He anchored the rope by looping it round and round the hinges of the manhole cover, then tied it fast.

The rope remained slack, so nobody was climbing up yet. Good! They must have gone to summon Riff.

He moved back into the shadows to wait. He kept his eye on the rope and his ears open for any sounds of approaching officers. After a while his thoughts started to wander.

They wandered back to his very first memory of Riff . . . two huge eyes staring out from under his bed. At that time he hadn't even known Filthies could speak. And when she'd emerged, he'd been amazed at how quick and agile she was. Only a few weeks ago—yet now it was impossible to imagine her any other way.

Then there was their second meeting, when she'd hidden under the very bed on which Quinnea was sitting. He grinned to remember the faces she'd pulled, peering out around his mother's legs. Afterward he'd wrestled her for his book . . . lucky for him she hadn't used her fighting skills then!

Lost in such thoughts, he was hardly aware of the minutes passing by, until he noticed a vibration of the rope. He hurried forward to take a look.

Yes, the rope was taut and thrumming with the weight of a climber. She was on her way up! He stood by the manhole, waiting for the top of her head to appear round the curve in the pipe.

That was when another memory came back to him. The one memory he'd instinctively steered clear of, even in daydreams . . . of standing on this very spot, beside the open manhole, when she'd put her arms round his neck and kissed him.

So strange, so intimate . . . the sensation of her lips pressing and opening, melting against his. Mingling breath to breath. The memory flooded through him in overpowering flashback.

And what if he'd given a tiny pressure back? How far could the melting go? His insides churned with nervous excitement at the thought.

The rope was thrumming more than ever. She must be coming up close already. What a climber! Was there anything she wasn't good at?

He bent forward and prepared to reach down an arm to help her out . . . both arms. And he'd say . . .

But she was too quick for him. In one moment he saw her appear round the curve in the pipe, a vision of blond-and-black hair, bare shoulders, thin muscular arms moving like pistons. In the next moment she had planted her hands on the rim of the manhole and was springing up and out. She landed lightly on the other side of the chute.

He blinked. Her cheeks were streaked with grime, and there were sooty smuts on her nose and chin. Yet her teeth gleamed all the whiter, and her eyes were all the more brilliant.

"You're . . ." He had been holding his breath so long that his words disappeared in a gasp.

"What?"

He could only stand there stupidly grinning at her. The real Riff was better than any daydream. .

"Let's get out of here," she said, and swung away.

He started to follow, then remembered the rope. "Wait."

Instead of waiting, she vanished into the shadows. Still in a state of euphoria, Col untied the rope. He didn't want to spend time recoiling it, so he threw it into the chute and let it drop. Then he closed the cover and slid home the bolts.

By the time he caught up with Riff, she had advanced to within sight of Door Seventeen. Obviously, she remembered the way.

"I did it," he said. "I kept my promise."

"Yeah. Took yer time about it too."

He blinked. Why was her tone so cold and unfriendly?

"I couldn't do it before," he said. "My family—"

"Just open the door."

He'd expected gratitude; he'd expected her to be as glad to see him as he was to see her. This wasn't working out right at all. He felt clumsy and confused.

Hardly bothering to check that the coast was clear, he went up to the door and spun the wheels to 4, 9, and 2. He shielded the numbers with his body as Riff darted through.

On the other side she went on ahead once more. When Col came up, she was at the top of the steps, peering out at the piled stores and dimly lit aisles of First Deck.

"Here's where I say good-bye," she said.

"What? No. Aren't you coming with me?"

She shook her head. "I got more important things to do."

Col couldn't believe it. She was no sooner back in his life than she was leaving again. Suddenly he remembered his original reason for bringing her up from Below.

"I want you to help me."

"Oh?"

"I want you to train me to fight like you."

"Impossible."

"Why?"

"You're Upper Decks. Too stiff and slow."

"I can learn. I can get better."

"I don't have time."

"You owe me."

"How do you work that out?"

"I just brought you up from Below."

"Huh. That was because you owed *me*." She scowled. "Or was it so's you could ask me a favor?"

Col could only scowl back at her. Why was she being so unfair? Why couldn't she understand?

"Bye," she said.

"But . . ."

She sprang up the last two steps and flitted away across First Deck. Col stared helplessly after her. He wanted to run and grab her, stop her, hold her, something, anything . . .

He still hadn't moved by the time she swung down an aisle and disappeared from view.

 B ack in his room he paced the floor for hours. What a fool he'd been! She wasn't interested in him but only considered her fellow Filthies. She was on her own spying mission, and he had no part in it.

When he climbed into bed, he still couldn't sleep. *I got more important things to do.* He pictured her scouting around the juggernaut, making mental maps of every deck, planning for the Filthies' revolution. He felt used and betrayed.

Finally he dropped off . . . only to wake up the next morning with the same thoughts rushing instantly into his head. *I got more important things to do.* How could he have been so stupid? It was like his first mad act of letting her hide in his cupboard—and now he'd done it again!

Even at breakfast he seemed cut off from the world by a pane of glass. He hardly cared what happened to him at school. The Squellingham group would beat him up, if not today then tomorrow, if not tomorrow then in a week's time. He couldn't avoid it now.

In fact nothing happened all day. He sat in class or stood in the yard wrapped up in his own painful reveries. The worst thought of all was of Padder with the stubbled chin, the member of the Revolutionary Council who'd exchanged looks with Riff. There was some close connection between them, no doubt of it. The more Col thought back over the scene, the more he felt sure they were partnered. Padder was the one she *really* kissed.

Col flushed to remember his feelings from last night. The nervous excitement as he'd waited for her by the food chute, the warm tingle as he'd pictured the kiss she'd given him once before. It was almost as though he'd wanted it to happen again. He *had* wanted it to happen again.

Mad! Warped! Monstrous! He hated himself, but he couldn't deny it. He'd wanted Riff to train him, but that wasn't why his heart had leaped at the prospect of seeing her once more. He'd had another motive all along. . . .

He stabbed the back of his hand with the nib of his pen. Shameful! He stabbed harder and brought forth a bead of blood. He was hurting, and he *deserved* to hurt. Shameful, shameful, shameful!

The rest of the day passed in a dreary blankness. He had no daydreams left to dream. After school he headed home along Thirty-seventh Deck, automatically following his usual route.

Septimus Trant was walking ahead of him, an unmistakable spring in his step. He must be on his way to the Norfolk Library. Was he still researching the history of Filthies and juggernauts with Professor Twillip? Col had no interest in any of that anymore.

He turned and went up toward Forty-second Deck by way of the Westmoreland Gallery. The gallery was a long hall lined with oil paintings on one side, potted hydrangea bushes on the other.

He was halfway along when a female Menial emerged from a side door and shuffled across in front of him. He should have ordered her out of the way, but instead he halted to let her pass. Strangely, she halted too.

Even more strangely, she turned to face him. This was unheard of!

"Didn't recognize me, did ya?" she said, and poked her tongue out at him.

She stood in the hunched manner of all Menials, wearing the usual sacklike, pajama-like uniform. Her hair was gray and pulled back in a bun. It was Riff in disguise.

"Over here," she said, and stepped in among the hydrangeas.

Col followed and found himself hidden behind luxuriant foliage. "How do you do that?"

"Good, ain't it?"

She must have bulked out the uniform with padding and put some kind of powder through her hair. She performed a full rotation in front of him, letting her shoulders slump and her face go slack.

Col shuddered to see her looking so much like a Menial. "Stop it."

"Yeah, well." Her face went back to its normal animation. "I can go all over the Upper Decks like this."

"Where did you get the uniform?"

"Plenty of 'em hangin' up in my new dormitory."

"Dormitory?"

"Menials' dormitory on Twenty-first Deck. That's my sleepin' place now."

"You'll never get away with it."

"Sure I will. I can act anyone. Doin' a Menial's easy."

"What about supervisors?"

"They never bother to check. There's always empty beds. And the real Menials . . ." She shrugged and left the rest of the sentence unspoken.

Col couldn't think what else to say; his emotions were so jumbled up.

Riff snapped her fingers. "Anyway, I've been thinkin'. You want me to teach you fightin'. I'll do it if you teach me, too."

"Teach you what?"

"Readin'."

"Reading books?"

"Of course books! What else?" Her eyes flashed. "Don't you think I can do it? I'm a fast learner."

"Why do you want to learn reading?"

"Why do you want to learn fightin'?"

Col shook his head. He didn't want to explain that he was in danger of getting beaten up at school. "That's my business."

"So's mine. Decide."

Col hardly needed to think about it. "It's a deal. When?"

"Tonight. I'll come to your room. Right?"

"Right."

Her jaw sagged, and her eyes went blank and mindless. She was putting on her Menial act again. She stepped away and checked the gallery in both directions. Then, with a rustle of foliage, she was gone.

Col hung back a minute and waited for his pulse to slow. He could have hugged himself. His world had turned upside down for the second time.

39

Col wasn't sure what to wear for training, but obviously not his best clothes or his nightgown. In the end he changed into an old pair of breeches and a sleeveless sweater. He lay down on top of his bedspread, planning to stay awake until Riff appeared.

Instead he drifted off into a pleasant drowse. The next thing he knew was that someone was shaking him by the arm.

"Wakey-wakey!"

A Menial bent over his bed, looking down at him. No—Riff in her disguise as a Menial.

He came fully awake and swung off the bed.

She made a face at the sight of his clothes. "What's that you're wearin'?"

"Isn't this right?"

"You'll get hot."

"Better than a jacket and shirt."

"Yeah, but not as good as bare to the waist."

Col was shocked. Strip off in front of her? Unthinkable!

She saw his reaction and grinned. "Okay. Take off yer shoes and socks, though."

Col eyed her bulky Menial uniform. "What about you?"

She sniffed. "Trainin' you ain't gonna make *me* hot."

However, she did remove the padding from her uniform: rolled-up lengths of cloth. Col removed his shoes and socks.

She nodded. "Now we take turns at trainin'. Right?"

"Right. Me first."

"Why you?"

"I thought of it first."

"So?" She shrugged. "Okay. Stand in front of me."

She made him poise on the balls of his feet. But she wasn't satisfied.

"You're too stiff. Don't be so *controlled* about everything."

"I'm doing what you tell me."

"You gotta loosen up. Give yerself a good shakin'. Like this."

She flung and flopped her arms, legs, and head in every direction.

"What's that for?"

"Just do it. Let yourself go."

"It's ridiculous."

"Know what's wrong with you? You're not just stiff in the body, you're stiff in the *head*."

Col still thought it was ridiculous, but he did the all-over shaking for several minutes. Perhaps she *wanted* to make him act like a fool. . . .

"Better. Now we start with defense." She thought for a moment. "I know."

She turned to his antique wardrobe and opened the door. Of course she remembered the contents. She selected one of his ties, dark blue, embossed with a gold *P* for Porpentine.

"Try to stop me hitting you," she said, and flicked out at him suddenly with the tie. He raised his arm, but the tip caught him a stinging cut on the cheek.

"Hey! That stung!"

"Block it."

She danced around him, wielding the tie like a whip. He tried to ward off lashes from all sides.

"Don't get angry," she warned. "Ignore the pain. Stay balanced."

He was soon hot and sweaty, and smarting in a hundred places.

"Dodge, but don't dodge too much," she said. "Be prepared for the next blow, and the next after that."

After ten minutes he was hardly conscious of what he was doing. The practice went on and on, until every move seemed to have happened a dozen times before.

"Okay, you're gettin' the idea," she said, and stopped. "Now stay still and watchful. Open and alert. Like this."

She stood motionless on the balls of her feet, but with a kind of vibrating readiness. Col remembered what she'd said once before: *Keep your mind wide and your senses open.*

Suddenly, her arm swept up and the tip of the tie nicked him on the shoulder.

"Hey, you never said—"

"This is fightin'. You don't get a warnin'."

For another ten minutes she made him stand in a state of readiness. At unpredictable moments she would launch into another attack: sometimes three lashes one after another, sometimes nothing for a whole minute.

Finally, she delivered a nonstop barrage of blows, striking almost faster than he could see. He whirled this way and that, until his feet tangled and he fell to the floor.

He looked up, beyond embarrassment. He was panting and running with sweat, while she wasn't even breathing heavily.

"I was better, wasn't I?"

"A bit. Not much."

"I only lost my balance right at the end."

"It's more than balance. You put too much effort into the way you move. You gotta unlearn old movements before I teach ya new ones."

"I'll unlearn them, then." Col stuck out his chin. "What next?"

"My turn."

He didn't want to stop, but he didn't argue. Riff went across to his bookcase and selected a book: *Heroes of Empire: True Tales for Boys.* She sat on the bed, and he sat beside her. He was very much aware that his bare arms were only inches away from hers.

He'd never considered how to teach reading, but he supposed you began with the sounds of the separate letters. He pointed to the *H, e, r,* and *o* on the book's title page.

"Huh . . . ee . . . rrr . . . oh."

She repeated the sounds with an exact echo of his pronunciation, through every letter of the alphabet. She had a real talent for mimicry.

It was a different matter when he pointed to the letters without saying the sound himself. She squinted at the print and made wild guesses. She couldn't believe that such similar-looking letters could go with such different sounds.

"But this one's the same as that!"

"No, this one's got an extra bit sticking out at the bottom. See?"

"Oh, *that!* That's nothing!"

He had to keep telling her to take her time and study the shapes more closely.

"Huh!" she huffed. "Readin's so *slow!*"

She went to the other extreme, pronouncing the letters with exaggerated deliberation.

"Now you're making it sound stupid," he complained.

"Well, it *is* stupid."

She remained supremely confident. When she finally managed to produce most of the right sounds for most of the right letters, she turned to Col with an expression of triumph. "Told ya I was a fast learner. I'm nearly readin' already, ain't I?"

He shook his head. "We haven't even started on words yet."

"Oh?" Riff looked blank. "There's more?"

Col held back a biting reply. "Just concentrate on learning this first."

He kept her pronouncing sounds for letters until she was perfect every time. Then it was his turn for training again.

Riff closed the book reluctantly. "Okay. We'll do something new."

"Attack?"

"No, still defense." She stood facing him. "Look into my eyes."

Her eyes were so large and brilliant it seemed too personal to look right into them. *This is a training exercise,* he told himself. But he found it hard to concentrate.

"Always watch your enemy's eyes," she said. "Soon as anyone means to hit you somewhere, their eyes get ready for it first."

"Even you?"

"Yeah, even me. Watch for a tiny, tiny movement of my eyes."

She reached forward suddenly and tapped him on the elbow.

"Did you see it comin'?"

"Mmm." Col wasn't sure what he'd seen.

"Try and block me. By watchin' my eyes."

She tapped him on his shoulder, the top of his head, his knee. Not once did he pick up the movement in advance; not once could he block her.

"You're not tryin'. Watch harder."

She jumped forward and back, hands shooting out at him. Some of her taps were more like punches.

"Worse and worse." She stopped after a while. "You're goin' backwards. What's wrong with ya?"

Col knew what was wrong, but he couldn't tell her. It wasn't only the effect of her eyes but also her physical closeness. She came right up against him when she tapped him. He could even feel the warmth of her breath on his face . . .

"You need another good shakin'," she said. "Do it again."

Once more she demonstrated the rag-doll flopping and flapping. Col flopped and flapped so hard he could barely hold himself upright afterward.

"That's enough. Now watch my eyes."

He found it easier this time. It was true—her eyes always flickered toward their target before her hand shot out. He stopped wondering what else was in her mind and thought only about where she intended to strike.

"Much better," she said after twenty minutes. "Now my turn again."

For Riff's second turn Col tried to get her to put sounds together to make a word.

"Ee . . . em . . . puh . . . eye . . . arrr."

Under his instruction she said it faster and faster, but she still couldn't merge it into a single word.

"Empire," he told her at last.

"'Empire'? Oh, *empire*. You say it a funny way."

Col realized the size of the problem. His teaching was right for Upper Decks pronunciation, but Riff had a different accent.

"You'll have to learn to say it like me," he said. "I can't teach you any other way."

There was another problem too. "What about the *e* at the end?" she asked. "Empire-ee?"

Col tried to explain that the letter *e* didn't always sound the same, and sometimes didn't sound at all.

"So how do you know?"

"You just do."

"Phuh! So it doesn't work!"

"What?"

"Your system. I make the sounds like you tell me, and then you say they're wrong."

"It works most of the time. Do you want to do this or not?"

"Yeah, we got a deal. I just thought you'd be a better teacher."

Col gritted his teeth and turned to a full page of text. For the rest of Riff's turn he tried to pick out words that sounded the way they were spelled. After a while he began to suspect that his system didn't work even most of the time. Teaching Riff was proving to be just as hard as learning from her.

At the end of her second turn she yawned. "I reckon we've done enough for one night. You need to practice what I showed ya."

"How?"

She pointed to his full-length mirror. "In front of that. Practice keeping yer balance. What about me? What can I do?"

"Practice letters and sounds. You can borrow *Heroes of Empire*."

"Nah, too big. I'll just take a bit of it."

She took hold of a page and ripped it clean out of the book.

"Hey! No!"

"What's the matter? You've still got plenty of pages left."

"There'll be a gap in the story."

"Huh?"

It was too difficult to explain, he decided, and too late anyway. "Forget it."

Riff folded the page and slipped it into a pocket of her Menial's uniform. She put the padding back in her uniform too.

"Same time tomorrow night?"

Col nodded.

"Sleep well. Practice hard."

"You too."

He stared at his cabin door long after it had closed behind her.

40

They met for midnight training sessions all through the week. Riff had new things to teach every night: how to avoid an attack from behind, how to duck under a blow, how to cope with several simultaneous attacks. For the simultaneous attacks she used rolled-up socks, which she threw at him two, three, or four at a time. They moved his bed back against the wall to make more space.

Col improved steadily. He would never acquire Riff's acrobatic agility, but his coordination was better, and he was lighter on his feet. When they went back to the tie-flicking exercise one night, he was surprised at the speed of his own reactions.

Riff made progress with her reading, too, though never as fast as she expected. Col devoted a great deal of thought to better ways of teaching her. He worked out how the sound of a particular letter was often influenced by its position in a word and other letters that came before or after it. Riff still had problems spotting clusters of letters in a word, but she was very sharp at switching from Filthy pronunciation to Upper Decks pronunciation.

"I do believe I shall be a most refined lady reader," she told him in a perfect Upper Decks accent, elegantly wafting her fingertips.

He thought less and less about the Riff of his daydreams,

more and more about their training together. He grew used to talking to her, sitting on the bed beside her, even making contact with her when he blocked her blows. Working toward practical goals, she became somehow real and familiar—as well as prickly, impatient, and competitive.

She was tight-lipped about her spying activities, and he didn't try to quiz her. She could explore and plan as much as she liked, but she couldn't do anything without the numbers for unlocking the door to Bottom Deck. The only question he asked was about the Changing Room.

"Have you found that room? You know, where Filthies get changed into Menials?"

"I thought you didn't believe in it?"

"I don't."

"So why ask?"

"Because you haven't found it, have you?"

"Not yet. But I will."

Their training sessions together were the one bright spot in his life. His days at school were at best dreary and at worst threatening. The hostility toward him was building up.

Every recess he saw the Squellingham group doing the rounds, talking to groups of boys they would normally have had nothing to do with. He knew he should try to talk to other students too, make an effort to counteract the rumors. But somehow he couldn't be bothered. A stubbornness was growing in him, a spirit of resistance. He was sick of the whole world of school.

His marks in tests went downhill too. Now he scored below the elite group, though still above the rest of the class. He wondered how long it would take before Mr.

Gibber dropped him below the climbers and crawlers.

Meanwhile, the campaign against impure thoughts continued. Mr. Gibber managed to introduce the word "filthy" into every lesson. There were filthy countries, filthy adverbs, filthy fractions, and filthiest reflex angles. He treated Col as a blank space in the classroom that he was quite unable to see.

At the end of the week he nearly went a step further. He had taken to hiding behind the blackboard and jumping out to fire sticks of chalk at pupils he suspected of harboring impure thoughts. All of the grindboys and most of the crawlers and climbers had been hit at least once. On Friday he got so carried away that he jumped out and took aim at Col.

Col saw him. "Don't you dare!"

The tone of authority might have come from Sir Mormus himself. Mr. Gibber lowered his arm and went very red in the face.

Then he bounced back. "Of course not! The grandson of our supreme commander! How could I think of it? No such grandson could ever have impure thoughts."

Col shook his head, not sure how to respond. Mr. Gibber began to put on a performance, capering around and throwing out his arms.

"You have to excuse me, please. I'm only a humble schoolteacher. Who am I to doubt the thoughts of a Porpentine? Not on the same level at all." He struck his forehead with the heel of his hand. "I was forgetting my role in life. Miserable, wretched nobody that I am! Pathetic, insignificant worm!"

Now that he'd discovered his role in life, he began reveling in it. "Yes, a pathetic, insignificant worm!" He appealed to the class. "What am I, boys?"

"A worm, sir!"

"Louder, louder!"

"*A worm, sir!*"

Mr. Gibber struck himself so hard on the forehead that a spare stick of chalk fell out from behind his ear. For a moment he appeared to have trouble focusing.

Then he went to sit behind his desk, wearing a smirk of self-satisfaction. He lifted up the wastepaper basket and tickled Murgatrude for the rest of the afternoon.

The confrontation was over. Col had the feeling that he'd lost in the end, even though he'd won.

41

Col expected all his time on the weekend to be taken up with social events. But Grandmother Ebnolia's list of engagements had recently thinned out—and the same had happened to the other branches of the Porpentine family. There was troubled discussion after dinner in the Northumberland Room.

"The Ollithorpes canceled their coffee morning."

"We didn't receive an invitation to the Sprouds' at-home."

"The Tremencys made excuses to put off Sunday luncheon."

"No choir practice at Lady Hallidom's."

"No children's games at the Trumpingtons'."

"We're being treated like pariahs. Something has to be done."

Ebnolia smiled and bobbed her head. "It's only temporary."

"Not if the Squellinghams can help it, it's not," boomed Sir Mormus. Everyone turned to him. "They're behind it all. Sir Wisley is impossible."

After Sir Mormus's boom Ebnolia's voice was a tiny, birdlike twitter. "Is this about the Executive meeting, dear?"

Sir Mormus nodded, visibly struggling to contain himself. "He outmaneuvered me. When we make landfall on the coast of Burma, we can head for Hong Kong by way of Siam, or Singapore by way of the Malay Peninsula. We're low on coal, and we need to restock. I planned for Singapore."

"You weren't outvoted?" Leath Porpentine exclaimed in horror.

Sir Mormus's face had turned an ominous shade of puce. "We've read a signal from the Prussian juggernaut that says they're heading toward Hong Kong from central China. If they get there first, we'll have to wait while they restock. No trade for a week. But Sir Wisley said we *ought* to have the speed to arrive before them, and no one dared to say otherwise."

"You *were* outvoted," groaned Leath Porpentine.

"No, I wasn't outvoted." Sir Mormus looked like a volcano ready to explode. "I had to back down before I could be outvoted. I could see Haugh and Fefferley were going to vote against me."

"What about Turbot?" asked Rumpley Porpentine. "Surely the chief helmsman would side with the supreme commander?"

"He could have gone either way. Self-serving coward! He *knows* the Singapore route is best. But his wife influences him to be ambitious for his family. He'll switch over to Sir Wisley if he thinks it's in his interest. I couldn't take the chance. I had to turn around and support the Hong Kong route *myself*!"

The Porpentines fell silent, their faces grim.

"Turbot is the key, isn't he?" asked Ebnolia.

Sir Mormus grunted in the affirmative.

"So we need a bribe." Ebnolia stood thinking, muttering, tapping a dainty finger against her chin. "An offer that the Squellinghams can't match. We're still the most important family on this juggernaut. Mmm . . . yes!" She fluffed herself out triumphantly. "I have a solution!"

The Porpentines clamored to be told, but Ebnolia only turned to her husband and whispered in his ear.

"Discussion with family heads first," he announced. "Everyone else to leave the room."

All the Porpentines filed out except for Morpice, Rumpley, Leath, and Oblett. Col left too. He had the impression that his grandmother's gaze followed him with special attention.

Was he involved in her solution? He couldn't imagine how.

It wasn't a question that stayed in his mind for long. He had other, more urgent things to think about. With no social engagements outside his own family, he was able to spend more hours in his room, practicing what Riff had taught him in front of his full-length mirror.

He felt that he was improving all the time. His reactions were quicker, his timing more precise. Riff was impressed with him, he was sure, though she didn't say so.

He was certainly impressed with her. Once she'd stopped being annoyed over the different sounds for the same letter, she'd made amazing progress. Already she could read through whole sentences, slowly but accurately, in an imitation Upper Decks voice. It was like dealing with two different people when she swapped from one voice to the other.

He practiced in every spare moment, determined to keep up with her.

42

Back at school on Monday Col discovered that his place in the classroom had changed. His own desk had been emptied out. No one spoke, but everyone was watching him.

On the other side of the room one of the grindboys cried out in surprise, "I've got someone else's books on top of my desk!"

Mr. Gibber bounced across. "Your desk, Hattimer? I don't think so." He pulled a succession of grimaces, trying to keep a straight face. "Why do you think it's yours?"

"Because, because . . ."

"Because because, *sir*," Mr. Gibber corrected. "Whose name is on the books?"

Hattimer took a look. "Porpentine's, sir."

"Well, then." Mr. Gibber turned to the rest of the class. "Let's use our brains and work it out, boys. Name on books, books on desk, desk belongs to . . ."

"Porpentine!" came the general response. "Sir!"

Col understood that he had been moved to sit among the grindboys. He didn't mind. He was sick of sitting with the Squellingham group. The grindboys might not be friends, except perhaps Septimus, but they weren't enemies. He collected his satchel and stood up.

The final rearrangement of desks required a complicated series of hierarchical swaps: Haugh shifted back to the desk that Col had occupied, a climber shifted to the desk that Haugh had occupied, a crawler shifted to the desk that the climber had occupied, and Hattimer finally shifted to the desk that the crawler had occupied.

Col didn't expect the grindboys to make him welcome, not in front of the other students. But they did much worse than that. They shifted as far away as possible from Col on their benches, as though avoiding infection. They were putting on a show for the rest of the class.

Septimus was at the desk directly behind Col. Col had more sense than to appeal for his support. But in Mr. Gibber's geometry lesson Septimus asked if someone could lend him a ruler. Other students, even grindboys, were always stealing Septimus's possessions. Right now they were busy with their own rulers.

"When I've finished."

"Wait a minute, Trant."

Col had two rulers. He dug into his desk and brought out his spare.

"Here." He turned round and held it out.

Septimus kept his arms at his sides and stared at a spot over Col's shoulder. Col waved the ruler in front of his nose, and still he refused to see it.

"Don't touch it," said one of the grindboys. "You don't know where it's been."

There were guffaws on all sides. For one moment Septimus's eyes met Col's. Then he deliberately looked the other way.

Col gave up. He had shared secrets with Septimus, taken him to the Norfolk Library . . . and now it counted for nothing.

His mouth compressed to a thin, tight line. He was angry and hurt.

He kept to himself through the school day. A few times he glanced round and caught Septimus looking at him with a shamefaced expression. Col made no response. If Trant wanted to run with the pack—so be it.

In the recesses Col took a book with him and pretended to read. He sat by himself on the ramp leading up to the first-floor gallery and stared unseeing at page after page. Sitting on the ramp was probably forbidden, but the master on duty ignored him in the same way as everyone else did.

At least there was an end to his ordeal. In the afternoon Mr. Gibber announced that exams would be held this coming Thursday, and school would break up on Friday.

Col's spirits lifted. Starting school in midterm, he'd never thought about the end of term or holidays. With Professor Twillip his studies had continued all year round. Now he had only four more days to go! If he could survive to the end of the week, he'd have all the holidays for training and perfecting his fighting skills.

He was heading back home after school when he heard footsteps hurrying behind him. He turned and saw Septimus Trant.

"Don't be hard on me," Septimus pleaded as he came up. "I'm not as strong as you."

Col kept walking.

"I'm a coward. I know it. I deserve everything you're thinking." Septimus was almost as tall as Col, but there was something frail and shrinking about him. "Please talk to me."

Col scowled. "You have to stand up for what you believe."

"I can't. You can. You never back down or suck up to any-one. I'd give anything to be more like you."

He sounded so hopeless and wistful that Col couldn't stay angry with him. Though nothing was said, Septimus must have sensed the change in mood. He matched Col's pace stride for stride.

"I've got some good news," he said. "I've been wanting to tell you all day."

"What?"

"Our history project. Me and Professor Twillip have been working on it."

Col took a moment to remember. "Oh, right. Where the Filthies came from. The beginning of juggernauts."

"Yes. It took ages to find any books at all. We made the big breakthrough two days ago."

"You found out the truth?"

"Yes. Enough."

"So tell me."

"Not here. Professor Twillip wants to tell you too. Come along to the Norfolk Library."

43

Professor Twillip was sitting at the central table under the electric light. He looked up over the top of his glasses. "Well, well, here you are, Colbert."

"I said you wanted to tell him too," said Septimus.

"Ah, a small vanity on my part, I'm afraid." Beaming, Professor Twillip gestured toward some books spread out on the table. "We've been gathering material for your history project."

"That's all? Six books?"

Professor Twillip nodded. "And only two of them are really on the topic. It's hard to believe so little was written on such important events."

"Or so little preserved in this library," said Septimus.

"True." Professor Twillip pursed his lips. "Perhaps nobody thought to bring the history collection up to date when *Worldshaker* was launched. Everyone was so familiar with recent events, they didn't realize that later generations could forget."

"Or there were books, and someone destroyed them," said Septimus.

"Oh, no, no, no." Professor Twillip was genuinely shocked. "I'm sure no one would ever destroy books on purpose."

"These were the two with the most information." Septimus drew Col's attention to one volume titled *Europe in the Age of the French Revolution,* and another titled *Napoleonic Warfare: Strategy and Tactics.*

"Most of the others had only bits of chapters," Professor Twillip agreed. "We had to assemble the facts with a degree of conjecture."

"I bet we got it right," Septimus insisted.

"Your friend has real talent as a scholar." Professor Twillip directed a smile from Col to Septimus. "Whereas, I confess, I'd forgotten the few facts I *did* know. I didn't even remember the Peace of Brussels until I read about it again."

"In 1842," said Septimus. "Ended the Fifty Years' War and launched the Age of Imperialism."

"Yes." Professor Twillip's smile broadened. "And I knew the names of many major battles in the Fifty Years' War. Jemappes. Wattignies. Marengo. Esternay. Liegnitz. Magdeburg. Bratislava. They were only empty names to me, though."

"You'd never heard of Dartford," Septimus put in.

"No, not the Battle of Dartford. Nor the Battle of Crawley or the Surrender of Aylesham."

"Hold on!" Col shook his head. "Start at the beginning."

"The beginning? Yes, of course." Professor Twillip steepled his fingers and rested his chin on them. "I suppose the best place to begin is the French Revolution."

"The what?"

"A revolution by the French people against their king. Britain was rapidly industrializing, but France still had an old-fashioned economy and a semifeudal system of administration."

"Britain? That's the same as the Old Country, isn't it?"

"Yes. Perhaps I should have begun with the Industrial Revolution. . . ."

"No, go on, go on."

"Well, in 1789 the French middle classes seized power and created what they called the National Assembly. Then the middle classes themselves were overthrown by the lower classes. Workers and the urban poor. Uneducated people."

"But not stupid." Septimus spoke directly to Col. "They demanded equality."

"Hmm." Professor Twillip frowned. "Perhaps not stupid, but they behaved very brutally. They executed their royal family, then started executing anyone who disagreed with them. They called it the Great Terror. They wanted to overturn everything. The new ideas spread to Britain and unsettled the lower classes there, too."

Septimus pointed silently to one of the open books. Col read a chapter heading: "Robespierre and the Reign of Terror."

"Then a general called Napoleon Bonaparte took over the revolution," Professor Twillip continued. "He waged war against every other country in Europe."

"And kept beating them," Septimus put in. "The start of the Fifty Years' War."

"By 1802 Prussia, Russia, and Austria had all pulled out, and only Britain still stood against him. So he invaded."

Col gasped. "How could he? That's . . . that's . . ." He couldn't find the words to express how wicked it was.

"I know." Professor Twillip was blinking behind his glasses. "But he didn't care, because he was a revolutionary. He couldn't beat the British navy, so he had an alternative idea. Or an engineer called Albert Mathieu-Favier did. The

French dug a tunnel under the English Channel from Calais to Dover. It took two and a half years, working in secret. No one in the Old Country had any suspicion until a hole suddenly appeared in the ground, half a mile inland."

Septimus leafed through to a page in the other book, where a map showed the tunnel as a dotted line from France to Britain. He pointed to an X at the end of the tunnel on the British side. "September 1804," he said, "the French troops came pouring out."

"Who won?" asked Col. "We must have defeated them, didn't we?"

"Not as simple as that," Professor Twillip said. "Napoleon marched on London and issued proclamations promising liberty, equality, and fraternity. The lower classes in London believed him and rose up against King George the Third. So the British army was betrayed behind its back and lost the Battle of Dartford. They retreated north, but then the lower classes in Birmingham and Manchester went over to Napoleon too."

"Birmingham and Manchester were new industrial towns," Septimus explained. "Coal mines, steam power, factories."

"Only one thing saved the Old Country." Professor Twillip's cheeks were glowing with excitement. "Prussia and Austria saw their chance to attack while Napoleon was away over the Channel, so they declared war and marched on Paris. Napoleon had to rush back to defend his capital. The French troops left in southern England lost confidence, and Britain discovered a great general of its own, called Arthur Wellesley, Duke of Wellington."

Col felt as if his head would explode from so much new

information. He could hardly keep up. "So this Duke of Wellington beat the French?"

"Yes, but not at first. First he marched against the lower classes, while the French stayed put and did nothing. All the people who'd betrayed their king—Wellington defeated them at the Battle of Crawley."

"In 1805," said Septimus. "The same year Napoleon crushed the Prussians at the Battle of Esternay. It's all in *Napoleonic Warfare: Strategy and Tactics*."

"Napoleon still couldn't return to the Old Country, though," Professor Twillip resumed. "Wellington spent the rest of 1805 dealing with the lower classes, then turned against the French. Outflanked them and took control of the mouth of the tunnel behind Dover. First he filled it in, then he flooded it. The French troops finally laid down their arms at the Surrender of Aylesham."

Col remembered Professor Twillip's earlier reference to the Surrender of Aylesham. He also remembered why he had invented this history project in the first place. "What about the Filthies?" he asked.

"Coming to them, coming to them." Professor Twillip sat back on his chair. "Britain had to assist its Continental allies, so the whole nation was put on a war footing. Industrialization was the path to victory. Factories turned out more and more guns and ammunition, new inventions, new machines, amazing progress. Napoleon was getting left behind."

"Until he started to industrialize too," said Septimus. "He exploited coal seams in northern France and the Low Countries and copied our iron and steel industries."

Professor Twillip nodded. "By the 1820s Prussia was also

industrializing, and Russia and Austria by the 1830s. France couldn't defeat the allies, and the allies couldn't defeat France. For all the great advances and retreats, it always ended up in stalemate."

"But what about the—"

"Filthies? They weren't given that name until much later. They were the labor force that made mass industrialization possible. They became the factory slaves."

"Yes, but where did they come from? How did they arrive in the Old Country?"

"They'd always been there. They were the lower classes."

"What?" Col thought back. "You mean the workers? The urban poor?"

"Yes, them. In the Old Country they were the ones who'd betrayed their king. The other European countries simply followed the British system. Even Napoleon. He was hardly different from any other ruler by the end. More interested in winning the war than in being a revolutionary."

Col struggled to stop his emotions from showing on his face. *The urban poor! Born and bred in the Old Country!*

He turned to Septimus. "So the Gibber *was* wrong,"

"Yes. Not loaded on Noah's Ark."

"Less than two hundred years ago."

"They were the same as everyone else. But without money."

"Extraordinary, isn't it?" Professor Twillip pushed up his spectacles to perch above his eyebrows. "I'm sure your teacher will be fascinated to hear the real facts."

Septimus gave an ironic grin, but Col remained deadpan.

"Yes, the Fifty Years' War turned history upside down," Professor Twillip went on. "The endless battles had made

Europe into a wasteland. Along with the smoke and pollution from the factories. By the time of the Peace of Brussels, agricultural production was decimated, and vast areas were uninhabitable."

"The Peace of Brussels ended the war," Septimus explained. "After the first Napoleon died, the second Napoleon gave up trying to expand his empire, and the other countries recognized the Bonapartes as the royal family of France."

"Then they started building juggernauts," said Professor Twillip. "The Age of Imperialism."

Col's head was in a whirl. So he'd been right all along, ever since he'd let Riff hide in his cupboard. His instinct had told him what his mind couldn't accept: Filthies were just as human as anyone else. The Upper Decks people were living a lie. They were wrong, wrong, wrong!

He was only half listening as Septimus and Professor Twillip continued the story into the Age of Imperialism. He took in the facts: how the population of Europe had escaped from their ruined continent in vast juggernauts, traveling and trading over the rest of the world . . . how the British had built *Worldshaker*, the French the *Marseillaise*, the Prussians the *Lebensraum*, the Austrians the *Grosse Wien*, the Russians the *Romanov* . . .

But his thoughts were elsewhere. What would Riff say when he told her tonight?

As it turned out, the revelation didn't excite Riff at all.

"Yeah? What did you expect?"

"Don't you understand? It proves Filthies and Upper Decks people are all the same."

"Right. Except we're better."

"Why better?"

"'Cause we've had to learn to be faster and smarter. Your lot's had two hundred years of takin' it easy."

It was after midnight in Col's room, and they were sitting on the side of the bed. Col had been ready to say, *It proves you and me are the same,* but somehow the moment had passed.

"Anyway," said Riff, "I've made a bigger discovery than that."

"What? You've found the Changing Room?"

"No." She jumped up. "You have to see this for yerself. I'll show ya."

"What about our training?"

"Later." She grabbed his hand and pulled him upright. "Come on."

"Where? How far? What if we're seen?"

"I'll be a Menial carryin' somethin' for ya." She picked up the jacket that Col had changed out of and rolled it into a bundle. "This'll do okay. Give me orders if anyone gets suspicious."

They set off, heading aft. Riff led the way down successive staircases to Thirty-first Deck. Here were the manufacturing workshops, all closed, with shutters pulled down for the night.

Still they continued aft. Four times they ran into officers or supervisors. Col made a show of giving orders to his servant.

"Move it! And don't drop anything!"

Riff gritted her teeth, even as she maintained her dull Menial expression.

They had been walking for half an hour before she arrived at a particular intersection and swung to the right. The lights grew dimmer, the workshops dirtier and dingier. Finally they left behind the manufacturing area altogether. Up ahead was an arched entrance closed off by a revolving turnstile.

"Follow me," whispered Riff.

As they approached, Col could see the padlock on the turnstile. Riff glanced around, then vaulted lightly over the top. Col did the same, not quite so lightly.

Beyond the turnstile was a passage with walls painted white. Riff padded forward to a second turnstile, which they also vaulted over.

Col whistled in amazement. Now they had reached the side of the juggernaut! He was standing in a strange metal tray, fifty feet square, open to the night sky above. In the middle of the tray was a pile of assorted vegetable matter.

He looked up at the pale round orb of the moon. So bright, so cool, so silvery! So different from the way it looked in paintings! It made the hairs on the back of his neck stand up.

"See there." Riff's pointing finger drew his attention lower down.

At the outer edge of the tray was a huge steel arm. He recognized it from the time when he'd stood and looked out from the platform above the bridge: a crane. Sir Mormus had told him that the juggernaut's cranes were for trade and loading cargo.

This one was moving. As he watched, a scoop as big as a house came into view. Then the arm swung round and the jaws of the scoop opened to deposit their load on top of the pile of vegetable matter. Col made out a tangle of vines and corn, bananas and coconut palms. There was even something that might have been a beehive and four upward-pointing legs, like the legs of a cow.

"When they've got enough stuff, a gang of Menials will come along and sort through it," said Riff.

"You've seen that?"

"Yeah. It started when the juggernaut began travelin' over land."

Col remembered what he'd heard about *Worldshaker* making landfall on the coast of Burma. He also remembered Sir Mormus's explanation of the principles of trade.

"These are raw materials," he explained to Riff. "We trade our manufactured goods for raw materials."

Riff snorted. "What manufactured goods?"

"I don't know."

"Nah, but I do. That's what I'm gonna show ya next."

So their expedition wasn't finished yet. Col watched as the crane swung away and lowered its scoop over the side again.

Then Riff led the way to a hole like a drain in the corner of the tray. She lowered herself in and disappeared from sight.

Col didn't like the look of it; the hole brought back

unpleasant memories of dropping down the food chute. But he took a deep breath and followed after her. His feet landed with a splash.

As his eyes adjusted, he saw he was in a round pipe, large enough for standing upright. A stream of scummy liquid flowed along at the bottom. He almost gagged from the smell of decayed vegetable matter.

"It runs all the way to the back of the juggernaut," Riff told him.

She turned and scuttled off. Col ran awkwardly after her, straddling the stream.

The drain sloped steadily down toward the stern. Other drain holes let in light at regular intervals.

Then there was a different light ahead: the circular shape of the end of the pipe. Riff slowed down.

"Careful," she warned. "The pipe hangs out over the back here. Nothin' to hold on to."

For the last few paces the pipe made a different, hollow sound under their feet. Riff advanced to the rim and halted. Col peered out over her shoulder.

It was unreal, uncanny. The panorama was no wider or more spectacular than he had seen from the platform with Sir Mormus, but it was transformed under the moonlight. The distant outline of mountains, the vague blur of woods, the numerous rivers and lakes . . . Everything had taken on a blue metallic sheen.

And something else, too. "What's that?"

Riff leaned to the side to give him a better view.

Col traced a great ugly gash across the landscape. A gash of flattened earth, a churned-up strip of ruin. It cut through hills and dammed rivers, growing steadily wider as it approached the stern of the juggernaut. It was exactly the same width as the stern of the juggernaut. . . .

"Well?" Riff prompted.

Col remembered the three hundred and forty rollers, each weighing eight hundred tons. Of course *Worldshaker* would mash everything it rolled over! Of course it would leave behind a trail of destruction! Why had he never thought of it before?

"See the villages on either side?" Riff pointed. "See, there and there and there? But not where we've been."

Col understood. He could see the pale patches of settlements dotted across the plain. But there were no settlements in the strip where the juggernaut had passed. Sir Mormus's words came back to him: *On the ground, we're traveling faster than a galloping horse.*

He would have liked to think that *Worldshaker* steered to avoid the villages in its path. But the unswerving line of the gash refuted him. Looking at the scarlike corrugations of plowed earth, he knew that the natives never had a chance.

"Yeah, take a good look," said Riff. "That's what you do all around the world."

Col imagined the thunder of approaching rollers, the unbelievable convulsion and upheaval of the earth. Whole villages must have been swallowed up. The lucky victims would have been instantly crushed to death; the unlucky ones would have been buried alive. . . .

"We never stop," he said slowly. "How could we trade when we never stop?"

Riff laughed a harsh, humorless laugh. "Oh, you trade, all

right. You want to see what the natives get from you?"

Riff propped herself against one side of the pipe so that he could squeeze forward on the other. She hooked a hand into his belt to steady him. Cautiously, he bent forward and looked down where she indicated, over the curved rim of the pipe.

It was like looking down the face of a cliff, a dizzying thousand-foot drop. The stern of the juggernaut was a vertical wall of metal broken only by the projecting ends of many pipes. She pointed to one particular pipe far below.

"That one comes out from Fifth Deck," she told him.

It was too distant for Col to see clearly, but something like a thin stream of droplets seemed to be issuing from the end of the pipe. Something like a very fine rain, falling and glittering in the moonlight.

"Fifth Deck," Riff repeated. "Don't you remember?"

Col cast back, but the memory wouldn't come. What was on Fifth Deck?

"Those plaster things," said Riff.

Then he remembered the statuettes of the imperial family: Queen Victoria seated, or Queen Victoria standing, or Queen Victoria and Prince Albert seated, or Queen Victoria seated and Prince Albert standing. He remembered the racks of shelves stocked with millions upon millions of painted plaster replicas. *Worldshaker's* manufactured goods!

"Very useful, huh?" Riff dripped sarcasm. "Just what you need when yer village has been wiped out."

Col shook his head. "I never knew. I thought trade meant . . . trade."

"Nah. It means cruelty and bullyin' and tramplin' on anyone weaker. Some get crushed underneath, and some get crushed inside. While your lot stays on top and rides over everyone." She clenched her fists. "That's why there *has* to be a revolution."

The word "revolution" gave Col a start. It *was* cruel and bullying, but . . . to turn everything upside down?

Yet how else could it be changed?

"You Upper Decks people are good at not knowin' what you don't want to know, ain't ya?" Her lips twisted in a bitter expression. "Well, you know it now. Just start thinkin' about whose side yer on."

She turned and headed back up the pipe. After a while Col turned and went after her.

45

Col had only four days to survive until the end of term, but every day was harder than the last. Showing more and more of his true attitude, Mr. Gibber began to act out the myth that Col was a source of infection.

On Tuesday he kept wandering toward Col's desk as if by accident. Then he would pretend to realize where he was, clap a hand over his nose, and backpedal away to safety. The students joined in with calls of "Danger zone, sir!" and "That was a close one, sir!"

On Wednesday he progressed to a further stage of provocation. Now he made a display of deliberately walking into danger, tiptoeing toward Col's desk one step at a time. The students waited until he was two paces away before they roared out a warning.

"Don't do it, sir!"

"We don't want to lose you, sir!"

"Think of Mrs. Gibber and the little Giblets, sir!"

Mr. Gibber put on a comical expression of shock and horror and skipped back to the front of the class.

Col refused to be provoked. He could see that Mr. Gibber was only looking for an opportunity for more playacting. He summoned up the latest fighting techniques that Riff had taught him and rehearsed them in the privacy of his mind.

It wasn't so easy to ignore the note that was waiting for him when he came back to class after the Wednesday lunch break. He opened the lid of his desk, and there it was, scrawled on a sheet of paper in red ink.

WE DON'T WANT YOU IN OUR SCHOOL
WE KNOW WHAT TO DO WITH FREAKS LIKE YOU
YOU MAKE OUR CLASSROOM STINK
FILTHY-LOVER!

Who was it from? He scanned around, but everyone seemed to be looking the other way.

It had to have been one of the Squellingham group, of course. But when could they have left the note in his desk? He was sure they'd been standing around their hamper all through the lunch break. Perhaps another student acting under their orders?

He was thankful that Thursday was taken up by end-of-term exams. Under conditions of strict silence Mr. Gibber had lost his audience. He stalked around with his tweaker and applied it to selected students, but he didn't dare use it on Col.

There was a history and geography exam, followed by an algebra and geometry exam, then a physics and chemistry exam in the afternoon. Col wrote his own answers regardless of Mr. Gibber's teaching. He had no doubt his marks would plummet no matter his answers.

Thursday also brought another threatening note. Someone had managed to slip it into his satchel, and he didn't discover it until the end of the day. It was written in the same red ink and the same block capitals:

GO BACK WHERE YOU BELONG
GET OUT WHILE YOU 'RE STILL IN ONE PIECE
OR MEET YOUR FILTHY FATE
WE 'LL FIX YOU TOMORROW!

It was coming to a head. He was a far better fighter than ten days ago, but he still couldn't take on the whole Squellingham group at once. He needed more attacking moves. Riff had insisted on teaching him defensive moves first, which she said was the proper order. But now he needed to do more than dodge and block and counterthrust . . . and he needed to be able to do it by tomorrow.

46

The Porpentines maintained their rituals in spite of everything. On Thursdays the Sir Mormus branch of the family met for afternoon tea in the Somerset Room, and Col was required to attend after school, as usual.

Today the atmosphere was glacial. Gillabeth had already arrived, immaculate in her school uniform, and Ebnolia, Orris, and Quinnea were sipping tea. Nobody spoke to Col.

Ebnolia was preoccupied with her favorite Menial, Wicky Popo. Extraordinarily, he had been allowed to sit on one of the Somerset Room's elegant, satin-upholstered chairs. Grandmother's well-known kindness toward Menials had transcended all bounds.

In fact he was more slumped than sitting. His cheeks were hollow, his eyes protuberant, and he could barely support the weight of his own head. He looked very sick indeed.

"Poor, poor Wicky Popo." Ebnolia stood before him, shaking her head. "What a big, sad, unfair world it is, isn't it? What's it all for? Where will it end?"

The Menial turned large, liquid eyes toward her. Ebnolia made patting motions over his head, though without actually touching him.

"So unhappy and suffering. So unwell, just when you want to be strong. Look at your poor, thin arms and legs! Look at your chest! Not eating properly at all."

She continued tut-tutting quietly to herself. Wicky Popo's silence didn't discourage her. No one else spoke, and she obviously didn't expect it.

Then the door swung open, and Sir Mormus marched in. One of the serving Menials poured a cup of tea and handed it to him. For a moment the cup rattled on the saucer.

"It's happening." His voice seemed dredged up from some deep, dark place. "A no-confidence motion tomorrow. Sir Wisley got his way. Their Imperial Majesties will be asked to attend a special session of the Executive." He turned to Ebnolia. "Our future is in your hands now."

Ebnolia left Wicky Popo and came across to him. She took the cup and saucer from his quivering hand and put them down on the nearest table.

"Negotiations are going well," she said brightly. "Hommelia is in favor. Now I must go and talk to Turbot himself. We'll have a yes or no before tomorrow, and I think it will be yes."

Sir Mormus's gloom scarcely lifted. "It still needs the queen's approval."

"Well, now, we just have to hope, don't we?"

"She hasn't let me talk to her since . . . the incident. It's ridiculous to let her make decisions by herself." He lowered his voice. "She doesn't have the brains."

"Shush, dear." Ebnolia fluttered her hands. "Don't worry. I'll go and talk to Turbot now."

She pattered to the door and went out, leaving behind a sweetness of strawberry-scented perfume.

There was absolute silence for the next three minutes. All the fire seemed to have gone out of Sir Mormus. Finally, he roused himself.

"You can go," he told Col. "You too," he told Gillabeth.

Gillabeth made a tiny curtsy, but she wasn't quite ready to be dismissed. "Don't you want to hear my report, sir?" Her eyes flicked toward Col.

"No. Tell your grandmother later." Sir Mormus turned away to the cake stand. "If there is a later . . ."

Col was glad to escape from the room. He hadn't uttered a word from start to finish. But he did have a question to ask Gillabeth, as soon as they were out in the corridor.

"You know what it is, don't you? This plan of Grandmother's?"

Gillabeth merely nodded, as though her knowledge were a matter of course.

"Well?"

"Well what?"

"What is it?"

"Not for your ears."

"But it's about me. Isn't it?"

"Oh, everything's about you. It was you that got our family into this mess. You and your undisciplined behavior. Flying in the face of convention. Do you have any idea what you've done to this family? Do you even realize how you've dragged our name down?"

She glared at him vindictively for a moment, then strode on ahead. Col was left stunned.

Were all older sisters like this? Always correct and perfect? He had never been able to live up to Gillabeth's expectations.

47

"Why do you need more attacking moves?"

"It's time I learned."

"I decide when you're ready to learn. Why tonight?"

Col didn't want to admit that students in his class were planning to beat him up tomorrow. In the end, though, he had to tell Riff the whole story. It came out in a great hot lump.

Riff frowned. "'But I thought you were top dog? Goin' to be supreme commander or somethin'?"

Col explained how the situation had changed since he'd returned from Below. Riff thought about it.

"Who's writing the notes?" she asked.

"Don't know. Probably one of the Squellingham twins."

"Who uses red ink?"

Col was amazed at her sharpness. It was true—the students all wrote in blue or black in their exercise books. He'd never considered it before.

"Someone must have a bottle of red ink in his desk," he said.

"You should've told me all this before." Riff pursed her lips. "Okay, I'll teach ya as many attackin' moves as I can. I'll go without my readin' lessons for tonight."

They moved the bed back against the wall, and Col loosened up with his all-over shaking exercise. Then Riff demonstrated the spots to hit and how to hit them.

"Short and sharp to the nerve spots—use the points of yer knuckles. Deeper to the muscles and flesh spots—drive in with yer full fist. Yer target's always below the skin, see, so aim for it."

The training began in earnest. She rolled one of his blankets into a tight cylinder and held it up in front of her, while he struck at it with different types of blows.

"Full fist!"

"Short and sharp!"

"Straighter! Don't swing!"

Next she tossed aside the blanket and told him to aim his blows at her, limiting him to one fist at a time. He was half-hearted at first, until he got used to the idea that he couldn't hit her anyway. She was fast enough to swerve aside, but she could always tell where the blow *would* have landed.

"No, lower!"

"From the left!"

"Forward and back! Hit and pull out!"

Faster and faster they went at it, panting and grunting. Col could feel the improvement in himself: a rhythm and rightness to all his movements. After a while Riff couldn't just swerve aside but had to use her hands to deflect his blows.

Then she called a break. "Good, you're gettin' it," she said. "Remember, never get boxed in. You say there's a whole gang against ya. Stay arm's length and keep yer freedom of movement."

Col's sleeveless sweater was soaked through with sweat. It had been gathering sweat night after night and now smelled sour and rank.

Suddenly Col didn't care about propriety. So what if he

looked like a male Filthy? He wanted to fight like a Filthy; he might as well look like one too. . . . He pulled off the sweater and stood bare to the waist.

"Yeah, better," said Riff, eyeing him curiously.

They resumed training. Riff devised a new exercise involving the rolled-up blanket and Col's pillow and socks. Arming herself with the socks, she propped the pillow on one end of his bed, the blanket on the other. He had to deal with opponent after opponent as she called out in random order, "Blanket!" "Pillow!" "Me!" He swung around and around, hitting and dodging, while socks came flying at him through the air.

Everything became a blur. He hardly knew what he was doing, yet he was strangely infallible. His body had taken over from his mind. He wasn't thinking about tomorrow or school or anything. Just this instant . . . and the next . . . and the next . . . Movement flowing into movement! He wanted to shout and laugh with the intoxication of it.

"Me!" called Riff.

He ducked under a sock, pivoted, and aimed at her solar plexus. Almost too quick! She missed his fist with her hand and only half blocked it with her forearm. The blow caught her glancingly just above the hip.

"Uff!" she gasped.

Before he could draw back, she grabbed his arm, twisted, knelt, pulled, and flipped him over her right shoulder.

In one split second he was hurtling toward the bedroom wall . . . in the next split second he reacted and countered. He met the wall with hands and feet, absorbing the impact like a spring, then recoiled and launched straight back at her.

He caught her by surprise and tumbled her to the floor. They sprawled together in a tangle of arms and legs.

So close, his bare chest weighing down on her arm, his face above hers . . .

He couldn't tell whether she was spluttering with laughter or with anger. All he knew was the blood pounding in his ears and a sensation of drowning in a dark wave. It was like the time when she'd kissed him. . . .

He leaned forward, closed his eyes, and pressed his lips to hers.

At once she twisted aside. A moan of disappointment came out of his mouth.

When he opened his eyes, she was looking at him. Raised eyebrows, quizzical expression.

"Full of surprises, ain't ya?" she said.

She didn't seem especially shocked. But he was. He couldn't believe what he'd just tried to do. His behavior would have been unacceptable even for a Filthy. And the moan that had escaped from his lips . . . like an animal! There was no excuse and no justification. Where did it come from, that dark wave rising up in him? Where had it been hidden? It was like someone else's personality. He would never be able to trust himself again.

She disengaged her arms and legs and jumped up. "Okay, come on, let's get back to it."

The training resumed, but Col's heart wasn't in it. When they practiced the same exercise, Riff dodged his attacking moves with ease. He wasn't afraid of hitting her; he was afraid of letting go. He didn't dare risk his body taking over from his mind again.

"What's wrong with ya?" she asked after a while.

He didn't answer. He kept picturing the way she'd twisted aside. Of course, if she was partnered with Padder, she couldn't let just any boy kiss her. Shame and mortification twisted a knot in the pit of his stomach.

Finally, Riff called it quits. "I guess you ain't fit enough to train nonstop."

"I'm not tired."

"I reckon you are. You're slowin' down."

"I wish I had more time. I'm not ready to fight tomorrow, am I?"

Riff shrugged. "You can still win. Just think like a winner."

Col nodded, but he didn't believe it.

48

There were no lessons on the last day of term. Mr. Gibber patted Murgatrude in his wastepaper basket and allowed the class to amuse themselves. Mostly they played games of hangman or tic-tac-toe, swiveling in their seats to form pairs. Col wasn't surprised that no one offered to include him in a game.

He *was* surprised that a few of the grindboys and crawlers looked a tiny bit sorry for him. Everyone must know what the Squellinghams intended to do. The peaceful lethargy in the classroom was like the calm before the storm.

Morning recess was the first danger period. Col stayed close by the master on playground duty, hovering in the middle of the yard while Mr. Dandrum puffed on his pipe and swung back and forth on his swing. He hated himself for doing it. *Only one day,* he told himself. *I'll be better trained after the holidays.*

The Squellingham group didn't approach, but roamed round the yard in a pack. They were coopting new members. By the end of the recess they had added two climbers from 4A, Prewitt and Melstruther, and two older boys from 5A. The odds had climbed from six against one to ten against one.

The next danger period was the lunch break. Now Mr. Gortliss swung on the swing, while Mrs. Stummer stood talking to him. Even better. Col pretended to be studying cracks in the surface of the yard.

But he was famished. The trestle table where two Menials served out food was twenty paces away. Perhaps when the queue of students had gone . . .

He checked around for the Squellingham group. They weren't in a pack, but had split up and ranged themselves round the sides of the yard.

Five minutes, ten minutes passed. The savory smells of pies and sausage rolls made him salivate.

Finally, there were no more students waiting to be served. Mrs. Stummer was still talking to Mr. Gortliss. He made his move.

But two girls from 3B moved first. They lined up at the food table in front of him, and he had to stand and wait his turn.

The two of them discussed the merits of cheese or chutney sandwiches. They couldn't make up their minds.

Already his enemies were starting to come forward, converging toward him. Surely they wouldn't attack with two teachers only twenty paces away?

But when he looked again, Mrs. Stummer was walking off. The conversation was over, and Mr. Gortliss was facing the other way.

No time! He lunged forward between the two girls, snatched up a sausage roll, turned to run—and someone grabbed him by the elbow.

Fefferley! His fat, buttery face was one big smirk of triumph.

Col squashed the sausage roll over the bridge of his nose, right between the eyes.

Fefferley staggered, and Col broke free. The rest of the Squellingham group rushed toward him. Impossible to get back to the safety of Mr. Gortliss; they'd cut him off first.

He took off in the other direction, narrowly evading Lumbridge's outstretched arms. The toilets were his only hope of refuge. He swerved round other students or knocked them out of the way.

He reached the toilets just ahead of his pursuers. He swung into the first empty cubicle, slammed the door, and fastened the catch.

There was no light inside, only nameless smells and the sound of dripping water. All toilets were kept dark to preserve the modesty of those who visited them. The toilet bowl was a mere pale ghost of a shape. Col lowered the wooden seat and sat on it.

Voices outside. "Come out, Porpentine!"

"Come and get what's coming to you!"

Col stayed where he was. The smell was stomach-churning. Shadows of feet moved back and forth in the narrow band of light under the door.

Then they began pounding on the door with their fists. The thumps and bangs were deafening in the small closed space, but the door was made of solid wood. Mere noise wouldn't drive him out.

After a while the banging stopped. He could hear them whispering. Then something moved in the crack at the side of the door.

It was a ruler. They were planning to lift and unhook the catch! Col leaped forward and seized hold of the end before they could work it upward. He pulled the whole ruler in through the crack and out of their hands.

There was a baffled cry from outside. He snapped the ruler

in half, kicked the two bits out under the door, and returned to his seat.

Time passed. They were still out there, still whispering. What next?

A massive weight crashed against the door. Someone was shoulder-charging the door, trying to batter it down. Lumbridge, at a guess.

Col jumped up, planted his feet, and braced himself against the wood.

A second run-up, a second crash. The impact jarred his bones and rattled his teeth.

"More! More! More!" came the chant from outside.

Crash after crash after crash. Col's shoulder was bruised and aching. He guessed that the hinges would burst before the wood broke. Already the screws were coming loose. Probably another two or three charges . . .

He decided then. Even though he couldn't outfight them all, he wouldn't be caught like a rat in a trap. He'd take a few of them by surprise, at least.

"Let's get it over with," he muttered, and prepared to raise the catch.

But he dropped his hand when the bell rang for the end of the lunch break.

Reprieved!

"We'll get you after school, Porpentine," hissed a voice through the crack. "We'll get you ten times worse."

He listened to the receding sounds outside. Gradually the schoolyard hubbub faded to silence. By the time he came out, everyone had gone except for the two Menials.

They were preparing to pack up the food table. Still, there

was one sandwich left. Col swooped on it: cheese and ham. He ate it in three bites as he made his way up the ramp and back to the 4A classroom.

Mr. Gibber rubbed his bobble of a nose but made no comment on Col's late return. The Squellingham group didn't even glance in his direction. Everyone had gone back to their games of hangman and tic-tac-toe.

When Col opened the lid of his desk, he found a new note waiting for him.

YOU'LL WISH YOU'D NEVER BEEN BORN!
THIS IS THE END FOR YOU!
YOU'RE DEAD!

How could they have done it? He stared at the red letters and remembered Riff's idea. Who had a bottle of red ink in his desk?

He was still thinking about it when there was a gentle knock on the classroom door.

Dr. Blessamy poked his head in. "Colbert Porpentine? Your father is here for you. Come along now."

49

Col didn't care about the reasons; he was just grateful to escape. It turned out that his father had come to escort him up to Fifty-first Deck. With his sad, bulging eyes Orris could never look happy, yet he seemed less hangdog than usual. In fact Col began to suspect that he was actually elated.

He refused to reveal why Col had been summoned. "Your grandfather doesn't want me to tell you."

"Are we going to the Executive Chamber?"

"Yes."

"Is there a meeting of the Executive?"

"Your grandfather doesn't want me to tell you."

Twenty minutes later they approached the door of the chamber. Orris didn't enter, but turned off into a small oak-paneled anteroom.

Inside sat Grandmother Ebnolia, perched on the room's only chair. She was dressed in her very best clothes, with her waist corseted almost out of existence.

Col was becoming more curious. "What's happening?" he asked her.

"Shush." She nodded toward a farther double door.

A murmur of voices filtered through from the other side. Col recognized Queen Victoria's clear-cut enunciation and the rusty bass of Prince Albert.

There was a crack where the two halves of the door didn't quite meet in the middle. While Orris stared at the floor and Ebnolia remained sitting, Col sidled up to it. No one said anything to stop him when he leaned forward and applied his eye to the crack.

It *was* a meeting of the Executive. The tables were arranged in a semicircle, as for the Imperial inquiry. Sir Wisley Squellingham paced up and down, in and out of Col's field of vision. He was making a speech to the queen and the Executive.

"It has come to the point, Your Imperial Majesty, where your supreme commander no longer commands automatic trust and respect from the members of your Executive. Although he bears the keys of office, I am sorry to say that his judgment is suspect. He has failed to show leadership since a certain event of a fortnight ago."

Sir Mormus rose in his seat on the queen's right-hand side. Col expected a contemptuous blast of rebuttal. But Sir Mormus said nothing.

"It is a grave step we propose, Your Majesty." Sir Wisley stabbed the air with his forefinger. "A motion of no confidence in your supreme commander. But we must have unity on the Executive. We have asked for this vote to be taken in your presence."

Prince Albert harrumphed. "And if Porpentine loses?"

Sir Wisley opted for humility. "I leave it for my queen to decide what should happen."

Queen Victoria turned to her supreme commander. "Well, Sir Mormus?"

"Certainly." Sir Mormus was at his most magnificent. "Let Squellingham have his vote, if he wants. I have more important things to think about."

"More *important*?"

"Your Imperial Majesty, I have a request to make on behalf of the Porpentine and Turbot families."

Sir Wisley swiveled to shoot a venomous glance at Chief Helmsman Turbot. Then turned back to Queen Victoria. "The motion comes first," he hissed.

But he had been caught off balance, and his protest lacked conviction.

"No, no," said Queen Victoria. "Let's see what can be more important than a no-confidence motion."

Sir Mormus turned to face the double door, as though looking straight at Col. "My grandson Colbert," he boomed. "Let him step forth."

Suddenly the two halves of the door were flung open. Col realized with surprise that his father had come up on his left and his grandmother on his right.

He found himself ushered out into the middle of the chamber. The members of the Executive gaped at him.

"What is this?"

"What's going on?"

Sir Mormus addressed himself exclusively to Queen Victoria. "My grandson wishes to get married, Your Majesty."

Gasps came from all around the chamber—and one of them was Col's.

"He asks for your permission to marry Sephaltina Turbot," Sir Mormus went on.

On Col's left, Orris was nodding his head in silent approval.

Queen Victoria knitted her brow. "Isn't he rather young?"

Sir Wisley broke in. "Impossible! Of course it's impossible! He's not twenty-one. Nowhere near twenty-one."

"He's sixteen." Ebnolia dropped a hint of a curtsy toward Her Imperial Majesty. "Sephaltina Turbot is seventeen. They can still get married by special dispensation from the queen."

"It's not right!" Sir Wisley was livid. "It's against all precedent!"

"There have been precedents." Ebnolia's sweet tones cut through his bluster like a knife. "Three times before. It's all in the records of the Imperial Church. I can show you, if you'd like."

Sir Wisley took a deep breath. "There must have been reasons before. Reasons of state, reasons of something. There are no reasons now. Except for a plot to frustrate the will of the Executive."

Queen Victoria spoke up. "What reasons, Sir Mormus? What reasons, Lady Porpentine?"

Ebnolia answered with her most grandmotherly smile. "They love each other, Your Majesty."

Chief Helmsman Turbot rose to his feet. He pointed to a matching double door on the opposite side of the chamber. "Let my daughter present herself."

The second double door flew open, and Sephaltina stepped forward, accompanied by the Honorable Hommelia Turbot.

Col stared in surprise. The last time he had seen Sephaltina, she had been wearing her school uniform. Now her flaxen hair was dressed in elaborate plaits and bound with blue ribbons. Her cheeks had been powdered, and her rosebud mouth seemed even smaller and rosier.

"Let them stand together," said Sir Mormus.

Ebnolia and Hommelia shepherded Col and Sephaltina into position, side by side. Sephaltina nibbled bashfully at her lower lip.

"Don't they make a lovely couple?" murmured Ebnolia.

"Too young," snarled Sir Wisley.

Queen Victoria waved him to silence and spoke to Col and Sephaltina. "And where did the two of you meet?"

"At Dr. Blessamy's Academy," said Sephaltina.

Queen Victoria clapped her hands. "How delightful! And do you really and truly love each other?"

"Say yes," murmured Orris in a low voice that carried only to Col's ear.

"Yes," Col answered Queen Victoria. "Your Majesty."

"And the young girl?"

Sephaltina blushed and lowered her eyes.

"She's been quite insistent." Hommelia spoke up for her daughter. "Hasn't she, Turbot?"

"Indeed," said the chief helmsman. "Very determined on the idea."

Queen Victoria's long horse face was almost girlish as she turned to her consort. "What do you think, my dear? Shall I grant my special permission?"

Prince Albert pulled on one end of his mustache, then the other. "They could get engaged now. Married later."

"They don't want to wait," said Ebnolia. "They want to get married as soon as possible."

"How soon?" asked Queen Victoria.

"A week from now, Your Majesty."

Everyone goggled. Col had the sense that his fate was

being decided, but it had nothing to do with him. Marriages were arranged all the time between young men and women of the elite. If this alliance saved the Porpentines from the disaster he'd caused, then he had no objection.

Queen Victoria stifled an unseemly giggle. "Such a hurry! Dear, oh dear! They must be very much in love." She turned to her consort. "Do you remember how we were, Albert, when we first met, all those years ago?"

"Not so many years," Prince Albert answered gallantly. "Seems like yesterday."

"You came on board at Gibraltar. We were supposed to have at least eighteen months of being engaged."

"But you wouldn't hear of waiting longer than six months." Prince Albert rested his hand on the table next to Queen Victoria's hand. "After we set eyes on each other, you put your foot down."

"I did, didn't I?"

They were leaning closer and closer. Their arms might have touched if Queen Victoria hadn't pulled herself together with a little shake.

"I'm going to allow it," she said. "These two young people can get married as soon as they like."

"Thank you, Your Majesty," said Sir Mormus.

"Thank you, Your Majesty," echoed Chief Helmsman Turbot.

Orris let out a deep sigh of relief.

"May we hope that Your Majesty will conduct the ceremony herself?" asked Ebnolia.

"Of course, of course!" Queen Victoria clapped her hands. "I'd love to."

There was a smattering of applause around the chamber. The mood had changed in the Porpentines' favor.

"Well, well." The queen adjusted her face to a serious expression. "I suppose we should get back to the business of the meeting. Sir Wisley, you were saying?"

Ebnolia and Hommelia drew Col and Sephaltina away to the side. Col was aware of Sephaltina glancing at him, blushing prettily on and off. He might have thought her extremely attractive if he hadn't grown used to Riff's different kind of looks.

Sir Wisley had the center of the room for pacing up and down again. However, he seemed to have lost the inclination.

"We proceed to a vote on your no-confidence motion, then," said Queen Victoria.

There was a bitter twist to Sir Wisley's mouth as he scanned the members of the Executive. "Your Majesty, I would like to withdraw the motion."

"Withdraw? Oh, if you wish." Queen Victoria was not amused. "Is there any other business?"

Chief Helmsman Turbot had remained on his feet. "Your Majesty, I have another motion to propose."

Receiving the queen's nod of approval, he took the floor. He spoke of the probability that the Prussian juggernaut would reach Hong Kong before *Worldshaker*, and proposed a change of route to the coaling station at Singapore.

The vote was a foregone conclusion, even without the chief helmsman's arguments. Sir Wisley's supporters recognized a shift in the wind. They voted in favor, while Sir Wisley abstained.

Then Queen Victoria declared the meeting closed. She left the chamber with Prince Albert, while the members of the Executive stayed talking among themselves. Col left with Orris and Ebnolia.

A little breathless cry brought them to a halt. "Oh, Lady Porpentine."

It was Hommelia Turbot sailing up behind, her trotterlike feet twinkling below the hem of her floral dress.

"Ah." She subsided and recovered her breath. "Lady Porpentine, do you think the young couple should have a meeting together before their wedding?"

Ebnolia tilted her head and thought about it. "Yes, that would be proper. Chaperoned, of course."

"Then we positively must pay you a visit."

"I shall be taking the family for a holiday on Garden Deck."

"When, dear Lady Porpentine?"

"We set off this afternoon. As soon as Colbert and his sister come home from school."

"Then a visit on Garden Deck. How nice. Would Thursday be available?"

"Perfectly available. Yes."

Ebnolia continued on along the corridor, followed by Col and Orris. Hommelia made elaborate gestures of farewell.

Col's head was still spinning from the scene in the chamber, but the mention of school brought him back to the immediate present. Sir Mormus might have won over the Executive, but Col hadn't won over the Squellingham group. They hadn't changed their minds about beating him up.

"Grandmother." He caught up with Ebnolia. "Do I have to go back to school now? I could start getting my things ready for the holiday."

Ebnolia didn't even consider it. "Plenty of time for that afterward, Colbert. Your father will escort you back."

50

Orris escorted Col as far as the entrance arch of the academy. Col thought of slipping across the yard to hide in the toilets, but he couldn't do it with his father watching. Like a prisoner going to execution, he went up the ramp and returned to class.

The Squellingham group grinned and gloated when they saw the victim delivered back into their hands. Col knew they would be lying in wait for him after school. Probably under the entrance arch, since there was no other way out from the academy.

But what if he stayed inside? They wouldn't expect that; they wouldn't know where he'd gone. Waiting for the last bell of the day, he pondered a plan of survival.

Clang-clang-clang!

End of term! The students gave a great cheer. Even Mr. Gibber couldn't outyell them. They were uncaged animals frantic for freedom. They snatched up their satchels and rushed for the door all at the same time. For several minutes there was a wild mêlée of jostling, shouting students.

The turmoil was exactly what Col needed. He collected his satchel but didn't follow the crowd. Instead he ducked down and hid under his desk.

Had he been noticed? He waited for someone to call out and give him away. But no. The shouting faded, and the classroom was empty. Col raised his head to take a look.

Only Mr. Gibber remained, standing in the doorway. He cracked his knuckles and seemed in high good humor.

"Good riddance!" he muttered. "Stinkers! Scum! Degenerates! Bartrim Gibber is ten times as good as any of you."

He came back into the classroom and played a drumroll on his desk. Whistling through his teeth, he wiped down the blackboard. Then he went out and closed the door behind him.

Col left his satchel under his desk and crawled as far as possible away from the door. He hid in the farthest corner, cross-legged beneath Pugh's desk. Here, he could be spotted only if someone knelt down to peer between the desk legs.

He willed himself to patience. When would the Squellingham group realize they'd missed him? And what would they do then? He would have to stay hidden for a very long time.

The empty classroom was a world transformed, silent and still and eerie. Now that the initial excitement was over, he fell into a blank state of boredom. Five minutes, ten minutes went past.

Then a thought popped into his mind. The red ink! Someone must have a bottle of red ink in their desk, someone like Hythe or Pugh. Now was the perfect opportunity to investigate.

He waited a while, but his curiosity had been aroused. He *had* to know who had been writing those notes. He felt sure he would be able to hear any footsteps approaching along the gallery outside.

He came out from his hiding place. Pugh's desk first. He opened the lid and found a stack of answer papers from yesterday's geography exam. But the only bottle of ink was blue.

Hythe's desk contained the answer papers from the algebra exam . . . but no bottle of ink at all. Col went through Haugh's desk, and Flarrow's, Lumbridge's, and Fefferley's. Still nothing.

What about one of the climbers, writing notes under instructions from the twins? Col moved farther and farther out across the room. He looked inside the desks of the climbers, then the crawlers, then even the blockies and grindboys. Nobody had a bottle of red ink.

Only one possibility remained: Mr. Gibber himself. Col could hardly believe it, but he had to make sure.

He crossed to the teacher's desk and pulled out the left-hand drawer. It contained only assorted bric-a-brac that Mr. Gibber had confiscated from students during the term.

He went to pull out the right-hand drawer, when a sudden loud crash made him jump.

The classroom door had been flung wide open—and there in the doorway stood Hythe and Pugh.

The rest of the gang crowded behind them. There was an ugly grin of triumph on every face. They had discovered him after all.

They filed in and closed the door. Not only the six members of the group, but Prewitt and Melstruther and the two boys coopted from 5A. At a word from Hythe, Prewitt and Melstruther dragged a desk across in front of the door.

So this is it, Col thought. *Ten against one.* He gave himself an all-over shaking, as he did at the start of his training sessions.

His enemies jeered. "Look at him shaking in his shoes!"

"He's cracking up already!"

They advanced across the room, Lumbridge, Haugh, and Flarrow at the front. As wise generals, Hythe and Pugh stayed out of harm's way at the back.

Col was still behind Mr. Gibber's desk. When the twins shouted, "Get him!" he pushed the desk forward into the charging pack. The front three doubled up as the wooden edge smashed into them at waist level.

Col sprang on top of the desk and aimed a kick at Flarrow—where Riff had shown him, right on the Adam's apple. Flarrow fell backward with a kind of gurgle. Col aimed another kick at Haugh, but missed his spot. Haugh clutched at the side of his jaw and stayed upright.

Lumbridge had already moved around the desk and was trying to catch hold of Col's ankles. Col danced back, then jumped right off the desk and onto Lumbridge's shoulders.

As his most dangerous opponent went down in a heap, Col delivered a punch to the nape of his neck. But his timing was wrong. Lumbridge roared and struggled to heave him off.

Rolled from side to side, Col collided painfully with a desk leg. Then his fingers touched Mr. Gibber's wastepaper basket.

He grabbed the basket with one hand, the back of Lumbridge's head with the other. Quick as a flash he pushed Lumbridge's face down in the basket.

There was a bloodcurdling *"Rrrrrr-ow-rrrrr-eeow!"* Murgatrude didn't tolerate strange faces intruding on his personal space.

Col sprang away as Lumbridge screamed. There was a frenzy of snarling and scratching inside the basket. It was jammed so tight on Lumbridge's head he couldn't pry it off. He reared up on his knees, then collapsed forward again.

Col retreated as Haugh and Fefferley came to Lumbridge's aid. No one was grinning now. They knew that their victim would put up a fight, and there was a vicious look in their eyes.

"Everyone together!" ordered Pugh.

They came at Col from all sides. Too late he remembered Riff's advice about keeping his freedom of movement. He was getting boxed into a corner.

He focused on his tallest opponent, one of the 5A boys. He lunged forward, switched direction, and struck twice: first deadening an arm with the point of his knuckles, then hitting the solar plexus with his full fist. But the boy was stepping back as he struck the second blow. The gang closed ranks, and Col was forced to withdraw.

He danced on his toes and feinted this way and that, but nobody would take him on one-to-one. They were working to bring him down by sheer weight of numbers.

"Throw things!" shouted Hythe.

Col swayed out of the way as a huge dictionary came flying toward him. Hythe had dug it out of someone's desk. Soon they were all opening desks and hurling missiles. Books, compasses, pencil boxes . . .

Col dodged easily. He'd had enough practice with Riff throwing socks. But behind him were piles of books and papers stacked ceiling-high against the wall. He brushed against them and started an avalanche. As the whole lot came crashing down over him, he stumbled and fell forward on his hands and knees.

"Now!" cried the Squellinghams.

Whooping and hollering, they charged. With no time to

regain his feet, Col dived under the nearest desk. He kept on going, scuttling under desk after desk.

For a moment he had broken out of the circle, and the gang had lost sight of him.

Then Flarrow yelled, "There he is! Over there!"

Col jumped to his feet and raced for the door. He heard Pugh shouting, "Use the canes! Use the canes!"

Canes?

The door was blocked by the desk that Prewitt and Melstruther had dragged in front. When Col tried to pull it away, it caught under the doorknob. He tilted it, worked it free, pulled again—

There was a roar of rage from behind. Col glanced over his shoulder and saw a figure of horror. Lumbridge was bleeding from scalp to collar, his face ripped by a thousand scratches. But he was back in action, and his eyes gleamed with lust for revenge.

The rest of the gang advanced in a semicircle behind him. They had armed themselves with Mr. Gibber's canes, which they cut and swished from side to side.

Too late to open the door. Col knew he was beaten, yet he didn't feel beaten. Now that he had no hope, he felt strangely inspired. *Think like a winner,* Riff had told him.

He waited, clear and composed, until the very last moment . . .

Then he exploded like an unbound spring. First Lumbridge: a straight, sharp jab to the nose that made him yelp. Then Haugh, then Prewitt, then one of the boys from 5A. Punch after punch struck home: to jaw, to groin, to kidneys. He kept at arm's length, poised and spinning on his toes. He felled the other 5A boy with a kick behind the knees; he swung Fefferley by the arm to crash against Melstruther.

It was as though everything had fallen into place. Once he threw himself into nonstop fighting, he was caught up in the rhythm and his timing was perfect. He didn't need to remember about watching for intentions in his opponents' eyes—he just did it. He didn't need to decide about different punches for different targets—his body decided for him. He was like Riff herself, in a trance of sure-footed motion.

Their canes only made them clumsy. They missed him and ended up hitting the furniture—or their fellow attackers. Col snatched Flarrow's cane from his hands and poked him in the chest with it.

Soon half the gang was on the floor. The two boys from 5A slipped round to the door and started to drag the desk away. Fefferley staggered to his feet and headed the same way. Hythe and Pugh shouted orders but held back from the fighting themselves.

Lumbridge was the only one still pressing forward. Col saw him coming out of the corner of his eye, whirled round, and drove him back with a punch over the heart.

The bully blinked, shook his head, and came barreling in once more. As if in slow motion Col saw him swing a huge right hook. It was aimed at Col's chin, but Col did what Riff had done to Scarface: caught hold of his fist and overbalanced him with his own momentum.

As Lumbridge crashed to the floor, Col delivered a paralyzing chop to the back of his neck. The bully grunted and lay still.

All the others were now sidling toward the door, even

Hythe and Pugh. Col didn't care if the rest escaped—but not the twins.

He sprang across and drove Pugh back beyond the teacher's desk. When Hythe tried to wriggle past on the other side, Col tackled him to the floor. He knelt with one knee on the small of his back.

"You're a sneaking coward, Hythe Squellingham. You make other people do your dirty work."

Hythe struggled to break free. "No."

"You and Pugh."

Col pressed down with his knee. Hythe gasped and spluttered.

"Not us," said Pugh from behind the teacher's desk.

"Who did you get to write those notes, Hythe?"

"Nobody."

Col spotted the wastepaper basket nearby. He pulled it closer. He could tell by the weight that Murgatrude wasn't inside, but Hythe didn't know that.

"You want me to stick your face in here?" He twisted Hythe's head. "You want to join Murgatrude?"

Hythe's eyes were wide with fear. "No, please, no!"

"Tell me the truth about those notes."

"She wrote them."

"What? Who?"

Hythe could no longer speak for blubbering. Instead it was Pugh who answered. "Your sister, Gillabeth. She's been organizing everything all along."

51

Col's triumph had turned to ashes. The twins not only stuck to their story but filled in the details: how they'd had secret meetings with Gillabeth, how she'd left the notes in his desk. The one thing they couldn't explain was why she'd been doing it.

Col sat for a long time in the empty classroom after they'd gone. He was in a state of shock. His secret enemy was his own sister. And yet she was always so committed to the family's interests—why would she work with the Squellinghams against the Porpentines? He felt as though he'd been punched in the head, far worse than any punch from Lumbridge.

When he got back to Forty-second Deck, his mother's servant Missy Jip was waiting at the door of his room to help him pack. He had to select enough clothes for seven days. Apart from Sir Mormus himself, the entire Sir Mormus branch of the family was going on holiday.

There was no chance to confront Gillabeth alone. When the party descended to Garden Deck, Gillabeth walked along behind Grandmother Ebnolia, holding Baby Brother Antrobus by the hand. Her manner was as self-consciously upright and virtuous as ever. Of course, she couldn't know that Col had discovered her secret.

Twelve Menials accompanied the party, ten of them laden with boxes and baggage. The eleventh was Grandmother's favorite, Wicky Popo, who was far too weak to carry anything. The twelfth Menial was needed just to support him.

Only the elite families were entitled to take holidays on Garden Deck. It was an open deck with more than fifty acres of varying botanical zones. Each zone recreated a particular scene from the Old Country. By the time they arrived, the sun had sunk below the enclosing walls and the sky was a glorious wash of orange and mauve.

Grandmother had reserved five side-by-side cottages in a zone of parkland: one for Col, one for herself, one for Orris and Quinnea, one for Gillabeth and Antrobus, and one for the twelve Menials. The parkland scenery was all rambling paths, clover-scented lawns, trees in buried pots, and a central bandstand. The bandstand and cottages were built to scale, halfsize.

The first hour was spent settling in. From the outside Col's cottage appeared to have two stories and many tiny rooms, but inside there was only one normal-size room, containing a normal-size bed, cupboard, and chest of drawers. Col did his unpacking in his own time, without help from any Menial.

He had just finished stowing his socks when he heard a cry of distress outside. Grandmother?

He hurried to see. Doors opened and faces peered out from every cottage. In the dim twilight Ebnolia stood gazing at a pale figure at her feet.

It was Wicky Popo, facedown on the grass. The twelfth Menial hovered nearby, and two other Menials watched from a distance.

"Oh dear, oh dear!" Ebnolia prodded her favorite with the toe of her shoe. He groaned and stirred. "He should never have come to Garden Deck. Too loyal and devoted. He just can't bear to be away from me. How could I say no?"

"What happened?" Col asked her.

"He fell down. No reason at all. Doesn't it break your heart? All he ever wanted to do was serve his mistress faithfully."

"You mustn't upset yourself," said Orris.

"Oh, yes, I must! I must! He was so fine and healthy when I got him. As fine and healthy as Wassam Boy and Baba Goom ever were."

She was so agitated, hopping back and forth, that she seemed to have forgotten the nearby Menial.

It was Gillabeth who gave the necessary command. "You. Lift him up. Take him back to your cottage."

The twelfth Menial raised Wicky Popo upright, holding him under the armpits. Still, Wicky Popo sagged in every joint. His lips were drawn back from his gums, and his teeth were almost transparent.

"Oh, look!" Ebnolia pointed. "He's got dirt on his face! And a bit of grass on his little nose! If only he had the power of speech! If only he could tell us why he fell down!"

Indeed, it did seem that Wicky Popo had a question on the tip of his tongue. He looked at Ebnolia with intense, yearning appeal.

Ebnolia made cluck-clucking noises in the back of her throat. "I can't stand to see him fading away like this. I'll be heartbroken if he dies. And he'll be so sad to leave me." She pulled herself together and turned to the twelfth Menial. "Take him to *my* cottage."

The excitement was over. But Wicky Popo's accident had turned the evening upside down. Ebnolia was too distracted to make arrangements for dinner, so everyone ate snacks and sweets, then went to bed early.

Although Col was tired, and his muscles were sore from the fight, his mind refused to go to sleep. His thoughts kept shuttling from Gillabeth to Riff and back again.

What would Riff do when she turned up at midnight and found no one there? Would she worry that he'd been beaten up so badly he'd been moved from his room? It was her turn for a full night of training, he remembered. If only he'd thought to leave her a note, since she could read simple sentences. . . .

It would have been so good to share his victory over the Squellingham group with her. Now that he knew what it was like to share things, he experienced aloneness as never before. And the revelation about his sister's treachery—he wished he could have told her about that. They could have talked it over together. . . .

His thoughts circled back around to the mystery of Gillabeth. Tossing and turning on his bed, he came to a decision during the night. He would visit his sister in her cottage tomorrow, before anyone else was up.

52

"It's me."

"What do you want?"

Gillabeth stood blocking the doorway, but Col pushed past. The interior of her cottage was predictably spick-and-span.

"You've woken Antrobus," she grumped, closing the door.

Antrobus was sitting up in his cot bed, peering with owl-like eyes through the wooden bars. He looked well awake already.

"Why?" Col demanded. "Why did you do it?"

"What are you talking about?" With her chin held high Gillabeth was supremely irreproachable.

"You plotted with the Squellingham twins."

Gillabeth's mouth came open for a moment, then snapped shut.

"You wrote those notes and put them in my desk."

"No."

"You tried to get me beaten up."

"Nonsense."

"Hythe and Pugh told me themselves. You had secret meetings with them."

"You've been listening to lies."

"Why? Did you want to make me drop out of school? I don't understand."

Gillabeth's lower lip was trembling with suppressed fury. "You never understand anything."

"You admit it, then?"

She shook her head. She was like a blank wall—and at the same time a bomb primed to explode.

"You deny it, then?"

The bomb went off. "You're the curse of our family!" she shouted in his face. "You, you, you!"

"Me? I'm not the one who worked with the Squellinghams."

"You're the one who fell down among the Filthies. You should've been disowned. You should've been properly punished. Instead they all back you up and lie for you. No one else would've got off the way you did."

There was a wetness around her eyes even as she ranted and raged. She was red in the face and red down the sides of her neck. Col was amazed that his starchy sister had such violent emotions in her.

"And now you're getting married to the Turbot girl. Everyone will be celebrating. More success! You get it all handed to you on a plate. You never do anything to deserve it. I despise you! I *hate* you!"

"What have I ever done to you?"

"What have you done? You've been the son! The male! Everything centers on you. I'm the eldest, but I don't matter. Just because I'm a girl I spend half my time looking after Baby Brother and the other half organizing Mother because she can't organize herself. Those are my jobs, because I'm female!"

She took a breath and returned to the attack. "And you're the future of the Porpentines! All our hopes depend on you! Only boys can grow up to be supreme commanders! Always a male! No matter how stupid they are! *I'm* the one who's like our grandfather! *I'm* the true Porpentine!"

She thrust out her chest like their grandfather and bellowed like him too. If words were blows, Col would have been bludgeoned to a pulp.

"I never knew any of this," said Col.

"I had to fight for every tiny scrap I ever got. I had to find things out, and plan and plot. No one gave me anything but dumb piano lessons. I'm only at school to report on you. No one cares about *my* marks!"

"I never knew you felt—"

"Because you're a simpleton. Shielded from the real world. All you know is *ethics*, that your useless tutor taught you. You'd be the worst supreme commander in the world. I'd be a hundred times better."

"Except you can't be."

"Antrobus can."

She bit her lip and fell silent. Col reflected on what she'd just said.

"You mean, when he grows up and starts to speak?"

Gillabeth held her tongue.

"So he'd become supreme commander in name, but under your control? You'd give orders through him?"

The main blast of Gillabeth's anger had passed, leaving only small gusts of contempt. "Work it out for yourself, if you can."

Col shrugged. "The Squellinghams would have got in first. You'd have had to push them aside for Antrobus."

"Yes, well. They're almost as pathetic as you." She shepherded him toward the door. "Now go and tell tales on me to Grandmother. Just get out of my cottage."

Col was too shell-shocked to resist. He hardly knew how it happened, but he found himself suddenly out in the open, with the door slammed shut behind him. He stood blinking in the early light of dawn.

What most astonished him was that Gillabeth had such strong feelings about him. She had always seemed to treat him like a cuff that needed straightening or a lock of hair out of place. They were more alike than he'd ever suspected.

In spite of everything there was an odd satisfaction in that discovery. He certainly didn't intend to tell tales on her to Grandmother Ebnolia.

53

The holiday week went past in a haze. Every afternoon Ebnolia took the family on an excursion to some particular zone of Garden Deck. On Sunday it was a flower garden with roses and hedges around a sundial, on Monday a farm with bales of hay and sheaves of wheat, on Tuesday a village green with a cricket pitch, and on Wednesday a beach scene with sand, deck chairs, and striped umbrellas, but no actual sea.

Between excursions Ebnolia fussed over Wicky Popo, and Gillabeth minded Antrobus. Quinnea spent most of her time in a hammock, while Orris sat in a wicker chair and drank endless cups of tea.

Col spent his time wondering about Riff. When would he get to see her again? Would she have given up coming round to his room every night? He conducted imaginary conversations and explanations with her in his head.

He had forgotten all about the chaperoned meeting with his bride-to-be. The meeting, like the marriage, had been arranged by other people and hardly seemed to concern him personally. He remembered on Thursday, though, when Hommelia and Sephaltina turned up with half a dozen of the Turbot family Menials.

Hommelia wore a flower-bedecked hat and carried a fan that she waved constantly in front of her face. Her many chins cascaded in a landslide of flesh all the way down to her chest. Today the ribbons in Sephaltina's hair were pink.

The Porpentine family Menials had prepared a patch of lawn in the dappled shade of Old Country elm trees. Red and white potted geraniums added color to the scene, and every insect had been removed over an area of thirty square yards. The ladies reclined in garden chairs under parasols, while the gentlemen stood. Sephaltina sat very straight, with ankles crossed and hands folded.

Hommelia took an iced lemon drink from a tray held by a Menial. She gestured for Col to stand beside Sephaltina's chair.

"Only three days till the big day now," she said. "*What a happy couple!*"

Ebnolia turned to Col. "What do you say to your bride-to-be, Colbert?"

Col smiled politely. "How do you do?"

"Oh!" Sephaltina's eyes went wide, and she blushed on and off like a beacon. Finally, she recovered her composure and answered, "How do *you* do?"

Hommelia nodded at her daughter as if to say, *There, that wasn't so bad, was it?* When she nodded, her many chins all quivered at once.

Quinnea was already overcome by the emotion of the event. She produced a handkerchief and dabbed at her eyes.

"What shall we talk about?" asked Sephaltina.

Col wasn't sure where the question was directed, but it was Grandmother Ebnolia who replied. "Something nice, dears. Something tender and true."

"Tell me about yourself," Col suggested.

"Oh, no!" Sephaltina blinked very fast. "I couldn't. I'm still too young."

"What do you like to do?"

"I don't know yet."

There was a long silence. Ebnolia gave a signal, and four Menials came forward bearing plates of sugarcoated bonbons. Sephaltina took a plate and rested it on her lap. She gazed at it wistfully but made no move to eat.

After another minute of silence she turned to Col. "Did you say something?" She inclined her head and composed herself to listen.

"Er, not yet."

"Are you thinking about me?"

He fumbled for an answer. "I . . . er . . ."

"You should, you know."

The petals of Sephaltina's mouth were ever so slightly pouting. Col noticed that his grandmother was giving him a pointed look.

"I never stop thinking about you," he said at once. "I can hardly wait till the day we're married."

A glow of satisfaction came over Sephaltina's face. "You'll have to, though," she said.

Hommelia murmured approval. "Very good, very proper."

Sephaltina preened. "Do you like me like this?" she asked Col.

"Of course. Like what?"

"With these ribbons in my hair. Everyone says they make me look pretty."

"They do." Col struggled to sound convincing. "Very, very pretty."

"Which part of me is the prettiest?"

"Um . . . all of you?"

"What about my ears?"

Her plaits covered her ears. Was this some kind of a test? "I can't see them."

"No, because we're not married yet. Do you think you'll like them?"

"I'm sure I will, yes."

"Shall I do a smile for you?"

"Er . . . if you want."

Hommelia gave a warning cough.

"Perhaps not yet," said Sephaltina. "Perhaps I could turn my head instead." She paused, but the cough wasn't repeated. "Would you like to see my face from the side?"

"I, um . . . yes . . . no . . ."

"I'm always willing to please, you know. It's part of my appeal."

Col was getting desperate. He couldn't keep this up much longer. Fortunately, Ebnolia intervened. "I think we're ready for a little presentation."

She beckoned to a particular Menial, who stepped forward with a box wrapped in pink paper. "A gift from you to your bride-to-be," she told Col.

Sephaltina passed her plate to her mother so that she could receive the gift. Remarkably, the bonbons had gone and the plate was empty. Col thought he'd been watching her the whole time, but his attention must have wandered elsewhere for a few seconds.

He took the box from the Menial and held it out to Sephaltina. "Please accept this token of . . . my feelings."

She took the box from him. "It *matches!*" she exclaimed in delight.

She meant that the pink wrapping paper matched the pink of her ribbons.

She might have opened it there and then, except for another cough from her mother. "No, Sephaltina. One doesn't open a present in front of one's husband-to-be. When we get home."

"Yes, indeed," Ebnolia agreed. "Innocence should be maintained between young people."

"And now it's time we were leaving." Hommelia rose to her feet.

Ebnolia also rose, with a delicate creaking of stays. "Such a pleasure," she said.

"Such a pleasure," said Hommelia.

The Porpentines watched as Hommelia glided across the lawn like a stately galleon, with her daughter one pace behind. Orris and Quinnea hadn't said a word for themselves during the entire meeting.

For Col it was a disconnected interlude like a dream. He never did find out what was in the box he'd given his bride-to-be.

54

The excursion on Friday afternoon was to another zone of Garden Deck, a recreated scene with a water mill. The water-wheel actually turned, and real ducks paddled on a rush-fringed duck pond. The mill also served as a tea shop.

Grandmother led the family inside. There were doilies and fine white china on the tables, and a Menial dressed in a frilly apron like a waitress brought a teapot, scones, and jam. The Porpentines' own Menials waited outside.

Seated directly opposite Col, Gillabeth refused to look him in the eyes. She'd been avoiding him for days now. She kept the door of her cottage locked and obviously didn't want to talk to him again. But Col wanted to talk to her.

Ebnolia took charge of the teapot while the scones were passed around. Then a loud thump and clatter outside made everyone prick up their ears.

Ebnolia tut-tutted. "Go and see what's happened, dear," she told Gillabeth.

Gillabeth rose and went out. Col saw his opportunity. "I'll go too," he said.

He walked round the side of the mill and found Gillabeth giving orders to the Porpentines' Menials. Wicky Popo lay on the path, along with the Menial who had the job of support-ing him. The sick Menial must have collapsed so suddenly that he'd dragged the other one down too.

Gillabeth's face darkened at the sight of Col. "I'm taking care of it," she said.

"Gillabeth, I don't want to be your enemy."

"No?"

"I didn't tell tales on you, you know."

If she was thankful, she didn't show it. "Why not?"

"We're similar, you and me."

"I don't think so."

"We both have improper thoughts."

"Speak for yourself."

"No, don't you see? You question things that nobody else does. Why do supreme commanders always have to be male?"

"It's unfair."

"But nobody else sees that. Where did you get the idea? It didn't come from Grandfather or Grandmother."

"You're talking nonsense," said Gillabeth—but faintly, automatically.

"You want to overturn male supreme commanders and keep the rest of the world the same. But if supreme commanders could be different, everything could be different."

Gillabeth took a backward step, staring at him. "You're dangerous. You ought to be reported."

"Not by you."

Of course she couldn't report him without having her own secret revealed.

"Think about it," Col went on. "All those things we grew up believing before we could even think about them—maybe we don't *have* to believe them. Maybe they're not so natural and necessary after all. I never thought a girl could want to be supreme commander until you said it."

This time Gillabeth didn't disagree. She pondered in silence for a while.

"Anyway, you're right about being supreme commander." Col grinned. "You'd be a hundred times better than me."

Gillabeth nodded. "I'm more practical. I've had to learn how things work."

"You said it. I've been shielded from the real world."

"You still think people behave the way they're supposed to behave. You always think the best of them."

Col shrugged—when suddenly there was an interruption. Wicky Popo swayed forward and almost knocked into them. The Menial who had the job of supporting him had managed to lift him upright but couldn't hold him steady.

"You." Gillabeth pointed to a second Menial. "Take his other arm."

The support of the second Menial kept Wicky Popo upright, though his legs dangled rather than stood on the ground. His cheeks were cavernous, and his breath came in short, shallow gasps.

"Poor Wicky Popo," said Col.

"Don't speak like that," Gillabeth snapped. "You sound like Grandmother."

"Why not? I feel sorry for him being so sick."

"He isn't sick."

"I thought—"

"He's starving to death."

"What?"

"Take a close look. No fever, no infection, no swellings or cough. The only thing wrong with him is not eating."

"Why can't he eat?"

"Because Grandmother doesn't feed him."

"I don't understand."

"She's been gradually cutting back on his food for weeks. Now he only gets water."

"But he's her favorite. She feels so sorry for him."

"She *likes* feeling sorry for him."

Col shook his head. It didn't make sense.

Gillabeth had a harsh grimace fixed to her face. "The more he wastes away, the more she can grieve over him. It's her favorite feeling for her favorite Menial. She'll have a lovely flood of tears over him when he dies. Do you remember Wassam Boy, who was last year's favorite? Or Baba Goom the year before? They both died from mysterious sicknesses."

"Starved to death?"

"Yes. Just the same. Being Grandmother's favorite is a death sentence."

Col struggled to believe it. His sweet old grandmother, with her smell of kindness and strawberry perfume?

"That's horrible," he said. "Why doesn't someone tell Sir Mormus?"

"He already knows. He probably thinks it's a harmless little hobby. There are always plenty more Menials."

Col felt as though he'd been kicked in the stomach. Gillabeth was observing him closely.

"Welcome to the real world," she said. "Now you see what it's like, knowing what goes on."

She turned away and retraced her steps to the tea shop. As Col watched her go, echoes of his grandmother's voice came back to him.

I just love his cute little nose. . . .
Look at his poor thin arms and legs. . . .
Not eating properly at all. . . .
Doesn't it break your heart. . . .
So adorable . . .
So sweet . . .
So fine and healthy when I got him . . .

Col hurried toward the duck pond, thinking he was going to throw up. He didn't . . . but he stood for a long while among the green rushes, watching a flotilla of ducks that paddled around on the calm water.

55

Early the next day the family returned to Forty-second Deck, while the Menials stayed behind to clean up and pack. The holiday was over; the wedding ceremony was the day after tomorrow.

Col still hadn't worked out how to save Wicky Popo. He had to find a way to feed the poor Menial—but how? The sick feeling over his grandmother's monstrous behavior had driven even the thought of Riff from his mind. The thought of his bride-to-be was a million miles away.

He stayed all morning in his room, brooding over the problem. He hardly heard the light tap-tap on his door. In the next moment a lumpy figure in a gray uniform entered. She turned to close the door, turned again—and the dull face of a Menial transformed into Riff's familiar features.

Col jumped up. The sight of Riff raised his spirits instantly.

"Where've you been?" she demanded. "I saw you all coming back this morning."

"Family holiday on Garden Deck. I—"

"So what happened?"

Col didn't understand. "What?"

"You and the gang at school. Did you fight them?"

"Yes." Col grinned. "I beat them! Ten against one, and I beat them!"

"Yay!" She sprang forward and wrapped her arms around him.

He couldn't believe how good it felt. To have her pressed against him, her arms tightening around him, to squeeze her in return. He burst out laughing.

She laughed too, and he felt her warm breath in his ear. He had no idea how long it lasted. He could have gone on hugging and laughing for an eternity.

But she drew back a little, her face alive and dancing. "Tell me about it."

"I fought the way you taught me. I didn't even have to think what to do."

"I always told you not to think too much."

"My body took over from my head."

She nodded. "That's how you were at the start of our last training session. Until you lost it, remember?"

Col remembered. He wished she didn't.

"After you tried to kiss me," she added.

He felt suddenly awkward to be standing so close. A hot blush rose to his face. She looked at him curiously.

"No harm tryin'," she said, and leaned forward suddenly to give him a kiss on the cheek.

"No!" he jerked away. "You can't!"

"I just did."

"I mean, you mustn't."

"Why not?"

"What would Padder say?"

"Padder? He'd disapprove. He'd tell me off."

"You don't care?"

"He's overprotective, is all."

"Overprotective?"

"Big brothers are like that."

The world stood still a moment for Col.

"Brother?"

"Yeah."

"Padder's your brother?"

"Yeah."

"You're sure?"

"Course I'm sure. How dumb a question is that?"

Col could have burst into song. He just gazed and gazed at her.

She had to wave a hand in front of his face. "Hello? You still there?"

Col couldn't trust himself to speak. He was beaming like a fool from ear to ear.

"What did you think? Did you think me and him was partnered?"

"No . . . yes."

"Ah, right. Glad that's sorted." She sat down on the bed and patted the bedspread beside her. "Now tell me everything about the fight."

Sitting close beside her, he described the battle blow by blow. He could see her clenching her fists and going through the actions in her mind. It was almost as good as hugging, to share it with her.

At the end he arrived at the revelation about Gillabeth.

Riff whistled. "Yer own sister! Is she mad or what?"

Col had temporarily forgotten about Wicky Popo, but now

the sick feeling came flooding back. He told Riff about his two confrontations with Gillabeth, and how his grandmother was starving her favorite Menial to death.

Riff's lips compressed to a thin line. "So what are you goin' to do?"

"I don't know. Try to feed him somehow. What would you do?"

"Join the revolution, of course."

Col shook his head. "It's not just yer grandmother," Riff insisted. "It's the whole Upper Decks."

Col reflected. "My grandfather knows," he murmured, more to himself than Riff.

"If they don't starve us to death, they steam us to death. They're out of their heads. It's all the same cruelty."

Col shook his head, though he half suspected she was right.

"Listen." Her tone grew more intense. "You're almost on our side already. You already let me up here to prepare and make plans for the revolution."

"I never meant—"

"Oh, you *knew* all right. I been workin' out our strategy. Places to capture first. Passages to block and staircases to hold." She tapped the side of her head. "It's all in here. What d'ya think about that?"

Col was breathing fast, with a kind of excitement and a kind of horror.

"All we need is for you to open that door and lower a rope," she went on. "Or not even go through the door. Just unlock it and walk away."

Col's ethical education with Professor Twillip wouldn't

allow him such easy excuses. "There's no difference."

They argued it back and forth and round and round. Riff had a hundred arguments, but her strongest persuasion was when she placed her hand over his on the side of the bed. He went hot and cold and hot again.

Still, he couldn't quite accept the idea of betraying his own people and his own family. In spite of what Riff said, they weren't all bad and wrong . . . not his father, nor his mother, and certainly not Professor Twillip. He continued to shake his head.

In the end she released his hand and rose to her feet. "I won't let up, you know. I'm gonna keep on and on about this."

Col didn't mind how long she kept on, so long as she kept holding and squeezing his hand at the same time. But now she was leaving.

"This Wicky Popo." She stopped with her hand on the door handle. "How do I recognize him?"

"He's as thin as a skeleton. He can hardly stand upright. Why?"

"I'll feed him."

"You?"

"You'll never do it."

"I . . . thank you."

Riff shrugged, opened the door, and looked out into the corridor.

"When will I see you again?" he asked.

But Riff was already closing the door behind her.

Only afterward did he realize he hadn't even mentioned his forthcoming marriage.

56

In the afternoon, preparations for the ceremony speeded up. Col was escorted down to Thirty-eighth Deck, where a barber cut his hair; then to a manicurist on Thirty-seventh Deck. In the evening normal dinner was replaced by a buffet in the Somerset Room.

When Col turned up, the Somerset Room was filled with people and buzzing with conversation. The members of the Sir Mormus branch of the family were all present, along with assorted uncles and aunts from other branches. Col took a cup of tea from a Menial and helped himself to cold chicken and potato salad from the buffet table.

On all sides the only topic of conversation was tomorrow's great event. He kept his head down and concentrated on his food, but he couldn't help overhearing.

"Over four hundred guests. Can you believe it?"

"No expense spared."

"And not only the elite families."

"No indeed, the better middle-class levels too."

"But all the elite families *are* coming?"

"Oh, yes. They wouldn't dare stay away."

"Not now Sir Mormus has the queen's favor again."

"We're back in our proper place. First family."

Keeping his head down, Col didn't notice Gillabeth until he was right in front of her. She rolled her eyes significantly, directing his attention to a particular corner of the room. There on a chair sat Wicky Popo.

Col swung back to question her, but she was already moving off. He threaded his way through the crowd to Wicky Popo's corner.

Close up, the change was plain to see. Wicky Popo had regained a spark of life in his eyes and a faint shade of color in his cheeks. He remained as thin as ever, but there was no doubt about it. Riff must have managed to feed him.

How had she done it? So soon! Not for the first time her powers seemed almost supernatural.

He was still gazing at Wicky Popo when his grandmother passed by. She stopped, a tiny frown forming between her delicately arched eyebrows.

"Ah, you're pitying my poor, sad Wicky Popo. He won't be with us much longer, I fear."

"He looks better today."

"Hmm. Temporary recoveries, misleading appearances. We must hope for the poor dear, but we mustn't expect too much. He'll probably go downhill again shortly."

She sounded puzzled and a little vexed. Suddenly the sweetness of her strawberry-scented perfume made Col want to gag.

Then there was an announcement from the other side of the room. Sharp as a bird Ebnolia switched her attention and nodded her head.

"At last. The Honorable Hommelia Turbot has arrived. Put down your plate and come with me, Colbert."

Col did as he was told. Hommelia was advancing into the room with her daughter a pace behind. As soon as she saw Ebnolia, her chins quivered and she gushed over with delight.

"*Dearest* Lady Porpentine. And the handsome groom. Our future son-in-law. So pleased to see you. Aren't we, Sephaltina?"

How-do-you-dos were exchanged all round, followed by a few minutes of small talk between Hommelia and Ebnolia. Then Hommelia cast an almost roguish eye toward Col and asked, "Have you told him what will happen at the ceremony, Lady Porpentine?"

"Not yet."

"May I have the honor?"

"Please do."

"Well, Colbert." Hommelia's face was wreathed in smiles. "You enter the Imperial Chapel first with the groom's party. You stand beside your grandfather facing the queen. Pretend I'm the queen and stand . . . just so, just so. You wait until Sephaltina enters with the bride's party and stands next to you."

She motioned her daughter into position. "Hold up your head, Sephaltina. Enough sweets for now."

She waved away a Menial who was hovering nearby with a plate of sweets. The round bulges in Sephaltina's cheeks disappeared as if they had never existed.

"Then the queen will speak about the duties of holy matrimony. You should both keep your eyes slightly lowered. Then she will ask, 'Do you, Colbert Porpentine, take this woman to be your lawful wedded wife?' And you reply, 'I do.'"

"I do," Col repeated.

"Then, 'Do you, Sephaltina Turbot, take this man?' and

the same reply. Finally, the exchange of rings. Do you know which is the finger for the marriage ring?"

Col shook his head. Sephaltina nodded and extended the third finger of her left hand.

"Very good. So, Colbert, when your grandfather hands you the ring, that is the finger you put it on. Very tenderly and lovingly, please. And, Sephaltina . . . what's that in your mouth?"

Sephaltina's cheeks bulged with new bulges, and her rosebud mouth was in constant sucking motion.

"I said, enough of those!" Hommelia stamped her foot at the Menial who had reappeared behind Sephaltina's shoulder with a plate of sweets. "Go *away*!"

Sephaltina swallowed. Tears sprang to her eyes, and for a moment she appeared to have stopped breathing.

"So, Colbert, you hold out the same finger, and my daughter puts her ring on it." The beatific expression was back on Hommelia's face. "And then it's all done. Husband and wife bonded forever." She turned to Ebnolia. "And the Porpentines and Turbots bonded forever too. Won't the Squellinghams hate that!"

Hommelia and Ebnolia began a conversation about ranking and precedence. Hommelia was in a hurry to displace the Squellinghams as *Worldshaker*'s second family; Ebnolia advised caution. Sephaltina made painful gulping noises over a lump in her throat.

Col's role was finished. He backed away, step by step, merging in with the crowd. Six steps away he bumped into someone and spun round with an apology on his lips.

It was only a female Menial . . . in fact, it was the same Menial with the plate of sweets. Before, she had been a Menial like any other Menial, and he hadn't registered her face.

But it registered now. As she continued to stand right in front of him, the dull, mindless features transformed into Riff's features. Her eyes flashed with emotion—with anger.

"Outside," she whispered from the corner of her mouth. "Talk. Now."

57

Outside in the corridor she shuffled away from the Somerset Room, and Col followed. She turned left into an intersecting passage, then left again into a short cul-de-sac. No one was likely to see them here.

"You must be mad," he said.

She looked mad. She was rocking back and forth on the balls of her feet. "*I do,*" she mimicked. "Oh, *I do.* Tenderly and lovingly."

"Why take such a risk?" he demanded. "In front of all my family."

"I went to feed that starving Menial. For *your* sake."

"Oh, right. Wicky Popo. I could see he'd been fed."

"Don't change the subject. I know what it means about lawful wedded wife. It means gettin' partnered."

"Yes, but—"

"You and her. You and that pretty-pretty doll. That's what you like, is it?"

"It's not what you think."

"No? Then why did you try and hide it from me?"

"I didn't."

"Yes. This morning. You never said a thing."

"I forgot."

"*Forgot!*" Riff sneered. "You *wanted* to forget, more like."

Col opened his mouth, then closed it again. He couldn't deny a twinge of guilt. Perhaps he *had* wanted to forget.

"One of yer own kind. So refined! Phh! Stuffin' sweets like a little girl."

"She's a year older than me. Three years older than you."

"Don't you compare me and her. Don't you dare."

"Just let me explain."

"Oh yeah. Explanations are what you're good at. Your kind can always *explain*."

"My family arranged it. It's only an alliance between the Porpentines and Turbots. It's not important."

"Not important! You get partnered with her, you live with her, right?"

"I suppose."

"You talk together, eat together, share the same bed. And that's not important?"

"It doesn't change anything. I don't love her."

"You don't care for her?"

"No."

"Not even a little?"

"Not at all."

"What's *wrong* with you?"

He stepped back away from her clenched fists. "Huh?"

"If you're goin' to get partnered, you *oughta* care for her."

Col was completely at a loss. "What do you want me to say?"

"I don't want you to say nothing. Just shut up. I thought you were different, but you're the same as the rest of your lot. You don't feel anything for anyone."

"I do. You don't know what—"

"You're all screwed up in the head. There's a bit missing.

No Filthy would ever let someone else arrange partners for them. We're not dead inside like you."

She was quivering with rage. Col prepared to dodge the first blow, watching in her eyes for the telltale indication, quite certain she was going to hit him.

Instead she swung away and whacked the wall with her fist. "Sephaltina!" She turned the name into a mockery. "Seph-al-teen-aaah!"

"Why does she matter so much to you?"

"Doesn't. Not if you don't see it."

"Okay, then."

"Okay. Go and get partnered with your pretty-pretty doll." She lowered her fists and glared at him eyeball to eyeball.

"But . . . I still want to see you," he said.

"Too bad."

"Won't you—?"

"Next time you see me, you'll wish you hadn't."

"What are you going to do?"

"You'll find out."

"What?"

"A surprise." She smiled maliciously, spun on her heel, and marched off.

"Wait!"

He followed her as far as the main corridor. A senior signals officer was approaching, and she changed her gait to a slow Menial shuffle.

Col dropped back into the passage out of sight. By the time the signals officer had gone past, Riff was nowhere to be seen.

58

There was no visit from Riff in the middle of the night. Col couldn't believe that everything had plummeted so suddenly. Next day the wedding preparations continued to advance, as inexorably as the great juggernaut itself. He wanted to say, *Stop! Not yet! Too fast!* But he was swept along in the grip of an irresistible current.

It was midmorning when his mother summoned him to her dressing room. His father was there too, along with Mr. Prounce and three Menials from the tailor's workshop. The room was draped with items of discarded clothing and littered with knickknacks and jewelry boxes.

Mr. Prounce bowed with an obsequious smirk and held up a tailcoat and matching breeches in charcoal gray. "I made them from your previous measurements, Master Porpentine. Also four shirts, hand-sewn, finest quality. Who would have thought a wedding suit would be needed so soon after a school uniform?" He gestured toward a screen in the corner of the room. "If you would care to try on your outfit, Master Porpentine . . ."

Col tried on the suit and all four shirts. He let Mr. Prounce decide which shirt was the best fit. The tailor declared that only the smallest alterations were needed and set his Menials to work with needles and thread.

Meanwhile Quinnea dithered over her own ensemble. She sat on a velvet stool in front of her dressing-table mirror, wearing a loose protective wrapper over a sumptuous dress of green watered silk. Coordination was her particular worry. She experimented with countless gloves and necklaces, earrings and brooches, hair combs and bracelets.

"This necklace doesn't match my eyes," she fretted. Or, "My ears don't go with my hair." Or, "Oh, no! My face is all wrong with my bracelets!"

Several times she shook everything off in despair, turned her hair back into a bird's nest, and started all over again.

Mr. Prounce stroked his pencil mustache and offered compliments. "Most harmonious, my lady. . . . A symphony of synthesis, ma'am." He kissed the tips of his fingertips to emphasize his sincerity.

Quinnea only became more and more agitated. "It's no use! Look at the state of me! I'm all askew! I'm falling apart!"

Orris patted her gently on the shoulder. "Don't upset yourself, my dear." He turned to Col. "Your mother is upset because you'll be leaving us. She'll miss you, you know."

"So young! So young!" Quinnea wailed. "I can't help it! It's too sudden! I can't cope! Nobody can cope!"

"We'll cope because we must, my dear." Orris found her bottle of smelling salts and held it briefly under her nose. He recorked the bottle and turned again to Col. "I shall miss you too, Colbert. We haven't been the best of parents, not as strong and firm as we should have been. I know I haven't. But we have always cared for you a great deal."

There was a gleam of wetness in Orris's eyes. A mass of muddled emotion welled up in Col until he felt like crying too. It might have been for what his father had lost, or it might have been for what he had lost himself. . . .

"I wish I could have been the one to stand beside you and hand you the ring," Orris went on. "But I forfeited that right long ago. Now it's more appropriate for your grandfather to act in my place. But I shall be beside you in spirit, Colbert. Beside you in spirit."

For one crazy moment Col wanted to go across and give his father a hug. But that was impossible, of course. The only person he'd ever actually hugged was Riff. . . .

After a while his mother calmed down and went on with her toilette. The Menials finished the alterations to Mr. Prounce's satisfaction, and Col dressed in his new wedding clothes.

A little later a male Menial entered, bearing a selection of pink corsages and boutonnieres in a basket. With fluttering fingers Quinnea fixed a single boutonniere in the lapel of Col's tailcoat.

"Sephaltina chose the color," she told him. "All the flowers and ribbons in the chapel are pink."

"And the decoration of your bridal suite," Orris added. "Pink carpet and pink curtains."

Col emerged from his mood of distraction. "Bridal suite?"

"Where you'll go with Sephaltina on your wedding night. It's on Forty-third Deck."

"Nobody told me . . ."

"Oh, *child!*" His mother flung up her hands. "What did I say? Too young! Too young!"

Orris patted her shoulder and spoke to Col. "You won't be going back to your old cabin, Colbert. Not when you're a husband with a wife. Didn't you realize?"

Col's heart sank. No, he hadn't realized. It was blindingly obvious, but he'd never given it a thought. So when Riff came looking for him in his old cabin, he wouldn't be there. *If* she came looking for him . . .

He had the sense of his path separating irrevocably from hers. It brought a tightness to his chest to think how alone he would be without her. He remembered the smell of her hair, the curve of her neck, her funny expressions. It wasn't just that she was exciting to be with, it was that no one else was even alive compared to her. His world would be unutterably flat and dull if she wasn't in it.

The wedding preparations rolled on regardless. An hour later the door of Quinnea's dressing room opened, and Grandmother Ebnolia looked in.

"Is everyone ready?" She clapped her hands. "It's time to begin."

59

For Col the whole wedding ceremony went past in a kind of dream. His body was involved, but his mind was a long, long way away.

First there was the procession up to the Imperial Chapel on Forty-fifth Deck. Col walked with his grandfather and grandmother at the head. Ebnolia wore a strawberry-colored dress pinched in so tightly at the waist that it seemed impossible for blood to circulate between her upper and lower halves. Sir Mormus was resplendent in a figured blue waistcoat, over which hung the inevitable gold chain and keys of office.

Orris and Quinnea came next in the procession, then Gillabeth with Antrobus. Antrobus looked like a miniaturized adult in a tiny tailcoat with pink boutonniere. Behind them marched the Porpentine Menials with trumpets and drums. Wearing braided tunics over their gray uniforms, they beat out a solemn rhythm and played a fanfare on just two notes.

When they came to Forty-fifth Deck, they passed through a crowd of well-wishers and spectators. There were wedding guests too, those who were important enough to be invited to the reception but not to the actual service. Col noticed Dr. Blessamy, smiling benevolently, and Flarrow and Lumbridge, not at all benevolent. The higher-ranking Squellinghams would have seats inside the chapel.

The entrance to the chapel was a relic from the Old

Country, a carved arch similar to the one outside the academy. At the top of the arch was the imperial family's coat of arms: a shield bearing the letters V and A with a lion on the right and a cannon on the left.

"Drummers and trumpeters, halt," Sir Mormus ordered.

As the drumming and trumpeting came to an end, the sound of organ music could be heard filtering out from the chapel. The wedding party marched on under the entrance arch.

Inside it was suddenly dark and dim. The chapel was small, and every pew was packed. Stained-glass windows cast a red and purple light over the congregation. Col had a vague impression of stone pillars and stone statues—more relics from the Old Country. Many of the pillars were broken at the top, and none reached all the way to the ceiling.

Grandmother Ebnolia fell back a pace as they walked down the aisle toward the queen and her consort, seated on their imperial thrones. Queen Victoria wore a robe that Col had never seen before: creamy white, with long, loose sleeves, embroidered with religious symbols.

Sir Mormus's every stride was a statement of success and domination. The front rows were occupied by the Porpentines on one side and the Turbots on the other. All the men wore formal suits and waistcoats; all the ladies wore lace-trimmed gowns and jewelry. While those in the groom's party took their places, Sir Mormus and Col advanced to stand facing the queen.

"Chest out," Sir Mormus rumbled. "Remember who you are."

While they waited for the bride's party to arrive, Col's mind wandered off into daydreams. If only he could be the revolutionary Riff wanted him to be! He imagined creeping down to Bottom Deck with her, unlocking the door, and lowering the rope. Then welcoming the Filthies as they appeared . . . leading them up through the Upper Decks. With Riff at his side, he would make a great speech against tyranny . . . and the officers would be ashamed of their cruelty . . . the elite would recognize the Filthies as human beings . . . everything would change . . . with Riff at his side. . . .

A murmur rippled through the congregation and jerked him back to the present. He glanced over his shoulder and saw that the bride's party had entered the chapel.

Sephaltina advanced on the arm of her father. In pearl choker, pearl tiara, and pearl-beaded dress, she had never looked prettier. She was both modest and radiant, her cheeks glowing with the same shade of pink as her bouquet. She took up position beside him.

Col bit his lip and looked away. Inside his head was a voice saying, *If you're goin' to get partnered, you oughta care for her.*

He didn't hear the first part of the service. Queen Victoria spoke, Prince Albert read out passages from a book, then Queen Victoria spoke about the duties of holy matrimony. Something about a husband loving and honoring his wife, a wife loving and obeying her husband.

It was all impossible, all a mistake. He couldn't love and honor Sephaltina. His feelings were taken up with someone else. He ought to stop this wedding right now. He ought to turn around and walk out of the chapel.

Still, the service progressed exactly as the Honorable Hommelia Turbot had said. Queen Victoria looked straight at Col and asked the fateful question. "Do you, Colbert

Porpentine, take this woman to be your lawful wedded wife?"

He knew he ought to say, *I do not*; he ought to face the consequences. But he couldn't even begin to imagine the consequences.

The queen smiled at him, awaiting his reply. Col felt as if he were tearing apart. *I do not, I do not, I do not . . .*

"I do."

Even as he said it, he seemed to hear the clang of a door slamming shut.

"And do you, Sephaltina Turbot, take this man to be your lawful wedded husband?"

"I do," said Sephaltina in a whisper.

"Then, by the authority vested in me as head of the Imperial Church, I declare you man and wife. Now you may exchange rings."

Sir Mormus held out a gold ring in the palm of his hand. Col stared at it as if it belonged in some other reality. Then he took it and turned to face Sephaltina, as she turned to face him.

If only it had been someone else. If only it had been blond-and-black hair, sharp cheekbones, large eyes. But Sephaltina was fair and rosy-pink. She was a complete stranger.

She held out her trembling finger, and Col slipped the ring onto it.

60

The reception took place an hour later in the Grand Assembly Hall. With more than four hundred guests the domed oval space was a sea of faces. Sprays of pink flowers adorned the marble pillars, while banners strung between the central chandelier and walls bore the motto PORPENTINES & TURBOTS. Around the sides of the hall were tables of food and drink, discreetly hidden under snow-white linen. An army of Menial servants and supervising officers stood lined up behind the tables.

The queen and her consort made a formal entrance, followed by the newlyweds. Col made a conscious effort to slow his steps to a dignified gait.

The imperial thrones had been carried in from the chapel and set up on a dais at the side. When Queen Victoria and Prince Albert took their seats, a brass band struck up at the back of the hall.

Victoria leaned toward her consort. "I do love a wedding. Do you remember our nuptials, dear?"

"How could I forget!" Prince Albert twirled his mustache. "What a day! And what a night!"

Victoria coughed behind her hand so vigorously that she almost lost her crown. Prince Albert helped readjust it.

With shining eyes Victoria turned to Col and Sephaltina. "Go and dance, my dears. The dancing can't begin until you start it off."

Sephaltina took Col's arm, and they moved across to the dance floor. The band struck up a well-known dance tune, very stately and respectable.

This particular dance involved a great deal of promenading back and forth and bowing or curtsying to one's partner. Col remembered the steps from his dance practice with Mrs. Landry. After the first dance a score of other couples joined them on the floor.

"Are you happy?" asked Sephaltina with a blush.

Col answered automatically. "Very happy."

"And excited?"

"Yes. Are you?"

"Of course. But not as excited as you."

"You're not?"

"The man always has to be more excited. It wouldn't be right for the bride to be as excited as the groom."

"Oh."

More bowing and curtsying. Then Sephaltina asked, "How long should we stay at the reception?"

"I don't know. Before what?"

"Before we go to the bridal suite."

"I don't know."

"Mama thinks we should stay about two hours."

"What do you think?"

"I think about two hours. It's all in pink, you know."

"What?"

"The bridal suite. My favorite color. Are you imagining it now?"

"Er, no. Yes. No." Col had no idea of the correct answer. "Are you?"

She shook her head. "No, that would be forward of me. I want it to be a surprise."

Another round of bowing and curtsying. Col found it hard to concentrate and kept putting his feet in the wrong places.

"I expect I'll faint," Sephaltina told him.

"You'll faint?"

"When I see the bedroom."

"Why?"

"I faint very easily. I'm very good at it."

"But . . ."

"I don't mind. I want to be the perfect wife for you."

Col gave up trying to understand. Communicating with an Upper Decks girl was like communicating in a foreign language.

They danced another three dances together, and Col continued to put his feet in all the wrong places.

"You're not getting any better, are you?" said Sephaltina with a hint of sharpness. "I can say that, now I'm your wife."

Col shrugged. "Would you like to dance with someone else?"

As if on cue Leath Porpentine came forward to ask if he might have the honor of a dance with the bride. Col backed out willingly.

By now the tables had been uncovered, and food was being served. Groups stood around with plates or glasses, talking as they ate. Col drifted from the dance floor and mingled with other guests. Everyone wanted to shake his hand, congratulate him, and admire the ring on his finger. He had to listen to words of praise for Sephaltina and utter the same polite replies a hundred times over.

For thirty minutes he was passed on from group to group, not so much circulating as being circulated. Then, out of the blue, he spotted Professor Twillip. Detaching himself from a group of bridge officers and their wives, he went to talk to his old tutor.

Professor Twillip seemed to be having a good time, though he was completely out of place in a social gathering such as this. He floated between groups, beaming vaguely in all directions.

"Colbert, Colbert!" His smile widened as Col came up. "Felicitations! I am so happy for you."

"I'm really pleased you were invited."

"Yes, isn't it wonderful? Fancy someone thinking of *me*."

"Is Septimus here?"

"I don't think so. I haven't seen him."

Col had hardly expected otherwise. The Trant family ranked several levels below Professor Twillip on the social scale.

"We've been continuing our researches into the Age of Imperialism." Professor Twillip nodded his fleecy white head. "For example, the coaling stations. Did you know that the countries of Europe once had colonies in every continent?"

"Colonies?" Col didn't even know the word.

"They took control and ruled over the natives. But the Fifty Years' War focused everyone's attention on Europe, and the colonies were left to wither away. The natives regained control and drove the colonists back into a few defended outposts. You see?"

"What?"

"Those are the coaling stations. Hong Kong, Botany Bay, Kingston, and so on. Small independent territories that survive by servicing the great juggernauts. If you ask me—"

Col cut him off with a warning cough. Sephaltina was approaching through the crowd with a petulant expression on her face.

"There you are!" She spoke to Col as though Professor Twillip didn't exist. "I was looking for you."

"I thought you were enjoying the dancing."

"Felicitations, Miss Turbot." Professor Twillip performed a little bow. "Or as I should now say, Mrs. Porpentine."

Sephaltina ignored him. "I stopped enjoying it ten minutes ago. There's a girl attracting everyone's attention. I'm the bride so I ought to be the center of attention. And you ought to want to dance with me."

"I'm not much of a dancer."

"That's not the point. What's the use of a husband who doesn't attend to his wife?"

Professor Twillip blinked and looked bemused. Col decided it was time for introductions.

"This is Professor Twillip, my old tutor. And this is—"

"Yes," said Sephaltina. "And now I'd like something to eat, please."

Since Professor Twillip seemed unaware of the snub, Col decided against making a scene. "What would you like?"

Sephaltina pouted. "Something sweet."

With an apologetic smile to Professor Twillip, Col turned away and threaded a route to the tables at the side of the hall.

A vast array of desserts was on display: shortbread and cup-
cakes, rice pudding and trifle, jelly and blancmange. In the
end he pointed to a parfait glass of yellow jelly, and a Menial
handed it to him with a spoon.

Sephaltina had already abandoned Professor Twillip's company. Scouting about for her, Col passed a group of Fefferley
family members clustered around Lord Fefferley. They were
wagging their heads over some kind of trouble on the dance
floor. Col paused to listen.

"It's not right."

"Not respectable."

"Millamie came back unescorted."

"The Dollimonts' daughter too. She didn't like the music."

"The young men keep encouraging the band to play
faster."

So Sephaltina wasn't the only one to leave the dance floor.
Col hadn't noticed before, but it was true that the music had
speeded up.

"I hope our son isn't there."

"She's a bad influence."

"Having a bad effect."

"If she were *my* daughter . . ."

"Does anyone know whose daughter she is?"

Col had a sense of foreboding, though he didn't know
why. He headed to the dance floor to see for himself.

He had to push through a ring of young men packed
shoulder to shoulder. There were half a dozen couples still
dancing, but all eyes were upon one particular pair. It was
Haugh from Col's class and a girl with long blond ringlets.

Haugh had a glazed grin, and his quiff drooped over his forehead, damp with sweat. The girl wore a long cream dress and silver earrings. She looked every inch an Upper Decks lady, but she wasn't. Col's very worst fears came true when he saw her face and recognized Riff.

Col watched in horror. It was madness. Yet she wore the long dress as though she'd been wearing such clothes all her life. He shuddered to think where she'd stolen it—and the blond wig and earrings.

Her dancing was faultless, too. She must have picked up the steps just by watching others on the dance floor, yet she carried it off as if she'd had years of practice. Incredible.

He heard the young men talking nearby.

"I'm going to ask her for a dance."

"You'd never dare."

"Why not? She dances with anyone."

"There are three ahead of you."

"I'll get the band to play the next dance *really* fast."

They had no suspicions, of course. They couldn't even begin to conceive of a Filthy in their midst, even if they knew what a Filthy looked like. Presumably, they thought she was from some family outside the circle normally invited to elite social functions. Yet they all sensed she was somehow different.

Col looked at the other dancers on the floor. Earlier on, when the music was slow and stately, Riff would have been dancing exactly like everyone else. But now that the music was faster, the others revealed their limitations. Whereas they were awkward and struggled to keep time, Riff flowed to the rhythm as effortlessly as ever.

She wasn't aware that she was giving herself away. The flaw in her imitation was that she was too good, too perfect. And the more the band speeded up, the more she would stand out like a peacock among pigeons.

It was near the end of the dance when their eyes met. She went through the final steps with redoubled vitality and finished off with an impromptu twirl that wasn't in the steps at all. There was a gasp of indrawn breath from the onlookers, and a smattering of applause. They were obviously in a state of rapt adoration.

Col felt a pang of what might have been jealousy—except that a much greater pang of fear drowned it out. She didn't realize how easily the mood of her admirers could change. He had to warn her.

The young men swarmed around her the moment the music stopped. However, she rose on her toes to look out beyond them.

"Why, Colbert Porpentine." She spoke in her reading voice, imitating Upper Decks pronunciation. "I wondered when I would see you again."

The young men fell back a little, eyeing Col enviously. Pugh Squellingham and Lumbridge were among them.

"The married man," she said. "Congratulations."

Col stood before her but couldn't speak with everyone watching. He willed a silent message through his eyes. *Why are you doing this?*

She only smiled. "You must be so happy with your beautiful new bride."

Obscurely, he sensed that she was getting back at him.

His frowns had no effect on her. She was flaunting her success in his face.

"Isn't the dancing fun?" Her smile grew more brilliant again. "I'm enjoying it so much."

Still, he had to warn her; he had to speak to her alone. "May I have the honor of the next dance?" he asked.

"I'm afraid not. I've already promised somebody else."

"Me," said a young man at her elbow.

"Then me," said another young man.

"Then me after that," growled Lumbridge.

"So you see, you'll have to wait quite a while," she said.

Urgent, urgent, urgent! Col willed through his eyes. But she was enjoying her triumph too much to stop. The band struck up for the next dance, and she began tapping her foot in time. The rhythm was impossibly fast!

He was desperate. "I have the right to go first, because it's my wedding."

It was a bluff, but Riff didn't know the rules of Upper Decks etiquette. An uncertain crease appeared on her forehead.

"What about your bride?" she asked. "Shouldn't you be dancing with her?"

"Yes," said Pugh Squellingham. "Dance with Sephaltina."

"Here she comes now," said Lumbridge.

The crowd parted, and Sephaltina advanced. She planted herself in front of Col, her whole body an expression of pouting indignation.

"What are you doing?" she demanded. "Talking to *her*. You were meant to fetch me something sweet."

Col looked down and realized he was still holding the parfait glass and spoon.

"Here it is," he said, and put it into her hands.

Sephaltina was not mollified. The glass shook in her hand, and so did the yellow jelly.

Riff stared at it. "What's that stuff?" she asked.

Obviously, she hadn't noticed the jelly before. Now that she'd noticed it, she was entranced. Her promised partner was trying to lead her away for the next dance, but she brushed him aside.

The other young men were all eagerness to explain. "It's a dessert."

"Jelly."

"You eat it."

Col's heart was in his mouth. Anyone from anywhere on the Upper Decks ought to know about jelly. How much longer before they worked her out?

Forgetting her manners, she leaned forward for a closer inspection. The jelly quivered in the glass.

"May I?" she asked Sephaltina. "Do you mind?"

Her language was polite, but her behavior wasn't. She plucked the spoon from Sephaltina's fingers, steadied the glass with a hand over Sephaltina's hand, then scooped up a big blob of jelly.

"So wibbly-wobbly!" She laughed.

It was the wrong sort of laugh, coarse and vulgar. Col was in the grip of a nightmare. He foresaw disaster but didn't know how to make it stop.

She opened her mouth wide and carried the spoon toward it. She was going cross-eyed as she followed the precariously balanced blob.

Sephaltina could take no more. With a quiet "Oh!" she rolled up her eyes and fell backward in a faint.

Riff lost concentration. An inch from her mouth the jelly slipped from the spoon, bounced on her chin, and vanished down the front of her dress.

There was a thump as Sephaltina hit the floor, then a crash as the parfait glass shattered on the floor. Then a sort of tremulous giggle from Riff.

"It tickles!" she gasped. "I'll have to wriggle it down."

No, don't! Col screamed in the silence of his mind.

But she did. She began to shimmy in time to the dance music. She was breathless with laughter, tickled out of control.

"Hah-ah! Ooo-ah!"

She seemed to have forgotten the surrounding crowd. Her focus was all upon the jelly slithering its way down under her dress.

"Whee-hee! It's a-comin'!"

If she had been graceful before, now she undulated like a snake. It was blatant and shocking. Faster and faster she jiggled and joggled. Everyone could hear the change in her voice as she went back to her own natural accent.

"I got it! Hoo! Nearly there! Ah! Ah! Ah! *Whoopsie!*"

She lifted the hem of her dress and stepped away. Where she had been standing, a small blob of yellow jelly lay on the floor. She brushed tears of laughter from the corners of her eyes.

"Done it!" She pointed.

But a sudden space had opened up all around. She focused on Col with a look of appeal. . . .

"What's going on here?" boomed a familiar voice.

The young men made way as Sir Mormus strode forward. He glared at Sephaltina, still flat on the floor, then directed his attention to Riff.

Riff had recovered her composure and her Upper Decks accent. "A tiny accident. I *do* apologize."

"That's not her real voice," said one of the young men.

"She's *different*," said Pugh.

Sir Mormus's expression was like a thunderstorm about to break. But he held himself in.

"Go back to your dancing, everyone." He gestured toward Sephaltina. "Someone look after her. And someone call the security officers. As for *you*"—he rounded on Riff—"I'll talk to you in private."

62

Sir Mormus marched Riff off the dance floor, away from the crowd. He stopped her in a quiet area between a row of white pillars and a row of aspidistras in huge brass urns. Pugh, Haugh, and Lumbridge followed, and so did Col, by a parallel route. He watched proceedings from the aspidistra side, while they watched from the pillars.

"Well?" Sir Mormus growled at Riff. "Your name?"

"Um." Riff's body language was modest and submissive. "Riffaltina, sir."

"Riffaltina?" Sir Mormus rumbled. "What sort of a name is that? What's your family?"

"Er. Por . . . bert . . . ing . . . ton."

"Porbertington?"

"Yes, sir."

"Never heard of them. What does your father do?"

Riff was saved from having to answer by the arrival of Ebnolia. Gillabeth came up a moment later, towing Antrobus. She must have scented a scandal.

"The security officers are on their way." Ebnolia bobbed to a halt before her husband. "Some disturbance, dear?"

"Indeed. Did you invite a family by the name of Porbertington?"

"No, not on my guest list. Nor Hommelia's, I'm sure."

Sir Mormus turned on Riff. "So nobody's heard of you. Nobody knows who you are."

"*He* does!" Pugh Squellingham called out. His finger was raised and pointing at Col.

He stepped out from the pillars, with Haugh and Lumbridge on his heels. Reluctantly, Col emerged from the shelter of the urns and aspidistras.

"What's this?" Sir Mormus rumbled ominously. "Come here, Colbert. Come here, all of you."

They lined up in front of him.

"She knew his name," said Pugh. "She said, 'I wondered when I would see you again.'"

On the spur of the moment Col could only think to deny it. "You're a liar."

"I heard her too," said Haugh.

"He was desperate to dance with her," added Lumbridge.

"Colbert, did you meet this girl before?" Sir Mormus demanded.

Col found himself looking straight into Riff's eyes. But what choice did he have?

"Never. Not until just now, when she made poor Sephaltina faint."

Riff gave him a stare that cut right through him. Her eyes were narrowed, and her lips were a thin white line.

Sir Mormus swung back to her with a snort. "You, girl, did you ever meet this boy before?"

Col was in a state of funk. He was sure she was going to expose him. He would have to shout her down, abuse her, anything to stop her going into details.

"No." Riff shrugged. "They're all liars. I only knew his

name because I knew Colbert Porpentine was the one who'd got married."

"Why would they make it up?"

"I don't know. Jealousy?" She gestured toward Haugh. "I *did* have a dance with that boy." Then Lumbridge. "And that one had asked me to do him the honor."

Haugh spluttered and went red with embarrassment. Lumbridge looked down at his feet.

Sir Mormus dismissed them all. "Get out of my sight. Go."

Haugh, Pugh, and Lumbridge were happy to take off and avoid further interrogation. Col withdrew, then looped back around. He took up a position behind Gillabeth just as the security officers arrived.

There were ten of them, strong burly men with red armbands. They isolated the disturbance by forming a ring around Riff, Sir Mormus, and Ebnolia.

Riff had sized up the situation. She addressed Sir Mormus in a sheepish, apologetic tone. "I have a small confession, sir. I *did* come here without an invitation. I was never on anyone's guest list. So why don't I just go quietly now? Shall I? No scene, no fuss."

"Not so fast," said Ebnolia. She had been looking Riff up and down for a while. "What is it about your hair?"

She reached up and snatched hold of Riff's ringlets. Too late Riff tried to knock her hand away. The wig came loose and tumbled off—revealing the wild black-and-blond mass of Riff's own hair.

Sir Mormus and the security officers were still goggling when Riff exploded into action. She raised her fists and launched forward to break through the ring. But the unfamiliar heels of her Upper Decks shoes betrayed her. She overbalanced and went down, crashing headfirst into one officer's shins.

She swiveled on the floor, kicked off her shoes, and sprang up in another direction. But the moment she'd lost had been enough for Sir Mormus to stamp down on the hem of her long cream dress. As she sprang forward, the dress jerked her to a halt, and she went sprawling a second time.

"Stamp on her!" Sir Mormus bellowed.

At once the security officers stamped down on other parts of Riff's dress. She struggled to fight free, with loud sounds of ripping fabric, but there were too many of them. One officer caught her hands behind her back and clipped iron handcuffs onto her wrists. Another did the same for her ankles. In vain she bucked and arched and twisted.

Sir Mormus raised his foot and stepped away. "No one to approach," he ordered. "I don't want our guests to see this."

He joined Ebnolia, who had already dropped back, not far from Col and Gillabeth. Though they spoke in lowered voices, Col could hear enough to guess the rest.

"You know what she is?" Ebnolia whispered.

"I do. She must have . . ."

"The scandal will ruin us."

"I can keep the officers quiet."

". . . still need to get her out of here unnoticed."

"There'll be talk if I'm seen leaving the reception."

"Why don't I look after it?"

"Good . . . usual place?"

"I'll have her taken there immediately."

Sir Mormus nodded. Ebnolia cleared her throat and gave

instructions to the officers in her normal voice. "Lift her up. Take her to the Changing Room."

It took Col a second to register what he'd heard. So there *was* a Changing Room! And Riff was being taken to it! The place she most dreaded!

The look of absolute despair in her eyes confirmed it. He shuddered to think of her transformed into a shambling, speechless, mindless Menial.

Four officers gripped her by the arms and shoulders while the rest shielded her from view. Her cream dress now hung in tatters. Col watched her being frog-marched away.

"You'd like to go after her, wouldn't you?"

He blinked. Gillabeth! She studied him with an appraising look.

"Yes," he answered without thinking.

He could almost see the calculations ticking over in his sister's mind. How much had she managed to work out?

"You'll be noticed if you do," she said.

"Why—?"

"Unless I take you there a different way."

"Where?"

"The Changing Room, of course."

"You know all about it, then?"

"I've always known about it. Well?"

"Yes," he said. "Take me there. Please."

63

They left by a door on the other side of the Grand Assembly Hall. As soon as they were out in the corridor, Gillabeth picked up Antrobus and carried him.

Col didn't care about her motives—whether she really wanted to help him or just wanted him to damn himself forever. He cared only about saving Riff.

They went past two descending flights of stairs, then swung into a short dead-end corridor. Gillabeth walked up to the green velvet curtains at the back and parted them to reveal a set of wooden swing doors. Then she opened the doors to reveal the vertical rails and chains of a steam elevator.

"We'll go the quick way," she said.

"Are you allowed to use this on your own?"

"I'm not allowed to use it at all."

She certainly knew how to work it, though. She clicked a switch, and a rattling, clanking sound started somewhere high above. When the platform arrived, they stepped on, and she raised a lever to go up.

"The Changing Room is on Forty-eighth Deck, but the entrance is on Forty-ninth," she told him.

Even the quick way seemed agonizingly slow to Col. Clouds of steam billowed around as they ascended to Forty-ninth Deck.

Coming out through another set of swing doors and green curtains, they passed through a warren of glass-fronted offices. Inside the offices were black boxes glowing with tiny lights, and cubicles where officers sat with pencils in their hands, metal cups over their ears.

"Wireless telegraphy," Gillabeth explained. "The signals come in as Morse code and get turned into messages. We plot the routes of other juggernauts from their messages."

"Come *on!*" Col only hurried all the faster. "The Changing Room."

Several officers looked up and frowned at them through the windows. One came and stood in a doorway, staring after them. But nobody challenged their right to be there.

They left the wireless telegraphy offices behind and turned into a blank-walled corridor. At the first corner Gillabeth gave a warning gesture and stopped dead. Together they peered around into the next corridor.

Up ahead were more blank walls, with a single door at the far end. Grandmother Ebnolia was holding it open, while the ten security officers struggled to force Riff through.

"That's the entrance," Gillabeth whispered. "Wait."

Riff's resistance was short-lived. The security officers overpowered her and frog-marched her inside. Ebnolia went in last, closing the door behind her.

"She didn't lock it, lucky for you," Gillabeth told Col. "What are you going to do?"

"Don't know. What about you?"

"I'm taking Antrobus back. I've helped you enough."

"Why help at all?"

Gillabeth scowled. "You can never do anything on your own. You're hopeless."

She went off without another word.

Col couldn't understand her and didn't try. He crept on down the corridor to the door at the end. It was labeled NO ADMITTANCE and had an elaborate locking mechanism of levers and bars. But as Gillabeth had said, it wasn't locked.

He entered and found himself in a long empty passage leading to another door. A small square pane of glass was set into this door at head height. He came up to it and peered through.

On the other side was the top of a metal spiral staircase and, beyond that, a yawning open space lit by a cold silvery glow. There was no floor on level with Forty-ninth Deck here; the floor of the Changing Room was a whole deck lower down.

He edged the door open. The first thing that hit him was the smell: sharp, biting, antiseptic. He slipped inside and crouched at the top of the metal steps.

Looking down, he took in tall white cabinets, baize-topped tables, zinc washbasins, and fans swishing slowly around and around. The room was dim apart from two pools of light that shone over two high leather chairs. Beside each chair a black metal tree held out enamel trays and equipment at various heights.

A male Filthy was already strapped into one of the chairs. Two figures bent over him, wearing gowns, caps, and face masks. One was evidently a surgeon, the other his Menial assistant. While the assistant held scissors, the surgeon did something to the male Filthy's mouth.

Riff was in the process of being strapped into the other

chair, which had been tilted back at an angle to receive her. The security officers had unclipped the iron cuffs from her wrists and ankles and were now fastening her arms onto armrests, her feet onto footrests. A particularly wide strap went round her neck, and a kind of leather cup enclosed her chin.

Then they drew back, leaving her immobilized. Her eyes looked out above the leather cup, huge and fearful.

"There, there, there," said Ebnolia, coming forward. "Let's remove that jewelry, now you won't be needing it anymore."

The sweetness of her tone made Col shiver. With dainty fingers she unpinned the earrings from Riff's ears. Riff couldn't speak properly with the cup round her chin, but she growled like a wild animal.

Ebnolia tut-tutted. "Hush, dear. You'll be better soon. Much less savage and intractable. You won't need to make such ugly noises when they fix up your tongue."

Choosing his moment, Col descended two whole turns of the spiral staircase. He was briefly in view, but no one looked up. He ducked down out of sight again.

The only sound was the *swish-swish-swish* of circulating fans overhead. Ebnolia continued to talk, and Riff continued to growl.

"Let me show you the wire they use for sewing." Ebnolia swung one of the trays on the metal tree closer. On the tray were half a dozen bobbins of bright golden wire.

"The very finest wire, you see." She held one bobbin in front of Riff's face. "Not only for the tongue, but all parts of the body. They'll sew you up inside, where nobody can see. You have far more movement than you really need, you know."

She pulled another tray closer, a tray that bore a small box.

She opened it up to display row upon row of shining needles nestled in beds of red velvet.

"And here are the needles for doing the stitches. Such a neat, tidy job they'll do." She passed one of the needles back and forth in the air. "Of course, it's far more difficult than it looks."

A grunt from the surgeon announced the end of the operation in the other chair. He stepped back to admire his handiwork, then went to wash his hands. His assistant untied a white bib, now spotted with blood, from around the male Filthy's neck.

"There, that other one has had his changes done. When he recovers, he'll be a fine new Menial."

The changed male Filthy twitched and shivered, then slumped back against the headrest of his chair.

"So peaceful and contented," Ebnolia pattered on. "That's how you will be too. But even better, dear, because I think I'll make you into my favorite Menial." She rested a thoughtful finger on the point of her chin. "Yes, I think I will. I'm feeling quite fond of you already. Such big appealing eyes you have."

The assistant came across and tied a fresh white bib around Riff's neck.

Col scanned the room. Was there a way to rescue Riff while keeping his identity secret? Then he noticed a spare gown draped over one of the sinks and a spare cap and face mask on a shelf above the taps. Yes, there was a way. . . .

Meanwhile the assistant had gone off again. He returned with a stoppered glass bottle and a felt pad.

"Ah, the anesthetic to numb the pain," said Ebnolia. "For when your limiters are inserted."

Riff struggled hopelessly in her straps.

"Oh, that's not very well behaved, dear." Ebnolia tinkled with amusement. "Don't you want less pain?"

The assistant returned with a dish of what looked like golden buttons. He placed them on a tray behind Riff's head. Ebnolia held one up for Riff to see.

"And these are your limiters, to limit your mind," she explained. "You have so many more thoughts than you really need. When you've been limited, you'll still have lots of nice small thoughts, but no nasty big ones. Won't you like that?"

The surgeon, who had now finished drying his hands, strode up to Riff's chair. Ebnolia made way for him.

"Here comes the surgeon to mark out your skull," she told Riff. "He has to insert your limiters into exactly the right parts of your brain."

The surgeon had a pair of calipers in one hand and a marking pen in the other.

Col didn't wait to see more. He swung silently down the last two turns of the staircase, then darted off and hid behind the nearest table.

No shouts of alarm; nobody had seen him. Bent double, he scuttled round by the cabinets and came to the sinks.

He didn't need to stand to take hold of the gown. He tugged on the end and pulled it to the floor. The rubbery green material made scarcely a rustle as he gathered it in.

He still needed the cap and face mask, though. Taking a gamble, he jumped up without looking, snatched the two items from the shelf, and ducked down again. Once more he was in luck. Everyone's attention remained focused on the operation.

He put on the cap and slipped into the gown. With frantic

fingers he buttoned the gown and tied on the face mask.

The surgeon must have finished marking out Riff's skull, because a whirring, buzzing sound started up. Something metal, something spinning at high speed . . .

Now or never! Col jumped to his feet and ran forward.

64

Surprise was his only weapon. Seeing him in surgical cap and gown, the security officers didn't know what to make of him.

"Who are you?"

"Do you work here?"

Col ran on without a word.

The surgeon didn't know what to make of him either. "Is that you, Shannock? Pendleton?"

He held some kind of drilling instrument, which was what made the whirring, buzzing sound. His assistant carried the stoppered glass bottle and a pad of cotton wool.

Col pushed them aside and bent over Riff. Her forehead had been marked out with blue lines like a diagram. He unfastened the strap from her neck and yanked the leather cup away from her chin. In spite of his mask she recognized him.

"Thought you'd come," she breathed.

He started on the straps that clamped her arms to the armrests.

"Hey!"

"Stop!"

"He can't do that!"

The cries of outrage multiplied. When Riff's left arm came free, the surgeon dropped his drill and tried to grab at Col's hand.

Col reacted with one of Riff's fighting moves. He took a two-handed grip on the surgeon's wrist, then twisted and flung, using his hip as a pivot. The surgeon spun through the air and fell to the floor at Ebnolia's feet.

Col returned to the strap on Riff's other arm. His grandmother was shrilling at the top of her voice. "That's no doctor! Keep him away from her!"

Col kept his mind wide and his senses open. Even as he focused on his task, he remained fully aware of the officers approaching behind his back. He finished unfastening the last buckle just as the nearest officer leaned forward to grip him by the shoulders.

He dropped down on one knee and the officer gripped empty air. He seized the man by the calves and threw him over his head, over Riff, over the metal tree and the chair.

By now they were all coming.

"Do the rest yourself!" His voice was muffled through the face mask, but Riff understood.

He whirled to confront the next officer. He feinted a punch to the belly, then turned it into a punch to the chin. The officer's head snapped back, and his teeth came together with a violent crack. His eyes glazed over, and he toppled to the ground.

Suddenly wary, the other officers halted in their rush. They spread out to surround him on all sides. He glanced back at Riff, who was undoing the straps over her feet.

Ebnolia was still close by, but he hadn't thought of her as a threat. She took him by surprise when she bobbed up on tiptoe and pulled the mask down from his face.

Col stood revealed.

The officers gasped. "That's her grandson!"

"Master Porpentine!"

"Who just got married!"

Ebnolia's shock turned into a scream, which turned into a shriek of accusation. "Traitor!"

"Yes, and I know about you too!" Col shouted full in her face. "Murderer!"

"Traitor! Traitor! Traitor!" Her tiny white teeth looked ready to bite. "Kill him!"

The officers wavered. The idea of actually killing a Porpentine was more than they could absorb.

"Perhaps take him prisoner," one suggested.

"No, kill him." Ebnolia's features were distorted with hatred. "He's shamed us once too often. Sir Mormus disowns him. We want him dead."

Riff jumped out of her chair, the straps all undone. She sprang forward in front of Col and snatched the bottle of anesthetic from the assistant's hand.

"You evil old witch!" she yelled.

She flicked the stopper out of the bottle, took hold of Ebnolia's hair, pulled back her head, and poured liquid anesthetic down her throat.

"Have a taste of your own medicine!" she snarled.

Ebnolia spluttered and gurgled. When Riff released her head, she sank limply to the floor.

The officers had waited a moment too long. Now they charged forward from all sides.

Riff hurled the bottle at one officer and knocked him over with a hit to the temple. Then she danced forward and kicked another in the groin. In the same flowing motion she pirouetted and punched a third in the kidneys. He folded up and collapsed like an accordion.

Col brought down a fourth with a scything kick to the kneecaps.

"Who's next?" cried Riff.

"You can't beat us all," threatened one of the survivors.

"Wanna bet?"

The five officers still on their feet looked at one another and decided that yes, Riff and Col together could probably beat them all. They began to retreat.

"Reinforcements!" shouted the surgeon. "We need reinforcements!"

He was already halfway up the spiral staircase. With clattering boots the officers hurried after him.

Riff pulled the white bib from her neck with an "Ugh!" of disgust. She licked the back of her hand and rubbed her forehead, wiping away the blue lines.

"Let's go," she said. "Before they come back with reinforcements."

But Col was looking at Grandmother Ebnolia. She began jerking this way and that on the floor.

Twang! Twang! Twang!

It was the elastic of her stays bursting open.

Twang! Twang! Twang!

Then the jerking and twanging stopped. Ebnolia was almost unrecognizable, bulging in strange places. Her wasp waist had vanished completely.

"She's not moving," said Col in sudden alarm.

He knelt and touched the soft, suedelike skin of her cheek. It wasn't cold, but somehow lifeless.

"I think . . . she's . . ."

He couldn't say the word. Riff knelt down on the other side and pressed a finger to the side of Ebnolia's neck.

"She's dead."

"The anesthetic killed her."

"I didn't . . ." For a moment Riff's voice shook, and her expression wavered. Then she sucked in her lips and recovered control. "She deserved it. We have to go."

She rose to her feet, but Col stayed kneeling. He looked into the blankness of Ebnolia's eyes, and his own eyes misted.

"Come on," said Riff.

"I have to say good-bye."

Riff tried to pull him by the shoulder, but he shrugged her off.

"She was going to kill you, remember? She starved her Menials to death. She was going to do the same to me."

Col shook his head. The real Ebnolia Porpentine was a monster—he didn't deny it. What he'd lost was something else: the image he'd grown up with, the grandmother in his heart. He remembered holidays and Sunday picnics, high teas and family card nights. *Will you always love your favorite grandma?* she used to ask. She had been so much a part of his life, the only grandmother he'd ever known. His whole past flashed before him.

One memory stood out, particularly vivid . . . a memory of a family circle book reading. Sitting on a chair in the Somerset Room, with Grandfather, Mother, Father, and Sister

Gillabeth, listening as Grandmother read out a story. He must have been very tiny, because his feet couldn't reach the floor. There were Menials in obedient attendance and mugs of hot chocolate. He didn't understand much of the story, but it had a wonderful hero whose best friends were his cat and his dog. They lived in a town where the streets were made of cobblestones and the roofs were made of straw, and they went around helping people and doing noble things. Grandmother showed him a picture of the hero in the book. Everything was so noble and good . . . In his memory the taste of hot chocolate mingled with the colors of the picture and the carpet and chairs in the Somerset Room to create a feeling of absolute safety and rightness. And, encompassing it all, the strawberry-sweet scent of his grandmother's perfume, his grandmother's kindness. . . .

"Good-bye," he murmured, and it became a farewell to his childhood and all the things he'd once believed in.

He stood up, swallowing, rubbing the wetness from his eyes. It was as though the world of his past evaporated, leaving him clean and fresh and clear-headed. Now he knew exactly what he had to do.

"Okay, let's go," he said. "Time to start the revolution."

Riff stared at him, then gave a whoop. "Lower the rope? Bring up the Filthies?"

"Yes. Let's do it."

65

They descended by the same steam elevator that Gillabeth had operated before. Gillabeth had raised the lever to go up, so Col lowered the lever to go down. At Fourth Deck he moved the lever to a midway position to bring the platform to a halt. They hunted around in the repair stores and found spools of cable even better and longer than the ropes that Col had used before.

He wasn't sure what would happen with the steel door to Bottom Deck. He knew how to open Door Seventeen, but this would be a different door. In fact it turned out to be Door Thirteen. Would the same combination unlock it, or would they need to walk all the way to Door Seventeen?

No need to shield the numbers from Riff anymore. He spun the top wheel to 4, the middle wheel to 9, and the bottom wheel to 2.

Clack! The same combination did the trick!

They darted inside. The scene on Bottom Deck looked very familiar: rows of iron piers, black mounds of coal, occasional pools of blue-white light. For the moment the coast was clear.

"It'll be the same arrangement, I bet." Riff pointed. "Food chute should be over there."

They passed four piers, turned right at a bunker, passed another two piers . . . and there ahead was the cover of the chute. Bags and sacks of food were stacked behind it; mounds of coal rose up on either side.

A sudden shout spoiled their success. "Hey! You!"

An officer had spotted them. No matter! They ran on to the manhole, crouched down, and set to work on the bolts. They heaved the cover back on its hinges and lowered it to the floor.

The officer strode up, spluttering with fury. "You-you-you!"

Riff was poised and waiting. As the officer lunged for her, she twisted aside and hooked his feet from under him. Then she caught him by the ankles, upended him, and propelled him headfirst into the hole.

It was over in a flash. By the time he managed a scream, the soles of his boots were already disappearing round the curve in the chute.

"We've sent a message!" whooped Riff. "That'll wake 'em up Below!"

"They'd better be quick," said Col.

He held one end of the cable and flung the rest of the spool into the hole after the officer. It dropped all the way down to the bottom. He wound the end round the hinges of the cover, and Riff made it fast with a knot.

The officer's shouts had not gone unnoticed. Straining his ears, Col could hear distant voices asking questions.

"What was that noise?"

"Where was it?"

"Something's wrong."

Then the cable went taut. The Filthies were on the way up. Riff caught Col by the wrist and drew him away from the manhole.

They hid beside one of the coal mounds, with a clear view over the approach to the chute.

The distant questions had turned into commands. It sounded as though someone was organizing a search.

Col jogged Riff's elbow. "Look."

Away on one side of Bottom Deck the moving beams of flashlights cut through the gloom.

Riff pointed in another direction. "And over there."

More flashlights: a second search party. There was nothing to do but wait and hope. Col had never actually gauged the length of the food chute, but he knew the Filthies had a long way to climb.

The beams swept from side to side, but always coming closer. Although the officers weren't sure what they'd heard, the chute was surely one of the places they'd check.

"Arm yerself," whispered Riff.

She had a lump of coal in either hand. Missiles for bombarding the officers. Col gathered two lumps of his own.

The first search party was already approaching. The officers had fanned out, and only some carried flashlights. One appeared around the side of a bunker and began to investigate in the direction of the food chute.

Luckily, he was one of the ones without a flashlight and couldn't immediately see that the manhole was open, the cover flat on the ground.

"Mine," whispered Riff.

She drew back her arm. When the officer came in close range, she hurled a lump of coal and struck him a terrible blow just above the ear. He went down without a sound.

But now the second search party was meeting up with

the first. More commands rang out. "Spread wider. Check everywhere."

Riff rearmed herself with another lump of coal. "I'll lead 'em away," she whispered.

She was gone before Col could protest. Gliding around the side of the mound, vanishing into the shadows . . .

Still the Filthies hadn't reached the top of the chute. Two officers approached between the coal mounds—and this time they both had flashlights.

"Aaa-aghh!" One stumbled and clutched at the back of his head.

Col couldn't see, but he heard the clatter of Riff's missile bouncing away.

"Yaa-wagh!" A mocking imitation of the officer's roar of pain. "Here I am! Come and find me!"

There was instant fury, instant hubbub. But the plan mis-fired. While everyone else turned in the direction of the voice, the other officer with a flashlight still shone his beam forward—and spotted the prostrate form of Riff's first victim.

"Man down!" His urgent shout pierced the hubbub. "Looks like Dumfrey!"

Col flung one lump of coal, then the other. His aim wasn't as good as Riff's, and he hit the officer only on the arm and shoulder. Still, the blows made him drop his flashlight.

He shouted all the louder. "Here! Here! Over here!"

More flashlights appeared around the coal mounds, and many more uniforms. One beam ranged beyond the body on the ground and picked out the open manhole cover.

"Look!"

"Emergency!"

"Forget Dumfrey! Close that cover!"

Col had run out of options. He sprang forward from the shadows and took up a fighting stance, blocking the way to the chute.

Lights dazzled his eyes. There were cries of amazement. "Isn't that—?"

He yelled defiance. "Colbert Porpentine! Stay back!"

But they weren't going to obey his orders now. Half a dozen came rushing at him, fists raised, flashlights wielded like clubs.

He dodged and felled the leading officer with a punch to the solar plexus. As that one dropped, he spun and knocked another sideways. A third swung at him and missed, but still bore him to the ground, trapping his legs.

Before Col could wriggle free, a fourth loomed over him. A massive boot came crunching down toward his face—but never landed. Suddenly, the man crumpled and fell headlong, crashing to the ground somewhere behind Col's head.

Riff had arrived.

"On yer feet!" She grinned.

Did she see the two officers behind her back? Even as they reached for her, one let out a sudden gurgle of surprise. A long metal spike had skewered him through the throat.

The other barely had time to stare before a second spike flew through the air and impaled him in the chest.

"Yay!" Riff brandished her fist. "And about time, too!"

It was the Filthies. Col rolled over and saw them emerging from the manhole. One after another they sprang out, landed lightly on their feet, and ran forward. They were all armed with spikes or iron bars or blades.

The officers were nowhere near outnumbered, but they couldn't match the Filthies for weapons—or speed and agility. They dropped back as Riff led the Filthies forward. Col found himself in a quiet zone behind the line of action.

He freed his legs and levered himself off the ground. But one of the officers he'd brought down before wasn't giving up the fight. Col saw only the flashlight in the man's hand, whirling in a savage arc. The metal casing met the top of his skull with a tremendous crack. There was a moment of blinding pain . . . then oblivion.

66

When he came to, he was flat on his back, and Riff was cradling his head in her lap. Her face lit up when his eyes flickered open.

"Good!" was all she said.

She was pressing something against the top of his skull. His head felt sore and muzzy. He remembered the fighting. . . . He directed his gaze left and right. No officers now, only Filthies. They were like a sea flowing past on either side.

Then a cry went up: "Where's Riff?"

Riff stirred her legs. "That's the Revolutionary Council," she told him. "They need me."

An older Filthy in a red headband came pushing through the crowd. Col remembered her name: Fossie.

"Riff, you gotta come and explain the strategy," she said.

"Okay, okay." Riff nodded down at Col. "But someone has to look after him."

"I can do it."

So Fossie changed places with Riff. Col's vision blurred as his head was raised, then lowered into a new lap.

"Use this for the blood," said Riff.

She was talking about a strip of rag, which she passed across to Fossie. It had once been white but was now three-quarters red. Fossie made a wad of it and applied it gently to the top of his skull.

Col looked up into her face. A friendly face, attractive even with age, strongly etched with laughter lines.

"You're a member of the Council," he brought out. "You were in the hammock."

"Ah, you remember. I must've made an impression on ya, then." Her gray eyes twinkled. "And now you've got me all to yerself. So be quiet and recover."

There was a long period of comfortable silence. Filthies with spikes, bars, and blades continued to pad past, an ever-growing army. Some glanced at Col with curious or hostile eyes—but fleetingly. They were intent on more urgent business.

Col felt better all the time. He could hear orders being issued about twenty or thirty paces away. The Revolutionary Council seemed to be sending different teams in different directions.

"How's the attack going?" he asked after a while.

Fossie lifted the strip of rag. "Hmm. Bleedin's stopped," she announced. "How's the attack goin'? I expect we're half a dozen decks up by now. We capture and guard the staircases. They're the key."

"Everything's so well planned."

"Of course. We've been livin' for this day. Dreamin' about it. Riff most of all."

Col reflected back over the last few weeks with Riff on the Upper Decks. Their training sessions had been so important to him he'd hardly considered what she was doing the rest of the time. Now he saw a whole new side to her.

"She's amazing."

"Very clever and very determined," Fossie agreed. Her mouth quirked in a smile. "Not so pretty, though."

"I think she is."

"No? Really?"

Col half heard the note of teasing, but couldn't stop himself. "She's better than pretty. She's better than anything. She's . . . she's . . ."

Fossie laughed. "Oh, dear. Got it bad, ain't ya?"

"Have I? What?"

"Reckon you're in love with her."

Col explored the idea in the privacy of his mind. Was being "in love" something more than just "love"?

"You'll have to fight for her, though," Fossie went on. "She's got dozens of boys feel the same way about her."

Col knew he didn't stand a chance against any male Filthy, not yet. But he could learn, he could practice, he could *make* himself good enough. "If that's what it takes," he said.

"Unless she loved ya back." Fossie put on a thoughtful expression. "She wouldn't allow fightin' then. Not impossible, I s'pose."

"Do you think so?"

The laughter lines deepened in her face. "Oh, how should I know?"

Col made an effort and sat up straight. There was blood all over his shirt and tailcoat. When he touched his fingertips to his scalp, his hair was crusted with dried blood.

A passing group of Filthies stopped and stared.

"It's okay," Fossie told them. "He's on our side."

They muttered and moved on. Fossie shook her head at Col.

"It's your Upper Decks clothes," she explained. "You don't look like us."

Col considered his clothes, which were bloodstained anyway. "I could take off my coat and shirt."

"Yeah, better."

He slipped out of his tailcoat, and Fossie helped him take off his shirt, which was stuck to his skin in many places.

"Let's see what Riff would be gettin'," she said.

"Ow! Ouch!"

She laughed when he was finally stripped to the waist. "Well, hello to the handsome young hero! I never knew anyone could be so *pale*!"

She made him take off his shoes and socks, too. But she still wasn't satisfied.

"No, you're too clean. Wait."

She rubbed the palms of her hands on the floor and coated them with coal dust and grime. Then she patted him on the chest and back.

"Don't move!"

She seemed to enjoy his outrage as she left dirty smears all over his skin. She finished her handiwork by pressing her palms to his cheeks, then stepped back to admire the effect.

"You're a real Filthy now. Much improved. I could almost fancy you myself."

Col didn't know how to deal with her humor. "I think I can stand up," he said.

She steadied him as he rose. "Not dizzy?"

"No."

She watched him closely and nodded approval. He wasn't swaying in the least.

"Let's go join the Council, then."

Four members of the Revolutionary Council were engaged in animated discussion, including Riff. Riff's brother, Padder, was there, along with cold-eyed Shiv and Dunga, the tattooed girl.

When Fossie added herself to the cluster, Riff glanced at her, then at Col. Her smile of relief lasted only an instant—then she plunged back into the discussion.

He stood on the edge of the cluster and listened. They were talking strategy: Was it time to open up further food chutes on Bottom Deck? Riff was in favor, but Shiv had doubts. Riff's arguments sounded completely convincing to Col.

Padder, with his stubbly chin, looked exactly as Col remembered, yet he was somehow different. Now he seemed almost likeable. Col warmed to him more and more, especially when he supported his sister's arguments.

Finally, Shiv backed down and the Council prepared to organize teams for the new strategy. A far-off *crack-crack-crack* interrupted them.

"What was that?"

No one could guess.

"Maybe on Fifth Deck?"

"Higher."

More reports, like a distant stutter. Col had a sudden suspicion.

"I think I know." He stepped forward. "Gunfire. They're shooting guns."

"Guns?"

"Your weapons will be useless."

Riff bit her lip. "How many guns?"

"No idea. Officers don't normally carry them." Col had seen only one real gun in his life: the rifle carried by the ensign on guard outside the bridge. "There must be a store of them somewhere."

Riff stared up in the direction of the gunfire. "I can guess. There's a locked room I could never get into on Eighth Deck." She snapped her fingers. "We have to stop 'em now."

She didn't wait for the Council to reach a decision, but shouted out to all the Filthies on Bottom Deck, "I need fifty fighters! Come with me now!"

Col made sure he was one of the fifty. Fossie came too, and so did Dunga and Shiv. Padder stayed behind to direct the Filthies who were still coming up through the food chute.

67

They headed toward the sound of gunfire, ascending from deck to deck. More Filthies joined in on the way. The reports grew louder.

Crack! Crack! Crack! Crack!

Col ran as fast as anyone. His head was still sore, but the muzziness had cleared. Fired up by adrenalin, he felt fighting fit—or if he wasn't, he didn't intend to think about it.

The shooting came from an area on Eighth Deck both fore and aft of the room Riff knew. Approaching along Seventh Deck, they came to a staircase going up. Four Filthies sat on the bottom steps.

One clamped a hand over a bleeding hole in her leg; another nursed an arm half shot away below the elbow; the other two were openly weeping. The arrival of reinforcements hardly raised their spirits.

"Can't even get close," groaned the girl with the hole in her leg. "They shoot us down from a distance."

Riff halted her army. For the time being, the gunfire had stopped here. She crept up the stairs, followed by Fossie, Shiv, and Dunga. Col crept after them.

Trickles of blood ran down over the topmost step. Cautiously, Col raised his head to peer out. Some lumpy shape was blocking his view.

He didn't realize what it was at first, because the body was twisted at such an odd angle. A young Filthy boy lay with his cheek flat to the ground, his eyes staring sightlessly. He had freckles, a mop of ginger hair, and a gaping red hole in the side of his chest.

Col's stomach turned over. But there was worse to come. He raised his head a little higher and took in the whole corridor.

It was a slaughterhouse, with six or more Filthies lying dead. They looked as though they had been picked up and tossed about at all angles. Their blood spattered the walls and smeared the floor.

Beyond the slaughter, at an intersection of corridors, a line of officers knelt with long-barreled rifles. Their faces expressed no particular horror at what they had done.

Seeing Col, they came to life. The rifles swung instantly in his direction, and a volley of shots rang out. As Col ducked down, he heard the *smack-smack-smack* of bullets tearing into the dead boy's flesh. Then a scream and a curse on his right. Dunga had had part of her ear shot away and was bleeding like a stuck pig.

Everyone slid and scampered back down the staircase. No sounds of pursuit came from above.

Riff quizzed the girl with the hole in her leg, who was still sitting on the bottom steps. "How can we get to their store of guns?"

"Not past *them*." The girl hooked a thumb. "They're spreadin' out wider and wider across the deck."

"She's right," said Shiv. "We'll be wiped out in a head-on attack."

"Perhaps there's a way to sneak up behind their lines," Fossie suggested.

"A weak spot," Shiv agreed. "Somewhere unguarded."

Riff nodded. "Worth a try. Okay, I'll take a scouting party, see what I can find."

There were now seventy or eighty Filthies in the army gathered at the bottom of the staircase. Riff selected ten volunteers, including Col and Fossie.

"What's the signal if you break through?" asked Shiv.

Riff put two fingers to her lips and gave a soundless demonstration of a whistle.

"Right."

The scouting party set off at once. On Seventh Deck they could walk right underneath the officers who had just shot at them. But they still had to find a staircase to go up—and one not guarded by officers with guns.

Col strode beside Riff at the head of the party. "Do you know where the staircases are?" he asked.

"Of course. Don't you?"

Col didn't answer. He was from the Upper Decks, but he'd never explored these levels. Riff obviously knew the overall layout of the juggernaut far better than he did.

Then they passed a short dead-end passage with green curtains at the back, and he found he had something to contribute after all.

"Wait up!" he called.

"What?"

He darted into the passage to take a look behind the curtains. Yes! The wooden swing doors of yet another steam elevator!

Riff had followed and was peering over his shoulder. He opened the doors for her to see.

"Like the one we came down on!" Her eyes lit up with excitement.

While Col clicked the switch to summon the platform, she explained the plan to the others. "We can ride this thing to the deck above. If we're lucky, it won't be guarded."

Col thought they might indeed be lucky. Lower-ranking officers never used the elevators, so they wouldn't expect Filthies to use them either.

When the platform arrived, the whole party crowded on, nearly overloading the machinery. The engine wheezed and hissed and struggled to move. At last, with voluminous clouds of steam, they began to ascend.

One floor up Col brought the platform to a halt. He stepped off, opened the doors, and peeped out through the curtains.

The passage outside was identical to the one below. Deserted!

By unspoken agreement Col was now in the lead with Riff. The two of them went on ahead to the corridor at the end of the passage. Also deserted. Riff beckoned the other Filthies forward.

A continuous murmur came from somewhere nearby: shuffling feet, voices, the chink and clank of metal. Around the next corner they looked out on a foyer where many corridors converged.

"This is the place," whispered Riff.

A shutter had been raised in the back wall to reveal a kind of serving counter. Red letters on the wall spelled out the word ARMORY, and a line of officers queued for weapons. Behind the counter other officers moved back and forth, lay-ing out guns and clips of bullets. As each man collected his gun, he loaded a clip into the magazine and stowed spare clips in his pockets. A master lieutenant sent the armed men off along another corridor.

There was something else as well. In the center of the foyer two men sat beside a special type of gun: larger, heavier, mounted on a tripod. A belt of bullets fed into it from the side.

Riff directed Col's attention with a nudge. "What does it do?"

"Don't know."

"Hmm. Only one way to find out." She beckoned the rest of the scouting party forward. "Okay. We charge the counter and break into the gun room. I'll go first."

Col frowned. "Why first?"

"To deal with *that*." She pointed to the gun in the center of the foyer. "Everyone ready?"

She tensed herself to launch forward. Col never knew what made him do it. He pulled her back by the elbow and launched forward in her place.

Sprinting into the foyer, running for the special gun. The men behind it saw him and swung the barrel. Col's vision was a telescope focused on the trigger, on the finger starting to squeeze. He jinked sideways to avoid the first shot.

Rat-tat-tat-tat-tat-tat-tat-tat-tat-tat!

It wasn't just one shot, but shot after shot after shot! Spurts of fire flickered nonstop from the barrel's end. The first man kept his finger pressed on the trigger while the second fed the belt in at the side. The murderous swathe of fire angled toward Col.

He flung himself flat to the floor, and the bullets skimmed over his head. He was still sliding forward, but losing momentum. With outstretched fingers he just managed to grip one leg of the tripod.

The man behind the gun snarled and tried to change his aim downward. Col jerked the leg and shook the gun. A slew of bullets plowed across the floor.

The second man struggled to wrestle the tripod away from him. Col scrambled to his feet and seized hold of the barrel—so hot it made him scream. Still, he ripped the gun from its operators' hands, whirled, and flung it away across the floor.

"Yay-ay-ay-ay-ay!"

Filthies poured forward, yelling and waving weapons, rushing for the armory. The officers who'd been handing out guns stood frozen in disbelief.

Riff was first to vault the counter. The other Filthies were right behind her.

The officers inside had no chance to defend themselves. Still laden with clips of bullets and rifles, they were chopped to the ground or thrown bodily out into the foyer.

Col joined the rush. He was the last to vault the counter, even as Riff reached up for the shutter. With a thunderous clatter she pulled it down.

Other Filthies grasped what she was doing. They slid home the bolts at either end and locked the shutter in place. Now the armory was sealed off from the world outside.

68

Racks of guns filled the room from floor to ceiling. Polished metal parts glinted under the light of bare electric bulbs. The guns that had been handed out so far were a mere fraction of the total still in store.

The Filthies were already helping themselves to guns from the racks and clips of bullets from the shelves. Col did the same. The wooden stock of his rifle was engraved with the word WORLDSHAKER and the imperial coat of arms. But how to load the bullets?

"Like this!" cried Fossie.

She must have been watching how the officers did it before. She fitted a clip above the magazine, pushed the bullets down inside, then flicked away the clip holder. Everyone copied the action.

Then fists started hammering on the shutter outside. The corrugated metal shook and rattled.

"Take aim!" yelled Riff.

They raised guns to shoulders, rested fingers on triggers.

A shot smashed through the shutter from outside. Col felt the wind of it ruffle his hair. The bullet ricocheted off the racks at the far end of the room and went zinging through the air. He aimed toward the bullet hole and fired back.

Except he didn't. Nothing happened. He squeezed the trigger again and again.

The others were also aiming and shooting—in vain.

"What's wrong?"

"These things don't work!"

They were forced to duck down behind the counter as more shots were fired from outside. They shook their guns, banged them on the floor, swore at them. Useless! Col tried loading another gun, but the result was the same.

Then a new sound started up outside: *Rat-tat-tat-tat-tat-tat-tat-tat-tat-tat!*

Bullet holes blossomed in the metal of the shutter. The racket was deafening. One Filthy girl yelped as a ricocheting bullet struck her on the arm.

"It's that special gun!" someone shouted.

Col gritted his teeth. He should have done something to disable it when he had the chance. Bullet holes merged in continuous lines, carving the metal apart.

And still they couldn't make their own guns work.

In slow motion a large part of the shutter fell away. It toppled back onto the counter, bounced over their shoulders, and crashed to the floor.

For a moment the gunfire ceased. Col popped up his head to take a quick look. There were more and more officers flooding into the foyer all the time. They knelt or stood in a half circle with rifles raised.

"Advance!" roared the master lieutenant.

The officers surged forward, firing at random as they ran. Col dropped down just in time to avoid a hail of bullets.

They didn't climb in when they reached the armory, but stuck their rifles over the counter. Col saw the tips of barrels appear over his head, still firing. He swung his own useless gun like a club and knocked one away.

"Fall back!" yelled Riff.

The Filthies sprang up and darted toward the back of the room. Shouts and screams and a fusillade of shots. They took temporary shelter among the racks of guns.

If there had been injuries, no one was left lying on the ground. But one person hadn't fallen back at all.

"Fossie!" Col called out in horror.

There she was, the woman with the red headband, still crouched under the counter. She was still fiddling and experimenting with her gun!

The officers remained outside. Two men ran forward with the special nonstop gun and set it up on the counter, facing toward the back of the armory.

It was the end. The racks would be no protection when thousands of bullets began ricocheting around.

Then a single shot from Fossie's gun changed everything. She shrieked in triumph as the bullet smacked into the ceiling.

"Like this! Watch me!"

She held up her rifle to show a small catch on top. She slid it back, then forward.

"This bit has to be forward!" she cried.

She stood up, took aim at one of the men behind the nonstop gun, and shot him through the chest. He toppled backward, dragging the gun off the counter as he fell.

Col was already working the catch on his own rifle. He squeezed the trigger and—*crack!*

All around, the Filthies were doing the same. They came

out from behind the gun racks, firing from the hip.

Crack! Crack! Crack! Crack!

The officers hadn't expected anyone to shoot at them. They wavered and started to panic.

Riff put her fingers to her lips and whistled. It was like the two-tone whistle she'd once used to signal to Col, but a hundred times louder and more piercing.

"Hold your positions!" the master lieutenant bellowed at his men.

But they were no longer listening to orders. As the Filthies came up on one side of the counter, they dropped back on the other. Retreat turned into rout.

Riff vaulted out into the foyer with the Filthies behind her. The officers fled, blundering into one another, making for the safety of the corridors.

But one corridor seemed to be blocked. The officers who ran into it were forced slowly back into the foyer.

It was the army of the other Filthies, now advancing in response to Riff's whistle. They raised a mighty cheer as they came.

Dozens of officers were trapped. Pleading for mercy, they threw down their guns and lifted their hands in surrender.

Col was no longer watching. When the Filthies had vaulted out into the foyer, he had stayed in the armory—with Fossie. He bent down over her. She lay on the ground beside the counter in the middle of a pool of blood.

69

The lower half of her face was a gaping mess, and blood pumped out from her neck. Was she still breathing? There was a guggling, bubbling sound in her throat. The red of the blood matched the red of her headband.

Col dropped his rifle and knelt beside her. He tried to press down on the artery to staunch the bleeding, as Riff had done for the cut in his scalp, but the blood only spurted out faster. Fossie swiveled her eyes toward him, but her gaze focused on something a long way beyond.

"You'll be all right," he said. "You'll be all right."

But she wasn't. The look in her eyes was growing more distant all the time. Col was desperate. He raised her head, and the flow of blood diminished—but only because there was no more blood to flow.

"Don't," he muttered. "You mustn't, you mustn't."

The look in her eyes went out altogether. Something had departed; something had left.

Dead.

She had saved them all by working out how to fire the rifles . . . and now she had paid the price for them all too.

Irredeemably dead.

The laughter lines on her face were just lines without the laughter. He remembered her teasing: *I never knew anyone could be so pale!* And then making grimy handprints all over his skin. *Much improved! I could almost fancy you myself!* Her gray eyes would never twinkle with amusement over anything again.

He lowered her head to the ground and folded her hands across her chest. He didn't even know a prayer to say over her. Calling down blessings from Queen Victoria would have been a mockery.

The tears were still streaming from his eyes when he rose and looked out across the foyer. The fighting was now over. Several sad, huddled bodies lay dead on the floor, which was wet with blood and littered with debris. Woodwork and plaster had been shot away from the walls. The officers who'd surrendered stood in a corner guarded by armed Filthies.

Riff strode around examining bodies, rolling them over with her foot. She stopped when she saw the tears on Col's face.

"What's wrong?"

"Fossie. She's dead."

There were no tears on Riff's face. "So's Trella." She pointed to the body of one dead Filthy among the dead officers. "Another three hurt so bad they could die too." She pointed to three Filthies who lay stretched out on the far side of the foyer, while other Filthies tended to them. "It's a miracle we didn't lose more. The murdering scum."

Col wanted to say something about Fossie but couldn't think of the words.

"We'll make 'em pay." The expression on Riff's face was cold and clenched. "Oh, yeah. Now we got the guns and they don't."

The crack of a shot interrupted her. Col looked across and

saw Shiv and Dunga standing over an officer on his knees. The officer crumpled slowly to the floor.

"What—?"

"They shot him," said Riff.

"Why him? He surrendered. You can't shoot people who've surrendered!"

Riff shrugged. "They deserve it."

The two Council members focused on another officer and dragged him out from the rest. Shiv shouted at him, swung the barrel of his rifle, and knocked him to his knees.

"You have to stop them!" Col protested. "They're executing everyone. I won't be part of this!"

Dunga took aim and shot the officer through the back of the head.

"They've tortured us for years," said Riff. Her face was full of bitterness, though she sounded a little less certain than before. "You don't know what it's like, gettin' burned by steam and crushed by machinery."

"But they're just officers. They believed what they were told. Same as me. I accepted the way of *Worldshaker*. I was as blind and cruel as any of them. You know I was."

Shiv and Dunga had hauled out their next victim. This time it was Dunga who knocked him to his knees, and Shiv who aimed with his rifle. . . .

"Stop!" Col vaulted over the counter and ran across the foyer.

Shiv's gun swung toward him. Col skidded to a halt beside the officer, letting the tip of the barrel touch his chest.

"Shoot me too, then," he bluffed. "If you want revenge. I'm Upper Decks too, so go ahead and shoot me."

Shiv might have done it. But he glanced first at Riff, who came striding across after Col.

"No," she said. "Enough of the shooting."

Shiv had an ugly look in his eyes. "You don't make the decisions."

"Nor you. The Revolutionary Council never voted for executions."

"Never voted against it, neither."

Col eased the gun barrel away from his chest. Riff continued to confront Shiv, glare against glare. Col had a momentary flashback to the way she'd faced off against Scarface.

"No mercy." Dunga joined in. "Revolution is war."

"How many are you planning to shoot?" Col demanded. "Do you want to wipe out the whole Upper Decks?"

"Maybe. We don't need *your* opinion."

"But you need mine," said Riff. "There are thousands of people on the Upper Decks. We *can't* kill them all."

"And you've already won the decisive battle," added Col. "They couldn't match you hand to hand, and now they can't match you with weapons. All you have to do is arm every Filthy with a gun."

"Right." Riff snapped her fingers at Shiv. "Have you sent a message to Bottom Deck? Have you told everyone to come up and collect a gun?"

"Not yet." Shiv lowered his rifle.

"You?" She swung to face Dunga.

Dunga shook her head and looked uncomfortable.

"We're wastin' time, then." Riff was in full control now. She gave instructions to a Filthy girl who'd been guarding the officers. The girl nodded and hurried off with a message for Bottom Deck.

Col hadn't finished. "You have to give all Upper Decks people a chance to surrender," he said. "Otherwise you make them fight to the finish. They'll get wiped out, but you'll have deaths and casualties. How many more Fossies do you want?"

"What happened to Fossie?" The question came from a second girl who'd been guarding the officers.

"She's dead," Col answered.

"Trella, too," said Riff. She turned to Col. "So how do we give 'em a chance to surrender?"

Col considered. "Maybe the queen herself. I think she has the power, if I can get her to use it. I'll negotiate with her on behalf of the Filthies."

"No negotiation!" barked Shiv and Dunga in unison.

"No, we don't negotiate," Riff agreed. "They lay down their weapons and hand over the juggernaut. In exchange, no executions. That's all we're offerin'."

"And after?"

"If they don't like us in charge, they can leave. Clear off for good." She appealed to the Filthies at large. "Right?"

There were nods of approval from all sides. Seeing they had no choice, Shiv and Dunga nodded too.

Riff swiveled back to Col. "Go and make your queen see sense. Unconditional surrender, or it's no deal."

70

Col formed a plan along the way. With luck the queen would still be on her throne in the Grand Assembly Hall. He rode the steam elevator up to Forty-fourth Deck.

On the way up he tidied his hair and used spit and a handkerchief to clean the coal-dust smears from his face. To pass among Upper Decks people he needed to look more like them and less like a Filthy. But he was still barefoot, and unclothed and dirty above the waist.

He stepped off the platform at Forty-fourth Deck and came out through another screen of green curtains. He didn't recognize any of the corridors at first. But his sense of direction told him this last elevator was aft of the one he'd descended with Gillabeth. He headed forward, and the corridors soon began to look familiar. He was in the neighborhood of the Norfolk Library.

Someone was walking ahead of him with a huge leatherbound book under his arm. Col guessed who it was from the back of his head.

"Septimus!"

Septimus turned and almost dropped his book at the sight of Col.

"Why are you . . . ?"

He was goggling at Col's bare chest and feet. In that moment Col hit upon a solution to the problem of his appearance.

"Lend me your jacket and shoes," he said.

"What happened to yours?"

"Too long to explain. Just do it. *Please.*"

Septimus took off his jacket and passed it across. Col did up the buttons from top to bottom. Septimus knelt and unlaced his shoes.

"What about socks?" he asked.

"No. No time."

"Is this something big happening? I've been hearing noises from the library."

"It's a revolution. Filthies against Upper Decks."

Septimus handed over his shoes. "A real revolution? Wow!" He was hopping with excitement. "Like in the books! This is history happening! Where do you fit in?"

"I'm making it happen." Col knotted his new shoelaces. "Come with me if you want."

He sprang up and ran on down the corridor, clip-clopping awkwardly in Septimus's shoes. He didn't turn to see if Septimus was following.

As he approached the Grand Assembly Hall, he ran into more and more people. All in a hurry, all flustered and busy. One time a whole troop of officers rushed past and he was forced to flatten himself against the wall. No one paid him enough attention to see that he had no socks in his shoes or shirt under his jacket.

Outside the hall was a gathering of familiar faces: Sir Mormus and members of the Executive. They were still in their finery from the wedding reception, but there was no mood of celebration now. Officers scurried up, reported, listened to instructions, then scurried off again. Sir Mormus boomed out a constant stream of commands and curses.

Col only wanted to speak to Queen Victoria, but Sir Mormus saw him go past.

"You, boy! Stop there! Come here!"

Col couldn't shrug off the habit of a lifetime. He obeyed automatically.

"Where have you been? What happened to your shirt?"

"I need to speak to our queen, sir."

"You? You don't talk to her. You tell me if you have anything worth telling."

Col felt himself pinned down by the weight of Sir Mormus's will. Yet Queen Victoria was his only chance. Looking into his grandfather's implacable face, Col knew he had absolutely no hope of persuading *him* to surrender.

He struggled to break free—and suddenly the spell dissolved. He turned his back on Sir Mormus and marched on into the Grand Assembly Hall.

The reception was still in progress, and the band played on. But all of the younger males had left, leaving women, children, and the more elderly men. Many held glasses or plates in their hands and attempted to maintain an air of festivity. But there was a haunted look in their eyes and a hectic edge to their conversation. Panic eddied through the hall like a cold draft.

Col caught snatches of talk as he crossed the room.

"My son's gone down to fight."

"My husband, too."

"They'll soon put things to rights."

"No reason to worry."

"None at all."

He headed toward the side of the hall where the queen and her consort sat stiffly on their thrones. Two security guards now stood behind them on the dais.

He made a deep and respectful bow. When he straightened, there was an expression of commiseration on Queen Victoria's long horse face.

"Ah, Colbert, what an unfortunate development on your wedding day."

Prince Albert appeared puzzled. "What did you do with your clothes?"

Col dismissed the question with a shake of the head. "Your Majesties, the Filthies are armed with rifles."

"Don't listen to him!" boomed the unmistakable voice of Sir Mormus. He came forward through the crowd, puffing and blowing like a beached whale.

"They can't be stopped," Col went on.

"He's a liar!" Sir Mormus thundered.

Queen Victoria frowned. "He's your grandson."

"No."

"I'm sure he is. You just married him to Sephaltina Turbot. I just performed the ceremony."

"I disown him."

Queen Victoria was shocked. "Oh! You mustn't do that!"

"No, no." Prince Albert twiddled his mustache. "Poor form, Porpentine, poor form."

"Your Majesties." Col raised his voice. "It'll be a massacre if you don't surrender."

"Surrender?" Sir Mormus gave the queen no chance to speak. "Never! Over my dead body! I'll blow *Worldshaker* up first!"

"Why can't they be stopped?" Queen Victoria asked Col.

"Because they control the armory."

"What's an armory?"

"How do *you* know what they control?" demanded Sir Mormus.

"I'm here to speak to the queen on their behalf."

"On their behalf!" Sir Mormus swung round to the two security officers. "Arrest him! Take him away!"

"Calm yourself, Sir Mormus," said Queen Victoria.

But Sir Mormus wouldn't be calmed. "Take him away and execute him!"

The security officers advanced from the back of the dais until Queen Victoria raised a hand. "Wait. Stay where you are."

Sir Mormus's face went blotchy, white on purple. "Do as your supreme commander commands!"

The officers looked at each other and stayed where they were. They were in the habit of obeying Sir Mormus, but they couldn't ignore their queen.

"No," said Queen Victoria. With firm-set chin and level gaze, she had never looked more majestic.

"I'll kill him myself!" roared Sir Mormus, and lunged at Col with outstretched hands.

Col could never have imagined it in his wildest dreams. He dodged and avoided Sir Mormus's blundering rush with ease. Sir Mormus collided with the dais and fell forward. He clutched onto Queen Victoria's legs as he fell.

Prince Albert jumped up at once. "Take your hands off the queen!"

Sir Mormus was beyond hearing. He pulled on the folds of Queen Victoria's dress as he tried to haul himself upright.

Prince Albert raised a foot, planted it on Sir Mormus's shoulder, and shoved. Sir Mormus staggered backward and returned to an upright position.

"Move away!" ordered Prince Albert.

Sir Mormus stared at him with outrage and disbelief. "Don't tell me what to do! You—you figurehead!"

The queen drew herself up. "That's enough, Sir Mormus. You are speaking to the man I love. You will address him as 'Your Imperial Highness.'"

"You too!" Sir Mormus's veneer of convention and propriety had gone. "Don't start thinking you can make decisions for *Worldshaker*! You don't have the brains!"

Queen Victoria's firm dignity was the opposite of Sir Mormus's bluster. "Kindly step away, Supreme Commander." She turned to the security officers. "See to it that Sir Mormus remains ten paces from this dais. He can wait until I wish to hear from him again. *If* I wish to hear from him again."

The officers advanced to do her bidding. Sir Mormus saw and let out an inarticulate bellow. He was more like a madman than the unshakable, imperious figure of Col's childhood. He retreated of his own accord before the officers could step down to him.

Queen Victoria leaned forward to Col again. "Please go on with what were you saying."

71

By now a packed crowd had gathered around the dais. Sir Wisley Squellingham, Rear Admiral Haugh, and Chief Helmsman Turbot had come forward to follow the drama, and so had Professor Twillip. Septimus was there too, his shoeless, jacketless state unnoticed amid the excitement.

Col told Queen Victoria about the Filthies climbing up through a food chute, fighting their way to higher and higher decks, and capturing the armory. He explained about the guns in the armory and how some of the Filthy leaders wanted to kill every last person on the Upper Decks. He didn't draw attention to his own role, but he didn't deny it either.

"It's now or never," he said. "Order a surrender, or the killing will become unstoppable."

"But I don't understand." Queen Victoria shook her head and winced under the weight of her crown. "These Filthies sound so *organized*. And learning how to fire our guns. I thought they were more like . . . well, animals."

"No, nothing like animals." Col turned to Squellingham, Haugh, and Turbot. "Even the members of your Executive know better than that."

"Perhaps not animals," said Turbot. "But hardly human."

"Yes they are!" a voice called out.

It was Septimus. He stepped forward, looking almost stunned by his own effrontery.

Prince Albert frowned. "Who's this?"

Professor Twillip stepped forward to support Septimus. "A humble scholar and researcher, Your Imperial Highness." He bowed. "As I am myself. We have researched the historical origins of the Filthies and can prove they're exactly the same species as ourselves. The separation goes back less than two hundred years."

"I never heard of that," said Queen Victoria.

"Start at the beginning," Col suggested.

So Professor Twillip and Septimus began at the beginning. They held forth upon the Old Country, the French Revolution, and the start of the Fifty Years' War. Since talking to Col, they had learned new facts about vast prison camps where the Filthies had been confined after the Battle of Crawley.

Sir Mormus rumbled and the other members of the Executive muttered and scowled. The queen and Prince Albert listened in fascination.

Col was soon wondering how to change the subject. He needed to get back to the present and the business of surrender. When Septimus and the professor spoke of the building of *Worldshaker* and the construction of an impassable barrier between Below and the Upper Decks, he jumped in at once.

"But now they have passed it, Your Majesties. They're spreading up through deck after deck as we speak. You have to decide. Unconditional surrender or a massacre."

Prince Albert bristled. "I don't know about *unconditional*."

"Think of everyone in this hall." Col focused his appeal on Queen Victoria. "Look around and think of the slaughter. A sea of blood."

"What happens to them if I order a surrender?" she asked.

"There'll be no more killings, no revenge. That's the Filthies' side of the deal."

"But what do we *do*?" asked Rear Admiral Haugh.

"You can stay and take orders from the Filthies. Or leave."

"Leave? You mean, go on the *ground*?" Haugh was appalled. "Live like natives? Live in the jungle?"

Col ignored him. "Think of the lives you can save, Your Majesty."

The queen and her consort exchanged troubled looks.

"Follow your sense of duty, my dear," said Prince Albert.

"But *which* duty?" Queen Victoria spread her hands in a gesture of despair.

Sir Wisley Squellingham spoke up. "If I might offer a word of advice, Your Majesty."

He stepped up onto the dais beside the imperial thrones, bent over Queen Victoria, and whispered in her ear. Col didn't trust him an inch—especially when he caught the words "pretend" and "for the time being."

"No pretending, Your Majesty," he warned. "It's too late for playing games."

His words came true even sooner than he expected. There was a disturbance on the other side of the Grand Assembly Hall, cries of shock and horror. Then a two-tone whistle—and six Filthies sprang onto the food-serving tables. Riff was one and Shiv was another. Perhaps they had come up by steam elevator, or perhaps they had raced up the staircases unopposed.

They kicked aside dishes and glasses and pointed their guns at the crowd.

"Last chance!" shouted Riff. "Unconditional surrender, or we start shootin'!"

Queen Victoria gasped, though not with horror. "Oh, they speak our language!" she exclaimed.

"And always did," said Col.

The crowd shuffled away from the menace of the guns. Children screamed and whimpered; several ladies fainted.

Professor Twillip squinted over his spectacles. "Just like us," he murmured. "No signs of regression at all."

The queen came to a decision and rose with dignity to her feet. Meeting her gaze, Prince Albert rose too.

"I accept the terms of surrender." She spoke in a loud, clear voice. "Let every officer and citizen of the Upper Decks lay down their arms. Spread the news. As queen and head of the Imperial Church, I hereby hand over power to . . . to . . ."

"The Revolutionary Council," prompted Col.

"To the Revolutionary Council."

The two security officers on the dais produced their batons and laid them on the ground. Queen Victoria nodded approval.

"That is my last order as your queen. I shall now abdicate." She reached up for her crown and struggled to lift it. "Help me, my dear."

Prince Albert took hold, and together they managed to raise the massive weight of steel and gold from her head. The creases disappeared from her brow.

"That feels better." She actually smiled as they lowered the crown to the ground. "No more queen."

"No more prince consort." Prince Albert removed his own, much smaller crown.

"And no more Executive or supreme commander." Without her crown Queen Victoria was more sprightly, almost youthful. Suddenly she looked no more than thirty years old. "Let Sir Mormus hand over his keys of office to *Worldshaker*'s new masters. Where is he?"

Everyone stared at the spot to which Sir Mormus had retreated, ten paces from the dais. But he was no longer there.

"I saw him leave," cried a voice from the crowd.

"Me too."

"He was muttering about vengeance."

Gillabeth spoke up from the middle of the hall. "I heard him say he was going to the bridge."

Col had a flashback to a phrase Sir Mormus had used earlier. "He threatened to blow up *Worldshaker* rather than surrender." He turned to the members of the Executive. "That's not possible, is it?"

"No," said Sir Wisley.

"I don't know how," said Rear Admiral Haugh.

"I do," said Chief Helmsman Turbot.

The smile had vanished from Queen Victoria's face. "Explain."

"He'd have to increase to full steam, shut down the turbines, halt the rollers, and allow the pressure to build up in the boilers."

"But the safety valves," Sir Wisley objected. "They let out the steam when—"

"They can be overridden," said Turbot. "Then the pressure would keep building until the boilers explode."

"How long?" asked Queen Victoria.

Turbot shrugged. "Perhaps twenty minutes. Perhaps thirty."

"He has to be stopped!" Col spun on his heel.

"I'll come!" cried Septimus.

"The blackguard! The madman!" Prince Albert snorted and jumped down from the dais.

"Be careful, my dear," called Queen Victoria. "But brave and . . ."

Her words faded away. Something had changed. Everyone became aware of it in the same moment.

The juggernaut was always in motion, the turbines always turning. For as far back as anyone could remember, the vibration in the decks had been a constant condition of their lives. They noticed it no more than they noticed their own heartbeat. But now it had stopped.

They looked at one another in silence. The strange stillness continued.

"Come *on!*" cried Col, and rushed for the exit.

The six armed Filthies joined the rush, along with Professor Twillip, Orris Porpentine, Gillabeth, and the two security officers. Col headed for the nearest steam elevator. But there was a problem.

"The platform can't carry fifteen people," said Gillabeth. "It won't move."

She took charge of dividing the party into two groups. Col, Prince Albert, Riff, and the Filthies would make the first ascent; Gillabeth, Orris, Septimus, Professor Twillip, and the security officers would wait and go second.

In the first group it was Col who knew the way to the bridge. When the elevator reached the top of its shaft on Fifty-third Deck, he led the way forward past offices with glass doors and filing cabinets. Riff was right at his heels, followed by the other Filthies, and Prince Albert panting along at the back.

They came to the final flight of steps and ran up toward the bridge. Outside the door stood not only an ensign with a rifle but half a dozen high-ranking officers. They rapped on the door and called out in worried voices.

"Sir Mormus, what are you doing, sir?"

"Can we help, sir?"

"Is it an emergency, sir?"

"Yes!" cried Col, coming up behind them. "And *he's* the emergency!"

The officers turned, saw Col—and then saw Riff.

"Filthy!"

The ensign directed his rifle on her. Riff swung her own rifle to shoot first.

Col grabbed the barrels of both guns and pushed them aside. "No!"

The ensign tried to wrench his rifle from Col's grip. He didn't stop even when the other five Filthies ran up and menaced him with their guns.

Then Prince Albert appeared at the top of the steps

"Stop this!" he ordered. "Fighting's over. We've surrendered. Who's in charge here?"

A lieutenant commander with four stripes on his sleeve stood smartly at attention. "Your Imperial Highness. Did you say 'surrendered'?"

"Yes. Don't goggle at me, man." Prince Albert gestured toward the door. "Is Porpentine in there?"

The situation was defused. Col released the barrels he'd been holding; everyone lowered their guns.

The lieutenant commander nodded. "He ordered us all out. He's shut down the turbines. We've stopped in the middle of the Pahang River plain."

"Is it because of the storm, Your Highness?" asked another officer.

"Storm? What storm?"

The lieutenant commander explained. "We've run into a bad tropical storm, Your Highness. But *Worldshaker* never stopped for a storm before."

Prince Albert snorted. "No, nothing to do with a storm. Is that door locked?"

"We don't know, Your Highness."

"Well, try it, man. Try it."

The handle turned and the door opened. Riff jumped forward and slipped in first. Col darted after her.

The last time he had visited the bridge, it had been daylight and a scene of bustling activity. Now it was night, and the activity was all on the other side of the windows: driving rain and jags of lightning. Inside, the control units stood silent and deserted. The only illumination came from a pale line of overhead strip lights and the green and red glow of the dials.

There was no sign of Sir Mormus.

"Porpentine!" Prince Albert called out. "Show yourself! Enough of this!"

Officers and Filthies fanned out across the room. Sir Mormus must have been bending down behind a particular control unit, because he rose suddenly into view.

"Yes, enough!" he boomed. "Enough of everything! It's time to make an end!"

He sounded triumphant, with the old tone of absolute authority. He held up something that glinted in the dim light.

Then he turned and moved across under the windows. He was heading for the metal staircase that led to the platform above the bridge. He pulled down a switch as he went past, killing the strip lights.

"Forget him!" shouted Col. "See to the controls!"

Sir Mormus let out a laugh. His footsteps clumped heavily up the stairs.

"Reduce the steam!" Prince Albert ordered. "Start up the turbines! Open the safety valves!"

"Safety valves?" The officers gasped as they took in the implications.

Then they moved—fast. In spite of the darkness they knew exactly where to find the necessary wheels and levers.

"Number four boiler's coming up to danger pressure!" one warned.

"So's number two!"

"And number five!"

Col followed in among the control units, banging on unseen projections. "Open the safety valves first!" he yelled.

But there were cries of dismay from the officers.

"This lever won't move!"

"Same here!"

They redoubled their efforts, straining and grunting.

"Nothing works!"

"All stuck!"

"He's locked down the controls!"

Col didn't understand. "How? What does that mean?"

One of the officers let go of the wheel he'd been struggling to turn and pointed to a keyhole on the control unit.

"Every unit has a lock. He's locked everything in place with his keys of office."

Riff heard and made the connection. "Keys! *That's* what he was holding up!"

Col remembered the glint in his grandfather's hand. Of course—his keys of office! He remembered Sir Mormus toying with them on the gold chain round his neck, saying, *These aren't just ceremonial, you know.*

Then a new voice called out from the doorway, "What's happening?"

It was Gillabeth. The second party had arrived.

"He's locked down the controls and taken the keys," Col explained.

"After him!" cried Riff. "Everyone! Get those keys!"

73

They ran up the stairs to the turret at the top. The door of the turret was swinging back and forth in the wind. They pushed through and met the full force of the storm outside.

Col could hardly see as the rain smacked him in the face. Clouds surged and churned all around the platform. The peals of thunder were like growls in the throat of a great beast. Flickers of lightning opened sudden bright gulfs in the depths of the clouds, on-off, on-off.

Sir Mormus turned to face his enemies, standing against the steel barrier at the front of the platform. His hair was plastered to his skull, and his clothes stuck to his skin. In the moments of darkness he was a mere shadow; in the moments of lightning he loomed bigger and more overbearing than ever.

As the Filthies aimed their rifles, he extended an arm back over the barrier.

Riff lowered her rifle. "Hold your fire!" she yelled.

Sir Mormus had the keys of office in the hand he held out over the void. If they shot him now, the keys would drop and be lost a thousand feet below.

"Keep your distance," he roared above the howl of the wind.

"Don't shoot until I say," ordered Riff.

They spread out in a line across the back of the platform.

The deck under their feet was a shallow lake. The bare skin of the Filthies gleamed with running water.

"The keys, Porpentine," Prince Albert barked. "Hand them over. That's a command from the queen herself."

Sir Mormus gave him a look of infinite disdain. "So that you can hand them over to the Filthies? I think not. I prefer my own plan."

Col felt something nudge against his arm. Riff's rifle.

"Hold this," she whispered. "Keep him talking."

She stepped backward as he took possession of the rifle. When he glanced over his shoulder, she had vanished into the driving rain.

"You can't want to destroy *Worldshaker*, Porpentine." Prince Albert's tone was reasonable, though he had to shout to make himself heard. "Think of all the Upper Decks people. Think of family and friends. You can't want to put their lives at risk."

"No risk," Sir Mormus laughed. "Certainty. When one boiler blows, it will set off all the rest. An explosion of unimaginable force. Ten thousand lives gone in a blast of superheated steam. No survivors."

"You'll die too."

"The captain goes down with his ship."

"You're insane," said Orris Porpentine.

"Ah, my worthless son." Sir Mormus turned his attention on Orris. "Speak up. I can't hear you."

Orris raised his voice. "You're a madman!"

Sir Mormus thrust out his chest. "I am what I have always been. Better a madman than a spineless weakling. Look at you, standing beside Filthies! Choosing such creatures over your own kind. You make me sick. Warped and twisted, the taint in the bloodline."

"No, you're the one who's warped and twisted. I see it now."

Sir Mormus laughed louder than ever and scanned the line of his enemies. His gaze settled on Col. "And here's my tainted grandson. Not only spineless but treacherous. Working against me all along, until he thought he'd achieved his goal. No, boy, what you've achieved is universal annihilation." He shifted his gaze to Gillabeth. "And you, too? Standing with Filthies against your own grandfather? The world will be a better place when I purge it of such corruption."

There was no need for Col or anyone else to keep Sir Mormus talking; he was unstoppable. The thunder and lightning were a mere background for his performance.

"None worthy of me! None fit to follow in my footsteps!" He seemed exultant rather than disappointed. "I am the last of the Porpentines! I—"

He broke off as a shudder ran through the platform, rippling the lake around their feet. A deep-down shudder that came from the very bowels of the juggernaut.

"Ah, it begins, it begins." A smile of lofty satisfaction spread over Sir Mormus's face. "The boilers can hardly contain the pressure."

The Filthies turned to one another.

"We gotta act now."

"Rush him."

"Riff said to wait."

"Grab his arm."

"Where is she?"

Col shook his head. There was no way they could prevent

Sir Mormus from dropping the keys. But where *was* Riff?

Then he saw—and barely managed to hold back a gasp. Two hands were hooked over the top of the barrier, working slowly around toward the front. Riff was hanging down out of sight on the *outside* of the barrier!

Luckily, Sir Mormus was absorbed in his own oration. "Now you see who has the power! Now you understand how helpless you are! You don't count! You don't have the strength of will. I decide!"

"You have no right," cried Professor Twillip.

Sir Mormus didn't hear the interruption. "Only a few minutes to go. Prepare yourselves! I have decided for you all."

Out of the corner of his eye Col watched Riff's hands edge closer and closer. He was sure he wasn't the only one to have spotted them. Less than a yard and she'd be under Sir Mormus's outstretched arm. So long as he didn't look down . . .

"I disown everyone and everything!" Sir Mormus's rant drowned out even the thunder. "I recognize only *Worldshaker*! I am this juggernaut and this juggernaut is me! You can share in my death!"

"*Fire!*" shouted Riff.

The Filthies raised their guns, barely pausing to aim. A volley of shots smashed into Sir Mormus's head and chest. Voluntarily or involuntarily, he let the keys drop. Every eye stared as the glint of metal vanished from view on the wrong side of the barrier.

Sir Mormus keeled over and slumped to the deck.

Col hadn't fired. Instead he dropped his gun and raced forward. He splashed through water, leaped over Sir Mormus's body. Riff had only one hand hooked over the barrier.

He looked down and there she was, dangling over the void. The immensity of the juggernaut was hidden in clouds and rain. In her other hand were the keys of office.

She looked up at him, face clenched with effort. "I caught 'em! Help . . ."

Even as she spoke, she lost her grip and started to drop. Col stretched farther over the barrier and grabbed her by the wrist. A stab of agony shot through his shoulder as he halted her fall.

But now his feet had lost contact with the deck. Inch by inch her weight dragged him forward, toward the void.

For one endless second they were suspended in a strange stillness outside of time. The lightning flickered on-off, on-off. Riff rotated half a turn to the left, half a turn to the right. The whole world seemed to turn with her.

Then hands caught onto him from behind.

"Okay!"

"We got ya!"

"Pullin' up now!"

More hands reached down and gripped Riff. He clung to her wrist until the hands had a safe hold on her, under the armpits. Then he let go and fell back inside the barrier.

His shoulder was throbbing with pain, perhaps dislocated. In another moment Riff came tumbling over the barrier after him.

"Safety valves!" she gasped. "Go quick!"

Gillabeth swooped and snatched up the keys. "I'll do it," she said.

74

Gillabeth disappeared through the door of the turret. The Filthies ran after her, followed by Prince Albert, Orris, Septimus, Professor Twillip, and the officers. Col and Riff lay in an inch of water. Riff raised herself up and leaned back against the inside of the barrier.

The wind and rain had eased for a moment. From far below came a grinding, grating, creaking sound, almost a groan.

"Boilers close to bursting," said Riff.

Col nodded. "Turbot said twenty or thirty minutes."

"Must be twenty by now. They better hurry."

"Trust my sister. She'll take care of it. She always wanted to be in charge of things." Col sat up, gritting his teeth against the pain in his shoulder.

Riff took a closer look at him. "What's wrong?"

"I think I've pulled my shoulder out."

"I'll fix it." She swiveled and bent over him.

"Now?"

"Hold still. This'll hurt a bit."

It hurt a lot. Under her manipulations his shoulder turned to liquid fire. He let out a yowl . . . then felt a click as the bones slid into place.

"Better?"

He nodded, unable to speak. Someone else spoke, though.

"*Worldshaker* I am!" came the booming voice.

It was Sir Mormus Porpentine, with a gaping hole in his forehead and another in the region of his heart. He should have been dead, yet he tottered on his feet like an unstrung puppet. Rivers of blood pumped from his wounds and poured down over his face and chest.

"Iron colossus, mechanical mountain, predominator." He seemed to be talking to himself. "This juggernaut is me."

Col and Riff shrank as he shambled toward them. But he wasn't deliberately heading in their direction. Three paces away he banged up against the barrier. His stumbling route had left a red snail's trail of blood over the watery deck.

"He can't see," whispered Col.

"What's he doing?"

Clumsily, grotesquely, Sir Mormus began clambering up onto the top of the barrier. He was still raving to himself.

"Yes . . . yes . . . building up and up. My boilers are bursting. My metal is straining. I feel it coming . . . any second now . . ."

Col and Riff watched spellbound. Sir Mormus rose up on the barrier, overbalancing even as he rose. Flashes of lightning silhouetted the shattered shell of his body against the sky. Then he lifted his arms.

"The end of greatness!" he cried, and fell forward.

"The end of madness," muttered Riff.

He was gone.

They staggered to their feet and leaned out over the barrier. Down below, heavy clouds still swirled around the lower decks of *Worldshaker*. They could see only glimpses through the gaps.

"What's that there?" Riff pointed.

"Can't see him." Col shook his head. "What about there?"

"Where?"

"No. Nothing."

They were still looking for signs of Sir Mormus when they heard an almighty roar of escaping steam. Plumes of vapor shot out on either side of the juggernaut, submerging even the violence of the storm.

"The safety valves!" whooped Riff.

In a few minutes a vast blanket of billowing whiteness had covered the gaps in the clouds, and there was nothing more to see.

The weather had cleared, and the day's sky was a deep tropical blue. The great cranes were transporting those who had chosen to leave the juggernaut, twenty at a time. Scoops that had once raised plundered produce to the Upper Decks now lowered Upper Decks people to the ground.

Riff supervised the disembarkation from one particular sorting tray, aided by Dunga, the tattooed member of the Revolutionary Council. They carried rifles but used them only for pointing and directing. Though sullen and bitter, those departing were too cowed to disobey. Col sat at the side of the sorting tray and watched.

After several hours the queue was coming to an end. Three quarters of the Upper Decks population had chosen to leave, including many officers and most of the elite. Queen Victoria and Prince Albert had opted to stay, however, encouraging others to do the same. Orris, Quinnea, Gillabeth, and Antrobus were among the stayers, along with Septimus and Professor Twillip. For Septimus and Professor Twillip it was hardly a decision—they could never have abandoned their library anyway. As for Orris, he had been a new man since the overthrow of Sir Mormus, shedding years of gloom and guilt overnight. The four other branches of the Porpentine family were all leaving.

Finally, the scoop swept down to collect its very last load.

There were only eleven people left—all Squellinghams.

Col watched as Sir Wisley, his wife, Hythe, Pugh, three younger children, and a couple of aunts and uncles staggered forward under the weight of their luggage. Everyone departing had been allowed to take what they could carry in two hands, and the Squellinghams had managed to take more than most. Unaccustomed to doing their own carrying, they snapped and snarled and grumped at one another.

"Move!" ordered Riff when the scoop touched down on the tray.

Still snapping, they clambered in and settled their luggage around them. Col was sure that Hythe and Pugh had seen him, though they made a point of not looking in his direction. But when Riff gave the signal and the scoop lifted away, Hythe could contain his bile no longer.

"Filthy-lover! Filthy-lover!" he yelled. "They'll turn on you! They'll kill you in the end. Then you'll be sorry . . . you . . ."

His face turned a sickly shade of gray as the scoop swung out over the side of the juggernaut. The Squellinghams were all hanging on for dear life as they dropped slowly out of view.

Riff padded across to Col. "Friends of yours?" she asked ironically.

"Worst enemies. Do you think they'll survive on the ground?"

"Depends." She sat down beside him, cross-legged. "If they can do real work like anyone else. They'll have to learn not to be so useless."

"And the rest of us? The stayers?"

"You'll have to learn not to be so useless too."

"What'll happen, do you think? There are a lot of Filthies who still want revenge."

"Yeah, and a lot of Upper Decks people still look down on us."

"We're cooperating and showing you how to operate *Worldshaker*."

"Okay. Don't expect instant forgiveness, though."

"But in time . . ."

Riff shrugged. "Just have to hope, won't we?"

"What will you do with *Worldshaker* now?"

"Who knows? Keep travelin'."

"But not over natives and their villages."

"No. I expect we'll get off the land and travel only by sea. The Revolutionary Council will decide."

There was a moment of silence. Col's thoughts moved on in their own channel.

"What about you and me?" he asked.

"Hmm." She looked at him with eyebrows raised. Her face was so close, her eyes so large and bright. A knot of feeling rose in his throat. He couldn't help it; he leaned toward her . . .

"Just have to hope, won't you?" She grinned and jumped to her feet. "Dunga's waitin' for me."

The tattooed girl stood with hands on hips, looking impatient. But he was sure Riff *knew* he'd been about to kiss her.

"Where are you going?"

"Meeting of the Council. I'm goin' to propose a change of name for this *Worldshaker*. I'm goin' to propose *Liberator*. 'Cause we're goin' to light up the world and make it a better place."

He went to speak, but she swung on her heel and marched off to join Dunga. In another moment they had vanished through the turnstile at the back of the sorting tray.

Col sat on, gazing at the sky. A hundred questions tumbled through his mind. What would he find to do now that the Revolutionary Council was running the juggernaut? How would they get coal from the coaling stations? What would they do for trade? How would the other juggernauts react to the news of the revolution?

Yet those were only small questions compared to the mystery of Riff and her elusive grin. What did it mean?

He had the feeling that life would never be predictable again. It was strange that she could make him feel so good and at the same time so insecure. How could he ever know where he was with her?

"I guess I'll have to put up with not knowing," he muttered to himself. And suddenly the thought didn't seem too bad at all.

About the Author

RICHARD HARLAND is the author of fantasy, horror, and science fiction novels, including the Eddon and Vail series, the Heaven and Earth trilogy, and the Wolf Kingdom quartet (winner of the Aurealis Award). Richard was born in the UK and migrated to Australia at the age of twenty-one. For many years he was a songwriter and performer of folk-rock music. His first novel was the cult gothic fantasy *The Vicar of Morbing Vyle*, and as soon as he had the chance he became a full-time writer. *Worldshaker* took ten years to plan and five years to write.

Richard has put up a free 145-page guide to writing and publishing fantasy, horror, and science fiction at writingtips.com.au. For more on Richard, steampunk, and *Worldshaker*, check out worldshaker.info.